KT-501-144

# LES ŒUVRES COMPLETES DE VOLTAIRE

## 20B

VOLTAIRE FOUNDATION

OXFORD

2002

ISBN 0 7294 0754 3

Voltaire Foundation Ltd
99 Banbury Road
Oxford OX2 6JX

PRINTED IN ENGLAND

AT THE ALDEN PRESS

OXFORD

# *Le Fanatisme, ou Mahomet le prophète*

# *De l'Alcoran et de Mahomet*

# CONTENTS

# ILLUSTRATIONS

## ACRONYMS AND ABBREVIATIONS

a) *Printed sources*:

Barbier *Chronique de la régence et du règne de Louis XV*, [1857]-1866

Bengesco *Voltaire: bibliographie de ses œuvres*, 1882-1890

BnC BnF, *Catalogue général des livres imprimés*, Auteurs, ccxiv [Voltaire]

Brenner *A bibliographical list of plays in the French language*, 1947

BV *Bibliothèque de Voltaire: catalogue des livres*, 1961

D Voltaire, *Correspondence and related documents*, *OC* 85-135, 1968-1977

Desnoiresterres *Voltaire et la société française*, 1867-1876

*Essai* Voltaire, *Essai sur les mœurs*, 1963

Kehl *Œuvres complètes de Voltaire*, 1784-1789

Moland *Œuvres complètes de Voltaire*, 1877-1885

Registres H. C. Lancaster, *The Comédie française, 1701-1774*, 1951

*Rhl* *Revue d'histoire littéraire de la France*

*SVEC* *Studies on Voltaire and the eighteenth century*

*OC* *Œuvres complètes de Voltaire / Complete works of Voltaire*, 1968- [the present edition]

b) *Library symbols*:

Austria

A-V Österreichische Nationalbibliothek, Wien

Belgium

B-Br Bibliothèque royale, Bruxelles

B-G/U Centrale Bibliothek, Rijksuniversiteit, Ghent

Switzerland
CH-4 Bibliothèque publique et universitaire, Genève
CH-16 Zentralbibliothek, Luzern
CH-21 Zentralbibliothek, Solothurn
CH-178 Institut et musée Voltaire, Genève
CH-Yverdon Bibliothèque publique, Yverdon

Germany
D-17 Hessische Landes- und Hochschulbibliothek, Darmdstadt
D-22 Staatliche Bibliothek, Bamberg
D-51 Lippische Landesbibliothek, Detmold
D-185 Deutsche Staatsbibliothek, Berlin

Denmark
DK-C Det Kongelige Bibliotek, Copenhagen

Spain
E-M Biblioteca nacional de España, Madrid

France
F-Ang Bibliothèque municipale, Angers
F-Av Médiathèque Ceccano, Avignon
F-Beaune Bibliothèque municipale, Beaune
F-Chm Bibliothèque municipale, Châlons s/Marne
F-Dp Bibliothèque municipale, Dieppe
F-Lib Médiathèque municipale, Libourne
F-Lille Bibliothèque municipale, Lille
F-Nts Bibliothèque municipale, Nantes
F-P/Ar Bibliothèque de l'Arsenal, Paris
F-P/BnF Bibliothèque nationale, Paris
F-P/Cf Bibliothèque et archives de la Comédie-Française, Paris
F-P/U Bibliothèque de l'université de Paris à la Sorbonne
F-Qr Bibliothèque municipale, Quimper
F-S/Bn Bibliothèque nationale et universitaire, Strasbourg
F-Tls Bibliothèque de la ville, Toulouse
F-Vers Bibliothèque de Versailles

Great Britain
GB-Ad/U1 University library, Aberdeen
GB-Ma/S John Rylands University Library, Manchester
GB-Ld/U1 Brotherton Library, University of Leeds
GB-Lo/N1 British Library, London
GB-Ox/U19 Taylor Institution, Oxford
GB-Ox/U38 Merton College Library, Oxford
GB-W The Queen's Library, Windsor

Italy
I-F/N Biblioteca nazionale, Florence
I-Mo Biblioteca Estense, Modena
I-Pd Biblioteca universitaria, Padua
I-R/N Biblioteca nazionale, Rome
I-V Biblioteca Marciana, Venice

Luxembourg
L-N Bibliothèque nationale

Sweden
S-S/N Kungliga Biblioteket, Stockholm

USA
USA-CLSU University of Southern California, Los Angeles
USA-Cty Yale University Library, New Haven, Connecticut
USA-CU University of California Library, Berkeley
USA-CU-BANC University of California Library, Berkeley, Bancroft Library
USA-DLC Library of Congress, Washington, D.C.
USA-DFo Folger Shakespeare Library, Washington, D.C.
USA-FU University of Florida, Gainesville
USA-ICU University of Chicago Library, Illinois
USA-InU Indiana University Library, Bloomington
USA-IU University of Illinois, Urbana
USA-KU University of Kansas, Lawrence
USA-MB Boston Public Library, Massachussetts
USA-MdBJ Johns Hopkins University Library, Baltimore, Maryland

USA-MdBP Peabody Institute, Baltimore, Maryland
USA-MH Harvard University Library, Cambridge, Massachussetts
USA-MH-L Law School Library, Harvard University
USA-MiU University of Michigan Library, Ann Arbor
USA-NBuG Grosvenor Reference Division, Buffalo and Erie County Public Library, N.Y.
USA-NcD Duke University Library, Durham, North Carolina
USA-NjP Princeton University Library, New Jersey
USA-NN New York Public Library
USA-NNMor Pierpont Morgan Library, New York
USA-NRU University of Rochester, N.Y.
USA-OCl Cleveland Public Library, Ohio
USA-OCU University of Cincinnati Library, Ohio
USA-OrU University of Oregon, Eugene
USA-OU Ohio State University, Columbus
USA-PHC Haverford College, Pennsylvania
USA-PPL Library Company of Philadelphia, Pennsylvania
USA-PU University of Pennsylvania Library
USA-PU-F University of Pennsylvania, Furness Memorial Library
USA-ScU University of South Carolina, Columbia
USA-RPB Brown University Library, Providence, Rhode Island
USA-TxU University of Texas Library, Austin
USA-ViU University of Virginia Library, Charlottesville
USA-WU University of Wisconsin Library, Madison

# KEY TO THE CRITICAL APPARATUS

The critical apparatus, printed at the foot of the page, gives variant readings from the manuscripts and editions discussed in the introductions to the texts. For the grouping of the editions of *Mahomet* into nine separate 'families', each of which is identified by the appropriate letter in brackets, ranging from A to I, followed by an asterisk, see p.136-37.

Each variant consists of some or all of the following elements:

- The number of the text line or lines to which the variant relates.
- The sigla of the sources of the variant as given in the bibliography. Simple numbers, or numbers followed by letters, generally stand for separate editions of the work in question; letters followed by numbers are normally collections of one sort or another, w being reserved for collected editions of Voltaire's works and T for collected editions of his theatre.
- Editorial explanation or comment.
- A colon, indicating the start of the variant; any editorial remarks after the colon are enclosed within square brackets.
- The text of the variant itself, preceded and followed, if appropriate, by one or more words from the base text, to indicate its position.

Several signs and typographic conventions are employed:

- Angle brackets < > encompass deleted matter.
- Beta β stands for the base text.
- The forward arrow → means 'replaced by'.

- Up ↑ and down ↓ arrows precede text added above or below the line.
- A superior V precedes text in Voltaire's hand.
- A pair of slashes // indicates the end of a paragraph or other section of text.

# ACKNOWLEDGEMENTS

For the preparation of the present volume we are especially grateful for the assistance of W. H. Barber and of Nathalie Rizzoni (CELLF 17$^{e}$-18$^{e}$, équipe 'Voltaire en son temps').

The *Œuvres complètes de Voltaire* rely on the competence and patience of the personnel of many research libraries around the world. We wish to thank them for their generous assistance, in particular the personnel of the Bibliothèque nationale de France and the Bibliothèque de l'Arsenal, Paris; the Institut et musée Voltaire, Geneva; the Taylor Institution Library, Oxford; and the National Library of Russia, St Petersburg.

Among the libraries that have supplied information or material for this volume are: the British Library, London; the Bodleian Library, Oxford; the Bibliothèque-musée de la Comédie-Française, Paris; and the Bibliothèque publique et universitaire, Genève.

Lekain in the rôle of Mahomet. Engraving by P. Baquoy from a painting by J.-B. Lenoir.

'Aux mânes de Le Kain'. Lekain in the rôle of Mahomet.

# PREFACE

By the late 1730s the studious calm provided since 1734 by the refuge of Cirey was beginning to come to an end. Voltaire found himself torn between on the one hand Mme Du Châtelet, whom in 1739 he accompanied on an extended trip to Brussels, and on the other the increasing demands of his burgeoning epistolary friendship with Frederick, whom he met for the first time in 1740 at the château de Moyland. His relationship with the French authorities remained delicate, and he had been hurt by his quarrel with Desfontaines and the publication late in 1738 of *La Voltairomanie*. Voltaire sorely needed a success in the public arena of the theatre, and he started work on two plays, both on an oriental theme, *Zulime*, begun in 1738, and *Mahomet*, begun the following year. By September 1739 he was working simultaneously on both, and wrote to the actress Mlle Quinault: 'J'ay relu Mahom. j'ay relu Zulime; cette Zulime est bien faible, et L'autre est peutêtre ce que j'ay fait de moins mal' (D2071). He was disappointed, if not entirely surprised, therefore, by the poor reception given to *Zulime* the following year, and in June 1740 he vowed to d'Argental that he would now focus his energies on *Mahomet*: 'Je vous suplie de faire au plustôt cesser pour jamais les représentations de Zulime sur quelque honnête prétexte. Je vous avoue que je n'ay jamais mis mes complaisances que dans Mahomet. J'aime les choses d'une espèce toute neuve' (D2230); the play is, Voltaire believes, 'dans un goût nouveau' (D2048). It is precisely this search for 'une espèce toute neuve' which makes *Mahomet* and its accompanying texts such an intriguing work. Voltaire wasted no time, and only a month later he was able to write to Pont-de-Veyle, 'Je viens d'esquisser ce cinquième acte, à peu près tel qu'on l'a voulu' (D2266). It was very soon after this that Voltaire met Frederick for the first time, and he used the occasion to read to him *Mahomet*: 'Il nous a déclamé Mahomet I, tragédie admirable qu'il a faite', wrote the king. 'Il nous a transportés hors de nous, et je n'ai pu que l'admirer et me taire' (D2317).

The theme of fanaticism is one which had been prominent in Voltaire's work at least since *La Henriade*, and in the 'Avis' he makes this connection explicit: '[*La Henriade*] ne fait-il pas aimer la véritable vertu? *Mahomet* me paraît écrit entièrement dans le même esprit.' What is new is the translation of this theme to the stage, and Voltaire says as much to Frederick: 'On n'avait jamais mis sur le théâtre la superstition et le fanatisme' (D2048); a further innovation is the manner in which Voltaire associates fanaticism with hypocrisy, a link which was to remain constant in subsequent works. Many years later, in 1760, Voltaire would write to Damilaville: 'vous détestez le fanatisme et l'hypocrisie, je les ai abhorrés depuis que j'ai eu l'âge de raison' (D9414); and soon after to Diderot, 'Je vous regarde comme un homme nécessaire au monde, né pour l'éclairer et pour écraser le fanatisme et l'hypocrisie' (D9454). In the late 1730s Voltaire was beginning to collect material for the *Essai sur les mœurs*, which would include two judiciously balanced chapters on Mohammed and Islam. In *Mahomet*, on the other hand, Voltaire is writing not as a historian but as a polemicist, and his focus is less on Islam as such than on religious hypocrisy and the 'fondateurs illustres de la superstition et du fanatisme', as he calls them in the prefatory letter addressed to Frederick. The portrayal of Mohammed as an impostor owes much of course to the *Traité des trois imposteurs* (which in fact is more severely critical of Moses and Jesus than of Mohammed), and we know from the researches of Margaret Jacob that as early as 1722 Voltaire had been in personal contact with the group of clandestine thinkers in The Hague responsible for the treatise's wide circulation (*The Radical Enlightenment: pantheists, freemasons and republicans*, London 1981, p.103). In November 1739 the police seized Voltaire's *Recueil de pièces fugitives* which included, among other works, his *Ode sur le fanatisme*, and so it must have seemed tempting to try to turn the subject of fanaticism into the theme, indeed the title, of a classical tragedy. To have chosen a Christian setting for a theatrical discussion of fanaticism would clearly have been too controversial. Islam, on the other hand, was understood in the eighteenth century to be primarily the religion of the Ottoman Empire, and there was good classical precedent for introducing a 'Turkish' element into tragedy; the figure of Mohammed thus offered the advantage of oriental local colour, and a veil only just opaque enough to distract critics from the thought of other (unnamed) religious impostors.

In the first instance Voltaire conceived *Mahomet* as a drama for the stage, and the successful initial staging of the play in Lille in 1741, with La Noue in the leading role, was deliberately designed to create favourable publicity for the play in advance of its Paris première. Voltaire continued to make minor adjustments to the text, and wrote in January 1742 to d'Argental, 'j'ay fait ce que j'ay pu. Je le crois plus intéressant que lors qu'il fit pleurer les lillois' (D2584). When the play was perfomed in Paris later that year it enjoyed a short-lived success, but in the face of complaints from certain *parlementaires*, Voltaire found himself obliged to withdraw the play after the third performance. 'Ce célèbre Mahomet annoncé depuis tant de tems parut enfin lundi passé à Paris pour la première fois. On est assez surpris de ce que la police en a permis la représentation. La Politique y est pour le moins aussi maltraitée que la Relligion, c'est le triomphe du Déisme ou plustôt du Fatalisme', reported the abbé Le Blanc (D2635). The portrait of Mahomet was clearly understood by many as a critical portrait of impostors of all faiths: 'On a remarqué que toutes les religions paroissoient être attaquées dans cette tragédie, sous prétexte de blamer celle de Mahomet', wrote one journalist (D2641, commentary), echoing a view which Lord Chesterfield had formed the previous year: 'mais j'ai d'abord vu qu'il en voulait à Jesus-Christ, sous le caractère de Mahomet, et j'étais surpris qu'on ne s'en fût pas aperçu à Lille' (D2653). Voltaire countered this as best he could, by suggesting that the only objectors to his play were Jansenist *parlementaires*, 'nos convulsionaires en robe longue qui ne veulent pas qu'on joue le fanatisme, comme on dit qu'un 1er président ne vouloit pas qu'on jouast Tartuffe' (D2643). In the correspondence of this period, Voltaire repeatedly uses the example of Molière's *Tartuffe* to suggest that the target of attack is the religious hypocrite, not religion itself. He writes in these terms to César de Missy (D2648), and also to Frederick: 'C'est l'avanture de Tartuffe. Les hipocrites persécutèrent Moliere et les fanatiques se sont soulevez contre moy' (D2647).

Initially conceived as a work for the stage, *Mahomet* is reconceived by Voltaire as a work of polemic, as a text designed to be read as well as performed. Already in 1742, long before the appearance of the first printed edition, Voltaire had sent the play to d'Argental, urging that it should be read widely: 'Apropos vous avez mon Mahomet, madame de Tensin le lira, mr le cardinal le lira, qu'en auront ils dit? et mr Palu? On ne peut pas se dispenser de luy en acorder une lecture' (D2643). Inevitably, given that copies of the play were in circulation, pirated editions began to appear in advance of an 'official' edition, and in October 1742 Voltaire sent to Ledet in Amsterdam the first part of the manuscript for publication (D2667); the first authorised edition appeared in 1743, *Le Fanatisme, ou Mahomet le prophète* (43A): this edition distinguishes itself from the earlier pirated editions by the presence of an engraved frontispiece, and by the inclusion of two prefatory letters. In the first of these, the 'Avis de l'éditeur', Voltaire anonymously, but transparently, praises his own play, guiding the reader as to how it should be read: 'Plus j'ai lu les ouvrages de cet écrivain, plus je les ai trouvés caractérisés par l'amour du bien public; il inspire partout l'horreur contre les emportements de la rébellion, de la persécution et du fanatisme.' This flagrant piece of self-advertisement is then reinforced by the following piece, a letter addressed to Frederick II. This bears the date '20 janvier 1742'; the genuine letter (D2386), of which Voltaire must have kept a careful copy, is actually dated two years earlier, but the date here is changed so as to link the letter more directly to the performance of the work and so as to make the letter, as Voltaire himself observed, 'une espèce d'épitre dédicatoire' (D2682). In place of a conventional preface or dedication in which the author addresses the reader, the reader here is confronted with two Voltairean voices in two contrasting registers: in the first, the voice addressing the reader pretends not to be Voltaire's; and in the second the voice admits to being Voltaire's but pretends not to be addressing the reader. The literary and ludic interest of these two letters serves only to disguise the otherwise overt authorial guidance being given to the reader.

The continuing interdiction on performances of the play after 1742 did not of course prevent Voltaire from publishing editions of the play outside France; on the contrary, indeed, it probably encouraged him to keep the work before the public, in the hope of future performances. With the 1748 edition of the *Œuvres* published in Dresden (W48D), the play of voices in the paratexts surrounding the play increase significantly in complexity: this marks the high point of the presentation of *Mahomet* as a polemical text aimed at the reader rather than the spectator. In addition to the two letters previously described, Voltaire now adds, in Italian only, the letters of an exchange with Benedict XIV in which the pope apparently gives his blessing to the play. We now know, of course, that the crucial expression of support is a fraudulent addition by Voltaire, who was obviously gambling that his readers would be impressed by the papal authority, albeit in a language which they probably did not read fluently, and that the liberally inclined pope would either not notice the deceit, or not trouble to complain about it. Certainly the dialogism of these prefatory letters is enhanced by the addition of a further 'Voltairean' voice, this time speaking in Italian (French translations of the three letters would be added only in 1757).

At the same time as he added these Italian letters at the beginning, Voltaire also appended to the play his short essay *De l'Alcoran*, remarkable among the various paratexts as the only one in which the authorial voice addresses the reader directly. The interplay between these various paratexts in the 1748 edition is thus extraordinarily complex. The prefatory letters invoke the authority of a king and a pope, no less, to underwrite the argument of the work and in different ways they playfully prepare the reader for the work which is to follow. Having come to the end of the play, the reader now finds a short prose essay in which the highly tendentious discussion of Mohammed and the Koran serves to confirm and extend the preceding discussion. In 1757 Diderot would publish *Le Fils naturel* flanked by prose texts which refract our reading of the play; and while Voltaire does not disconcert the reader quite as radically as Diderot will do a decade later, it does seem that with the 1748 edition of *Mahomet*, Voltaire uses his play to create quite deliberately a literary structure designed to provoke and challenge his reader. Although later on *De l'Alcoran* would become separated from *Mahomet*, the essay was clearly originally conceived as a contribution to the paratexts surrounding *Mahomet*; the works remained together, as originally conceived, in another edition of the *Œuvres* published by Lambert in 1751 (W51), and also in a separate edition of *Mahomet* published by Lambert in the same year (BnC 1015-16). In the 1757 second editon of the Lambert *Œuvres*, *Mahomet* and *De l'Alcoran* appear in separate volumes, and they remain separated thereafter, so that in the Kehl edition, for example, *De l'Alcoran* is assimilated into the 'Mélanges de philosophie', far removed from the volumes of theatre.

*Le Fanatisme, ou Mahomet le prophète*, to give the work its full title, has therefore a double focus, as a polemical work both for the theatre and for the reader at home. As a play, after its initial difficulties, the work was brought back to the Comédie-Française in 1751, and thereafter established itself in the repertoire: the play was very widely translated, and the role of Mahomet became one of the signature roles of Lekain. As a polemical text, the work affords us an important insight into Voltaire's evolving public campaign against fanaticism. At the end of the 1730s he is still attempting to adapt the most august classical forms to the requirements of modern political debate, and it is only later that he will continue his struggle by experimenting with short prose essays; the prose texts which surround this play, perhaps his most political tragedy, mark an important stage in that development. In reuniting two texts which have generally been read separately, this volume allows us to appreciate to the full the complexity of the polemical work which evolved out of the play *Mahomet*.

NEC

# *Le Fanatisme,*

# *ou*

# *Mahomet le prophète,*

# *tragédie*

critical edition

by

Christopher Todd

# ACKNOWLEDGEMENT

I gratefully acknowledge a grant from the University of Leeds which helped me to purchase some of the microfilm needed in the collation of this much-published text. I am also grateful to the staff of the Voltaire Foundation for their help and advice in the preparation of this volume.

Christopher Todd

## CONTENTS

# INTRODUCTION

## 1. '*Mahomet*' and its historical sources

In his desire to give tragedy new local colour Voltaire had first turned to the Islamic world with success in *Zaïre*,[1] although the emphasis there was more on comparing civilisations as well as religions, showing 'les mœurs turques opposées aux mœurs chrétiennes' (D497).[2] With *Zulime*, he moved to North Africa, but with a plot which is 'toute d'invention, et roulant tout entière sur l'amour'.[3] It is only with *Mahomet* that Voltaire is seen to question much more directly the origins of Islam itself, while returning to the epic line developed from *La Henriade* through to the *Histoire de Charles XII* and beyond, in which all events reflect the presence of an overpowering central character,[4] in this case a cruel tyrant.

In France negative views of Islam as a religion of superstition and fanaticism dated back to the middle ages and the crusades.[5] They had, however, been notably reinforced from the end of the seventeenth century by Humphrey Prideaux's *The True nature of imposture fully display'd in the life of Mahomet*[6] on the one hand, and the article 'Mahomet' by Bayle in his *Dictionnaire historique et critique* (1697) on the other. Although differing in overall purpose

[1] See Jean-Luc Doutrelant, 'L'Orient tragique au XVIII^e^ siècle', *Revue des sciences humaines* 37 (1972), p.283-300.

[2] See the introduction by Eva Jacobs to her edition of *Zaïre* (*OC*, vol.8, p.279-82).

[3] Jean-François de La Harpe, *Lycée ou cours de littérature ancienne et moderne* (an VII [1805]), ix.409.

[4] See O. R. Taylor's introduction to *La Henriade* (*OC*, vol.2, p.139-40).

[5] French views of Islam leading up to the composition of *Mahomet* are fully recounted in Magdy Gabriel Badir's impressive *Voltaire et l'Islam*, *SVEC* 125 (1974), p.1-70.

[6] London 1697; translated into French in 1699.

Bayle acknowledged his debt to Prideaux and subscribed fully to his view of Mohammed the man:

Qui voudra voir une suite chronologique des actions et des aventures de ce faux prophète, soutenue de fort bonnes citations, et d'un beau détail de circonstances, n'aura qu'à lire l'ouvrage de M. Prideaux. Il a été traduit d'anglais en français depuis la première édition de ce Dictionnaire. On y voit entre autre choses beaucoup de preuves que Mahomet a été un imposteur, et qu'*il a fait servir* son imposture *à sa cupidité*.[7]

This harsh view was echoed by others. At a meeting of the Académie des inscriptions et belles-lettres on 17 November 1724 the abbé Vertot read a 'Dissertation sur l'auteur de l'*Alcoran*' in which he too sought to portray Mohammed as an ignorant man who took advantage of the stupidy of others.[8] Reviewing the history of Islam given in Granet and Desmolet's *Recueil de pièces d'histoire et de littérature*, the *Mercure de France* stressed how the author 'réfute en peu de mots [...] les principes de cette fausse religion'.[9] Yet in the *Nouvelliste du Parnasse* the abbé Desfontaines expressed grudging admiration for Islam, amid some distaste for the character of its founder:

J'ai toujours admiré l'adresse de Mahomet à gouverner ses passions; dévoré par l'ambition, tyrannisé par la volupté, il se prêta d'abord à l'une, pour satisfaire l'autre; et sachant combien la religion a d'empire sur les hommes, il adopta les opinions de différentes sectes, pour multiplier le nombre de ses disciples; son autorité étant affermie, il fit toujours servir la religion à ses passions. Il était bien difficile qu'un tel législateur ne séduisît pas des hommes corrompus.[10]

Desfontaines may have been influenced by a more sympathetic view of the Prophet which had appeared a year earlier with the

[7] *Dictionnaire historique et critique. Seconde édition* (Rotterdam 1702), ii.1987.

[8] See *Mercure de France* (December 1724), p.2577-80.

[9] *Mercure* (March 1732), p.510, reviewing François Granet and Pierre-Nicolas Desmolets, *Recueil de pièces d'histoire et de littérature* (Paris 1731-1732): this work was consulted by Voltaire in 1735 (D906).

[10] *Nouvelliste du Parnasse* (1731), i.388-89.

posthumous publication in 1730 of the comte de Boulainvilliers's *Vie de Mahomed*, Voltaire's main source for the plot of his play.[11] The French were given a more complete view of Mohammed with the publication in 1732 of Jean Gagnier's *La Vie de Mahomet traduite et compilée de l'Alcoran*, described as an 'enchaînement de faits, où à peine se trouve-t-il la moindre place pour quelque réflexion',[12] a book which Voltaire still possessed at the time of his death (BV1411), and which provided him with details for the stories of both Séide (Zeid) and Zopire (Abou-Soffian).[13] George Sale's English translation of the Koran (London 1734) was also in Voltaire's library at his death (BV1786). He may also have known the anonymous *Traité des trois imposteurs*, circulating in manuscript in 1719.

Under the influence of Boulainvilliers and others Voltaire himself eventually subscribed to a softer, more balanced, view of Islam.[14] In the *Essai sur les mœurs*, for instance, he directly echoes Boulainvilliers in stressing that Mohammed did not invent polygamy.[15] He also defends him against the charge of ignorance, and sees Islam as following an opposing path to Christianity by becoming progressively more humane and tolerant.[16] Mohammed may have been mistaken, using methods that could hardly be approved of, but his motives were not necessarily as black and self-seeking as previously painted: 'Il est à croire que

[11] Henri, comte de Boulainvilliers, *Vie de Mahomed* (London 1730). Ronald W. Tobin, 'The sources of Voltaire's *Mahomet*', *French review* 34 (1961), p.372-78, proves convincingly that Voltaire consulted Boulainvilliers rather than Prideaux, as has been suggested by some (see H. Lion, *Les Tragédies et les théories dramatiques de Voltaire*, Paris 1895, p.139-42; H. Carrington Lancaster, *French tragedy in the time of Louis XV and Voltaire, 1715-1774*, Baltimore 1959, i.203-205).

[12] *Bibliothèque française* (1732), viii.382.

[13] See R. S. Ridgway, *La Propagande philosophique dans les tragédies de Voltaire*, *SVEC* 15 (1961), p.122; Badir, *Voltaire et l'Islam*, p.127-30.

[14] See René Pomeau, *La Religion de Voltaire*, nouv. éd. (Paris 1969), p.156-58.

[15] *Essai sur les mœurs*, ch.7, ed. R. Pomeau (Paris 1963), i.269; all references are to this edition.

[16] *Ibid.*, i.259 and 275.

Mahomet, comme tous les enthousiastes, violemment frappé de ses idées, les débita d'abord de bonne foi, les fortifia par des rêveries, se trompa lui-même en trompant les autres, et appuya enfin, par des fourberies nécessaires, une doctrine qu'il croyait bonne' (i.257). While accusing Boulainvilliers of showing rather too much understanding for his hero, Voltaire too bore witness to the grandeur of the latter: 'Ce fut certainement un très grand homme, et qui forma de grands hommes' (ii.918). There is little of this less-damning view of Mohammed here and we can only suggest that its complexity hardly fitted Voltaire's long-affirmed dramatic purpose of producing tragedies based on 'de grands intérêts' (D940), and in which a truly tragic character is one who is 'furieux, terrible, auteur de crimes, accompagné de remords'.[17]

When Voltaire wrote from Cirey to thank La Noue for a copy of his *Mahomet II* – the success of which may well have encouraged him in his return to a Near Eastern subject[18] – he pointed out various historical inaccuracies in La Noue's plot, while admitting that it was not the duty of the dramatist to show a servile respect for historical truth (D1966; 3 April 1739):

Ce que je dis icy, je le dis en historien, non en poète. Je suis très loin de vous condamner. Vous avez suivi le préjugé reçu et un préjugé suffit pour un peintre et pour un poète. Où en seraient Virgile et Homère si on les avait chicannés sur les faits? Une fausseté qui produit au théâtre une belle situation, est préférable en ce cas à toutes les archives de l'Univers.

Whatever Voltaire's real views, and even if his play owes a great deal to Boulainvilliers, the overall attitude remains closer to that of Prideaux and Bayle,[19] and we must not expect to find in Voltaire's

[17] *Notebooks*, *OC*, vol.82, p.456

[18] See Badir, *Voltaire et l'Islam*, p.75-77.

[19] Indeed Haydn Mason sees the general influence of Bayle in the harsh way that Voltaire depicts Mohammed in his play (H. T. Mason, *Pierre Bayle and Voltaire*, Oxford 1963, p.50-51).

*Mahomet* a balanced view of Islam.[20] As the *Journal encyclopédique* commented in 1756, in a summary of the general reputation of each of Voltaire's major dramatic works, 'quelle peinture frappante des effets du fanatisme dans le tableau qu'offre *Mahomet*'.[21] Voltaire's play is propaganda, and inevitably entails simplification and the sacrifice of truth to the expression of a message.[22]

Sending the first act to Frederick the Great in July 1739, Voltaire portrayed it as the first attempt ever made to portray superstition and fanaticism on the French stage: 'Je prends donc la liberté de lui envoyer ce premier acte d'une tragédie qui me paraît, sinon dans un bon goût, au moins dans un goût nouveau. On n'avait jamais mis sur le théâtre la superstition et le fanatisme' (D2048). He explained his purpose even more clearly when he sent the last two acts in September of the same year (D2074):

> Votre altesse royale verra si les horreurs que le fanatisme entraîne, y sont peintes d'un pinceau assez ferme et assez vray. Le malheureux Said qui croit servir dieu en égorgeant son père n'est point un portrait chimérique. Les Jean Chatel, les Clements, les Ravaillacs étoient dans ce cas et ce qu'il y a de plus horrible c'est qu'ils étoient tous dans la bonne foi. N'estce donc pas rendre service à l'humanité de distinguer toujours, comme j'ay

[20] On Voltaire's treatment of Islam I acknowledge my debt to the notes and commentaries in Jean Humbert's edition of the play (Geneva 1825). The most detailed and comprehensive modern study of the play comes as the second part of Badir's *Voltaire et l'Islam*, p.71-146. A critical edition of the play was also the subject of a 'thèse pour le doctorat de 3$^{e}$ cycle' presented by Marie-Noëlle Basuyaux-Revel under the direction of Professor Jacques Truchet at the Université de Paris X-Nanterre in 1973. Although the critical apparatus covers a rather limited number of editions and manuscripts, there are some interesting comments in the introduction and the notes. While showing the debt to Boulainvilliers and others, for instance, Basuyaux-Revel nevertheless insists (p.xlvii) that it is borrowings from Prideaux that give the play its tone.

[21] *Journal encyclopédique* (December 1756), viii.109.

[22] For a study of how psychological truth is sacrified in the play, see Ahmad Gunny, 'Tragedy in the service of propaganda: Voltaire's *Mahomet*', in *En marge du classicisme: essays on the French theatre from the Renaissance to the Enlightenment*, ed. A. Howe and R. Waller (Liverpool 1987), p.227-42. Gunny says that *Mahomet* reads rather like a pamphlet, and finds it less dramatically convincing than *Zaïre*.

fait, la relligion de la superstition; et méritoi-je d'être persécuté pour avoir toujours dit en cent façons différentes, qu'on ne fait jamais de bien à dieu en faisant du mal aux hommes?

This was an idea which he stressed many times (D2106, D2221, D2386, D2584).

Commenting on the similarly expressed arguments in the 'Avis de l'éditeur',[23] the *Bibliothèque française* wrote:

A l'entendre, si son *Mahomet* eût été joué il y a cent-trois ou cent-cinquante-cinq ans, Henri III et Henri IV vivraient encore, ou pour parler plus sérieusement n'auraient point été assassinés par Clément et par Ravaillac. Mais il s'en faut beaucoup que les personnes judicieuses et sensées pensent ainsi. On lui reproche, au contraire, qu'une pareille tragédie n'est qu'une odieuse école de meurtre et d'assassinat, toute propre à former de pareils monstres.[24]

In *Mahomet*, therefore, the real Mohammed is misrepresented from the start. Not only is he transformed into a hypocritical, love-sick, ambitious and bloodthirsty villain,[25] but he is also seen as the lowest of the low, with an exaggerated view of his former poverty.[26] Voltaire casts middle-class scorn on the profession of camel-driver (act I line 231), for instance, although it is perfectly respectable in an Arabian context, and, contrary to what is implied, Mohammed was not banished from Mecca by the Senate (act I line 236), but left of his own accord. On his return after an exile which did not last fifteen years,[27] there is

[23] First published with the play in 1743 (43A3).

[24] *Bibliothèque française* (1743), xxxvi.178.

[25] See, for instance, act II lines 139-156, 189-196, 239-240, 315-316, 323-324, 345-347; act III lines 102-108, 141-142; act IV lines 9-11.

[26] Act I lines 203-205. Humbert comments: 'Mahomet, ayant perdu son père à l'âge de deux ans, n'hérita de lui que cinq chameaux et une esclave éthiopienne; mais quoiqu'il fût *sans biens*, on ne le vit pas "Ramper au dernier rang des derniers citoyens." Il était de la tribu des Koréischites, la plus illustre des tribus arabes.'

[27] Act II line 75. Humbert comments: 'L'exil de Mahomet n'avait pas duré *quinze* ans, puisque la Mecque fut prise la huitième année de l'*hégyre* (c'est-à-dire de la *fuite* du prophète).'

excessive emphasis on battle[28] and criminal trickery (act II line 166).

The starting point for the plot is the opposition to Mohammed by Abou-Soffian (the Zopire of the play),[29] which in the original account finally led to the Prophet retiring from Mecca. To quote Boulainvilliers:

Au contraire Abusophian, soutenu par un vieillard inconnu que les auteurs postérieurs ont imaginé avoir été le Diable, déguisé sous cette forme, prétendit prouver que Mahomed s'était rendu coupable de mort en attaquant la religion commune du pays; en tenant des assemblées particuliéres; et en s'efforçant de soulever le peuple par des harangues publiques, et des écrits séditieux qu'il répandait: lesquels ne contenaient que des menaces propres à troubler la société. [...]

Cependant Abusophian, le plus grand ennemi du Prophète, se trouva revêtu de la principale autorité dans la ville de la Mecque par la mort d'Abutaleb; circonstance peu favorable aux projets de Mahomed, et qui anima tellement contre lui les Koréishites (qui jusques-là avaient été retenus par le grand crédit d'Abutaleb) qu'ils commencèrent dès lors à s'opposer vigoureusement aux progrès considérables que le Musulmanisme avait déjà faits à la Mecque et aux environs. Ils y réussirent même si bien que plusieurs des disciples du Prophète, voyant qu'il n'y avait rien à gagner avec lui, et qu'au contraire il y avait tout à craindre, l'abandonnèrent lui et sa nouvelle religion.

Mahomed n'était pas homme à se rebuter, et les difficultés qu'il rencontrait ne servaient qu'à animer son courage, et à le rendre plus

[28] Act II lines 48 and 125. Humbert comments at line 125: 'Mahomet entra en effet dans la Mecque sans coup férir. Ses généraux avaient ordre de ne point combattre, à moins d'être provoqués. Une légère escarmouche ayant eu lieu aux portes de la ville entre les Koréischistes et les soldats de Khaled, Mahomet, qui s'en aperçut du haut d'une colline, s'écria: "Ciel! que vois-je? N'avais-je pas défendu de combattre?" Et il signifia d'épargner le sang.'

[29] The names of Zopire, Palmire and Phanor are invented, although the first two owe at least something to history. Zopyrus was a Persian who helped Darius to trick his way into Babylon (Herodotus, iii.153-160). Palmyra is the Greek name of the city-state of Tadmor, and seventeenth-century France saw three plays on its queen, Zenobia Septimia (J.-M.-B. Clément and Joseph de La Porte, *Anecdotes dramatiques*, Paris 1775, ii.281).

attentif. Voyant donc que les Mecquois étaient si fort prévenus contre sa doctrine, il jugea devoir céder au temps, et attendre des circonstances pour les amener à ses sentiments. Il sortit donc de la Mecque.[30]

It is on this basis that Voltaire constructs a tale of jealousy in which Mohammed disposes of his main opponent, whereas the real Abou-Soffian ended up as a convert to the religion of his former enemy:

Dès qu'Omar vit cet ancien ennemi du Prophète, il courut à Mahomed pour lui demander la permission de le tuer. Mais elle lui fut refusée, et Mahomed assura le chef des Koréishites qu'il ne lui serait fait aucune insulte dans son camp. Cette première entrevue fut suivie d'une seconde, dans laquelle Mahomed acheva de persuader Abusophian d'embrasser le Musulmanisme.[31]

To carry out the murder Voltaire's Mahomet uses one of the real Mohammed's lieutenants, Zeid, renamed here Séide, and turns him into a blind fanatic. There is no hint of this in the original tale, although as Boulainvilliers tells us the real Zeid – a former slave – was well-known for his absolute fidelity to his master, being Mohammed's second convert, and we can see where Voltaire found the source of the rivalry over love:

Le second prosélyte de la religion musulmane a été Zéid, fils de Hareth, cousin germain et beau-frère de Mahomet, duquel il est aussi qualifié *serviteur*, non seulement parce qu'il s'était intimement attaché à sa personne, mais plutôt parce que depuis l'élévation du prophète à la dignité de chef de la nation arabe, il a fait la charge de son ministre: fonction qui en ces termes de simplicité ne donnait encore à ceux qui en étaient revêtus que celui d'employé, ou de serviteur [...]. Au reste, ce Zéid est fameux dans cette histoire par rapport à l'injustice que Mahomet commit envers lui par l'enlèvement de sa femme, dont il était devenu amoureux et qu'il l'obligea de répudier pour l'épouser ensuite.[32]

[30] Boulainvilliers, *Vie de Mahomed*, p.302-303, 352-53.

[31] Boulainvilliers, *Vie de Mahomed*, p.392; see also Gagnier, i.416-21.

[32] Boulainvilliers, *Vie de Mahomed*, p.273-74.

Like his leader, Mohammed's uncle, the true Omar also suffers unfair transformation,[33] and the inhabitants of Mecca are also slandered. They are seen as the 'plus vils des humains' (act I line 234), just as it is suggested that the Arabs prefer slavery to death (act I line 131).

The scant respect for historical truth is compounded by a certain amount of invention. Mahomet's desire for revenge stems from the fact that Zopire has killed his son (act I lines 42, 288), whereas the sons of the real Mohammed died naturally in infancy. More for the sake of the rhyme than for any other apparent reason, Voltaire talks of fertile countryside around Mecca (act I line 166), where there is in fact nothing but dry desert. He also creates rather misplaced names for fictitious characters such as Hercide and Ammon (act II line 91). Voltaire also transposes to the Arabs the Turkish habit of insisting on a yearly tribute of young Greek Christians (act III line 264). There is a certain amount of anachronism. Obviously wanting to give the subject more prestige, Voltaire repeatedly refers to both Mahomet and the Arabs as great conquerors, long before they actually became so.[34] In addition, Mahomet is seen as using force to convert the infidel (act II lines 191-192) at a time when – as related by Boulainvillers – he still relied on persuasion:

Jusqu'alors Mahomed s'était contenté de prêcher une Doctrine, bonne ou mauvaise, qui n'influait pas directement sur le gouvernement de l'Etat: mais dans la treizième année de sa mission, il changea de langage: et l'on

[33] Act I lines 167, 266-269; act V line 35. Humbert comments at act I line 174: 'Omar fut un prince doux, modéré, frugal, simple dans ses mœurs, chéri de tous ceux qu'il abordait. S'il fit incendier la fameuse bibliothèque d'Alexandrie, ce fait prouve plus son ignorance que sa fureur. Econome pour lui-même, Omar était prodigue pour les autres; il distribuait tous les vendredis l'argent du trésor. Mais dans cette tragédie, Omar n'est que le vil satellite d'un tyran plus vil encore.'

[34] Act I lines 19, 258, 269; act II line 63; act III line 182. Cf. Humbert's note to act I line 19, for example: 'Vingt ans plus tard, on aurait pu parler des *trente nations* domptés par les Musulmans; mais à l'époque de la prise de la Mecque, Mahomet n'avait encore soumis que des tribus arabes et juives, battu une fois les Grecs de Syrie, et fait quelques prosélytes en Ethiopie.'

vit ce Prophète, qui d'abord se disait n'être envoyé du Ciel que pour ramener les hommes au culte de Dieu, et qui déclarait n'avoir rien à opposer aux persécutions de ses ennemis qu'une grande patience: on vit, dis-je, ce Prophète prendre des mesures pour faire la guerre à sa patrie; et supposer des ordres positifs de la part de Dieu, d'exterminer tous ceux qui ne croiraient point en lui, ou qui ne se soumettraient pas à son obéissance.[35]

There is little respect for the true spirit of Islam. The Prophet Mahomet carries out miracles,[36] is presented as the sole and exclusive interpreter of God's will,[37] and shows scant respect for his followers, from whom he expects blind unquestioning faith.[38] Mahomet is addressed as a king.[39] With repeated references to altars and incense,[40] Islam is seen as a form of idolatry, although this was one of the main features of earlier religions that the real Mohammed strove against:

Mahomed, maître de cette importante place, songea d'abord à abolir

[35] Boulainvilliers, *Vie de Mahomed*, p.358. See also the review in the *Mercure* of the succinct history of the real Mohammed, based on Abulfeda and others, which appeared in Granet and Desmolet's *Recueil de pièces d'histoire et de littérature*: 'Il fut cependant douze ou treize ans suivi d'un très petit nombre de disciples. La quatrième année près de quatre-vingts disciples se joignirent aux premiers, ce qui fit du bruit dans la Mecque. Les magistrats en craignirent quelqu'émotion et le chassèrent de la ville [...] Peu de temps après cette fuite, Mahomet eut recours à l'épée, qui lui réussit encore mieux que la parole' (*Mercure*, March 1732, p.514-15).

[36] Humbert comments at act I line 20: 'Mahomet n'a jamais prétendu pouvoir opérer des *miracles*, et même il blâma hautement ceux qui lui en demandaient. Voyez l'*Alcoran*, chap.XVII et XXI, A 5 et 6.'

[37] Humbert comments at act I line 146: 'Mahomet, il est vrai, s'est donné pour *envoyé du ciel*, mais jamais pour *son seul interprète*. L'Alcoran proclame à chaque page d'autres interprètes du ciel, et surtout Adam, Noë, Abraham, Joseph, Moïse, David, Jean-Baptiste, et Jésus-Christ.'

[38] Act I lines 23 and 146; act II line 121 and act IV line 28; act III line 177.

[39] Act II line 95; act III line 184.

[40] Act I line 258; act II lines 110, 142; act III lines 149, 262. Humbert comments at act II line 142: 'Les Mahométans n'ont pas dans leurs temples ni autel ni *encensoir* ni parfum. Leur culte est aussi simple que celui des Réformés. Il y a seulement, à l'extrémité des mosquées, une sorte de niche pour marquer la *Kibla*, c'est-à-dire l'endroit vers lequel on doit se tourner en priant (cet endroit, c'est la Mecque).'

entièrement le culte des idoles, qui y était pratiqué. Il renversa pour cet effet tous les simulacres qui jusqu'alors avaient été les objets de la vénération des Arabes. Il sanctifia ensuite par son exemple la visitation du Temple, et celle du Kaaba, en faisant le tour de ces lieux, réputés saints, par sept fois.[41]

By talking about 'un dieu' rather than God, Mahomet is even made to sound as though he believed in polytheism. His God is seen as a 'new' God, quite unlike that of the Jews or the Christians, even though an essential part of Islam is the link with earlier monotheistic faiths:

Mahomet pour profiter de ces divisions et pour réunir toutes ces sectes en une seule, pose pour principal fondement qu'il n'y a qu'un Dieu digne de nos adorations; ce principe établi avec les Chrétiens et avec les Juifs, il tâche d'y amener aussi les Ismaëlites ou les Arabes, en les faisant souvenir qu'ils sont enfants d'Abraham, et qu'Abraham n'a jamais adoré qu'un seul Dieu.[42]

As we shall see, the problem for Voltaire was to try and attack fanaticism, without casting unfair aspersions on true religious sentiment (see, e.g., act II line 351; act I lines 245-246).

## 2. *Composition*

Although the 'Avis de l'éditeur', published in 1743 and doubtless written by Voltaire, says that *Mahomet* was written in 1736, the first clear reference to it is in April 1739, when he writes to d'Argental: 'L'auteur de Mahomet 2 m'a envoyé sa pièce, elle est pleine de vers étincelants, le sujet étoit bien difficile à traitter. Que diriez vous si je vous envoyais bientôt Mahomet premier?' (D1962). La Noue's play was first performed in Paris on 23 February 1739. *Mahomet* was almost certainly also the subject of earlier allusions in Voltaire's correspondence during February and

[41] Boulainvilliers, *Vie de Mahomed*, p.393; cf. act II line 226.

[42] *Mercure de France* (March 1732), p.512-13; see act II lines 123, 216.

March (D1862, D1932, D1957). The correction of *Zulime* then seems to have taken up most of Voltaire's attention, but he was back working on *Mahomet* by the beginning of June (D2022), and before the end of the first week in July he had finished the first draft and was already thinking of having the play performed anonymously (D2040). By September he had sent the complete text to Frederick, as we have seen, and he also entrusted a copy of the manuscript to the actress Mlle Quinault and invited her to read it to her colleagues (D2071). He sent further corrections to her, care of Pont de Veyle, in January 1740 (D2131), and a performance by the actors of the Comédie-Française was expected (D2141, D2150).

At the same time Voltaire admitted to being hampered by having to be careful and not say all that he wanted to on such a delicate subject as religious fanaticism: 'La circonspection est une belle chose, mais en vers elle est bien triste. Etre raisonable et froid, c'est presque tout un' (D2148). On 31 January 1740, apparently as a result of some advice received from d'Argental, he decided that he was still far from happy with the text (D2154). He continued to revise it, asking Cideville, d'Argental and others for their advice.[43]

By July 1740 circumspection dictated the rather less obvious title of *Séide* (D2259). At the beginning of 1741 Voltaire even thought of having the play printed, but was discouraged by Mme Du Châtelet (D2399). The play was approved for performance on 10 January 1741, but withdrawn ten days later (see MS3, p.51). Voltaire continued to talk of a possible performance (D2415); he seemed at last to be satisfied that the play was ready to be performed (D2433, D2434) and continued to send instructions for the actors in Paris (D2443). Immediate performance in the capital was, however, made more difficult through the departure

[43] See D2137, D2193, D2194, D2218, D2230, D2247, D2251, D2266, D2408, D2459, D2523, D2525, D2533.

from the Comédie-Française of the actor Dufresne (D2459) on whom Voltaire had been counting for the role of Séide (D2170).

Voltaire abandoned hope of immediate performance at the Comédie-Française, therefore, and began to look to the provinces (D2439, D2423, D2455). While on a visit to his niece, Mme Denis, in Lille, he read his 'Mahomet premier' to La Noue, author of *Mahomet II* (D2444) and sent La Noue a verse comparison of the two plays (D2447):

> Mon cher Lanoue, illustre père
> De l'invincible Mahomet,
> Soyez le parain d'un cadet,
> Qui sans vous n'est pas fait pour plaire.
> Votre fils fut un conquérant;
> Le mien, a l'honneur d'être apôtre
> Prêtre, filou, dévot, brigand,
> Faites en l'aumônier du vôtre...

As well as being a playwright, La Noue was also the leader of a troupe of actors recently established in Lille, and it was they who gave the play its first performance on 25 April 1741 (D2456). La Noue wrote to Cideville: 'M. de Voltaire est à Lille et nous jouerons aujourd'hui pour la première fois son Mahomet. Il en a vu hier deux représentations; il est content du jeu que j'ay donné. Je vous écrirai demain ce que toute la ville aura senti, car nous serons pleins jusqu'aux fenêtres. C'est, selon moi, un magnifique ouvrage. Oh! Le beau quatrième acte!' [44] Four performances were given. La Noue played Mahomet and François Baron, Séide. The role of Palmire was apparently taken by Mlle Gautier. [45]

Voltaire and Mme Du Châtelet looked on the Lille performances as a kind of dress rehearsal (D2466) for later staging in the

[44] Léon Lefèvre, *Histoire du théâtre de Lille* (1905), i.235, quoted by Spire Pitou, 'Sauvé de La Noue: actor, author, producer', *SVEC* 117 (1974), p.99.

[45] And not Mlle Clairon, as suggested by Lefèvre (Lefèvre, i.235). On the Lille performances see also Louis Trénard, 'L'influence de Voltaire à Lille au XVIII$^{e}$ siècle', *SVEC* 58 (1967), p.1610-12, quoting the preface to the edition of the play by A. M. Gossez (Lille 1932), p.14-22.

capital (D2459): 'On dira que je ne suis plus qu'un auteur de province, mais j'aime encor mieux juger moy même de l'effet que fera cet ouvrage dans une ville où je n'ay point de cabale à craindre que d'essuyer encore les orages de Paris.' Voltaire was well satisfied with the play's reception in Lille (D2478), but Mme Du Châtelet's lawsuit called him back to Brussels and delayed his plans for the play in Paris (D2482). Both in Brussels and after Voltaire's return to Cirey, revision of the work continued off and on for the rest of the year and into the next (D2533, D2558). Immediate performance in Paris was, however, now prevented by the presence of the Turkish ambassador, Mehmed Sa'd Pasha, and the impossibility of performing such a play during his visit. A further complication was the fact that La Noue had been invited to Berlin by Frederick, and Voltaire had wanted him to repeat his success as Mahomet in Paris, despite his not yet being a member of the Comédie-Française.[46] The play was at last produced in Paris on Monday 9 August 1742.[47] Mahomet was played by Grandval, Séide by La Noue, Omar by Legrand, Zopire by Sarrazin and Palmyre by Mlle Gaussin. The play was given two further performances on the following two nights before mounting pressure forced Voltaire to withdraw it.[48]

## 3. *Reception*

At these first Paris performances *Mahomet* met with tolerable but mixed success, as the full account in the *Bibliothèque française* shows:

> Le célèbre, le rare, l'admirable, le charmant M. de Voltaire vient de nous donner aujourd'hui une nouvelle attendue, souhaitée. Je sors de la Comédie-Française; et j'aurais de la peine à vous dire ce que je suis après ce spectacle, et ce que j'ai été pendant la représentation.

[46] See D2569, D2574, D2583, D2584, D2585, D2592.

[47] *Bibliothèque française* (1742), xxxv(i), p.144-45.

[48] For the first of the three performances 1205 tickets were sold; for the second performance 1102 and for the third 998. Voltaire's share in the receipts was 774 francs (Lancaster, *French tragedy*, i.209-10).

*Mahomet* est-il reçu? Ne l'est-il pas? C'est encore un paradoxe, quoiqu'il ait été applaudi. Il semble que, par une certaine fatalité, jusqu'au jeux d'esprit qui portent le nom de ce célèbre législateur, tout ce qui en rappelle la mémoire, doive, comme la religion exciter du trouble et des combats, et ne s'établir que par la force. Aussi est-ce la route qu'a suivie M. de Voltaire dans son poème: il étonne, il étourdit la raison par des traits qu'on a plutôt applaudis qu'entendus. La terreur est le caractère dominant de cette tragédie. L'inceste, le parricide, le poison, le sacrilège en sont les ressorts.

Le premier acte a été peu applaudi: il est d'exposition, et n'intéresse pas beaucoup. Le second m'a paru plus fort de versification. Le troisième a fait beaucoup d'effet par la force du caractère de Mahomet qui s'y développe pleinement. Le 4ᵉ est le plus terrible et le plus touchant coup de théâtre qu'on ait jamais exposé sur la scène. Le commencement du 5ᵉ acte a été fort applaudi dans une tirade débitée avec feu par mademoiselle Gaussin. La catastrophe a fait un effet assez équivoque.

Le sieur Grandval fait Mahomet. Ce rôle demanderait une figure capable de répondre à l'idée extraordinaire que nous nous formons du personnage: et le législateur de l'Asie s'y présente sous la forme d'un fréluquet. Le rôle de Séid, jeune prince amoureux et fanatique, est rempli par La Noue. Celui-ci demandait sans doute une figure noble et grâcieuse. Le fond du caractère qui n'est pas bien élevé par lui-même, est encore dégradé, ce me semble, par l'action peu avantageuse de ce comédien, qu'on n'appelera jamais le Maquereau des vers. Si Le Grand qui fait le rôle d'Omar avait pensé l'apprendre par cœur, il s'en serait tiré assez bien. Sarrasin fait celui de Zopire, comme il fait la plupart de ses rôles, non pas comme il fait celui de Lusignan. Mademoiselle Gaussin a rempli le sien comme la Beauté secondée de toutes les Grâces est capable de faire.[49]

Even before its first performance, however, the play was causing disquiet in official circles, and it was staged without the approval of Crébillon, a royal censor as well as Voltaire's rival: 'Feu M. de Crébillon, alors Censeur de la Police, avait refusé son approbation. M. de Voltaire avait eu le crédit d'en faire entendre

[49] *Bibliothèque française* (1742), xxxv(i), p.144-45.

une lecture au cardinal de Fleury, qui donna l'ordre de la laisser jouer. La crainte de M. le procureur-général empêcha cependant les comédiens d'en continuer les représentations.'[50]

On 7 and 8 August the police spy Mouhy had written to the *lieutenant de police*, Marville, that the play was widely 'décrié', and that it was unlikely to succeed since its author had too many enemies.[51] In other words, there was already a plot to have it suppressed, perhaps, as Voltaire later alleged, with the abbé Desfontaines at its centre:

On a vu une cabale de canailles, & un abbé Des F........ à la tête de cette cabale au sortir de Bicêtre, forcer le gouvernement à suspendre les représentations de *Mahomet*, joué par ordre du gouvernement; ils avaient pris pour prétexte que dans cette tragédie de *Mahomet*, il y avait plusieurs traits contre ce faux prophète, qui pouvaient rejaillir sur les convulsionnaires: ainsi ils eurent l'insolence d'empêcher pour quelques temps les représentations.[52]

On 13 August the *procureur général*, Joly de Fleury, wrote to Marville (D2638): 'Sur ce que je viens d'apprendre, je crois qu'il faut défendre la pièce [...]. Tout le monde dit que pour avoir composé une pareille pièce il faut être un scélérat à faire brûler [...]. C'est une révolte universelle [...]. Ce soir on l'a annoncée pour jeudi: ne faudrait il point demain à l'annonce, en annoncer une

[50] Clément and La Porte, *Anecdotes dramatiques*, i.504. According to the Kehl editors: 'en 1741 M. Crébillon refusa d'approuver la tragédie de *Mahomet*, non qu'il aimât les hommes qui avaient intérêt de faire supprimer la pièce, ni même qu'ils les craignit; mais uniquement parce qu'on l'avait persuadé que *Mahomet* était le rival d'*Atrée*' (both plays involve incest and parricide, and both have a subplot of children who are ignorant of their father's existence). See also Charles Collé, *Journal et mémoires*, ed. H. Bonhomme (Paris 1868), i.349-50. For a survey of Crébillon's opposition to the play, see P. M. Conlon, 'Voltaire's literary career from 1728 to 1750', *SVEC* 14 (1961), p.171-72, and Paul O. LeClerc, *Voltaire and Crébillon père: history of an enmity*, *SVEC* 115 (1973), p.42-60.

[51] D2633; see also Barbier, viii.145; Desnoiresterres, ii.337. After the first performance Mouhy attributed what applause there had been to a hired claque among the groundlings (Barbier, viii.153).

[52] D9492; see also the 'Avis de l'éditeur' below, and Barbier, viii.156.

autre?'[53] Marville, feeling under attack himself, wrote to Maurepas (D2636), who in turn went to see the cardinal de Fleury with the result that it was agreed that one of the actors should pretend to be ill in order to stop a fourth performance on the Thursday (D2637). On 15 August Marville was able to report that Voltaire had angrily agreed to withraw the play (D2641). The following short note appeared in the *Mercure:* 'Le 9 août, les Comédiens français donnèrent la première représentation d'une tragédie nouvelle de M. de Voltaire, intitulée *Mahomet*, laquelle a été retirée par l'auteur après la troisième représentation. On en parlera plus au long.'[54]

The fuller discussion of the play did not materialise. Aunillion's commentary on the play printed in the *Nouveaux amusements du cœur et de l'esprit* adds an anecdote:

Voici quelque chose d'assez plaisant. On donna *Polyeucte* à la place de *Mahomet*; un homme d'esprit de nos amis dit que c'était une espèce d'amende honorable que le théâtre faisait au public: mais vous allez être bien édifié. Ces zélés qui avaient tant fait de bruit sur l'impiété de *Mahomet*, n'applaudirent de toute la tragédie de *Polyeucte*, que cette affreuse imprécation contre les Chrétiens que Corneille a mise dans la bouche de Statonice au troisième acte de sa tragédie:

> Ce n'est plus cet époux si charmant à vos yeux,
> C'est l'ennemi commun des hommes et des dieux;
> Un méchant, un infâme, un rebelle, un perfide,
> Un traître, un scélérat, un lâche, un parricide.
> Une peste exécrable à tous les gens de bien,
> Un sacrilège impie, en un mot un Chrétien.

Si l'on eût joué *Athalie*, ils auraient sans doute applaudi l'apostasie de Mathan et la confession de son confident.[55]

[53] See Paul Bondois, 'Le procureur-général Joly de Fleury et le "Mahomet" de Voltaire', *Rhl* 36 (1929), p.246-59. Bondois reproduces Joly de Fleury's notes from his reading of the play from his 'Avis et mémoires sur les affaires publiques'.

[54] *Mercure* (August 1743), p.1859.

[55] *Nouveaux amusements du cœur et de l'esprit* (1742), xiv.424-36.

Although Voltaire repeatedly maintained that, like Molière in *Tartuffe*,[56] he was not attacking true religion through showing its misuse in his play, many saw a general slur. For some the staging of the play was judged inexpedient in the light of the recent visit of the Turkish ambassador and of France's close links with the Ottoman Empire.[57] The abbé Le Blanc voiced widely felt criticism (D2635; 13 August 1742):

On est assés surpris de ce [que la p]olice en a permis la représentation. La Politique y est pour le moins aussi maltraitée que la Relligion, c'est le triomphe du Déisme ou plustôt du Fatalisme. Le caractère de Mahomet y est absolument manqué. [...] C'est Philoctète coëffé d'un Turban. Palmire, Zéïde & Zopire leur Père, sont le Luzignan, le Nerestan & la Zaïre de la Piéce qui porte ce titre. L'Horreur que le IV Acte peut inspirer est düe aux Imitations d'Atrée. Le Prétendu miracle qui fait le dénoûment de la Piéce ne m'a paru que puérile. En un mot ce n'est pas la plus mauvaise Tragédie que je connoisse mais la plus extravagante.

Lord Chesterfield was even more scathing:

Mais ce que je ne lui pardonne pas, et qui n'est pas pardonnable, c'est tous les mouvements qu'il se donne pour la propagation d'une doctrine aussi pernicieuse à la société civile que contraire à la religion générale de tous les pays.

Je doute fort s'il est permis à un homme d'écrire contre le culte et la croyance de son pays, quand même il serait de bonne foi persuadé qu'il y eût des erreurs, à cause du trouble et du désordre qu'il y pourrait causer; mais je suis bien sûr qu'il n'est nullement permis d'attaquer les fondements de la morale, et de rompre des liens si nécessaires, et déjà trop faibles pour retenir les hommes dans le devoir.[58]

Feeling, again like Molière, that he was the victim of a 'cabale'

[56] See for instance the 'Avis de l'éditeur' of 1743.

[57] *Bibliothèque française* (1742), xxxvi.181-82.

[58] D2653. Similar sentiments continued to be echoed after Voltaire's death. Some even accused Voltaire of making fanaticism attractive: 'Bornons-nous pour le moment au seul *Mahomet*, pièce atroce, où le crime triomphe de la manière la plus éclatante, où le plus scélérat des hommes inspire plus d'admiration que de haine, grâce au brillant coloris que l'auteur lui a donné' (*Année littéraire*, 1784, i.295).

of 'convulsionnaires en robe longue',[59] Voltaire once more left Paris and set off for Brussels with Mme Du Châtelet, where he started to plan the publication of the work. If it could not be performed, it could at least be printed.

The first performances of the play were greeted by a number of pamphlets, including the abbé Cahagne's *Lettre d'un comédien de Lille sur la tragédie de Mahomet*,[60] and *Sentiments d'un spectateur sur la tragédie de Mahomet, août 1742*,[61] Claude Villaret's *Lettre à Monsieur de V***, sur sa tragédie de Mahomet* (n.p. 1742), and Pierre Aunillion's *Lettre écrite à M. le Comte ***, au sujet de la tragédie de Mahomet, de M. de Voltaire* already quoted.[62]

Villaret says that he attended the first performance and wrote his complimentary account the next day. Cahagne's *Lettre* is written from the perspective of one closely connected with the Lille performances ('les cœurs glacés de nos Flamands ne purent résister à la force des ressorts que l'auteur a mis en œuvre pour émouvoir'); his *Sentiments* set out to be impartial ('Je parle sans intérêt et j'ose assurer que je ne suis conduit que par l'amour et l'équité de la raison. J'ai donné à la tragédie de *Mahomet* les éloges que j'ai cru lui devoir'). Aunillion relates the history of the cabale:

[59] D2643, D2644, D2647, D2649.

[60] *Lettre d'un comédien de Lille sur la tragédie de Mahomet. Contenant l'idée des caractères, de la conduite et des détails de cette pièce*, 14pp. (Paris, Prault, 1742); reproduced in *Nouveaux amusements du cœur et de l'esprit* (1742), xiii.518-30.

[61] *Nouveaux amusements du cœur et de l'esprit* (1742), xiv.331-72, followed by the editorial comment: 'L'auteur de cet écrit ingénieux aurait souhaité faire ces réflexions sur la tragédie imprimée de *Mahomet*. Ce n'est que depuis quelques jours qu'on en débite deux éditions pleines de fautes qui ôtent la mesure des vers, et les défigurent horriblement. Le lecteur voudra bien se souvenir qu'il échappe ordinairement à la mémoire quelques traits particuliers d'une pièce qu'on voit représenter et qu'on n'a point lue. C'est dans ce point de vue qu'il faut considérer les *Sentiments* de notre spectateur.'

[62] Ms Arsenal 2757; reproduced in *Nouveaux amusements du cœur et de l'esprit* (1742), xiv.424-46. See George B. Watts, 'Notes on Voltaire', *Mln* 41 (1926), p.118-22. Pierre Fabiot Aunillion was French ambassador to Cologne.

J'ai vu de ces pestes de la société, malheureusement pour eux, trop connues pour faire gloire de leur incrédulité, crier à l'impiété et se scandaliser que *Mahomet* ne prêchât pas les maximes de l'Evangile. J'ai vu de petits auteurs, aussi méprisés que leurs ouvrages, condamner au feu de leur autorité, l'auteur, la pièce, les comédiens, le parterre, et les loges; celui- ci, pour avoir fait, celui-là pour avoir joué, et les autres enfin pour avoir vu et applaudi *Mahomet*. J'ai vu la foule, des sots s'entend, car c'est toujours le plus grand nombre, adopter et répéter au hasard des sentiments si respectables. Dès-là, mon cher comte, vous croyez *Mahomet* tombé à la première représentation; point du tout, ces clabaudeurs y venaient en foule, ils y étaient pénétrés, ils y frémissaient; et pour mettre le comble au contraste de leurs déclamations et leur conduite, ils n'ont cessé de redemander, à grand cris, cette tragédie, depuis qu'on a jugé à propos de la retirer du théâtre.

He goes on to comment more seriously:

Pour la poétique, il me semble qu'on est assez généralement d'accord que M. de Voltaire n'a guère écrit de tragédie mieux que celle-ci, ni avec plus de force et d'imagination. La poésie en est exacte et nerveuse, les images nobles et toujours tirées de son sujet: ainsi il y a apparence qu'on n'a prétendu attaquer son *Mahomet* que par le fonds.

Quel est donc le plan de M. de Voltaire dans cette tragédie? c'est, si je ne me trompe, de faire voir que l'ambition désordonnée, et que le fanatisme, ou le faux zèle, sont capables de porter les hommes à tout ce qu'on peut imaginer de plus atroce.

Aunillion evidently sent his *Lettre* direct to Voltaire, who replied 'Votre lettre a été pour moi ce que la rosée est pour les fleurs, et les rayons du soleil pour le tournesol' (D2671). The remarks by Cahagne and Aunillion in particular were favourably received, and seen as both defending Voltaire's cause and echoing public sentiment.[63] Later criticism in Voltaire's lifetime included Rousseau's *Lettre à d'Alembert sur les spectacles* (1758), quoted in the notes to the text, and J.-M.-B. Clément's *Cinquième lettre à M. de Voltaire* (La Haye 1774).

[63] See *Bibliothèque française*, xxxvi.139.

Further performances in Paris remained central to Voltaire's aspirations after 1742, and in the light of what had happened to the first run these needed to be carefully prepared. The play required patronage and protection, and if French officials could not be counted on, Voltaire felt that he had to go above their heads. Immediately after the abortive first run of the play, he talked of dedicating it to the pope (D2643), and he was thinking of this again by the spring of 1745 (D3112). In August he sent the play to the urbane Benedict XIV, and prefixed both his letter and the pope's reply to editions of the play from 1748 onwards.[64] Voltaire now felt more secure (D4224). The possibility of a new run was in the air as early as 1749 (D3965), although it was not seriously planned until 1751 (D4390).

In the summer of 1751, while Voltaire was in Berlin, permission to revive the play was obtained with the help of the maréchal de Richelieu, who had to overcome last minute opposition again from Crébillon, as described in the *Anecdotes dramatiques*:

L'on demanda encore à cette seconde époque, l'approbation de M. de Crébillon, qui la refusa de nouveau. M. d'Argenson nomma M. d'Alembert pour censeur de cette pièce. Ce dernier s'en chargea, l'examina avec l'attention la plus sévère, fit quelques légers retranchements, et signa son approbation. Il offrit même à M. de Crébillon, de réfuter les raisons de son refus, s'il voulait les faire imprimer; et de joindre, dans la réponse qu'il y ferait, les motifs qu'il avait de permettre la représentation de cette tragédie.[65]

On 30 September *Mahomet* began a successful run of eight performances in Paris. It drew large crowds, 1021 tickets being sold for the first performance:[66]

[64] See the note below to the pope's reply to this letter, p.159.

[65] Clément and La Porte, *Anecdotes dramatiques*, i.504; see also D4539, D4557, D4561, D4576, D10069, D10070. On the significance of d'Alembert's role as censor of *Mahomet* in 1751, see Marta Rezler, 'The Voltaire–d'Alembert correspondence: an historical and bibliographical reappraisal', *SVEC* 20 (1962), p.21-22.

[66] Lancaster, *French tragedy*, i.210.

Les Comédiens français ont remis au théâtre, jeudi 30 septembre, le *Mahomet* de M. de Voltaire. Cette pièce que l'auteur avait retiré en 1742, après trois représentations, a été reçue comme le sont ordinairement les ouvrages de ce grand poète. Beaucoup de gens très éclairés prétendent que c'est celle de ses tragédies où il y a plus de beautés et des idées plus sublimes. Le but de cette pièce, comme tout le monde sait, est de rendre odieux le fanatisme, projet que M. de Voltaire avait ébauché dans *La Henriade*. Le voyage de Fontainebleau a interrompu le succès de *Mahomet* à la huitième représentation.[67]

It is difficult to say exactly who played what during this run, although we can guess. The manuscript register of the Comédie-Française[68] shows that the short play staged on the first night to accompany *Mahomet* was Regnard's *La Sérénade*, but the unpublished part merely lists, without giving other details, the names of the eleven actors and four actresses who were paid for working on 30 September 1751. In theory, seven of them should have been involved in the comedy, and eight in *Mahomet*, allowing for the non-speaking part of Ali. Somewhat surprisingly the list seems to give one actress too many (there are only two female roles in the Regnard play and only one in *Mahomet*) and to be thus one actor short. Eight of the eleven actors named for 30 September were paid for working on all of the twelve days on which *Mahomet* was performed during this run, which ended on 4 December 1751: Baron, Bonneval, Dangeville, Dubois, Grandval, Lekain, Paulin, Sarrazin. A number of these had been involved in the earlier production of the work, such as Sarrazin, Grandval and Paulin who had played Zopire, Mahomet and Phanor in 1742. The only actress paid for working on all twelve nights was Mlle Gaussin, who had played Palmire in 1742.[69] It would seem reasonable to suppose that the role of Séide was filled by Baron, who created it in Lille in 1741, but it may have been given to the

[67] *Mercure de France* (November 1751), p.143.

[68] H. C. Lancaster, *The Comédie-Française 1701-1774: plays actors, spectators, finances*, Transactions of the American Philosophical Society 41 (1951), p.768-69.

[69] On Voltaire's relationship with Mlle Gaussin, see Conlon, 'Voltaire's literary career from 1728 to 1750', p.133-34.

young Lekain, although he was not yet a full member of the troupe.[70] Omar could also have been played by Dangeville, who frequently took the part of the confidant, as he did in La Noue's *Mahomet II*.[71] Other actors named for 30 September – Armand, Bonneval and Deschamps – were usually employed in comic roles, although only the last two were paid when *La Sérénade* was performed with other works on 15 November and 3 December – as were Dubois, often a valet or a confidant, and Drouin, who played youthful lovers. Other actresses named for 30 September and again found for at least one of the two further performances of the Regnard play are Mlle Anne Lavoy, who usually played confidantes and ridiculous women, Mlle Beauménard – the future Rose Bellecour – who was often a 'soubrette', and Mlle Guéant, who specialised in young girls in love. The Registres of the Comédie-Française tell us that diamonds were provided for the troupe, together with babouches, an *écharpe* for Grandval, coats for Grandval, Dubois and Paulin, a turban for Dubois, five Turkish costumes, six *vestes*, further *écharpes* and wigs.[72]

Despite the interruption of the summons to Fontainebleau, Voltaire had planned the revival well, and *Mahomet* was soon paid the backhanded compliment of being parodied.[73] It was also to influence the more serious work of others,[74] and attract

[70] According to La Harpe, Séide was one of the roles taken by Lekain during his début (*Œuvres de La Harpe*, Paris 1820, iv.453). On the other hand, Lekain appears to have been also acquainted with the role of Mahomet (D4557).

[71] *Mercure de France* (April 1739), p.781.

[72] Lancaster, *French tragedy*, i.210.

[73] See G. L. van Roosbroeck, 'Une parodie inédite du *Mahomet* de Voltaire: *L'Empirique* [de Favart]', *Rhl* 35 (1928), p.235-40. See also the parody attributed to Collier or A. C. Cailleau, *Thomet ou le Brouillamini, parodie en un acte* (London 1755). Jean Humbert also reproduces a supposed exchange between Voltaire and Le Franc de Pompignan based on the interview between Mahomet and Zopire in act II scene v, which was first published in *Les Nouveaux Si et Pourquoi, suivis d'un dialogue en vers* (Montauban 1760), p.17-22.

[74] See, for instance C. H. Ibershoff, 'Bodmer's indebtedness to Voltaire', *Modern philology* 23 (1925), p.83-87, and Fred O. Nolte, 'Voltaire's *Mahomet* as a source of Lessing's *Nathan der Weise* and *Emilia Galotti*', *Mln* 48 (1933), p.152-56.

the attention of translators as illustrious as Goethe.[75]

*Mahomet* remained part of the regular repertory of the Comédie-Française for just over a century, with 273 performances up to 1852.[76] A number of actors made their début in the play, either in the role of Zopire[77] or more frequently as Séide.[78] Among the actors most notably to fall into the latter category was Molé at his début in October and November 1754, and again when he returned to the Comédie-Française in January 1760.[79]

[75] Goethe's debt to Voltaire has been the subject of a number of studies of which the most recent is that by Inborg H. Solbrig, 'The theater, theory and politics, Voltaire's *Le Fanatisme ou Mahomet le prophète* and Goethe's *Mahomet* adaptation', *Michigan Germanic studies* 16 (1990), p.21-43. On the influence of Voltaire's play in Italy at the end of the eighteenth century, see Renzo de Felice, 'Trois prises de position italiennes à propos de *Mahomet*', *SVEC* 10 (1959), p.259-66. A witness to the continuing success of the English version of the play by James Miller, even in the provinces, is the following article which appeared in *The Newcastle Courant* on Saturday, 5 July 1760, p.3: 'The play of *Mahomet*, which is now reviving at the theatre, and is to be perform'd there on Monday evening, was written originally by Mr Voltaire, and alter'd and adapted to the English stage by Mr Miller. It is universally allow'd to be one of the most finished pieces of that celebrated French author. The design is plainly to guard mankind from the dangers which wait upon bigotry and superstition. These are exemplified in the lives of the unfortunate Zephna and Palmire, who, being bred up under that imposter, Mahomet, were by him wrought up into a religious fury, to murder their own father. The whole play abounds with noble sentiments, the diction is elegant, and the passions are touch'd so masterly, they do honour to their author. N.B. This play will be decorated with an entire set of new dresses.'

[76] See A. Joannidès, *La Comédie-Française de 1680 à 1920: tableau de représentations par auteurs et par pièces* (Paris 1921), p.103. The breakdown is as follows: 1742 (3); 1751-1760 (35); 1761-1769 (24); 1771-1780 (37); 1781-1790 (50); 1791-1793 (12); 1799-1800 (4); 1801-1810 (25); 1811-1819 (15); 1822-1829 (25); 1831-1840 (22); 1841-1850 (20); 1852 (1). For further details of performances up to 12 February 1774, see *Registres*, p.738, 741, 768-70, 778, 780-81, 784, 787, 790-92, 794-96, 798-801, 803-805, 807, 809-10, 813, 815-16, 820-22, 825-26, 830, 832-33, 837-38.

[77] *Mercure* (June 1757), i.187; (July 1765), i.205; (July 1777), i.169.

[78] *Mercure* (June 1755), ii.179-80; (July 1756), p.188; (January 1764), i.153; (February 1771), p.176.

[79] *Mercure* (November 1754), p.1260-61; (December 1754), i.174; (February 1760), p.198.

After Voltaire's death, undoubtedly the most famous actor to have begun his career at the Comédie-Française in the role was Talma, whose appearance as Séide on 21 and 25 November 1787 was greeted with enthusiasm.[80] So standard a part of the repertory did the play become that it could be relied on as a stop-gap, as when Mlle Clairon fell ill during the first run of *Tancrède*. By the end of the 1760s the part of Mahomet had become one of Lekain's major regular roles, and La Rive took on the role as part of his second début in 1775.[81]

During the Revolution *Mahomet* once again fell foul of censorship, but it was seen to have a message for the times when it was revived after Thermidor at the Théâtre de l'Egalité on 5 vendémiaire an III (26 September 1794):

Honneur aux artistes de ce théâtre! Ils viennent d'y faire entendre des vers de Voltaire et de Corneille, que nous ne savons quels lieutenants de police avaient enveloppés dans leurs proscriptions. *Mahomet* et *les Horaces* ont attiré une foule immense. Dans la première de ces pièces, le public a accueilli d'un assentiment général ces deux vers:

> 'Exterminez, grands Dieux! de la terre où nous sommes
> Quiconque avec plaisir répand le sang des hommes.

Mouvement sublime et consolant, dont la philosophie s'applaudit, et qui fait honneur au peuple français, à ce peuple qu'on fait parler comme jadis les prêtres faisaient parler leurs dieux, en faveur des sacrifices humains.[82]

Judging from the takings at the Comédie-Française, *Mahomet* continued to be fairly successful well into the nineteenth century. On the other hand in the second half of the century – under the Second Empire and the Third Republic – interest seems to have declined. When it was revived at the Théâtre de l'Odéon on 16

[80] *Journal de Paris* (22 November 1787), p.1403.

[81] *Mercure*: Mlle Clairon: (February 1761), p.200; Lekain: (December 1769), p.165, (October 1774), ii.157, (April 1778), ii.165; La Rive: (June 1775), p.181.

[82] *Décade philosophique*, 20 vendémiaire an III (no.17), iii.112; see also *Journal des théâtres*, 8 vendémiaire an III (29 September 1794), iii.341-42.

March 1885, *Le Figaro* was more interested in Voltaire's letter to the pope, and Francisque Sarcey in *Le Temps* was extremely critical: 'Non, la lecture de *Mahomet* n'est plus soutenable, et l'audition en est pénible.'[83] In the present day the cult of political correctness makes it difficult to imagine a modern staging of the play.

## 4. *Publication*

After the first abortive run of the play in Paris in August 1742, Voltaire decided that it was time to publish it. He first attempted to do so in England – 'Il n'est permis aux poètes d'être philosophes qu'à Londres' (D2648) – with the help of César de Missy, a French exile living in London, but he was quickly overtaken by events not under his control. When he had given La Noue the play for performance in Lille in 1741, Voltaire had been able to trust him not to divulge the manuscript: 'Je luy ai confié ma pièce comme à un honnête homme dont je connois la probité', Voltaire wrote to d'Argental on 7 April, 'il ne soufrira pas qu'on en tire une seule copie' (D2459). He was less lucky with the actors in Paris. On 22 September 1742 Mme Du Châtelet wrote to d'Argental: 'Il y a plus d'un mois qu'on dit Mahomet imprimé à Meaux, mais à moins que ce soit [Mme] de chimai qui l'y fait imprimer je ne puis deviner qui c'est. M. de V. ne connaît pas un chat à Meaux' (D2660; Voltaire wrote along the same lines, D2661). This is presumably the edition 42X1, and we must assume that the place of publication is not given on the title-page.

On 20 October Voltaire learned that further pirated editions

[83] *Le Figaro* (18 March 1885), p.6; *Le Temps* (30 March 1885), p.1-2. The last public performance of the play that I know of was that given by the Théâtre Antique de la Nature at Champigny-la-Bataille (Val de Marne) in June 1913 (see *Comoedia*, 6 July 1913, p.3; 4 October 1913, p.4). At least eight posthumous editions of *Mahomet* appeared between 1778 and 1799, all of which contain early versions of the text. I have counted eighteen separate editions for the nineteenth century, but only five for the twentieth. Four appeared between 1905 and 1932 and one in 1979.

had appeared under the Brussels imprint (42B1 to 42B5): 'Je viens d'aprendre dans le moment qu'on a imprimé *Mahomet* à Paris sous le nom de Bruxelles. On me mande que cette édition est non seulement incorrecte, mais qu'elle est faitte sur une copie informe qui m'a été dérobée' (D2676). By that time, many copies of the different pirated editions were circulating widely in Paris (D2673). Speculating on how these editions had come about, and hoping to trace the culprit, Voltaire wrote to Marville: 'Je vous aurais, monsieur, la plus sensible obligation, si vous pouviez découvrir le dépositaire infidèle qui a trafiqué du manuscrit. Je ne me plains point des libraires, ils ont fait leur devoir d'imprimer clandestinement et d'imprimer mal; mais celui qui a violé le dépôt mérite d'être connu' (D2679; see also (D2674, D2675), and in a letter to d'Argental he accused the Paris bookseller Prault of being the chief culprit (D2683).

In addition to continuing to negotiate with Missy over a London edition of the play (D2659),[84] Voltaire also started to plan the first truly authorised edition, given by Etienne Ledet in Amsterdam in 1743 (D2683); see below 43A3 (p.77-80). Ledet had started printing the edition by November 1742 (D2690), and in April 1743, the *Mercure de France* printed an announcement, obviously designed to publicise an edition of the play that finally met with Voltaire's full approval: 'Il a paru à Paris trois éditions de la tragédie de *Mahomet*, toutes très-défectueuses et faites sur des manuscrits infidèles; le véritable ouvrage s'imprime actuellement à Londres et à Amsterdam.' *Mahomet* entered Voltaire's complete works in 1746 (W46). Pirate editions continued to appear. Revisions undertaken for 51B were carried forward to most collective editions after that date. For the families of editions of *Mahomet*, see below, p.136-37.

[84] Despite Missy having apparently found a willing *libraire* this edition did not see the light of day.

## 5. *Development of the text*

In the autumn of 1739, after completing the first draft of the play, Voltaire suppressed some repetition and developed further the importance in the plot of the mystery surrounding the birth of Palmire and Séide (D2106). He hesitated over the right moment for the disclosure of details of Hercide's letter revealing the identity of Séide and Palmire (see MS1, p.50), and he sought to put more emphasis on Zopire's feelings as a father by stressing the horror of Séide stabbing Zopire just when the latter was praying for his children and asking the gods to make them known to him (act IV lines 140-144).

After he withdrew the first version of the play from the Comédie-Française in January 1740, Voltaire reworked the beginning of act III. Initially he had had Mahomet planning Zopire's murder at the hands of Séide before and not after his interview with Palmire. The more he thought about this, the more he found the shift from horror to love-talk revolting (D2154):

> Il faut absolument que Mahomet avant d'avoir pris son party, surtout avant d'avoir parlé à Seide, soit piqué des froideurs de Palmire; il faut que ce soit une raison de plus pour le déterminer à la vangeance et non pas qu'après avoir résolu de se vanger du père et du fils, il vienne parler froidement d'amour à la fille.

At the same time he suppressed part of what Omar had said to Mahomet when Séide agreed to kill Zopire. He also continued to worry away at the fifth act, which was causing him particular difficulty.[85] He had even thought of putting Zopire's recognition of his children in the final act as a means of giving it greater vigour, but quickly realised that the natural place for it was at the end of act IV, when Zopire staggers in bleeding from the knife wounds inflicted by his son,[86] thereby bringing in a necessary moment of tenderness to counteract the preceding horror (D2170).

[85] D2155, D2158, D2218, D2266, D2267.

[86] D2160, D2161, D2200.

In March 1740 Voltaire declared that he was no longer in any hurry to see *Mahomet* performed (D2187), and during the following months he worked on the text almost every day (D2214, D2259). He continued to revise the scenes with Mahomet and Palmire (see MS1). He was still not entirely satisfied with the fifth act. After toying with the idea of a poisoned letter, in July 1740 he decided that Palmire should grab her brother's dagger and then kill herself with it. Even then, however, he was not entirely sure that this would bring about a satisfactory ending (D2266):

Mais il faut là de la promtitude. Il sera bien difficile que la douleur et le désespoir aient lieu dans l'âme de Mahomet surtout dans un moment où il s'agit de sa vie et de sa gloire. Il ne sera guère vraisemblable qu'il déplore la perte de sa maitresse dans une crise si violente. C'est un homme qui a fait l'amour en souverain et en politique, comment lui donner les regrets d'un amant désespéré?

In January 1741 we again find Voltaire trying to find satisfactory lines for Mahomet's final speech (D2408, D2411). He also shortened Mahomet's lines at the end of act II scene iv (166-172), and left until the final scene of the act the Prophet's description of his plans for Zopire and Séide (D2411). At this stage Séide was still poisoned when in prison rather than before stabbing Zopire (see below MS3).

As we have seen even after the first performance of the play in Lille in April 1741, Voltaire delayed printing it until it had been performed in Paris,[87] and in the meantime he continued to revise the text. He again asked Cideville's advice, suspicious of his easy success in Lille as 'une sentence de juges inférieurs' (D2488) and, following this in July 1741 he toned down act II scene vi, in which Mahomet plans Zopire's murder (D2521). In addition, where Palmire had previously been summoned in act V to plead for her brother's life, she now came on stage of her own accord. Voltaire was still unhappy about the ending, remarking that 'tout

[87] D2473, D2477, D2495.

le monde a[vait] exigé absolument quelques petits remords à la fin de la pièce pour l'édification publique' (D2515).

When unauthorised versions of the play appeared in the autumn of 1742 Voltaire was forced to speed up his negotiations with Missy as well as with Ledet. He started to send Missy various manuscripts (D2676, D2682, D2684) as well as at least one annotated copy of a pirated edition (see 42X1). In turn Missy sent Voltaire detailed advice on possible improvements to the play (D2689). As usual Voltaire listened, and was grateful for these suggested changes (D2699), many of which he incorporated into the first authorised version of 1743.[88] Although the 1743 text introduces changes that were to prove far more radical than any subsequent alterations, Voltaire continued to revise the play (see D2923, 28 January 1744, marquise Du Châtelet to d'Argental: 'Ie trouue Encore bien des choses à refaire à Mahomet, il y trauaille tous les jours'), and it was not until 1768 that it finally appeared in what we may consider to be its definitive form (see w68).

## 6. *The action and the characters*

The plot is from the beginning a little repetitive, as Zopire pours out his opinion of Mahomet first to Omar and then to Mahomet himself.[89] The action also takes some time to move, as for much of

[88] See 43A3, and references to Missy in the notes to the text.

[89] See the synopses in D.app.58 and Lancaster, *French tragedy in the time of Louis XV and Voltaire*, i.204-205, as well as the detailed synopsis by the abbé Cahagne in his *Sentiments d'un spectateur sur la tragédie de Mahomet I, août 1742* (*Nouveaux amusements du cœur et de l'esprit*, 1742, xiv.331-72). It would also be difficult to improve on the exhaustive 'analyse structurale' of the tragedy in Badir, p.99-125. See also the same author's 'L'anatomie d'un coup d'Etat ou la prise de pouvoir dans la tragédie de *Mahomet* de Voltaire', in *Eighteenth-century French theatre: aspects and contexts. Studies presented to E. J. H. Greene*, ed. Magdy Gabriel Badir and David J. Langdon (Alberta 1986), p.99-106. Ridgway presents *Mahomet* as a quintessential example of a 'tragédie philosophique' and concentrates on the opposition between Zopire and Mahomet (*La Propagande philosophique dans les tragédies de Voltaire*, p.113-136). Jack R. Vrooman sees the play as 'the struggle of two opposing forces

act I Zopire does little more than refuse to give Palmire her freedom. In true classical manner, however, in this first act Voltaire carefully prepares the audience for what is about to happen, with Mahomet, like that other hypocrite, Tartuffe, taking some time to appear.

Frederick preferred the first act to the second (D2072), which for some was too full of incidents and slightly confusing through beginning with a scene devoted entirely to Palmire and Séide. This does however complete the exposition by describing their situation thoroughly, and the curiosity of the spectator is still aroused before Mahomet and Zopire finally come face to face in act II scene v, a scene much praised by Rousseau among others.[90]

The author plays well on our fears with effective uses of soliloquy in act III scenes ii and vii. In the meantime Mahomet is shown eloquently trying to strengthen Séide's resolve (act III scene vi). Zopire's pity for Séide – when the latter is entrusted with killing him – makes effective use of dramatic irony (act III scene viii). This pity leads to sympathy and compassion, thus consecrating the usual Voltairean belief in the hidden voice of nature already suggested in the first scene of the act (line 29). Voltaire's love of peripeteia and of the alternating of hope and fear comes out nicely a little later in the act (line 285), when Séide finally runs off to renounce all intention of harming the old man. Even then, Voltaire brings in a further dramatic twist with the letter from Hercide, revealing to Zopire that his children are still alive (act IV scene xi).

Act IV – in which Séide at last mortally wounds Zopire, and in which his children discover who they are, the parricidal nature of their crime and the incestuous nature of their love – is commonly

to gain control of the State' with Mahomet showing devotion 'to himself rather than to his god' (*Voltaire's theatre: the cycle from 'Œdipe' to 'Mérope'*, *SVEC* 75 (1970) p.131-52, 177-79). According to Thomas M. Carr, the plot is based on a series of appeals by Mahomet for others to side with him ('Dramatic structure and philosophy in *Brutus, Alzire* and *Mahomet*', *SVEC* 143 (1975) p.36-45).

[90] In the *Lettre sur les spectacles* (1758), *Œuvres complètes*, éd. B. Gagnebin et M. Raymond (Paris 1979-1995), v.28. See the note to II.v. below.

held to be most awe-inspiring and moving part of the plot, although for some its success was mainly due to horror as in Crébillon's *Atrée et Thyeste*, a comparison which much shocked La Harpe.[91]

La Harpe also stressed Voltaire's debt to George Lillo's *The London merchant, or the History of George Barnwell.* This much-imitated play, which was to have a significant influence on the development of the *drame* in France, enjoyed an unbroken run of thirty-eight performances at Drury Lane in 1731. The first complete French version by Pierre Clément dates from 1748,[92] but a translation of the key scenes, in which the young man murders his uncle in the dark of Windsor Great Park, together with a description of the whole plot, is given in Prévost's *Le Pour et contre*, lettre XLV (iii.337-56).

The motives are obviously different. The main driving force in the English play is money rather than religious fanaticism. On the other hand, if Palmire does not exactly push Séide into committing his crime, she does not stop him and it is similarly to please a woman – admittedly a less pure one – that Barnwell crosses the moral divide. Having committed his murder, like Séide, Barnwell is immediately overcome by remorse and despair:

Il avait un oncle, riche et âgé, dont il était aimé tendrement, et qui l'avait déjà institué son héritier. Après quelques explications, la courtisane lui déclare nettement que ne pouvant le recevoir chez elle s'il ne la paie bien, il faut pour mériter ses faveurs qu'il aille voler son oncle. Barnwell lui représente que l'entreprise est impossible. Eh bien, lui dit-elle, qui vous empêche de le tuer? Vous en jouirez très vite de son héritage. Une proposition si horrible fait frémir le jeune homme, mais l'exécrable Millwood (c'est le nom de la Courtisane) ne tarde guère à l'y faire consentir. Il part, il étouffe tous ses remords, il assassine son oncle [...].

[91] La Harpe, *Commentaire sur le théâtre de Voltaire* (Paris 1814), p.212-13. The comparison to *Atrée et Thyeste*, made at the time of the first performances by Le Blanc (D2635), was most fully developed by Rousseau, and J.-M.-B. Clément (*Cinquième lettre à m. de Voltaire*, La Haye 1774, p.113-18).

[92] *Le Marchand de Londres, ou l'histoire de George Barnwell, tragédie bourgeoise* (n.p. 1748).

Barnwell, quoique mal accoutumé au crime, avait déjà commis le parricide. Mais le remords et la crainte l'ayant fait fuir aussitôt, il était revenu chez Millwood, les mains encore sanglantes, et la peur imprimée sur le front. Cette misérable femme le voyant rentrer chez elle dans cet état, et jugeant bien que le coup était fait, lui demanda avec empressement s'il avait eu soin d'aller au coffre-fort. Elle est fort surprise non seulement d'apprendre qu'il n'a point eu le courage d'ajouter le vol au meurtre, mais de l'entendre parler de l'action qu'il vient de commettre comme d'un attentat détestable dont il a autant de repentir que d'horreur.[93]

There are similarities of detail, although the two murders do not take place in exactly the same way. While Séide steels himself for action in Palmire's company, in act III, scene iii of *The London merchant* Barnwell is alone in the dusk:

Il me semble que le jour s'est tout d'un coup obscurci. C'est le soleil qui se cache derrière quelque nue, ou qui a précipité son cours, pour n'être pas témoin de l'action qu'on me condamne à commettre. Depuis que je me suis mis en chemin pour accomplir ce détestable dessein, je crois sentir à tous moments la terre qui tremble sous mes pieds. Le ruisseau que je viens de passer, et dont le chute forme dans cet endroit une cascade naturelle, m'a épouvanté par un bruit que j'ai trouvé cent fois agréable.[94]

When Barnwell's uncle appears, like Zopire, he is found to be saying his prayers:

Ha ... je vois mon oncle qui s'avance dans une de ces allées... Il est seul... Déguisons-nous. (*Il se couvre le visage d'un masque.*) C'est l'heure qu'il prend ordinairement pour faire ses prières. Hélas! C'est ainsi qu'il prépare tous les jours son âme pour le Ciel? Ha, conscience! point de remords (*Il achève de se déguiser, il tire de sa poche un pistolet, et il quitte le Théâtre comme pour s'aller cacher derrière quelqu'arbre*).[95]

For much of the following scene (scene iv) Barnwell listens while the uncle talks of death:

(*Barnwell ayant présenté encore une fois son pistolet, le jette enfin par terre.*)
BARNWELL: Ah! c'est une chose impossible.

[93] *Le Pour et contre*, p.340-42.
[94] *Ibid.*, p.351.
[95] *Ibid.*, p.353-54.

L'ONCLE: Un homme si proche de moi, armé et masqué? (*L'oncle tire son épée, et Barnwell pressé tire un poignard dont il lui perce le sein.*)

BARNWELL: Il le faut donc, puisqu'il n'y a point d'autre voie.

L'ONCLE, *tombant*: Oh! je suis assassiné. Dieu plein de clémence! écoutez la prière de votre serviteur expirant. Répandez vos plus précieuses bénédictions sur mon cher neveu. Pardonnez mon meurtrier, et recevez mon âme entre vos bras.

The nephew is thus already plagued by remorse even before finally carrying out his dastardly deed, which is neither quite so one-sided as that of Séide, nor quite so out of sight as French susceptibilities might demand.

The end of act IV in *Mahomet* is highly charged. It is once again the result of a sudden surprise twist of events, with Phanor turning up at just the right moment to bring the dreadful truth.

From early on, as we have seen, Voltaire was unhappy with the fifth act (D2149, D2154), and it remained short and not entirely satisfactory. Critics have had a field day pointing out its faults. La Harpe said that it was rather empty of action, since the great moment of the play is the catastrophe in the fourth act, after which interest dies away.[96] For the abbé Le Blanc 'le prétendu miracle qui fait le dénouement de la pièce' was puerile (D2635). Obviously, Séide has to die from poison just as he is about to unmask Mahomet, something which is not easy to arrange, although it is doubtful whether an audience would have the time to appreciate this. Also somewhat unbelievable is the lack of opposition. It should be obvious to all that Séide has been poisoned, and how is it that the people should believe Omar so easily when he says that Mahomet disapproves of Zopire's murder, especially as Séide is known to be a follower of Mahomet? The inaction of the Senate – previously presented as resolute in its opposition to Mahomet – also raises unanswerable questions. Voltaire himself was aware that it was a little unlikely that Palmire would be able to seize her brother's dagger (D2266). Mahomet's

[96] La Harpe, *Lycée*, ix.447-48.

final speech caused the author particular difficulty, as he reworked it several times and continued to call it a 'pantalonade' (D4557). Even as it now stands, we can still ask – seeing Mahomet's ruthlessness elsewhere – whether Palmire's death can really bring him feelings of remorse rather than simple regret.

It is indeed also all to easy to point to absurd and illogical happenings earlier in the plot, even if many of them are not immediately apparent in the heat of performance.[97] One basic difficulty raised in the action is Mahomet's very presence in Mecca, which could be judged foolhardy to say the least (when the real Mohammed sent an envoy to Mecca he was mistreated):

Arrivée à une journée de cette ville, il y trouva quelques députés des Koréishites, qui lui signifièrent que les Mecquois étaient résolus de ne point lui en permettre l'entrée. Arwa était chargé de cette commission, et Othman reçut ordre du Prophète d'aller de sa part trouver Abusophian, et de lui représenter qu'il avait entrepris ce voyage uniquement pour faire ses dévotions à la Kaaba, et y offrir des sacrifices. Abusophian ne se laissa pas éblouir par ce spécieux prétexte, et bien loin de rendre au Prophète une réponse favorable, il fit mettre aux fers le député musulman.[98]

Indeed, it would seem hardly prudent for Mahomet to enter a town still in the control of his sworn enemies, even if Voltaire invents a truce to explain it (act II line 183), and the placing of all the action in Mecca also suffers a little from an over-slavish respect for the unity of place. In addition, if there is a truce and Mahomet is in the town as an ambassador, why does he have guards (act II lines 169-170)? In any case, the latter soon seem quite unnecessary, as we then have the spectacle of Mahomet wandering around the city as he likes, plotting mayhem without, apparently, arousing suspicion. Similar implausible freedom of movement is given to Séide, who is supposed to be a hostage. Moreover, even if we are asked to accept that it was possible for the young man to put himself forward as a hostage without Mahomet's permission (act II

[97] See the lists of 'invraisemblances' drawn up by Clément; and also *Année littéraire* (1780), vii.156-80. The author of the latter article is possibly Geoffroy.

[98] Boulainvilliers, *Vie de Mahomed*, p.382.

lines 95-100), it is difficult to believe that such a humble slave would have much value in that capacity.

As in other plays by Voltaire, we can argue over the preparation of the catastrophe and the dénouement. It is tempting to ask why Hercide does not reveal to Séide who he is when the latter tells him about the plan to murder Zopire (act IV lines 5-7). Similarly, how is it that Zopire, when he realises that his children are still alive, does not try to find out more about Séide and Palmire, seeing the similarity of their situation?[99]

There is also illogicality in detail. Some lines do not tie up with the rest of the action. In act II scene v, Mahomet tells Zopire that he is the only 'dépositaire' of the secret surrounding the latter's children, whereas he had already revealed it to Omar in the preceding scene. Palmire is unintentionally made to sound like a hypocrite. When she is alone, she talks of the 'secrète horreur' inspired by the very name of Mahomet; yet, when she next sees him, she welcomes his presence as God sent (act III lines 52 and 58).

The greatest weakness in the plot stems from the depiction of Mahomet in love. Just as the question of love interest had worried Voltaire in earlier plays, so he wrote to Cideville on 19 July 1741 (D2515):

> J'aurois voulu pouvoir retrancher l'amour, mais l'exécution de ce projet a toujours été impraticable, et je me suis heureusement aperçu à la représentation que toutes les scènes de Palmire ont été très bien reçues et que la naïveté tendre de son caractère faisait un contraste très intéressant avec l'horreur du fonds du sujet.

Cideville was still unhappy about it (D2521), and he was not alone:

> Je ne sais où il a pris le trait qui forme le fond de sa tragédie; c'est-à-dire l'amour de Mahomet et de Palmire, fille du Shérif de la Mecque. S'il l'a imaginé, comme je le crois, c'est un grand défaut. Le fond d'une tragédie doit être historique, surtout lorsque cette tragédie porte un nom connu dans l'Histoire.[100]

[99] Act III lines 266-272; act IV lines 143-144.

[100] *Bibliothèque française*, xxxvi.182.

In fact, nearly all commentators on the play have continued to regret the presence of Mahomet's passion for Palmire as it gets in the way of more important action. The spectacle of Mahomet more interested in love than anything else on entering Mecca after his long exile (II.iii-iv), and jealous of a slave of whom he could easily dispose (III.iii-iv), is more than a little ridiculous. We are even asked to believe (act V line 172) that Mahomet did all for love and nothing else.

All in all, this love interest – forming a strange amalgam with brutal talk of hatred and revenge (act III line 118) – further undermines our belief in the character of Mahomet. As was to be expected, the general picture of him is black, as we see him plotting one atrocity after another, and cynically glorifying in spreading 'error' (act IV lines 13-34). Yet in the final act he is ingenuous enough to think that Palmire will listen to him after all he has done (act V lines 43-60), and the play ends with his asking Omar to hide his weakness for Palmire (act V lines 187-190).

We are supposed to see Mahomet as a past master in the art of cunning, but he spends most of his time revealing what he would do best to hide.[101] In this light, it is easy to agree with the abbé Le Blanc (D2635):

Le caractère de Mahomet y est absolument manqué. Loin d'y paroître cet habile imposteur qui veut qu'on le croye un Prophète, il avoüe de bonne foi qu'il est un Fourbe. Il n'inspire le Fanatisme qu'à une jeune Cervelle, qu'il veut sans raison entraîner dans le Parricide. Il y a plus le ton de la Garonne que le ton de Prophétie. C'est Philoctète coëffé d'un Turban.

The critic of the *Année littéraire* saw the character of Mahomet as the main victim of the faulty plot, which made him work against his own interests, and thus appear not only despicable but naïve:

Si Voltaire a manqué son caractère de Mahomet, c'est qu'il a mis en œuvre un moyen faux pour le développer; et cela pour répandre beaucoup de pathétique sur ce sujet dont il craignait l'austérité. Outre

[101] Act II lines 115-121, 189-264.

que le nœud de son intrigue est trop romanesque et n'a pas une lueur de vraisemblance, cette même intrigue avilit Mahomet et le rend absurde: car ce faux prophète s'annonçant d'abord pour un ambitieux et un politique habile, dont la tête est remplie des plus grands projets; et ne trouvant ensuite d'autre ressource pour *séduire tous les esprits*, que de faire assassiner un père par son fils, sans songer qu'il ne peut tirer de cet attentat d'autre fruit que d'être abhorré, est non seulement odieux en pure perte, puisque son propre intérêt combat cette atrocité; il est encore petit et méprisable, parce qu'il ne met aucune grandeur réelle ni apparente dans sa vengeance, et qu'il va, par les moyens les plus vils et les plus scélérats, directement contre son but, qui est d'*enchaîner les cœurs et de séduire les esprits*.[102]

Le Blanc also compares the other main protagonists to the main characters in *Zaïre*. Séide certainly shares Nérestan's rigid view of religion, but in Voltaire's mind the unfortunate Séide – as he referred to him – was to be compared to well-known fanatics who had committed the worst of crimes with the best of intentions (D2074). As for Palmire, she has the usual passive nature found in most of Voltaire's heroines, and shows above all unbelievable naivety, seeming to be quite unable to understand the nature of Mahomet's feelings for her (act III scene iii).

Like Lusignan, Zopire comes across as a strong father figure,[103] and his rigidity provides a necessary foil for Mahomet's cunning. As a character, Omar is less satisfactory than Zopire. Like his leader, Mahomet, he too talks when he would do best to remain silent. He is made to sound harsh and dogmatic whereas the real Omar – while fixed in his ideas – was known for his gentle manner and highly developed sense of diplomacy:

[102] *Année littéraire* (1781), ii.170-72.

[103] The contrasting attitudes of Zopire and Mahomet towards Palmire and Séide have been analysed by Haydn Mason, 'Fathers, good and bad in Voltaire's *Mahomet*', in *Myth and its making in the French theatre: studies presented to W. D. Howarth*, ed. E. Freeman, H. Mason, M. O'Regan and S. W. Taylor (Cambridge 1988), p.121-35. Mason also shows the shift in dramatic interest away from the Prophet to the young fanatic and makes some interesting suggestions on what drew Voltaire to the subject in the first place.

Omar, fils d'Alchattab homme d'une extrême considération parmi le peuple; prévenu contre les nouveautés; mais d'ailleurs judicieux, d'une inviolable fermeté pour la justice, et très accessible à tout ce qui pouvait se présenter à lui sous le titre de vérité [...].

Si la conversion d'Omar avait fait un grand éclat parmi le peuple de la Mecque, la conduite franche et sincère avec laquelle il rendait compte aux grands, et aux petits des motifs de son changement, et les liberalités qu'il faisait avec une espéce de profusion, ne firent pas un moindre effet pour justifier la nouvelle religion.[104]

Omar's main fault, however – dramatically speaking – is that he seems capable of arranging a quite unbelievable number of things and is always popping up mechanically like a Jack-in-the-box whenever the action seems to require a new dramatic twist.[105]

## 7. *Style*

Many passages from *Mahomet* have been praised.[106] Collé – who was critical of the plot – did admit that the play contained 'de grandes beautés' and called it 'une des tragédies les plus remplies de beaux vers'.[107] Even Francisque Sarcey – despite his general dislike for the work both in plot and style – could not resist the tempation of quoting from 'la fameuse tirade' by Mahomet when he faces Zopire in act II scene v, which many of his generation had learned by heart when at school.[108] Ever since the first performances, however, the general style of the play had not been without its critics. Some thought it had been written rather carelessly: 'Au fond la pièce de Voltaire est écrite négligeamment,

104 Boulainvilliers, *Vie de Mahomed*, p.289, 300, 301.

105 Act II scene vi; act IV scene vi; act V scene iii.

106 Among the lines highlighted for praise by Jean Humbert, in his edition of the play, are act I lines 1-6, 124, 150, 192, 261-264, 309; act II lines 186, 189-238; act III lines 18-32, 56, 137-142, 151-216, 285; act IV lines 183-194, 252; act V lines 61-90, 120, 126.

107 Collé, *Journal et mémoires*, i.351-52.

108 *Le Temps* (30 March 1885), p.1-2.

bien des endroits en sont mal versifiés. Cela n'est pas pardonnable à quelqu'un qui sait faire aussi bien des vers que lui.'[109]

Many lines have a Cornelian or Racinian ring,[110] and many of them hark back to the work of these and other earlier authors. Voltaire also imitates himself, as shown in the notes to the text.

There is a fair amount of line-filling,[111] and there is also stylistic repetition. Apart from the intentional echo in the *réplique* in act I lines 132-133, there are twenty-three repeated identical hemistiches,[112] plus two pairs of identical-sounding half-lines (act I line 22 and act V line 109; act III line 214 and act IV line 54). There are at least forty-two near echoes, often differing only in one small word or syllable.[113] There is much general repetition

[109] *Bibliothèque française*, xxxvi.182.

[110] See in particular act I lines 69, 118, 299; act II lines 34, 86, 238, 281, 335; act III lines 214; act V lines 29, 88. For a useful computer-based statistical comparison of the vocabulary of *Mahomet* and of Corneille's *Polyeucte*, see Keith Cameron, 'Aspects of Voltaire's style in *Mahomet*', *SVEC* 129 (1975), p.7-17. Cameron brings out Voltaire's love of sonorous vowels, adjectives and monosyllabic injections, stressing the declamatory nature of his work. He also shows how Voltaire uses expressions of which he disapproves in his *Commentaires sur Corneille*. Noted similarities with earlier writers are listed in Appendix IV.

[111] See in particular act I line 328; act II lines 178, 247; act III lines 30, 63, 112, 124, 206, 216, 279; act IV lines 136, 159, 199. For other examples of padding, often with an excessive use of exclamations such as 'eh bien! ô ciel! dieux!', see act I lines 95, 240, 255, 313; act II lines 24, 38, 54, 212, 252, 265; act III lines 14, 34; act IV lines 105, 138, 226; act V lines 3, 26.

[112] See act I lines 16 and 197; act I line 118 and act II line 30; act I line 153 and act IV line 244; act I line 313 and act II line 6; act II lines 46 and 151; act II line 226 and act III line 181; act II lines 294 and 332; act II line 351, act III line 151 and act IV line 111; act III line 72 and act IV line 208; act III line 279 and act IV line 136; act IV line 97 and V line 87.

[113] See act I line 24 and act V line 10; act I line 30 and act V line 107; act I line 42 and act III line 162; act I line 102 and act V line 40; act I line 111 and act V line 57; act II lines 49 and 255; act II lines 75 and 299; act II line 97 and act III line 45; act II line 247 and act III line 309; act II lines 294, 332 and act IV line 276; act II lines 296 and 318; act II line 319 and act III line 31; act II line 321 and act III line 271; act II line 351, act III line 151, act IV lines 111 and 244; act III lines 3 and 203; act III line 120 and IV line 199; act IV line 15 and act V line 1; act IV lines 81, 106 and 237; act IV line 232 and act V line 103; act V lines 56 and 187.

both in ideas and expressions and in the use of individual words.[114]

Voltaire likes enumeration (see act I line 49) and antithesis, though the latter frequently appears cold and rather artificial (see act II lines 182, 228; act V lines 182, 186). Another common fault is a superabundance of adjectives, piled one upon the another in lines where every noun somehow has to be qualified with an all too often trite epithet.[115]

As a writer of ideas who was anxious to encapsulate them in a striking form, Voltaire is fond of aphorisms, some of which work better than others.[116] At times they appear hardly designed to produce lasting dramatic effect. Even more striking and unfortunate are the instances of exaggeration and misplaced bombast. The characters frequently rant and rave when they should be quiet and diplomatic, or even gentle. The tone is nearly always harsh and extreme, full of insult and imprecation, and sometimes pompous.[117] What particularly shocked many contemporary critics was Mahomet's use of the language of power, even before he was the absolute master of Mecca:

Mahomet dans la position où on le représente, était un misérable chef de secte, qui n'avait d'asile que Médine, et de défenseurs qu'une poignée de disciples; cependant on le fait agir et parler en maître, et comme s'il eût eu sous sa domination l'Afrique et l'Asie. Ce défaut est familier à Voltaire. Il

[114] Compare, for instance, act I lines 4-6 and 277-278; act I line 22 and act V line 109; act I line 309 and act II line 268; act III lines 33 and 36; act IV lines 24, 29 and act 31; act IV lines 72, 96, 103, 114 and 129; act IV lines 115 and 117; act IV lines 235, 237 and 241; act V lines 149 and 152. There is a marked overuse of words such as 'cœur' (62 times) and 'sang' (43 times).

[115] See act I lines 7-8, 91-93, 154-156, 231-233; act IV lines 206-208; act V lines 96-102.

[116] See act II line 181; act III lines 78, 98, 273; act IV lines 31-32, 170.

[117] For possibly misplaced high-flown language and unnatural grandiloquence, see act I lines 188-191, 275-292, 320-329; act II lines 11-14, 50-53, 90-94, 100, 139-152, 175-176, 193-194, 256-258, 339-340; act III lines 61-63, 71-72, 173-199, 219, 237-238, 287-290, 304-306; act IV lines 41-42, 99-100; act V lines 10-15, 49-50, 155-156, 171-173, etc.

a peint les Romains dans son *Brutus* avec le même degré de puissance et de renommée que sous César.[118]

Another fault found not just in Voltaire, but in other classical and neo-classical playwrights, is a lack of true local colour. Regardless of the subject, the lines are full of Graeco-Roman and Christian imagery, with words such as 'autel' which not only sound strange in a Arabian context, but further pervert our understanding of Islam.[119] Another result of this untoward fidelity to the traditional language of the French stage is to make a number of lines sound either insipid[120] or even prosaic.[121]

Voltaire's respect for grammar reveals a certain amount of poetic licence,[122] and not all words are used entirely correctly.[123] The style is occasionally incoherent and inexact.[124] Some lines are awkward and rather ugly.[125] Others are unclear, either because of ellipsis or ambiguity.[126]

[118] *Bibliothèque française*, xxxvi.182.

[119] See, for instance, act I lines 59, 172, 212, 258; act II lines 95, 110, 123, 142; act III lines 149, 184, 262; act IV lines 76, 80. In the light of this, it is curious to note the judgement on Voltaire's style here by J. de La Porte and J.-M.-B. Clément: 'C'est sans contredit, de toutes les tragédies de m. de Voltaire, une des mieux versifiées, et de la manière la plus grande. Le style oriental employé avec raison dans ce sujet, est, comme on sait, celui de tous les styles le plus favorable à la poésie sublime' (*Anecdotes dramatiques*, i.504).

[120] See, for instance, act I line 93; act II lines 74, 109, 185, 299, 347, act III lines 50, 69, 235, 248; act IV line 164; act V line 10.

[121] See act I lines 157-158, 312; act II lines 331; act IV line 113.

[122] See, for instance, act I lines 98, 282, 338; act II lines 29, 102, 162; act III lines 68, 74, 124, 176, 198; act IV lines 134, 152; act V lines 29, 58, 75.

[123] See, for instance, act I lines 245, 302; act II lines 29, 64, 126, 133, 156, 160, 168, 180, 318, 322, 340, 343; act III lines 37, 100, 114, 174, 199, 302, 311; act IV lines 67, 70, 86, 94, 102, 110, 166; act V lines 51, 53, 62, 97, 115, 128, 142, 144, 178.

[124] See in particular act I lines 222, 281; act III lines 52-58, 102-106, 309; act IV lines 58, etc.

[125] See in particular act I lines 84, 193; act II lines 68, 92, 171; act III lines 101, 117, 136, 233, 288; act IV lines 97, 154, 241; act V lines 25, 76.

[126] See in particular act I lines 23, 120, 123, 138, 161, 174, 217; act II lines 12, 54, 70, 114, 123, 192, 261, 266, 296, 314, 334, 345, 347; act III lines 37, 53, 57, 74, 145-146, 151, 183, 225, 256, 298, 313; act IV lines 23, 29, 40, 108, 115, 152, 202, 263, 284; act V lines 12, 37-38, 48, 103, 105, 149, 170, 188.

Contemporaries also thought that more care could have been taken over the rhymes and the versification in general.[127] Purists have complained about rhymes based on a single letter (act II lines 263-264; act III lines 261-262, 313-314), on long words (act IV line 113) or on words with a common root (act V line 145-146). Perhaps more obviously objectionable is the repetitive nature of many rhymes, with the same sounds if not the same words recurring rather too often.[128] The flow of the verse is also sometimes monotonous, either because of the unvarying sound of the words (act III lines 57-64), or because of a regular caesura marked too clearly in the punctuation (act III lines 11-17).

The play is written with vigour, however, and the style is certainly elegant enough to serve as an efficient medium for what Voltaire wants to say. The overall harsh tone is merely a reflection of the author's desire to paint an unfavourable picture of the main protagonist.

## 8. *Bibliography*

### Manuscripts

#### MS1

– holograph of alterations in 8 quarto pages. (Brown G). It passed at two sales by Charavay: 18 December 1880, p.43, no.245 and 26 February 1887, p.37, no.156
GB-Ox/U19: VF.

MS1 is an early manuscript, revealing that a considerable number of lines were displaced as well as replaced, and showing how Voltaire later expanded at least part of his text. It gives the final version of act I lines

[127] See D2635. The following eight words appear there at least ten times: *cœur* (18), *humains* (noun) (10), *maître* (15), *moi* (11), *Séide* (18), *toi* (12), *vie* (16), *Zopire* (14).

[128] See in particular act I lines 115-116, 117-118, 155-156, 159-160, 201-202, 229-230, 281-282; act II lines 37-38, 45-46; act III lines 47-48, 51-52; act IV lines 109-100, 103-104, 107-108; act V lines 133-134, 137-138. There is a marked preponderance of words ending in '-eur'.

215-220, act II line 150, act III lines 126-127, 241, 243-246, 253-254, act IV lines 189-194, act V lines 89-90. Act II lines 151, 161, act III line 16, act IV line 137, act V line 170 appear as they do as in various earlier versions of the printed text. There are, however, important as well as minor variants not found elsewhere for act I lines 34-35, 37, 138 (with two additional lines by Zopire praising Palmire), 229-230, act II lines 1, 120, 156-158, 160, 166 (with six lines by Mahomet on how he will make use of Zopire's children), 169, 245 (offering two variants), act III 43-45 (giving a different version in two lines for the end of act III scene i, in which both Palmire and Séide express their trust in Mahomet). In act III scene iii (lines 77 etc., 101(?)-117) Mahomet's reaction to Palmire's description of her love for Séide is expressed in different terms. His anger is more quickly mastered, and his hypocrisy is rather more obvious and direct. In MS1 what would appear to be a variant for act III lines 118-119 in scene iv (in Mahomet's soliloquy on his true feelings over Palmire's love for Séide) precedes her confidence as given in scene iii, and appears under scene ii. Scene v begins as in the final text, but the manuscript version of the dialogue between Omar and Mahomet on making use of Séide (see lines 127-138(?)) would seem to owe at least something to the earlier scene on the same subject: act II scene vi (see in particular the final version of act II lines 321-332). A variant for lines 165-202 (glorifying further than in the printed text the joy of revenge) in what is now act III scene vi again appears under act III scene ii. There is a small variant for line 254. Towards the end of act III the reference to the letter from Hercide is moved from scene xi to scene viii, to just before Omar bursts in at the beginning of scene ix (lines 279-280, 293-294). A different version of Mahomet's threatening comments on Hercide's fondness for Séide, now given at the beginning of act IV scene i (lines 6-120), is placed in MS1 in act III scene v (around line 152). Act IV begins with acid comments in the stage instructions on the restrictions of the French theatre. When Séide returns after having stabbed Zopire, MS1 does not have the touching description of the old man with the dagger in his side (lines 195-211). In act V scene i (lines 23(?)-32, etc.), as Omar describes in different terms how the crowd has rushed to see Séide in his prison, and that the latter has been poisoned, Mahomet seems to show more hesitation and self doubt than in later versions of the text (see MS3, lines 5-57). In the final scene (lines 123-148), when Séide finally succumbs to the poison, Palmire is rather more harsh in her reaction, and we only have two lines (131-132) of the final ten-line version of Mahomet's exultation (lines 126-135). On the other hand, the manuscript has what would seem to be an additional short threatening speech by Mahomet before the crowd finally leaves (lines 159-161).

MS2

– holograph fragment of part of what is now act IV scene v. (Brown C). Printed at D2265n.
USA-NNMor: Ms.986.
[Inscribed:] Au Roi de Prusse ... 174 ...

This rather truncated version of the text begins with the final version of act IV line 243, and is given as the end of act IV scene iii and the beginning of scene iv. Séide's discovery that he is Zopire's son is phrased in a slightly different way (lines 229-231). In line 245, we have 'les mortels' instead of 'les humains'. The end of what is now scene v is missing. Immediately following Séide's attempt to kill himself (lines 247-249), Phanor makes his entrance (in a variant for lines 227-228). He thus appears after and not before Séide discovers his identity, leaving us to wonder who revealed it at this stage of the development of the text.

MS3

– contemporary copy with holograph corrections of act V, incomplete at the beginning, with official approbation and notice of withdrawal of same. (Brown D). It passed at a Charavay sale, 31 May 1924, no.147.
F-P/BnF: B24342. ff.23-28.
f.28 (verso):
Vu Permis de représenter. à Paris ce 10 Janvier 1741. A. Boilly.
[holograph:]

retiré la pièce pour n'être point jouée le 20 jan. 1741.

*M. Duval* me le gardera sans la montrer.

The manuscript begins in the middle of the speech by Omar that opens act V (lines 5-57, 59-60), with an expanded version of part of MS1 (see

MS1, lines 23(?)-32). Mahomet asks more directly than in the final version whether his orders have been carried out. Here Séide is poisoned while in prison, and not before or at the time of carrying out his attack on Zopire (see D2408). In Omar's description of the present state of Séide and of the plans for Palmire (lines 21-41), only lines 31-32 and 39 are as they appear when printed. MS3 retains in a slightly altered form Mahomet's reply to this, first seen in MS1, though the Prophet now shows rather less weakness and little hesitation. This immediately precedes line 42, which is given as printed. In scene ii Mahomet tries to impress on Palmire just how honoured she is that he should want to choose her as a wife. When Palmire turns on him, Mahomet does not talk of treachery, but tries to stress his magnanimity (lines 90-93). Part of the final text in line 95 is suppressed, and for line 103 Séide is reported to be proclaiming his guilt in a version not found elsewhere. In line 110 Voltaire himself replaces a variant not retained in print, and then seems to have wanted to suppress lines 109-111. Palmire's reaction when Séide stumbles is just as severe as in MS1, though the following two lines are reworked (lines 123-125). The first hemistich of line 132 is not as later printed, and neither is the end of line 138. In his dying speech Séide talks more of atoning for his crime, and only confronts Mahomet in his last complete line (lines 139-147). Mahomet then lingers a little over a description of the features of the dying Séide (lines 149-154), whereas in print he immediately exults and talks of divine revenge. Before the crowd finally withdraws (lines 157-161), as in MS1, Mahomet gets in an extra threatening speech, though several of the lines have now been been slightly altered. There are otherwise unrecorded variants in lines 165, 167, 170, 173. Line 175 appears as in 42X1 (A*). For the very end of the play (lines 183-190) – where the text has been much revised – the final lines on hiding Mahomet's real nature are given to Omar.

MS4

– contemporary copy by Collini with holograph corrections. pag.[ii].116. (Brown A).
GB-Windsor (Royal library).
[Front cover] No.23. Mahomet I. Tragédie de Voltaire, MS.
p.[i] Mahomet Premier, / Tragédie nouvelle, / en cinq actes / par Voltaire.

p.[ii] Acteurs.
MAHOMET, faux prophète ... Granval.
ZOPIRE, chérif de la Mecque ... Sarazin.
OMAR, disciple et confident de Mah[t] ... Le Grand.
PHANOR ... confident de Zopire ...
SÉIDE, fils inconnu de Zopire, frère et amant de Palmire ... La Noue.
PALMIRE, fille inconnue de Zopire, sœur et amante de Séide ... Mlle Gaussin.
Suite de Mahomet.
Peuple.
La scène est à la Mecque, dans le palais de Zopire.

This manuscript appears to date from 1742. It is somewhat carelessly transcribed, but is useful since it was looked at by Voltaire. It shows a close relationship with 42X1 (A*) rather than 42B1 (B*). MS4 follows both 42X1 (A*) and 42B1 (B*) in the following lines: I.53, 54, 58, 161, 163, 173-175, 180, 181-182, 198, 250, 254, 261-266, 285, 292, 321, 329, 333-334; II.12, 48, 86, 102, 135, 165, 308, 317, 336-337; III.12-17, 30, 32, 41, 60, 61, 112, 128, 146, 147, 179, 198, 211-212, 220, 231, 262, 266; IV.7, 10, 16, 33, 40, 41-42, 96, 159, 160, 234, 241, 260, 285, 287-290; V.11, 22, 27, 60, 76, 103, 105, 126-127, 132, 135, 148, 172, 173. However, it follows 42X1, 42X2 (A*) alone in 111 places: see I.7, 11, 15, 20, 56-57, 96, 98, 138, 143, 169, 177/178, 184-185, 196, 220-224, 241, 279, 306, 322-325, 330; II.51, 92, 106, 130, 137, 154, 263, 269, 273, 284-285, 293, 320; III.1-10, 11, 18, 35-36, 58, 59, 79-89, 91-99, 104, 108, 114, 133-136, 145, 152, 161, 167, 174, 199, 201, 213-214, 218, 223, 232, 248, 278-314; IV.1-3, 18-29, 64-66, 71, 73, 84, 86, 94, 107, 110, 119-121, 122, 125, 132/133, 132, 137, 144, 154, 156, 160, 168, 175-176, 188, 198, 208, 210, 223/224, 227, 233, 240, 242/243, 247, 254, 262-263, 267, 270, 277, 280-281, 284/285; V.68, 75, 79, 106, 114, 117, 119, 125, 138, 143-144, 166, 175. It adopts the text found in 42B2 etc. (B*) in only five cases: see I.160; II.21, 47; III.216; V.37.

Suppressed text is found for act I lines 128, 137, 140, 278, act II line 254, act III line 33, act II lines 75, 276, including the final version for act II line 114, replaced above the line by Voltaire. He makes similar corrections for act I lines 15, 20, 139, 144, 329, act II lines 91, 99, 246, act III lines 54, 223, acte IV lines 57, 164, 166, 219, 239, 258, 286, act V lines

86, 154. He also corrects the spelling in act I line 285 ('vain') and act IV line 262 ('libre').

There are miscellaneous minor differences – usually involving one word – in act I line 226, act II lines 99, 126, 174, 183, 299, act III lines 48 (cf. MS5), 186-187, 219, act IV lines 6, 8, 30, 177, 182, 223, 239 (cf. MS5). There are the usual small variants concerning articles (I.85, 108, 156, 167; II.329; IV.151; V.73, 101, 164), or prepositions (III.52). The tense is changed in act I line 208, act III line 170. The object pronoun comes before the auxiliary verb in act IV line 123.

MS4 lacks the first hemistich in act I line 165, and in act II lines 37-40, 296 are missing. Act IV lines 111-221 were initially missed out and had to be added at the end. Voltaire himself adds above the line act III line 178.

Despite Voltaire's corrections, there are many obvious mistakes (some of which give the clear impression that the script was noted down from dictation, and not always with respect for grammar or the rules of versification). See I.24, 35, 41, 48, 84, 87, 91, 101, 165; II.18-19, 83, 89/90, 138, 171, 241, 274, 283; III.208, 259; IV.52, 109, 246, 269; V.12, 108, 151, 185.

MS5

– contemporary copy of author's copy as submitted to the police.
pag.90.
USA-NNMor: MA.636.
p.1: Mahomet / Tragédie / Par M. de Voltaire.
Représentée à Paris pour la premiere fois le jeudi 9 aoust 1742; la seconde le samedi 11; et la 3$^{e}$. et d$^{re.}$ le lundi 13 dudt. Elle était le mercredi 15[*sic*]; annoncée pour le jeudi 16; mais elle fut supprimée ou retirée le d$^{t}$ jour,
Reprise et représentée le Jeudi 30 7bre. 1751.
Copié sur le manuscrit de l'auteur fourni à [...] le L$^{t}$ general de Police.
21 aoust 1742: 30 dud$^{t}$.
p.2:
Acteurs.
MAHOMET, faux prophète ... M. Grandval.

ZOPIRE, Cherif de la Mecque ... M. Sarazin.
OMAR, Disciple et confident de Mahomet ... M. le Grand.
Ali ...
PHANOR, confident de Zopire ... M. Paulin.
SÉIDE, fils inconnu de Zopire, frère et amant de Palmire ... M. de la Noüe
PALMIRE, fille inconnue de Zopire, sœur et amante de Séide ... Mlle. Gossin.
Suite de Mahomet.
Peuple de la Mecque.
La scène est à la Mecque dans le palais de Zopire.
p.3-90: Mahomet, tragédie.
p.90: Au S. La Noüe, par Voltaire. 12 aoust 1742.

This has the text of 1742 (with later additions and changes). On the line, there are a number of minor variants that are not found elsewhere: see I.36 (has 'accabler' instead of 'écraser'), 141 ('amitié' for 'bonté'), 187 ('teints' in place of 'pleins'), 300 ('acquis par' for 'le prix de'); II.91 (calls 'Morad' 'Moad'), 106 (removes the inversion), 109 (uses the direct imperative form in the first hemistich), 114 (has 'ne [...] point' instead of 'ne [...] pas' (cf. MS4), 227 (inverts the nouns), 308 (has 'rendus' for 'vendus'); III.48 (gives 'tant' instead of 'si', while the rest of the line is that printed in 1742 (cf. MS4), 101 (for 'arme' has 'a sur'), 131 (begins the line with 'Près de' in place of 'Tu vois'), 132 ('ton' becomes 'ce'), 273 ('point' replaces 'pas'); IV.52 (has 'des' instead of 'ces'), 211 (puts 'laissez' into the singular and omits 'moi'), 227 (puts the MS4, 42X1 (A*) version into the plural), 239 (follows MS4 with 'mon' and not 'mes fils'), 243 ('ma' is replaced with 'la'), 247 (replaces the first 'Rendez' with 'Donnez'), 268 ('mon' becomes 'son'), 276 (has 'témérité' instead of 'crédulité'); V.18 (instead of 'ou' gives 'et'), 175 (replaces in the MS4, 42X1 (A*) version the first 'ô' with 'Ah!'), 187 ('étouffe' becomes 'efface').

A number of other variants – some of them obvious copyist's mistakes – were crossed out: see I.42 (had 'mon fils' for 'son fils'), 239 (had written inadvertently 'de cités en cités'); II.67 (in line with Voltaire's preference, the plural is removed from 'mêmes'), 109 (hesitated over 'que' instead of 'et'); III.208 (had initially 'Qui' in place of 'Y'), 217 (had mistakenly written 'Zopire'); V.39 (through error had substituted 'ton pays' for 'ta patrie'), 130 (had the meaningless 'bras pour vous punir'), 143 (had put 'quel foudre' into the plural), 144 (had put 'Tremble' into the plural), 149 (wrote 'O' for 'Aux').

Further otherwise unrecorded variants – with some lines thoroughly revised – are given as a choice above the line. See I.47: (offers 'détruits et' for 'par ses mains'), 158: ('d'humanité' becomes 'du peuple humain', 160: (changes the tense), 247: (changes the tense of the first verb), 274: (instead of 'Et, las' there is 'Lassé'), 279-280: (a reworked couplet), 301: ('je' for 'se'); II.203-204: (gives 'enfin' for 'à la fin' and 'ignoré' for 'inconnu'), 247: (has 'voit-on' in place of 'vois-tu'); III.137-138: ('il est né pour le' becomes 'né l'instrument du' and line 138 is radically reworked); IV.274: (has 'sa' instead of 'ta'); V.62: (writes 'sang, je t'abjure' instead of 'sang, que j'abjure'), 148: (modifies the 1742 version with 'des' instead of 'ces').

In seventeen places, the final version of the text is given as an alternative above the line: see I.321-322, 324, 330, 332; III.41, 58, 59, 68, 76, 79-89, 91-99, 124, 133-136; IV.110; V.68, 79, 82. On the other hand, it is replaced in act I line 65, act II lines 92, 109, 161, act III line 174, act IV lines 53, 99, 275, act V lines 143-144, 189.

The following lines give the text as printed in all editions in 1742: I.53, 54, 58, 96, 116, 160, 161, 163, 173-175, 198, 220-224, 250, 254, 261-266, 285, 292, 321, 333-334; II.12, 48, 86, 102, 135, 165, 247, 317, 336-337; III.12-17, 30, 32, 35-36, 41, 61, 112, 146, 179, 198, 211-212, 220, 231, 262; IV.7, 10, 16, 33, 40, 41-42, 96, 155, 159, 177, 234, 241, 260, 285, 287-290; V.11, 22, 60, 76, 103, 105, 126-127, 132, 135, 148, 172, 173. Above the line, one also finds the 1742 printed version of act I line 329.

Like MS4, MS5 resembles more closely 42X1 (A*) than 42B1 (B*). In eighty-one places, the text on the line is that of 42X1 alone: see I.7, 108, 169, 185, 196, 227, 241, 306, 322, 323, 324, 330; II.29, 37, 40, 51, 92, 130, 137, 269, 273, 285, 320; III.1-10, 11, 18, 58-59, 68, 79-89, 91-99, 104, 114, 133-136, 167, 169, 201, 213-214, 223, 232, 248-249, 278-314; IV.1-3, 18-29, 64-66, 71, 73, 84, 86, 94, 132/133, 137, 144, 156, 160, 162, 168, 175, 182, 188, 197, 206, 208, 210, 223/224, 240, 242/243, 262, 263, 267, 277, 280, 284/285; V.50, 75, 79, 119, 125, 138, 143, 144, 166. It only adopts the text exclusively given in 42B1, etc. (B*) fourteen times: see I.1, 65, 68; II.35, 92, 292; IV.53, 119, 122; V.37, 45, 82, 170, 189. It also has the version of act III line 127 given in 42B5 (C*).

In nine places the 42X1 (A*) version is suppressed: see II.272, 284, 329;

III.176, 218; IV.119-121, 198; V.2, 117. It is, however, given as an alternative – usually above the line – in act I line 325, act V lines 106, 154-155. There are even more cases of the 42B1 (B*) version being added in this way. See I.69, 144; II.1, 92, 241; III.213-214; IV.53, 124-125; V.63, 75, 97, 138. It is suppressed in act V line 2, as is the general 1742 version of act III line 128. The version of act II line 161 first printed in 43A3 (D*) is added as a replacement for the final text.

### MS6

– contemporary copy (actors' copy). pag.79. (Brown B).
F-P/Cf: Ms.165.
[Inscribed] 9 viii 1742.
[title page] 7e. carton, no.120 d'ordre. / Voltaire / Mahomet Premier / Tragédie en 5 actes / de Voltaire 1742. / [in another hand] Com. Fr. 9 août 1742.
[preceding the text] 7e. carton, no.120 d'ordre. / Mahomet 1er. / Tragédie de Voltaire / 5 actes Voltaire. 1742.
[in another hand] une addition au rôle de Mr Molé.

There are number of later alternatives given above the line in another hand. See I.54 (replacing the 1742 version of this line with the final version first added to the printed text in W56), 96; II.12, 31 (which all give the final version of the text first printed in 43A3), 42 (in second hemistich has 'et Séide peut-être'), 277 (replaces 'fils' by the more logical 'enfants'), 285 (instead of 'Quoi!' gives 'Et'); III.213-214 (gives the 42X1 (A*) version); V.126-127 (retains from the 1742 version 'Mortels séditieux', but otherwise follows the final text).

The manuscript presents a number of particularities. See I.154 (by mistake: has 'Tous donnaient'), 258 (puts 'récompenses' into the singular again by mistake); II.320 (changes tense in 42X1 version); III.89 (changes tense), act IV lines 66 (adds 'en' before 'sais'), 87 (has 'majesté' instead of 'autorité'), 116 (adds 'en' in front of 'frémis'). Act IV lines 85-101, 153-156, 195-198 are added, but the manuscript lacks act III lines 245-258, 303-306, act IV lines 253-256, 261-264. There seems to have been hesitation over act III lines 287-291, and against act I line 1 the word 'nuit' brings in an extra stage instruction.

In several places we find changes adopted in 43A2*. See I.118 (has 'elle' instead of 'je'), 145 (gives 'révèrent' in place of 'adorent'), 154 (replaces 'cœur' with 'âme'), 191 (changes tense), 244 (for 'le' gives 'ce'), 329-334 (crossed out); III.256 (for 'lui' has 'moi'); IV.284-290 (lacking the final exchange between Zopire and Phanor, and ending the act with Zopire's still hoping that he can save his children); V.173 (has a different first hemistich). On the other hand, in four places the 43A2* version is finally suppressed. See I.175 (suppresses 'quel'); II.67 (crosses out 'nos' given for 'vos' (given above the line in 43A2*), 166 (had had 'leurs' in place of 'les'), 172 (for 'retenir' had had 'suspendre').

Other suppressions would seem mainly to be copyist's mistakes. See I.99 (different tense), 224 (had 'temple' for 'peuple'), 243 (had written 'vomissant' instead of 'écoutant'); III.91 (future for conditional), 223 (had omitted the object pronoun), 231 (a spurious 'Tout' at the beginning of the line), 263 (had had 'des' instead of 'ces'), 282 (had 'je suis frappé du' instead of 'je vois tomber la'); V.84 (had wrongly written 'Que' for 'soit'). In act III line 92, MS6 had had above the line 'des' for 'les', which is retained by Lekain (MS8).

Also crossed out is the text as printed in all 1742 editions in act I line 96, act III line 30, 128, 220, act IV line 96, act V line 11. In act I line 241 and act III line 16 the 42X1 (A*) text is suppressed, just as that of 42B1 (B*) in act II line 241, act III lines 130, 213-214, act IV line 7.

In eighteen places the final version of the text is replaced with additions above the line: see II.165; III. 87, 150-151, 169, 216, 266, 268, 278; IV.7, 18, 28, 52, 163-165, 177, 182 (giving two variants), 188, 244; V.3. It is replaced by the text as given in all 1742 editions in act II line 165, act III line 266, act IV lines 7, 177, by that of 42X1 (A*) in act IV line 188, and by that of 42B1 (B*) in act III lines 169, 216, 268, act IV lines 163-165, act V line 3.

MS6 has the text of all 1742 editions in thirteen lines: I.329; II.102, 135; III.32, 61, 198; IV.40, 234; V.132. It follows 42X1 (A*) in five places: I.177/178, 220-224; II.92; IV.86, 208, but retains the 42B1 (B*) version in sixteen cases: I.160, 322; II.58, 167; III.74, 110, 139, 229; IV.132/133, 233; V.45, 119, 125 (with a slight change), 165/166, 170, 184. This version is adopted above the line in act III line 209. It has the version given in 43A3 and 51B in act III line 48.

### MS7

– contemporary copy of various corrections. (Brown F).
CH-4: AT 177, no.15.

Gives the version found in all 1742 editions in act I lines 220-224. Replaces the 42X1 (A*) version with that of 42B1 (B*) in act III lines 213-214, act IV lines 119-121, but includes the couplet given at the first performance of the play and only printed in 42X1, 42X2 (act V lines 154-155).

MS8

– contemporary copy by Lekain of the title role. (Brown E).
Rôle de Mahomet de 465 vers. pag.17.
F-P/Cf: (Lekain 1754-59, no.1) MS.200015.
MAHOMET – Lekain.
ZOPIRE – Brisard.
OMAR – Dauberval.
SÉIDE – Monval.
PALMIRE – Mme. Vestris.
PHANOR – Vanhove.

Like MS6, this manuscript is useful as a guide to how the play was actually performed, and for act II lines 94-95 it gives an extra stage instruction. As in 43A2*, act II line 241 begins with 'Ainsi tout factieux'. MS8 does, however, contain a number of obvious copying mistakes. See II.154 (ignores the rhyme and miscopies the second hemistich), 190 (adds a superfluous 'jamais'), 242 (omits 'Il'), 286 (omits 'point'); III.76 ('vous attache à nous', in place of the more logical contrary). In act II line 349, Lekain had started by writing 'l'amour' after 'intérêt', but then crossed it out. Other changes are fairly small, and some of them could again be due to carelessness. See II.158 (gives 'les' for 'le' twice), 223 ('ces' replaces 'les'), 261 (gives 'mais' for 'et'), 320 (has 'les' for 'ces'), 321 (gives 'Ces' for 'Les'); III.92 (for 'les' has 'des', which is crossed out above the line in MS6), 133 ('Où' for 'Là'), 139 (has the same word order as in 42B1 (B*), but with the first two nouns put into the plural); IV.18 (puts 'ses mains' into the singular), 27 (has 'honneur' instead of 'bonheur'). There is 'ne [...] pas' rather than 'ne [...] point' in act II line 319, act III 163, act V lines 19, 49.

The text of all the 1742 editions is found in act II line 247, act III line 198, act V lines 11, 132, 148. Act III line 175 is given as in 42X1 (A*), whereas act III line 169 and act V line 184 follow 42B1 (B*). Act III line 136 adopts the 51B (F*) version.

MS Lekain

Manuscript in the hand of Lekain, *Cahiers de mise en scène*, 'Mahomet Ier de M. de Voltaire'.

Fonds de la Bibliothèque musée de la Comédie-Française, ms. 25035.

This manuscript gives detailed instructions for scene and lighting changes, costumes, and crowd movements, the cues for the latter being sometimes uncertain. The precise text followed by Lekain cannot be identified with certainty. Nothing precludes it being the text of MS6.

## Editions

(A*)

42X1

MAHOMET, / *TRAGEDIE.* / PAR M. DE VOLTAIRE. / REPRESENTE'E A PARIS / pour la premiere fois le Jeudi / 9 Août 1742. / [*ornament: flowers in an inverted triangle*] / [*thin rule*] / M. DCC. XLII. /

8°. sig.[].A-I$^4$, K-L$^4$, M$^1$; pag. [ii].89.[i blank]

[i] title; [ii] Acteurs; [1]-89 Mahomet, tragédie.

*ACTEURS.*

MAHOMET, faux Prophète. *Granval.*

ZOPIRE, Cherif de la Mecque. *Sarazin.*

OMAR, Disciple & Confident de Mahomet. *Le Grand.*

PHANOR, Confident de Zopire.

SEIDE, Fils inconnu de Zopire, & Amant de Palmire. *La Noue.*

PALMIRE, Fille inconnue de Zopire, Sœur & Amante de Séide. *Mlle Gossin.*

Suite de Mahomet.

Peuples.

*La scène est à la Mecque, dans le palais de Zopire.*

Bengesco 135.

F-P/BnF: Yf.6531; GB-Ox/U19 (as part of W39), USA-CtY.

42X1, 42X2 (A*) have the following particularities in the following lines: I.7 ('le' instead of 'ce'), 11 (this is missing in both editions, but is added in the errata of 42X2), 20 ('les' for 'ces'), 24 ('l'irreligion' for 'la sédition'), 40 ('Ce' for 'Le'), 56 ('le' for 'ce'), 57 (singular for plural), 98 (a tense change), 108 ('tumulte, ces camps' for 'tumulte des camps'), 138 (indicative instead of subjunctive), 143 ('le' for 'ce'), 169 ('jadis un tyran' instead of 'longtemps le tyran'), 177/178 (have the stage instruction: 'Elle s'en va'), 184 (a different tense), 185 (ten instead of six years), 196 ('Et t'apporte' instead of 'Et j'apporte'), 227 ('connais' instead of 'conçois'), 232 (a punctuation change), 241 (a line on the diaspora of the Mohammedans, later replaced at de Missy's suggestion (D2689), 259 ('aveuglé' for 'aveugle'), 279 ('dirai' instead of 'nierai'), 306 ('interroge' for 'intimide'), 322 ('ce' for 'ton'), 323 ('je vais' instead of 'je cours'), 324 ('te suis' instead 't'y suis'), 325 ('J'y défendrai' for 'Je défendrai'), 330 (for 'parmi nous, et l'épargner' there is 'en ces lieux, lui pardonner'); II.29 ('dont' in place of 'd'où', but adopted in 51B), 37 ('inflexible' instead of 'insensible'), 40 (with the object pronoun before the modal verb), 51 (with a comma instead of 'et'), 62 ('est tué' instead of 'est né'!), 67 ('mêmes' in the plural), 92 ('à' instead of 'vers'), 106 (a different tense), 113 (adds the instruction 'A Palmire'), 130 ('les' instead of 'ces'), 137 ('tu le vois' instead of 'c'est assez'), 154 ('Connais-tu' instead of 'conçois-tu' (see I.227), 175 (mistakenly gives 'vous' instead of 'nous'), 176/177 (has Zopire and Mahomet sitting down), 263 (prints 'je peux d'avoir', which was later corrected by de Missy; see D2689), 269 (has 'assemble' for 'rassemble'), 272 (gives 'Contre ses ennemis' instead of 'Entre ces ennemis'), 273 (a different tense), 275 (has 'ton bras me ravit' instead of 'mon bras te ravit'), 284 (gives 'bienfaits en mes mains' in place of 'bienfaisantes mains'), 285 (prints 'ne [...] pas' for 'ne [...] point'), 293 (for 'ton' gives 'son'), 320 (has 'veux' instead of 'dois' and 'porter' instead of 'lancer'), 329 (wrongly gives 'Des autres' for 'Tes autres'); III.11 (for 'me' has 'nous'), 16 ('Le prophète' appears as 'Le pontife') (but this is retained in 43A3 (q.v.), 18 (mistakenly replaces 'ait' by 'est' to make a nonsense of the line), 68 (gives 'ne [...] point' instead of 'ne [...] pas'), 76 (has 'Font' instead of 'sont'), 104 (for 'de vos vrais intérêts' gives 'de tous vos intérêts'), 108 (has 'les' in the place of 'des'), 109 (brings in a spurious pronoun in 'ciel l'ordonne'), 114 (for 'adore' one finds 'chérit'), 145 (mistakenly puts the verb in the singular), 152 (gives to Mahomet with a variant the part of the line now spoken by Omar), 161 (has 'le' instead of

MAHOMET,

TRAGÉDIE.

PAR M. DE VOLTAIRE.

REPRESENTÉE A PARIS
pour la premiere fois le Jeudi
9 Août 1742.

M. DCC. XLII.

*Mahomet, tragédie par M. de Voltaire* (n.p. 1742), title page.

'ce'), 167 (the noun is put in the singular), 174 ('L'on' appears rather unnecessarily instead of 'On'), 175 (gives 'ces' instead of 'les'), 176 (puts 'mêmes' in the plural), 199 (has 'vos' instead of 'mes'), 201 (adds the instruction 'en s'en allant'), 213-214 (a variant on Séide's summoning up his courage, that was probably given at the Comédie-Française (see 67C), 218 (has the rather odd 'Vois d'un cœur'), 223 (has 'soi' instead of 'moi'), 232 (has 'est ému' instead of 's'est ému'), 248 (gives 'le crime' for 'le piège'), 249 (instead of 'erreurs' has 'horreurs'); IV.43 (has slightly different stage instructions at the beginning of the act), 52 (prints by mistake an infinitive instead of a past participle), 71 (replaces 'ce' by 'et'), 73 (instead of 'sais que trop que' one finds 'sais, comme vous, que'), 84 (for 'éperdu' there is 'attendri'), 86 (a different tense), 94 (introduces indefinite articles, transforming the adjectives into nouns), 107 (places 'ainsi' after the auxiliary verb), 110 ('dot!' becomes 'loi!'), 119-121 (a variant as Palmire and Séide steel themselves to kill Zopire), 122 ('des' becomes 'les'), 125 (for 'Ces' there is 'Les'), 132/133 (gives a variant for the stage instructions at the beginning of act IV scene iv), 132 ('est glacé' instead of 's'est glacé' (see III.232), 144 (instead of 'en' gives 'dans'), 154 (through error gives 'sceptre' instead of 'spectre', and has 'les' for 'ces'), 156 (has 'mes pas' instead of 'mon bras'), 160 (gives 'crime' for 'meurtre'), 162 (replaces 'et' with a comma), 168 (has 'ou' instead of 'et'), 175 (removes the inversion with the pronoun and the verb), 176 (has 'quelle' instead of 'cette'), 182 (slightly alters the stage instructions here), 188 (has 'Le' for 'Ce'), 197 (has Séide sitting down), 198 (has 'te' in the place of 'le'), 206 (has 'ses' for 'ces'), 208 (replaces 'regards' by 'esprits'), 210 (instead of 'du nœud', one finds 'du Dieu'), 223/224 (gives slightly different stage instructions), 227 (puts the subject in the singular and has the adjective after the noun), 233 (omits 'en'), 240 (has 'ne [...] point' and not 'ne [...] pas'), 242/243 (gives slightly different stage instructions), 247 (instead of repeating the verb, has 'Rendez ce fer cruel à'), 254 (has 'honneurs' instead of 'horreurs', which is surely a mistake), 262 (gives the present participle instead of the imperfect), 263 (changes the tense), 267 (puts 'moments' in the singular), 270 (replaces 'enchaînez' with 'entraînez'), 277 (gives a different order to the soldiers), 280 ('tout' gives way to 'vous'), 281 ('votre Roi' becomes 'notre Roi'), 282/283, 284/285 (gives slightly different stage instructions); V.2 (gives the meaningless 'Le voit déjà sans front'), 37 ('son' becomes 'Le'), 50 ('destins' is given in the plural, as in 43A3 (D*), 68 (for 'deux' there is simply 'des'), 75 ('Le peuple' disappears to become 'sans doute on'), 79 (for 'ensemble' there is 'en cendre'), 106 (instead of 'On' there is 'Il'), 114 (has 'affermis' instead of 'raffermis' (see II.269), 117 (for 'les' gives 'me'), 119, 125 (gives slightly different stage instructions), 138 (for 'ses' has 'des'), 143-144 (puts 'crimes' and 'victimes' in the singular), 154-155 (gives the extra couplet spoken at the first performance), 159 (lacks stage instructions for the crowd), 166 (gives slightly different stage instructions), 175 (instead of 'fureur' gives 'douleur' (see 42B1 (B*)).

There are a fair number of obvious errors (I.11; II.175, 263, 329; III.18, 109, 145; IV.52, 154, 233, 254; V.2), and many of the other differences are slight (many only affecting articles, pronouns and possessive adjectives). The use of the plural for 'mêmes' (II.67; III.176) would not have met with Voltaire's approval (see D2699). Only act I line 241, act III lines 203-214, act IV lines 119-121, act V lines 154-155 present variants of any substance, not found in the Brussels editions of 1742 (see 42B1, etc. (B*)).

42X1 differs slightly from 42X2. It has a 'Pontife' instead of a 'prophète' in act III line 16. Like 42X2, it mispells 'je cours' in act III line 117, but in a different way. In act IV scene iv is misnumbered as scene iii (see lines 132/133). In act V line 11, there is 'de flots' rather than 'des flots'.

42X1*

– a copy of Bengesco 135 (42X1) with holograph corrections and additions. (Brown H). It passed at the Evans sale: 10 April 1824, p.18, no.460; A. A. Renouard sale, 20 November 1854, p.374, no.3660.
F-P/BnF: F12933, ff.74-123.

Besides adding the words 'ou le fanatisme' to the title, the following lines are changed to give the final text: I.7, 11, 20, 57, 96, 108, 138, 143, 161, 163, 184, 196, 227, 241, 250, 254, 285; II.51, 62, 67, 86, 154, 272, 284, 336-337; III.1-10, 79-89, 91-99, 117, 152, 176, 266, 278-314; IV.1-3 (following de Missy), 18-29, 33, 52, 71, 107, 110, 119, 137, 160, 176, 197, 198, 254, 262, 263, 270, 280; V.2, 22, 27, 37, 60, 106, 119.

Variants not recorded elsewhere also appear. See I.159-160, 261, 264; III.12-14, 81, 88, 98, 100, 213, 293-294, 309, 314; IV.26; V.166. Erased variants are found in act III lines 5, 17, 289, act IV lines 25, 27. The two extra lines at act V lines 154-155 – given at the first performance and printed in 42X1 – are also suppressed. Small errors occur in act III lines 6, 311, act IV line 154. As in MS5, in act IV line 227 the subject is put into the plural. Act I line 279, act III line 128 are left unchanged, although the anomalies are underlined. A small change in act III line 199 brings it in line with the version found in 42B1, etc. (B*).

42X2

MAHOMET, / *TRAGEDIE,* / PAR M. DE VOLTAIRE. / *REPRESENTÉE SUR LE THEATRE* / *de la Comédie Françoiſe.* / Le 9. Août 1742. / [*ornament: stars and other designs in an inverted triangle*] / [*thin rule*] / M. DCC. XLII. /
8°. sig.[].A8, B4, C8, D4, E8, F4, G8, H1; pag.[ii].34[=90] Sig.C3 is wrongly numbered as C4. The last page is misnumbered.
[i] title; [ii] Acteurs; [1]-34[90] Mahomet, tragédie.
Bengesco 134.
B-G/U.

According to the catalogue of the Bibliothèque nationale, the paper and the typography of this edition show that it was printed in Rouen.

As we have seen, 42X2 differs only slightly from 42X1, and adds the missing act I line 11 in its *errata*. It has the final version for act III line 16, act V line 11. It has its own particularities in the following lines: I.48 (changes the tense), 91 (misses out the partitive article), 307 (misses out the second verb), 332 (has 'son' instead of 'mon' (cf. MS5); II.78 (has 'ces' for 'ses'), 192 (makes a wrong agreement for the verb); III.25 (puts 'ces moments' in the singular), 117 (just as 42X1 spells 'cours' as 'course', so here we find 'courre'); IV.168 (follows 42B2, etc. in missing out the 'en'), 197 (puts 'suivez-moi' into the singular), 200 (for 'à l'aspect de' has 'dans le cœur de').

(B*)

42B1

MAHOMET, / TRAGEDIE. / PAR / M. DE VOLTAIRE. / *REPRÉSENTÉE SUR LE THEATRE.* / *de la Comédie*

*Françoiſe.* / Le 9. Août 1742. / [*ornament: limpet shells from above in an inverted triangle*] / A BRUXELLES, / [*thin rule*] / M. DCC. XLII. /

8°. sig.[].A-H4, I3; pag.[ii].70.

[i] title; [ii] Acteurs; [1]-70 Mahomet, tragédie.

GB-Ox/U19: Besterman 1973/46 V3.M2.1742(1); GB-Lo/N1: 11736.ccc.3(2).

*ACTEURS.*

MAHOMET.

OMAR, *général de Mahomet.*

ZOPIRE, *chérif du Sénat de la Mecque.*

SEIDE, PALMIRE, *enfants de Zopire élevés secrètement dans le camp de Mahomet.*

PHANOR, *confident de Zopire.*

*La scène est à la Mecque, dans le temple des faux dieux de Zopire.*

This rival primary version of the full text, which we call B*, does not appear to have met with Voltaire's approval.

41B1 (B*) has the following particularities in the following lines: I.1 (has 'ces' instead of 'ses', as in 51B (F*)), 14 (gives 'les' instead of 'vos'), 29 (introduces 'et' before 'a crainte'), 37 (for 'éternelle' gives 'immortelle'), 58 (instead of 'vous-même' has 'vos mains'), 65 (replaces 'Quoi!' with 'Qui' and 'la fraude' with 'l'erreur'), 68 (gives 'fureur' instead of 'faveur'), 69 (for 'aux bornes' there is 'vers la fin'), 81 (instead of 'vœux' there is 'yeux'), 87 (in place of 'vient' one finds 'approche'), 109 (puts the adjective in front rather than after the noun), 121 (replaces 'révère' with 'respecte'), 122 (gives 'en' instead of 'dans'), 125 (for 'ne [...] pas' has 'ne [...] point'), 130 (by mistake, puts 'esclave' in the singular), 131 (for 'nos' has 'les'), 139 (instead of 'abhorrez' gives 'détestez'), 144 (gives 'odieux' in place of 'inouïs'), 146 (has 'de Dieu' for 'du ciel'), 160 (instead of 'de pleurs' has 'des pleurs' (an understable variant retained in some later editions such as W72P), 166 (misprints 'Moad' as 'Morad'), 177/178 (lacks stage instruction for Palmire's exit, but gives a change of scene, which is more in accordance with classical practice), 200 (has 'donne' instead of 'rende'), 241 (another variant for a line over which Voltaire hesitated (see D2689), 272 (has 'moi' instead of 'nous', which in Omar's mouth is an obvious mistake), 290 (through error has 'sa colère' instead of 'ma colère'), 311 (gives the singular for the plural), 312 (has 'celui' instead of 'le nom'), 322 (has 'ce' instead of 'ton' and 'frivole' instead of 'fragile'), 325 (inverts the word order); II.1 (for 'cruelle' has 'affreuse'), 16 ('heure où de carnage et de sang' instead of 'heure de carnage, où, de sang'), 21 ('dans' replaces 'en'), 29 (gives the singular for the plural), 35 (prints in error 'D'aucun ombre'), 39 (for 'Mais le cruel enfin vient' has the rather awkward 'Mais! hélas le cruel vient'), 42 (instead of 'et ton amant peut-être' has 'et moi-même peut-être' (a variant which Beuchot preferred, see Moland, iv.119), 47 (has 'Ce' instead of 'Le'), 49 (gives 'yeux' instead of 'pieds'), 58 (gives wrongly 'nous' instead of 'vous'), 62 (replaces 'vos' with 'nos'), 76 (begins line with 'Il vient' rather than 'Il entre'), 90 (has 'grandeur' instead of 'pouvoir'), 92 (omits the object pronoun after the second verb, which may be less precise, but which certainly helps the flow of the alexandrine), 107 (has 'M'empoisonneriez-vous' for 'Empoisonneriez-vous'), 117 (gives 'longueur' for 'lenteur'), 150-151 (a reworked couplet, over which Voltaire hesitated (see MS1 and 43A2*), 159 ('deux ennemis' becomes 'dieux ennemis' which is an obvious mistake), 167 (has 'sur' in place of 'vers'), 171 (gives 'lancer' for 'hâter'), 180 (changes the tense), 206 (has 'par' instead of 'pour'), 210 (for 'splendeur' has 'grandeur'), 215 (puts 'culte' into the plural), 221 (gives 'chasser' instead of 'changer'), 241 ('tout factieux' becomes 'tout scélérat'), 259 (gives 'mais' instead of 'et'), 263 (gives 'puis' instead of 'peux', as in Kehl), 272 ('Entre' is given as 'Contre'), 273 ('ciment' is replaced by 'lien'; see D2689), 285 (changes the word order), 292 (gives 'tromper' instead of 'dompter', a variant which is adopted in Kehl), 302 ('ton culte' becomes 'l'erreur'), 313 ('Ce' is replaced with 'Le'), 314 (a line which Voltaire reworked several times; see 43A2*), 316 (has 'fut' instead of 'fit'), 319-320 (a much re-worked couplet; see 42X1, 43A2*, etc.), 338 (omits the second 'oui'), 339 (omits the definite article, thus failing to scan), 340 (gives 'ton' instead of 'son'); III.22 (has 'Elevait' instead of 'Enlevait'), 25 (has 'que' for 'où'), 40 (instead of 'qu'à l'envi' has 'que tous deux'), 42 ('me' in place of 'nous'), 43 (has 'le prophète roi' and not 'le pontife roi'), 59 (a much reworked line; see MS4, MS5, 42X1, 42B5, 43A3, etc.), 62, 74 (reworks the first hemistich in both these lines), 110 (gives 'les' for 'ses', which is surely an error), 114 (a reworked line), 120 (has 'M'enfonce' and 'le cœur', which were later corrected at de Missy's suggestion; see D2689), 127 (has 'vos pieds' and 'ses citoyens' instead of 'tes pieds' and 'nos citoyens'), 129 (replaces 'te' with 'le' and puts it after the modal verb; this is surely a mistake), 130 ('Il voit souvent Zopire' becomes 'Lui seul il voit Zopire'),

139 (changes the word order), 143 ('était' is replaced with 'semble'), 157 (gives 'cœur' instead of 'être'), 167 (gives the singular for the plural), 169 (for 'd'un' has 'du'), 172 ('nos' becomes 'mes'), 199 (has 'vos' for 'mes'), 209 (for 'Enfin Dieu m'a choisi' has 'Dieu m'a daigné choisir'), 213-214 (a much reworked couplet; see MS5, MS6), 216 (has 'la' instead of 'ma', something which is corrected by de Missy; see D2689), 221 (puts 'moment' into the plural), 222 (has 'suspendu' instead of 'retenu'), 229 ('Ah!' becomes 'Quoi!'), 268 (gives 'ton' instead of 'son', thus having Zopire addressing this line to Séide); IV.15 (misses out 'en'), 32 (replaces 'toujours' with 'souvent'), 43 (gives slightly different stage instructions), 45-50 (gives these lines in a separate scene (SCENE III), changes the numbers of the subsequent scenes, and thus again shows a greater adherence to classical custom; see I.177/178), 47-48 (a reworked couplet on Séide's inner resistance to Mahomet's orders), 50 (has 'hélas!' instead of 'ô ciel'), 52 (gives 'Te conduit' for 'Qui t'amène'), 53 (for 'Séide, la frayeur et' has 'La frayeur, cher Séide, et'), 58 (gives 'raison' instead of 'fureur'), 72-77 (lacks the lines 73-76 in which Séide summons up courage to kill Zopire), 82 (puts 'moins' after the auxilliary verb), 107 (replaces 'arrêté' with 'ordonné'), 117 (has 'sorti' instead of 'parti'), 119 (for 'vient d'emprunter' has 'a parlé par'), 122 ('des' becomes 'ses'), 124 (a reworked line), 125 (for 'affreux' there is 'cruels'), 129 (has 'dans' instead of 'sur'), 132/133 (gives slightly different stage instructions; see MS6), 142 ('en' becomes 'entre'), 156 (a reworked line, changing 'l'autel' to 'le lieu', and keeping – as in 42X1 – 'mes pas', rather than 'mon bras'), 163-165 (reworking the moment Séide disappears behind the altar to stab Zopire), 168 (has 'de me' instead of 'de m'en', which is a mistake), 181 (here the knees 's'abaissent' rather than 's'affaissent'), 186 ('Grand Dieu' takes the place of 'O ciel!'), 188 (a reworked line), 196 ('nous sommes' replaces 'vous êtes'), 197 (has Séide sitting down and getting up again, and gives 'Je meurs', thus omitting 'me' and breaking the scan), 206 (puts 'regards' into the singular), 208 (gives 'nos' for 'mes'), 214 (puts the adverb before the past participle of the modal verb), 218 (for 'effrayer' has 's'offrir à', and gives a slightly different stage instruction), 223 (for 'entraîne' has 'a vaincu'), 223/224 (gives slightly different stage instructions), 224 (has 'chancelants' instead of 'languissants'), 225 (misses out 'ingrat' and ends up with eleven syllables), 226 ('ta' is replaced both times by 'la'), 231 (a much reworked line), 233 (puts 'encor' after 'temps'), 235 ('d'un horrible' becomes 'de cet affreux'), 239 (redistributes who says what in this line),

242 ('cet affreux' is replaced by 'un si noir'), 242/243 (gives slightly different stage instructions), 247 (has 'le' instead of 'ce'), 247/248 (gives slightly different stage instructions), 261 (gives 'et' instead of 'ou'), 266 (for 'ils vont punir' has 'ils puniront'), 274 (gives 'attentat' instead of 'meurtre horrible'), 277 (a much reworked line; see 42X1), 280 (has 'sur' for 'par'), 282/283 (again following classical custom, there is a change of scene here; see in the same act, lines 45-50), 283 (misses out the first 'ô' and thus breaks the scan); V.2 (a much reworked line), 3 (has 'Les' for 'Tes'), 20 (a reworked line), 37 (gives 'Ce' instead of 'son'), 44 (has 'pressé' instead of 'pesé', which is surely a mistake), 45 (for 'Le' has 'Ce'), 46 (has 'secret' instead of 'mystère'), 47 ('à jamais' is replaced by 'par mes mains'), 52 (puts 'sur vous' after rather than before the verb), 58 (has 'monter' instead of 'penser'), 62 (for 'de' gives 'du', which – though ambiguous – is surely a mistake), 63 ('dernier' is replaced by 'cruel'), 75 (a much reworked line; see 42X1, etc.), 82 (has 'tes' instead of 'ses'), 83 (has 'la' for 'ta', which is nonesense), 85 (has 'les' instead of 'tes', retained in 43A3 (D*) and 51B (F*)), 97 (gives 'des' instead of 'ses'), 107 (has 'mêmes' in the plural, which despite Voltaire's known preference for the singular is again found in 51B (F*)), 114 (has 'contre moi' for 'comme moi'), 119 (gives slightly different stage instructions), 120 (puts 'peuple' into the singular, something which is again done in W72P and Kehl), 125 (gives slightly different stage instructions), 138 ('encor ses' becomes 'ici des'), 139 (lacks stage instructions for Séide here), 140 (a reworked line), 144 (puts the verb into the plural and has 'des' instead of 'ses'), 147 (has 'ce traitre' instead of 'le poison'), 150-155 (lacking the four lines in which Mahomet exults over the death of Séide: lines 151-154), 159 (omits the stage instruction for Palmire, but has the crowd leaving), 165/166 (gives slightly different stage instructions), 166 (brings in a redundant 'me' in 'Je meurs'), 170 ('le' is replaced by 'ce'), 182 (Mahomet admitting that he can make mistakes, the contrary of what is really implied), 184 (has 'ce' instead of 'le', as in 43A3 (D*) and 51B (F*)), 189 (gives 'veux' in place of 'dois').

Just as with 42X1 (A*), there are again obvious errors (see I.130, 166, 272, 290; II.35, 58, 159, 339; III.110, 129; IV.15, 197, 283; IV.44, 62, 83, 166, 182). Many other lines introduce small changes that may well again be errors, but which can be argued over (see 43A2*). Again there is 'mêmes' given in the plural (V.107). Because of the manuscript evidence the text here seems to have slightly less authority than 42X1 (A*), but variants particularly worthy of note are to be found in I.177/178, 241;

II.42, 150-151, 273, 292, 302, 314, 319-320; III.59, 62, 74, 114, 120, 130, 209, 213-214, 216, 222, 268; IV.32, 45-50, 47-48, 52-53, 72-77, 107, 117, 119, 124, 156, 163-165, 168, 188, 225, 231, 274, 277; V.2, 20, 47, 75, 85, 120, 140, 147, 150-155, 184.

As distinct from the other 1742 Brussels editions, 42B1 has 'dieux' rather than 'cieux' at the end of act I line 215, and changes the tense of the verb in act V line 160.

42B2

MAHOMET / TRAGEDIE, / PAR M. DE VOLTAIRE. / REPRÉSENTÉE SUR LE THEATRE / *de la Comédie Françoiſe.* / Le 9. Août 1742. / [*ornament: stars and leaves in an inverted triangle*] / A BRUXELLES, / [*thin rule*] / M. DCC. XLII. /
8° sig.[].A-I4; pag.[ii].71.[i]
[i] title; [ii] Acteurs; [1]-70 Mahomet, tragédie.
p.[72]: *ERRATA*. Au lieu de ZOPHIRE, *liſez*, ZOPIRE.
Bengesco 133.
F-Ang: BL2236(1); F-P/BnF: 8°Yth.10623; GB-Ox/U19: V3.M2.1742 (3).

Similar to 42B1, but with minor changes. Zopire is transformed to Zophire throughout, and act I line 78 gives the past participle instead of the third person present singular of the verb 'remplir' (something which is followed in 43A1, 43A2 and 47A). As in 42B4, in act II line 43 'Car' is mistakenly printed as 'Ca'. Like 43A1, it turns 'Me cachât' into 'Ne cachât' in act III line 24. It repeats some of the errors of 42B1 in act II lines 35, 159, act IV line 119, act V line 60.

42B3

MAHOMET, / *TRAGÉDIE*, / PAR M. DE VOLTAIRE. / REPRÉSENTÉE SUR LE THEATRE / *de la Comédie Françoiſe.* / Le 9. Août 1742. / [*fleuron, with leaves and berries*] / A BRUXELLES. / [*double rule*] / *M. DCC. XLII.* /
8°. sig.A-D8, E4; pag.72.
[1] title; [2] Acteurs; [3]-72 Mahomet, tragédie.

Bengesco 132.
F-P/BnF: 8°Yth.10620.

Similar to 42B1, but correcting errors found in act II line 35, act IV line 119, act V line 60. On the other hand, it makes its own mistakes in act II line 195 (omitting the object pronoun), act III line 234 (omitting 'et'). It also has 'ta' for 'la' in act V line 13.

42B4

MAHOMET / TRAGÉDIE, / PAR M. DE VOLTAIRE. *REPRESENTÉE SUR LE THEATRE / de la Comédie Françoiſe.* / Le 9 Août 1742. / [*fleuron, with leaves, tassels, etc.*] / A BRUXELLES, / [*thin rule*] / M. DCC. XLII. /
8°. sig.A-I4, K3; pag.78.
[1] title; [2] Acteurs; [3]-78 Mahomet, tragédie.
Bengesco 131.
F-P/BnF: 8°Yth.10621.

Again similar but not identical to 42B1. 42B4 follows 42B3 in correcting act IV line 119, but reproduces the errors of 42B1 and 42B2 in act II line 35 and act V line 60. It follows 42B2 in act II line 43. On the other hand, it corrects act II line 159 and gives the final text in act II line 340, act IV line 16 and act V line 189.

(C*)

42B5

MAHOMET, / *TRAGEDIE,* / Représentée sur le Théatre de la Comédie / Française / *Le neuviéme Août* 1742. / [*ornament: stars, asterisks and small floral designs in an inverted triangle*] / A BRUXELLES, / [*thin rule*] / *M. DCC. XLII.*
8°. sig.A-F4; pag.48.
[1] title; [2] Acteurs; [3]-48 Mahomet, tragédie.
p.48:

Cette deuxième Edition a été revuë & corrigée par l'Auteur même, qui est actuellement à Bruxelles. Celle que l'on annonce en Hollande ne peut être que très imparfaite.

F-P/Ar: Rf.14.321.

Similar (but less so than others) to 42B1.

42B5 (C*) gives the final version of act I line 130, act II lines 259, 339, act IV lines 15, 142. It also has variants not found in 42B1 (B*) in the following lines: I.27 (has 'nous' instead of 'vous'), 69 (has a variant that is even further away from the final text than that given in 42B1 (B*)), 70 (has 'mortelle' instead of 'honteuse'), 118 (has 'd'où' instead of 'dont'), 206 (gives 'ces' in place of 'tes'), 231 (for 'grossier' gives 'ancien'); II.148 (by mistake gives 'avec moi' instead of 'avec toi'), 340 (has 'mon' instead of 'son'); III.59 (reverts to the version found in 42X1 (A*) and retained in 43A3 (D*)), 127 (keeps – as in 42B1 – 'ses citoyens' instead of 'nos citoyens', but has the definitive 'tes pieds'), 129 (as in the final version, this has 'te' rather than 'le', but keeps the word order of 42B1 (B*), with the pronoun placed in front of the infinitive); IV.119 (while Séide's part of the line still has the text as given in 42B1 (B*), Palmire now says: 'Qu'entends-je?'), 215 (has 'affreux' rather than 'horrible'), 225 (corrects the 42B1 version, by adding 'Ah!').

In act V line 17 42B5 has rather strangely the partitive 'des' rather than 'de' with 'secrets chemins'. This variant is retained right the way through to W75G. Further variants in this act are found in lines 76 (has 'Le ciel vient' instead of 'Leurs bras vont'), 114 (has 'avec moi' instead of 'comme moi'), 165 (puts 'horreur' into the singular).

Three mistakes made in 42B5 are corrected in the editions that it inspired (52B, 60B, 78B). It lacks act IV line 244. It follows 42B1 with 'suivre' in the infinitive in act V line 60 and a superflous 'me' in act V line 166.

### 42B5*

– a copy of 42B5 (F-P/Ar: Rf.14.321), with what appear to be holograph corrections. This is possibly Brown I: a copy of a 1742 edition with holograph corrections (present whereabouts unknown) (see D.app.62), which was formerly in the collection of A. A. Renouard; see his *Catalogue de la bibliothèque d'un amateur*, iii.71.

The following lines are changed to the final version: I.1, 14, 65, 68-70, 81; III.222; V.2, 165-166. Small variants are found for act I line 146 and act IV line 188. A small variant, later found in 78B, is crossed out.

42XX

MAHOMET, / *TRAGÉDIE.* / DE / MONSIEUR / DE VOLTAIRE, / *Repréſentée ſur le Théâtre de la Comédie Françaiſe,* / Le 9. Août 1742. / [n.p.n.d].
12°. sig.A-D[12], E[4]; pag.104.
[1] title; [2] Acteurs; [3]-104 Mahomet, tragédie.
USA-PU.

This is an odd hybrid text, influenced by all but not following entirely any one of the various 1742 editions.

The general 1742 text is given in many places. See I.53-54, 58, 96, 116, 161, 163, 173-175, 180-182, 198, 220-224, 261-266, 285, 292, 329, 333-334; II.12, 48, 86, 102, 135, 165, 247, 308, 317, 336-337; III.12-17, 30, 32, 35-36, 41, 48, 60-61, 112, 128, 133-136, 146-147, 179, 198, 211-212, 220, 231, 262, 266; IV.7, 10, 33, 40-42, 96, 137, 155, 159, 177, 234, 241, 260, 272, 285, 287-290; V.22, 27, 60, 85, 103, 105, 123, 126-127, 132, 135, 138, 140, 148, 172-173.

It follows 42X1 (A*) alone in seventeen places. See I.7; II.40, 67, 92, 275; III.1-10, 104 (with a slight difference), 108, 218; IV.64-66, 122, 144, 210, 254; V.37, 68, 114. However, it has closer links with the text as given in 42B1, etc. (B*), which it follows exclusively in one hundred and thirty-three places. See I.29, 37, 65, 68, 81, 87, 109, 121-122, 131, 139, 144, 146, 160, 166, 177/178, 241, 250, 254, 290, 312, 321-322, 325 (with a slight variant); II.1, 16, 21, 29, 35, 39, 42, 47, 58, 76, 90, 92, 107, 117, 150-151, 159, 167, 171, 215, 221, 241, 263, 272-273, 285, 302, 313-314, 319-320 (with a slight difference), 338; III.22, 40, 42-43, 62, 74, 110, 114, 120, 130, 139, 143, 167, 169, 199, 209, 213-214, 221-222, 229, 278-314; IV.1-3, 18-29, 32, 43, 45-50, 52-53, 58, 72-77, 82, 107, 117, 124-125, 132/133, 156, 163-165 (with a slight difference), 168, 181, 186, 188, 196-197, 206, 208, 218, 223-226, 231 (with a slight difference), 233, 235, 239, 242/243, 242, 247/248, 247, 261, 266, 274, 277, 280, 282/283, 283; V.2-3, 20, 46-47, 58, 62, 75, 82, 97, 107, 119, 120, 125, 139, 144, 147, 150-155 (with a mistake), 159, 165/166, 166, 170, 182, 184, 189. In a further fifteen places, it has the lines as given in 42B1-42B4 (B*), but not in 42B5 (C*) and its related editions. See I.69, 130; II.339-340; III.25, 58-59, 79-89, 91-99 (with a printing mistake ('distiguée')), 127, 129; IV.15-16 (partly as also found in 42X1), 119, 142, 197, 225; V.76 (also found in 42X1). Act II line 43 is that given in 42B2, 42B4 and 43A1. On the other hand, it follows 42B5 (C*) in act V line 17, and gives the final versions of act II line 62 and act V line 11 as they first appeared in 43A3, though as these are small changes, this could be due to the vagaries of printing. There is a mistake in act II line 153, and the similarity with MS4 in act I line 85 is again probably unintentional.

### 43A1

MAHOMET / TRAGEDIE, / PAR M. DE VOLTAIRE. / *REPRESENTÉE SUR LE THEATRE* / *de la Comedie Françoiſe*, / Le 9 Août 1742. / [*ornament: stars surrounding four small ornate decorations*] / A AMSTERDAM. / [*long thin rule*] / M. DCC. XLIII. /

8°. A-D⁸, E⁶; pag.76.

[1] title; [2] Acteurs; 3-76 Mahomet, tragédie.

GB-Ox/U19: Besterman: 1973/47 V3.M2.1743(1).

The text is similar to that of 42B1 (B*) – see in particular II.259, 340; III.127; IV.15, 142, 197 – but with some inaccuracies. Most noticeably, it reproduces mistakes already found in 42B2. In act I line 78 it follows 42B2 with 'Rempli', and in act II line 43, like 42B2 and 42B4, it has with 'Ca' instead of 'Car'. In common with 42B2, it omits 'dit' in act IV line 119. It has its own careless mistakes. Act III line 156 is missing, and act V lines 179-180 are merged into one. There are also obvious errors in act II lines 88 (omitting 'et'), 131 (having 'Que' for 'Qui'), 174 (giving, as in MS4, 'revoir' for 'recevoir' and thus lacking a necessary syllable), 320 (having 'porteront' for 'partiront' as given in 42B1, etc.), act III 65 (printing 'notre' for 'votre'), 112 (omitting 'en'), 152 (having 'Enfin' for 'Enfant'). Other small changes are also probably due to carelessness. See I.31 (has 'nos' for 'vos'); II.91 (spells 'Morad' as 'Morade'), 98 (changes the tense), 116 (has 'trouve' instead of 't'ouvre'), 125 (gives 'en' for 'dans'); III.165 (has 'nos' for 'vos'), 247 (has 'le joug' instead of 'un joug'); IV.18 (has 'dans' for 'de' in the 1742 version of this line); V.119 (omits 'et'). It is probable a mere coincidence that has led to the printing of the final version of act V line 184 (with 'le' instead of 'ce').

### 43A2

MAHOMET / TRAGEDIE, / PAR / M. DE VOLTAIRE. / *REPRESENTEE SUR LE THEATRE* / *de la Comédie*

*Françoise.* / Le 9. Août 1742. / [*woodcut: on a pedestal a seated cherub-like muse being crowned by two others, flags, two horns of plenty, a caduceus and various other instruments radiating from an astrolabe*] / AMSTERDAM, / [*thin rule*] / M. DCC. XLIII. /
8°. sig.A-D⁸, E⁴; pag.68.[ii blank]
[1] title; [2] Acteurs; [3]-68 Mahomet, tragédie.
F-P/Ar: Rf.14.323.
Bound in with Cahusac's *Zénéide, comédie en un acte, avec divertissements* [music by N. R. de Grandval] (Paris, Prault, 1743). This was performed at the Comédie-Française on 13 May 1743 (see *Mercure de France*, May 1743, p.1010).

Except in act II line 203, where 43A2 has by error printed the conjunction 'et' instead of the verb 'est', it will be followed almost identically by 47A. Both editions are based on 42B1 – 42B4 (B*). They follow 42B1 (B*) rather than 42B5 (C*) most noticeably in act I lines 27, 69-70, 118, 130, 206, 231, act II lines 148, 259, 339, act III lines 59, 129, act IV lines 215, 225, act V lines 17, 76, 114. On the other hand, they do follow 42B5 (C*) in act III line 127 (with 'tes' for 'vos') and act IV line 142 (with 'en' rather than 'entre'). They correct act IV lines 15 and 197. Following 42B2 and 43A1, they have 'Rempli' for 'Remplit' in act I line 78. Like 42B2, 42B4 and 43A1, they also make a mistake in act II line 43, but have 'si' instead of 'Car'. In act II line 340 they follow 42B4 and give the final text.

43A2*

– a copy of the [second] Amsterdam 1743 (43A2) edition with ms corrections (pag.134). (Brown J). From the collection of François Joseph Talma, it passed at the Comte Emery Sale (Paris 14 juillet 1870), p.16, no.199.
F-P/Ar: Rf14.323.
[Facing title-page:]

Je crois cette impression de Mahomet la 1ère et les ratures surchargées, petites pièces écrites et détachées, de la main de Voltaire. Ce volume, dites-vous, a appartenu à l'acteur Talma; je l'ai payé 3fr. au bouquiniste

Givant, rue du Carrousel qui m'a vendu bien des fois des livres bons et rares et aussi des mauvais dans tous les genres.

Je ne garantis rien. Je dis seulement que les notes de ce Mahomet ont l'air d'être de la main de Voltaire. Je les ai comparées avec 3. chants de la Pucelle qui sont écrits et mis au net par lui, et où il me semble qu'il y a analogie. A.B. [Beuchot].

The following lines are changed to give the final version: I.37, 53, 58, 65, 69, 81, 87, 109, 121, 130, 144, 146, 161, 163, 173-175, 200, 241, 250, 254, 261-266, 285, 290, 292, 311, 312, 321, 325, 335; II.16, 39, 47, 48, 62, 76, 86, 92, 107, 117, 151, 165, 171, 206, 210, 215, 221, 259, 272, 273, 285, 302, 316, 336-337; III.1-10, 35-36, 40, 41, 42, 59, 61, 62, 79-87, 89, 91-99, 114, 120, 133-136, 143, 146, 157, 169, 209, 216, 222, 231, 262, 266, 268, 278-314 (though retaining some variants); IV.1, 3, 7, 10, 16, 18-29, 41-42, 47-48, 52, 53, 58, 64, 66, 72-77 (added), 82, 117, 119, 122, 124, 125, 129, 137, 163-165, 177, 181, 186, 188, 214, 223-224, 225 (as an alternative), 235, 239, 241, 242, 247, 260, 266, 272, 274, 277; V.2, 20, 44, 63, 75, 76, 82-83, 85, 103, 105, 135, 140, 144, 148, 172, 182.

Act III lines 88, 309, act IV lines 2, 65 remain unchanged, as they are found printed in 43A2. In several places, 43A2* cuts out the definitive version, most noticeably to follow the actors' copy as given in MS6 (see I.118, 145, 154, 191; II.31, 166, 172). Other variants already following the same source are also to be found. See I.244, 329-334; II.67, 92; III.16, 48; IV.284-290; V.173. Act III lines 303-306, act IV lines 253-256, 261-264 are suppressed here, just as in MS6. 43A2* also suppresses act III lines 245-258, act IV lines 85-92, 97-100, 195-198, 286, and amalgamates act IV lines 153-156 into one. In act II line 161, the final version of the text is replaced by that first found printed in 43A3. For act V lines 187-190 a choice of two variants is given in place of the final text, illustrating well Voltaire's hesitation over the closing speech (see also MS3 and D2408, D2411). In act I line 7 and act IV line 208 the changes bring the text in line with that of 42X1 (A*). A word missing in 42B1 and related editions (B*) is supplied in act II line 92. Other miscellaneous small variants not found elsewhere are given in act I line 175, act II lines 241, 314, 320, act III 200, 289, 297, act IV 50, 132/133, 231, 248, act V 127. Small mistakes appear in act III lines 179 and 296.

(D*)

43A3

LE / FANATISME, / OU / MAHOMET / LE PROPHETE, / *TRAGÉDIE.* / PAR / M$^{R}$. DE VOLTAIRE. / [*fleuron*] / *A AMSTERDAM,* / Chez ETIENNE LEDET & Compagnie. [*in some copies*: Chez JACQUES DESBORDES] / M. DCC. XLIII. /

8°. sig.*$^{6}$, [], **$^{4}$, A-G$^{8}$; pag.[xxii].112.

Bengesco 136.

F-P/BnF: 16°Yth.1831; GB-U/19: V3.M2.1743(2, 3).

Title-page in red and black.

[i] title; [iii-x] Avis de l'Editeur (A Amsterdam le 18 de Novembre 1742. P.D.L.M.); [xi-xxii] A Sa Majesté le roi de Prusse, &c.&c.&c. (A Rotterdam ce 20 de Janvier 1742. Voltaire) [1] faux-titre: LE / FANATISME, / OU / MAHOMET / LE PROPHETE, / *TRAGÉDIE.* / [2] Acteurs / [3]-105 Le Fanatisme, ou Mahomet le prophète, tragédie; [106]-112 Lettre de l'auteur à Mr. de S*** ['S Gravesande] (A Cirey [Bruxelles] le 1 de Juin [août] 1741) (D2519).

*ACTEURS.*

MAHOMET.

ZOPIRE, scheich ou schérif de la Mecque.

OMAR, lieutenant de Mahomet.

SEIDE, PALMIRE, esclaves de Mahomet.

PHANOR, sénateur de la Mecque.

Troupe de Mécquois.

Troupe de Musulmans.

*La scène est à la Mecque.*

Frontispiece (facing title-page: hors-texte): of Palmire stabbing herself. L.F.D.B. inv. P. Tanjé sculpt.

43A3 (D*) brings the text much nearer to the final version, with major and minor alterations to all earlier editions in the following lines: I.53 (toning down Zopire's association of death with glory), 96 (introducing a linguistic repetition), 116 (having 'des combats' for 'de la guerre'), 161:

LE

FANATISME,

OU

MAHOMET

LE PROPHETE,

*TRAGÉDIE.*

PAR

M^R. DE VOLTAIRE.

*A AMSTERDAM,*

Chez ETIENNE LEDET & Compagnie,

M. DCC. XLIII.

*Le Fanatisme, ou Mahomet le prophète* (Amsterdam, Ledet, 1743), title page.

(replacing 'Oui' by 'Ah!'), 163 (giving 'oui' instead of 'non'!), 173-175 (removing a rather awkward introduction of Séide's name), 180 (a tense change), 181-182 (plural for singular), 198 ('Nous accorder' instead 'Me proposer'), 220-224 (cutting out Omar's invocation of God to justify his actions, and removing a direct reference by Zopire to the erroneous nature of the Muslim faith), 250, 254 (stressing even more Omar's admiration for Mahomet), 261-266 (adding five lines on Zopire's persecution of the Mohammedans), 285 (rephrased), 292 ('devoir' replacing 'savoir'), 321 (strengthening Omar's dislike of the senate), 329 (rephrased), 333-334 (for the final couplet of act I, Zopire attacks tyranny, where he previously simply followed the path of virtue); II.12 (correcting a small error), 48 ('Le' for 'Ce'), 86 (introducing alliteration), 102 ('dans' replacing 'dès'), 135 ('tes' replacing 'les' and thus stressing how the Mohammedans belong to Mahomet), 165 (a tense change), 247 (singular for plural), 308 (removing an ambiguity by replacing the singular by the plural), 317 (a tense change), 336-337 (rephrasing to stress how Séide is a victim of superstition); III.1-10, 12-17 (reworking the beginning of act III, displacing Palmire's distrust of Zopire and of the senate, and cutting out a reference to Zopire's having asked to see Séide and Palmire in secret), 30 (a tense change), 32 (a tense change), 35-36 (rephrasing, toning down the repetition of the word 'sans'), 41 (Séide announces more explicitly that he is going off to swear to what Mahomet asks of him), 58 (Palmire's impersonal reference to Mahomet in the third person becomes a direct appeal to him), 60 (correcting a small error), 61 ('douleur' rather than 'terreur'), 79-89 (developing with four extra lines Palmire's description of her love for Séide), 91-99 (toning down Palmire's defence of Séide, and stressing the mystery surrounding Mahomet's plans), 112 ('ne [...] pas' for 'ne [...] point'), 128 (correcting a small error), 133-136 (rephrased, stressing the error of Zopire's faith rather than his fanaticism), 146 (toning down the alliteration), 147 (giving the plural for the singular), 179 (replacing the repetition of 'songez-vous' by that of 'savez-vous'), 198 (a tense change), 211-212 (plural for singular), 220 ('nos ennemis' becomes 'mes ennemis'), 231 ('Prêt à verser son sang' replaces 'Tout prêt à le frapper'), 262 (introducing a verb), 266 (Zopire no longer addresses this line directly to Séide), 278-314 (a radical reworking of the end of act III, from the beginning of scene ix: Zopire now reads Hercide's letter after and not before Omar's precipitious entrance, and no longer does he do it in the presence of Séide. Zopire's suspicion that Palmire and Séide may be his children is reworked, and the act no longer ends with a soliloquy by Zopire, with Phanor off the stage); IV.1-3 (Omar's warning to Mahomet at the beginning of act IV that Séide has revealed the plot to kill Zopire is rephrased), 7 (the line is simplified), 10 (the threat against Hercide is less explicit), 18-29 (a reworking with four extra lines of Mahomet's plans for Séide and Palmire after Zopire's death), 33 ('à mes yeux' replacing 'crois-moi'), 40 ('m'immoler' for 'immoler'), 41-42 (a rephrasing of Omar's description of Séide's anguish at the thought of what he has to do), 64-66 (a rephrasing of Palmire's belief in Mahomet's absolute authority), 96 (God rather than a god dictates what Séide has to do), 137 (a rephrasing of a line on the imminence of war), 159 ('ne [...] point' becomes 'ne [...] pas'), 177 ('terrible' becomes 'triste'), 234 ('le fer' becomes 'ce fer'), 260 (the word order is inverted), 272 ('du crime' replaces 'de crime'), 285 ('Déjà' replaces 'Enfin'); V.11 ('de flots' replaces 'des flots'), 22 ('le secret' becomes 'ce secret'), 27 (Séide is now punished before rather than at the same time as he commits his crime), 60 (correcting a grammatical mistake), 103 (rephrasing a line on Séide's horror at having committed parricide), 105 ('Il semble respirer' replaces 'Il respire à demi'), 123 (introducing stage instructions, in which Palmire runs to her brother), 126-127 (rephrasing Mahomet's triumph as Séide falls victim to the poison), 132 (changing the word order), 135 ('à l'instant' replaces 'devant vous'), 148 ('désormais' is replaced by 'contre moi'), 172-173 (Mahomet's realisation that he has lost Palmire is rephrased).

43A3 still follows the initially printed text as given in all 1742 editions in act I lines 54, 58, act III line 48, act IV lines 155, 241, 287-290. It follows 42X1 (A*) in act III lines 16, 59, act V line 50. Act III line 59 also appears this way in 45B5, and 43A3 shares with the latter its version of act IV line 17. Already found in 42B1 (B*) as given here are act V lines 85, 97, 107, 184. All 1742 editions except 42B5 have the versions found here of act IV lines 16 and act V line 76.

### 45A

LE / FANATISME, / OU / MAHOMET / LE PROPHETE, / *TRAGEDIE.* / [*fleuron (as in 43A3)*] / *A AMSTERDAM*, / Chez ETIENNE LEDET & COMPAGNIE. / M D C C X L V. /

8°. sig.*6, [], **4, A-G8; pag.[xxii].112.

B-Br.: FS23 A.

This not just a reissue of 43A3, even though it has the same layout, with the same lines on each page. Not all the typographical ornaments are the same, and the text has been reset, with minor differences on almost every page. In act I line 166 there is the more usual 'Moab' for 'Moad'. In act V line 17 there is the more correct 'de secrets chemins'. Other corrections are 'du' for 'de' in act I line 150, 'débris' rather than 'd'ébris' in act II line 214 , and 'repris' in place of 'reprit' in act IV line 4. Supplying the object pronoun missing in act II line 2 in 43A3, 45A creates the variant 'je te revois'. At the same time, in act IV line 164 it adds a superfluous 'me' with 'Je me meurs'. There is a misprint in act I line 251 ('quannd'), but 45A itself corrects a number of similar mistakes made in 43A3. Thus one finds 'L'inspire' for 'Linspire' in act I line 26. Similarly, 'fortfaits' is replaced by 'forfaits' (I.300), 'Vien y' by 'Viens-y' (I.326), 'noyez' by 'noyés' (II.106), 'Di' by 'Dis' (II.251), 'Répond' by 'Répons' (II.275), 'pren' by 'prends' (IV.217), 'hates-toi' by 'hate-toi' (IV.237), 'Qu'entens-je?' by 'Qu'entends-je?' (V.61). On the other hand, in act II line 273, 'répond-moi' becomes 'répons-moi'.

The use of accents varies considerably. Acute 'e' is frequently added. 'Seide' and 'SEIDE' become 'Séide' and 'SE'IDE' throughout. Similarly, one now finds with their proper accent 'bénir' (III.44; IV.255), 'Déserts' (I.108; II.147, 205), 'Déserteur' (I.188), 'hélas' (II.242; IV.55, 112, 143, 173, 204, 224) – though not in act III line 253 – and 'intérêt', both in the singular (IV.27) and the plural (III.104). The odd accents in 'fléxible' (I.162 and IV.162) and 'l'infléxible' (I.157; II.69) are removed. On the other hand, there is now a spurious accent in act I line 111 with 'prémiers', and the erroneous 'ensévelir' (II.205) is retained in both editions. The accent is, however, suppressed rightly in act III line 164 ('Exécuteur') and act II line 75 ('exil') and wrongly in act III line 89, where 'Réprouver' becomes 'Reprouver'. Similarly, the acute is replaced by the grave in act V line 45 ('évènement').

Although 43A3 already had grave 'e' in some places, as in 'zèle' (see I.7, 9, 22, etc.), it is now added even more systematically where it was lacking in nouns like 'Mèque' (I.18, 30, 31, etc), 'père' (I.32, 134; II.59, etc.) and 'mère' (II.182), and where it is needed in adjectives like 'chère' (I.141) or in parts of verbs such as 'lèvent' (I.114), 'revère' (I.121), 'pèse' (I.207), 'amène' (II.53), 'sème' (II.179), 'mène' (III.98), 'cède' (IV.222), and 'achève' (V.112) and 'achèvera' (V.40). There is still no accent for 'frère' in act V line 160, but it given with other occurrences of the word (see I.49; II.338; IV.238; V.136, 165). 'Prophète' is now found throughout with the grave accent in place of a circumflex (see I.18, 193; II.6, etc.). In the plural 'fiers' remains untouched (III.199), but in the singular it attracts an unwanted grave accent: 'fièr' (see II.27, 339, 347; IV.78). The accent is removed in act II line 157, which had had 'n'ès', but for some unknown reason it is replaced by the acute in act II line 220 ('Donnérent'). Grave 'a' now appears 'Déjà' (IV.285; V.2).

The diaeresis is removed from 'obéir' (I.219; III.200; IV.12, etc), 'obéissance' (III.106; IV.50), 'desobéissance' (IV.113) – still written without an acute accent in the first syllable – and 'déifié' (V.162). It also disappears from 'Ismaël' (I.8, 180). The circumflex over 'a' is cut out in 'flame' (III.117) – still spelled thus – and 'nager' (V.78), but added in 'nâquit' (III.186; IV.29). The circumflex over 'i' is removed from 'connoît' to give 'connoit' (III.240; IV.36), but added to the subjunctive 'Vînt' in act II line 26. Similarly, it now appears over 'u' in 'Eût' in act I line 138, but is removed for some reason or other from 'brûle' (V.186), 'brûler' (II.17), 'brûlans' (II.147), 'coûter' (III.80), 'coûte' (IV.50) and 'sûreté' (III.139). More understandable is its disappearance from words such as 'ajoutez' (III.213), and 'assuré' (V.71), 'assurons' (IV.44), 'blessure' (IV.258), 'couteau' (II.184), 'flame' (I.45), 'rassurer' (II.120), 'rassurez' (III.102), 'vue' (II.50; IV.218). In act V line 179 'blasphêmé' becomes 'blasphémé'.

As far as spelling is concerned, the 'c' cedilla is removed from all forms of the verb 'sçavoir' to make 'savoir' (see I.19, 209; II.99, 139; III.30; IV.66, etc.), except in act I line 77, where it was not present anyway.

In some places, capital letters are replaced by lower case ones, as with 'caverne' (I.238 (twice), 'esprit' (II.20, 334), 'esprits' (II.69), 'élite' (II.77), 'murs' (I.314), 'patrie' (III.262), 'port' (I.54), 'remparts' (II.48) and 'serment' (III.5). Sometimes, the movement goes the other way, as with 'Ami' (II.121), 'Amour' (IV.111), 'Armes' (II.142), 'Conducteur' (I.231), 'Humains' (II.20), 'Enfans' (II.130), 'Glaive' (II.191), and 'soutien' (II.63). A hyphen is added in act I line 45 for 'cachez-en' and act II line 92 for 'instruisez-le'. Another hyphen appears in 'Genre-Humain' (I.327), and 'grand Homme' becomes 'Grand-Homme' in act I lines 250, 270, 308, act II line 62. Although one still finds 'long-tems' in act II line 204, in act I lines 169 and act II line 15 it appears as 'longtems'.

In the same way, 'bien-tôt' becomes 'bientôt' (I.242; III.14; V.31), and 'si-tôt' becomes 'sitôt' (IV.17), while 'sur-tout' remains unchanged in act II line 202.

45A wavers somewhat over double consonants. In both editions, one finds 'abatus' (II.255), 'abatu' (V.2), 'falu' (IV.77) and 'rafermis' (V.114), but 'appaiser' (I.60; V.159). Although 'appelle' is still given with two sets of double consonants in act I line 25 and act IV line 173, and even so as 'appelloit' in act IV line 83, in act I line 68 one now finds 'apeller'. The general tendency is to reduce to a single consonant in the case of 'p' ('aprens' (II.158-159), 'aprendre' (III.93), 'Aprenez' (V.93, 147), 'aprit' (V.129), 'Aproche' (II.175), 'aprocher' (V.15), 'aprouver' (III.94), 'suplice' (I.150, 332; II.313; IV.14; V.176)) or 't' ('flater' (I.6, 123), 'flate (V.168), 'flaté' (I.123), 'flater' (III.300), 'lutant' (IV.219), 'quiter' (IV.123), and giving them their usual form: 'souhaité' (III.48), 'traite' (I.307)). At the same time, in act II line 49 'abatuë' becomes the more recognisable 'abattue'.

There is a good deal of hesitation over the spelling of 'vengeance' and 'venger'. In at least one place (I.10), 'vengeance' is written in the usual way in both editions. On the other hand 'venger' is frequently spelled as 'vanger' in both 1743 and 1745 (see II.328; III.154, 158, 190; IV.260, 269, 271; V.48, 82, 100, 105, 119, 128, 132, 184). However, 'van' becomes 'ven' in act I line 48 and act II line 157, whereas 'ven' becomes 'van' in act III lines 197, 277, act IV line 114, act V lines 7, 24, 72, 111, 149, 152. In similar fashion, the word 'penchant' becomes 'panchant' in act I lines 77, 153, 156, act III line 87. In one place (II.164), 43A3 had the more Voltairean 'connaitre', but this now becomes 'connoitre', as elsewhere.

Though 'y' – acting as a vowel or as part of a diphthong – remains unchanged in at least four places (see I.38 ('playe'); III.226 ('azyle'); IV.98 ('proye'); V.144 ('s'essaye')), in such cases it is usually changed to 'i'. See I.22 ('enivrée'), 82 ('azile'), 216 ('Aieux'); II.16 ('enivré'); III.135 ('enivré'), 301 ('croie'), 302 ('joie'); IV.253 ('m'envoie'), 254 ('joie'); V.109 ('enivrés'). Going the other way 'i' becomes 'y' in act I line 169 ('Pays').

The punctuation is now more in line with that of later editions of the play. A superfluous comma is removed from 'sans, patrie' in act I line 130. Commas are added in act I lines 271 ('croire,'), 288 ('fils,'), act II lines 254 ('Enseignes,'), 298 ('père,'), act IV lines 31 ('force,'), 44 ('Viens,'), 85 ('tendresse,'), 233 ('tems,'), act V lines 79 ('Médine,'), 185 ('jour,'), but removed from line 136 ('eh quoi'). Commas become exclamation marks after 'Dieux!' in act I line 199, act III lines 293, 311, act IV line 139, act V line 65. They are turned into semi-colons in act II lines 31 ('pieds;'), 197 ('Mahomet;'), 313 ('suplice;'), act IV line 92 ('pitié;'), act V line 86 ('Loix;'). On the other hand, semi-colons are replaced by commas in act II line 128 ('ressorts,'), act III lines 41 ('redoutable,'), 259 ('servi,'), act IV line 69 ('Il l'est,'), by full stops in act I lines 14 ('étincelle.'), 27 ('unis.'), 104 ('liens.'), 112 ('ans.'), 217 ('Maître.'), 266 ('Terre.'), 288 ('main.'), 325 ('Patrie.'), act II line 153 ('Epouses.'), act III line 56 ('suis.') and by colons in act I line 16 ('séditieux:') and act II line 202 ('guerre:'). A colon replaces a full stop in act I line 34 ('esclavage:'). In act I line 222 ('fanatique;'), the full stop has given way to a semi-colon. In act I line 39 ('ressentimens,') its place is taken by a comma. Exclamation marks appear instead of full stops in act I line 36 ('tous!'), act II lines 64 ('Citoyen!'), 96 ('moi!'), 306 ('impitoyable!'), act IV line 136 ('fois!'). In act I line 109, the full stop gives way to a question mark ('abandonne?'). Similarly, an exclamation mark is replaced by a question mark in act I line 317 ('Lui?'). On the other hand, an exclamation mark replaces a question mark in act II line 265 ('nous!'), and in act III line 71 the place of the question mark is taken by a comma ('dites-vous,'), and by a semi-colon in act V line 66 ('j'adorai;').

## W46

ŒUVRES / DIVERSES / DE MONSIEUR / DE VOLTAIRE / *NOUVELLE EDITION*, / Recueillie avec soin, enrichie de Piéces / Curieuses, & la seule qui contienne / ses véritables Ouvrages. / *Avec Figures en Taille-Douce.* / TOME DEUX-IEME./ [*vignette*] / A LONDRES, / Chez JEAN NOURSE. / M. DCC. XLVI. /
ii.[361]-471.
[361] LE / FANATISME / *OU* / MAHOMET / LE PRO-PHETE. / *TRAGEDIE.*
[362] blank; [363]-368 Avis de l'Editeur; [369]-377: A Sa Majesté le Roi de Prusse; [378] Acteurs; [379]-472: Le Fanatisme, ou Mahomet le prophète, tragédie.
D-22; F-P/BnF: Rés.Z.Beuchot 8.

This follows essentially 43A3 (D*): as shown in particular in act I line 195, act II lines 161, 205, 256, act III lines 48, 59, act IV line 144, act V lines 91, 107, 119. On the other hand, it follows earlier and later editions in act I lines 150, 157, 236, 327, act II line 2 and act V line 50. It reverts to the 1742 text in act III line 146. It has its own minor oddities in act I lines 129 ('connaissions' for 'connaissons'), 247 ('oses-tu' instead of 'osas-tu'), act II line 291 ('leur fers'), act III lines 133 ('ces' in place of 'ses'), 159 ('en' for 'par').

47A

MAHOMET / TRAGEDIE, / PAR / M. DE VOLTAIRE. / *REPRESENTEE SUR LE THEATRE / de la Comédie Françoise.* / [*woodcut: astrolabe behind an open book, with compasses, a harp, a palette, a bust, etc. within a ornate frame of leaves*] / AMSTERDAM, / [*long rule*] / M. DCC. XLVII. /
8°. sig.A-D$^8$; pag.62.
[1] title; [2] Acteurs; [3]-62 Mahomet, tragédie.
F-ChM: gt.10635$^2$.

47A is identical to 43A2, except in seven places. Act V line 162 is missing, and there are minor errors in act I line 57 (having 'ces' for 'ses'), act II line 331 (omitting 'tous'), act III line 111 (having 'les' for 'ses'), act IV lines 4 (giving 'la' for 'sa'), 6 (spelling Hercide as Hercine). It begins act III line 8 with 'Palmire et mes serments'),

(E*)

W48D

OEUVRES / DE / M$^r$. DE VOLTAIRE / *NOUVELLE EDITION* / REVUE, CORRIGÉE / ET CONSIDERABLEMENT AUGMENTÉE / PAR L'AUTEUR / ENRICHIE DE FIGURES EN TAILLE-DOUCE. / TOME QUATRIEME. / [*engraving*] / *A DRESDE 1748.* / CHEZ GEORGE CONRAD WALTHER / LIBRAIRE DU ROI. / *AVEC PRIVILEGE.* /
iv.[349]-454:

[349] LE / FANATISME, / OU / MAHOMET / LE PROPHETE. / *TRAGEDIE.* /
[350] blank; 351-54 Avis de l'Editeur en 1743; 355-61 A Sa Majesté le Roi de Prusse; 362 Lettre de Mr de Voltaire au Pape Benoît XIV; 363-64 Lettre du Souverain Pontife Benoît XIV à Mr de Voltaire; 365 Lettre de remerciement de Monsieur de Voltaire au Pape; [366] Acteurs; [367]-448 Le Fanatisme, ou Mahomet le Prophète, tragédie; 449-54 De l'Alcoran et de Mahomet.
S-S/N: Vu.36a.

W48D introduces the final version of the text in act I lines 58, 333-334 (a new couplet to end act I), act III line 146. It comes nearer the definitive text, but with a different tense, in act IV line 241. It retains the text as printed in 43A3 in act I lines 54, 195, act II lines 161, 256, act III line 48, act IV lines 155, 287-290, act V lines 2, 17, 85, 107, 184. There are three oddities: in act I line 77 (introducing a comma after 'sais'), act II line 3 (having the impossible 'des tous'), act V line 165 (having 'amour pleins').

W50

[*half-title*] OEUVRES / DE / MONSIEUR / DE VOLTAIRE. / *TOME QUATRIE'ME.* /
[*title-page*] / LA / HENRIADE / ET AUTRES / OUVRAGES / *DU MEME AUTEUR.* / NOUVELLE EDITION. / Revuë, corrigée, avec des augmentations considérables, / particulières & incorporées dans tout ce Recueil, / Enrichi de 56. Figures. / TOME QUATRIE'ME. / [*ornament*] / A LONDRES, / *AUX DÉPENS DE LA SOCIETE'.* / M. DCC. LI. /
iv.[419]-538:
[419] LE / FANATISME, / OU / MAHOMET / LE / PROPHETE. / *TRAGEDIE.* /
[420] blank; 421-26 Avis de l'éditeur, en 1743; 427-35 A Sa Majesté le Roi de Prusse; 436 Lettre de Mr. de Voltaire au Pape Benoît XIV; 437-38 Lettre du souverain pontife à Mr. de Voltaire; 439 Lettre de remerciement de Mr. de Voltaire au Pape; [440] Acteurs;

[frontispiece (hors texte): the death of Palmire]; [441]-538 Le Fanatisme, ou Mahomet le prophète, tragédie; 539-546 De l'Alcoran et de Mahomet.
F-GBl.

w50 gives the correct version of line 1350, and follows 47A with 'ces' for 'ses' in act I line 57. It still has the 43A3 version of the text in act I lines 54, 195, act II lines 161, 256, act III line 48, act IV lines 155, 287, act V lines 2, 85, 107, 184.

(F*)

51B

LE FANATISME, / OU / MAHOMET LE PROPHETE, / *TRAGÉDIE.* / PAR M. DE VOLTAIRE. / [*thin rule*] / *XXX. SOLS.* / [*thin rule*] / [*fleuron*] / A BERLIN. / [*thick-thin rule*] / M.D.CC.LI. /
8°. sig.a[8], [], b[1]; A-F[8], G[1]; pag. xix.[i].99.[i blank].
Page 33 is numbered 49.
[i] title; [ii] blank; [iii]-xiii A sa majesté le Roi de Prusse (A Rotterdam, le 20 Janvier 1742); [xiii]-xiv Lettre de Monsieur de Voltaire au pape Benoît XIV (Parigi, 17 Agosto 1745); xv-xvii Lettre du souverain pontife Benoît XIV à Monsieur de Voltaire (19 Sept.1745); xviii-xix Lettre de remerciement de Monsieur de Voltaire au Pape; [xx] Acteurs; [1]-90 Le Fanatisme, ou Mahomet le Prophète, tragédie; [91]-99 De l'Alcoran et de Mahomet.
Acteurs, etc., as in 43A3.
Bengesco 137.
F-F/BnF: Yf.12119; GB-Ox/U19.

51B was published in Paris by Lambert. It generally follows 43A3, but three lines echo the text of all 1742 editions: I.182 (reverting to 'Image' in the singular); II.247 (with the plural for the singular); V.60 (reproducing the erroneous infinitive for 'suivre'). In act II line 29 the new edition reverts to the text of 42X1 (A*) with 'd'où' for 'dont'. In follows the text of 42B1 (B*) in act I lines 1 (having 'ces' instead of 'ses'), 122 (with 'en' for 'dans') and act II line 21 (with 'dans' for 'en'). Unlike most later editions, in act V line 17 it corrects 'des' to 'de'. On the whole, the changes are fairly minor. 51B gives the final version of act I line 58, act III lines 16, 59, act IV line 241, act V line 50. Small differences are found in act I lines 108 (has 'Ces tumultes des camps'), 214: has 'la' instead of 'leur'), 300 (has 'tes' for 'ses'), 313 (puts 'aux bords' into the singular), act II lines 61 ('de' for 'du'), 91 (like 43A1, spells Morad as 'Morade'), act III lines 7 (has 'sous' in place of 'pour'), 111 (like 47A has 'les' instead of 'ses'), 136 (has 'pour' and not 'par'), 172 (gives 'mes' for 'nos'), act V line 42 (has 'les' and not 'mes').

### W51

ŒUVRES / DE / M. DE VOLTAIRE. / NOUVELLE EDITION, / Considérablement augmentée, / *Enrichie de Figures en taille-douce*. / TOME VI. / [*ornament*] / [*thick-thin rule*] / M. DCC.LI. / [*thick-thin rule*] /
vi.[121]-244:
[121] LE / FANATISME; / OU / MAHOMET / LE PROPHETE. / *TRAGEDIE*. / [*thick-thin rule*] / Représentée pour la premiére fois, / le Jeudi 9. Août 1742. /
[122] blank; 123-28 Avis de l'éditeur, en 1743; 129-37 A Sa Majesté le Roi de Prusse; 138-139 Lettre de monsieur de Voltaire au pape Benoît XIV; 140-41 Lettre du souverain pontife Benoît XIV à Monsieur de Voltaire; 142-43 Lettre de remerciement de monsieur de Voltaire au Pape; [144] Acteurs; [145]-236 Le Fanatisme ou Mahomet le prophète, tragédie; [237]-44 De l'Alcoran et de Mahomet.
Frontispiece (hors texte, facing p.[121]) (C. Eisen, inv., Aliémet, sculpt.)
F-P/Ar: 8°BL.13057$^{1-4}$; GB-Lo/N: 630.a.27-37.

W51 follows on the whole the text of 51B (see I.1, 58, 108, 122, 300; II.29, 91; III.7, 16, 59, 111, 136; IV.241; V.17, 42, 50, 60, 185). On the other hand, it returns to the definitive versions of act I lines 182, 214, 313, act II lines 61 and 247 as given in 43A3.

(G*)

W52

ŒUVRES/ DE / M^r^. DE VOLTAIRE / *NOUVELLE EDITION* / REVUE, CORRIGEE / ET CONSIDERABLEMENT AUGMENTEE / PAR L'AUTEUR / ENRICHIE DE FIGURES EN TAILLE-DOUCE. / *TOME DEUXIEME.* / [*engraving*] / *A DRESDE 1752.* / CHEZ GEORGE CONRAD WALTHER / LIBRAIRE DU ROI. / *AVEC PRIVILEGE.* /
ii.[309]-402:
[309] LE / FANATISME, / OU / MAHOMET / LE PROPHETE. / TRAGEDIE. /
[310] Avertissement; 311-14 Avis de l'éditeur en 1743; 315-321 A Sa Majesté le Roi de Prusse; 322 Lettre de monsieur de Voltaire au pape Benoît XIV; 323-24 Lettre du souverain pontife Benoît XIV à Monsieur de Voltaire; 325 Lettre de remerciement de Monsieur de Voltaire au Pape; [326] Acteurs; [327]-96 Le Fanatisme, ou Mahomet le prophète, tragédie; 397-402 De l'Alcoran et de Mahomet.
A-V: *38 Li (2).
Frontispiece (as in 43A3).
p.[310]: 'Avertissement.'

On a cru devoir placer cette tragédie à la fin de ce second tome, parce qu'il y règne un esprit philosophique ainsi que dans tout ce volume. La digression sur Mahomet et sur l'Alcoran, et le petit chapitre sur la police des spectacles appartiennent de droit à ce tome. On y a joint aussi pour le rendre complet la tragédie de la mort de César avec la lettre de M. le comte Algarotti.

W52 adds notes to the *Avis de l'éditeur*. As far as the play itself is concerned, on the whole W52 follows W48D and gives the new version of act I line 58 which is also found in 51B. It gives the final version of act IV line 241, as suggested by W48D and finalised in 51B. Unlike either W48D or 51B, however, it gives the earlier 1742 and now definitive version of act II line 161. There are three oddities. In act I line 70, the prophet's name is written as 'Mohomet'. Like W48D, W52 puts a comma after 'sais' in act I line 77. In act IV line 246, it has the meaningless 'de plus' for 'le plus'.

52B

MAHOMET, / *TRAGEDIE,* / PAR M. DE VOLTAIRE. / Repréſentée ſur le Théâtre de la Comédie / Françaiſe à Paris. / *NOUVELLE EDITION.* / [*ornament (same as 42B3)*] / A BRUXELLES, / [*thin rule (broken in two places)*] / *M. DCC. LII.* /
8°. sig. A-F⁴; pag.48
[1] title; [2] Acteurs; [3]-48: Mahomet, tragédie.
Bengesco 138.
F-P/U: R.874 (2).
Has the same post-script as 42B5 on p.48.

Based on the text of 42B5, 52B only differs from that edition in a few places. In act V line 60, it corrects the misuse of the infinitive 'suivre', but inadvertently has 'murs' in place of 'mœurs' in act II line 219. For other changes, see I.91 (follows MS4 in having the less correct 'des' for 'de'), 146 (adopting a suggestion made in 42B5*, while adding a necessary 'et'); II.136 (has 'ne [...] pas' for 'ne [...] point'), 272 (has 'ses' instead of 'ces'); III.52 (replaces 'son' with 'ce'); V.2 (replaces 'sans' with 'son', but keeps 'se voit').

53A

LE / FANATISME, / OU / MAHOMET / LE PROPHETE, / *TRAGÉDIE.* / PAR / M$^{R}$. DE VOLTAIRE / [*fleuron (as in 43A3)*] / *A AMSTERDAM,* / Chez ESTIENNE LEDET & COMPAGNIE./ M D C C L I I I. /
8°, sig*$^{6}$, [], **$^{4}$, A-G$^{8}$; pag.[xxii].112.
Reissue of 43A3, but with title-page in black only [some copies].
F-P/BnF: Rés.Z.Bengesco.55.

53A obviously follows closely 43A3 and reproduces most of the punctuation, spelling and other miscellaneous minor changes introduced in 45A. There are again different ornaments, and this time many of the page breaks are different, with one or two lines frequently carried over on to the following page.

As far as accents are concerned, 53A does not follow the odd use of accents found in 45A in 'prémiers' (I.111), or 'fièr' (II.27, 339, 347; IV.78). On the other hand, where 45A removed the superflous circumflex in 'Ajoûtez' in act III line 213, this is retained here. Even more strangely, in 53A 'e' grave is systematically replaced by 'e' acute, thus producing the correct 'zélés' (II.329), but otherwise oddities such as 'premiére' (I.14, 232; III.63), 'misére' (I.98), etc. 'Trêve', which previously appeared as 'Trève', is now given as 'Tréve' (II.183, 309; III.14, 221; IV.261). In act V line 160, 45A had left 'frere' without an accent. This is now printed as 'frére'. Whereas 45A had mistakenly given 'évènement' in act V line 45, 53A returns it to the correct form already found in 43A3. 53A also adds 'e' acute to the one case where 45A failed to do so with the word 'hélas' (III.253). The circumflex is also added to 'idolâtrie' (III.181), to 'hâte-toi' (IV.237) and 'connoître' (II.164). In the last two cases, 53A follows 45A in the spelling.

The bizarre 'quannd' (I.251) of 45A is silently corrected, and 53A fails to follow 45A in its printing of 'quiter' instead of 'quitter' in act IV line 123. In act II line 319 'pers' now becomes 'perds', but in act II line 325 we find 'répons' rather than 'réponds'. Act II line 66 has the more usual 'surtout' in place of 'sur-tout', but in act I lines 221, 223, act II line 86, act IV line 29, act V line 141 'en vain' is merged to become 'envain'.

In twenty-one places, additional words now begin with capital letters: 'Bruit' (II.122), 'Epoux' (I.126), 'L'Ecole' (II.252), 'Joug' (II.131), 'Maître' (I.126, 134), 'Objet' (I.89), 'Public' (I.46), 'Pére' (I.134, 142; II.259, 298, 314; IV.40, 248, 283; V.29, 52), 'Raison' (I.243; II.70). Four new words now begin with a lower case letter instead of a capital: 'enfans' (II.279), 'peuple' (IV.15), 'imposteur' (V.167), 'victime' (V.171).

The punctuation tends to follow that of 45A, but with some differences. A semi-colon is replaced by a comma in act I line 126 ('maître,') and by a full stop in act III line 115 ('Appui.'). A comma disappears in act II line 219 ('Rois') and is replaced by a semi-colon in act II line 81 ('encore;'). Full stops give way to exlamation marks in act I line 4 ('Non!') and act V line 164 ('lumiére!'). Exclamation marks are replaced by question marks in act II line 59 ('Lui?') and act IV line 179 ('Zopire?'), and by a comma in act V line 80 ('d'hypocrisie,')

There are three obvious printing mistakes: 'Jadmirois' (III.20),

'Remes-toi' (III.278), 'Fait-il' rather than 'Faut-il' (V.18). Such is surely also the source of 'ses' instead of 'ces' in act I line 113?

T53

[*thick-thin frame*] / LE / THEATRE / DE / M. DE VOLTAIRE. / *NOUVELLE EDITION,* / Qui contient un Recuëil complet de toutes les Piéces de Théâtre que l'Auteur a / données jusqu'ici. / TOME PREMIER. / [*ornament: a basket of fruit*] / A AMSTERDAM, / Chez FRANÇOIS-CANUT RICHOFF, / près le Comptoir de Cologne / [*thick-thin rule*] / M.DCC.LIII. /
i.[291]-390:
[291] LE / FANATISME, / OU / MAHOMET / LE PROPHETE. / *TRAGEDIE* /
[292] blank; 293-99 Avis de l'éditeur du Fanatisme ou Mahomet le Prophète en 1743; 299-307 Lettre à Sa Majesté le Roi de Prusse; 308-309 Lettre de Mr. de Voltaire au Pape Benoît XIV; 310-11 Lettre du Souverain Pontife Benoît XIV à Mr de Voltaire au Pape; 312-13 Lettre de remercîment de Mr. de Voltaire au Pape; [314] Acteurs; [315]-82 LE / FANATISME / *OU* / MAHOMET LE PROPHETE. / TRAGEDIE. /
383-390 De l'Alcoran et de Mahomet.
F-P/Ar: Rf.14.090.

This tends to follow the text of W48D. In act II line 35, however, it reproduces an error found in all the 1742 Brussels editions: 'D'aucun ombre'. Again in common with these editions, T53 has 'Les prophètes' in act V line 5. In act V line 80, it puts 'fureurs' into the plural.

54V

LE / FANATISME, / *OU* / MAHOMET / LE PROPHETE / *TRAGEDIE* / PAR MONSIEUR / VOLTAIRE. / EN CINQ ACTE. / [*fleuron*] / *VIENNE EN AUTRICHE* / Chez JEAN PIERRE VAN GHELEN, Imprimeur de / la Cour de Sa Majeſté Imperiale & Royale. / [*thin rule*] / M. DCC. LIV. /

8°. sig.A-G⁸; pag.110.
[1] title; [2] Acteurs; 3 Lettre de Mr Voltaire au Pape Benoît XIV; 4-5 Lettre du souverain pontife Benoît XIV à Mr de Voltaire; 6-7 Lettre de remerciement de Monsieur de Voltaire au Pape; 8-110 Le Fanatisme ou Mahomet le prophète, tragédie.
F-P/Ar: Rf.14.327.

54V owes at least something to W48D (see I.77; II.3). Printed abroad, it appears to have been produced by printers with only a rudimentary knowledge of French. Apart from 'ACTE' for the plural on the title-page, one finds a number of oddities in the text itself. See I.105 ('l'écoutser'); II.26 ('le violence'), 251 ('De plutôt'); III.301 ('fuit-il que'); IV.10 (', ist est chargé'), 284 ('qui m'assissine'); V.67 ('cumplots').

(H*)

W56

[*half-title*] COLLECTION / COMPLETTE / DES / ŒUVRES / *de Mr. de VOLTAIRE*, / PREMIERE EDITION. / TOME HUITIEME. /
[*title-page*] OUVRAGES / DRAMATIQUES / AVEC / *LES PIECES RELATIVES A CHACUN*. / TOME SECOND / [*vignette*] / [*thick-thin rule*] / MDCCLVI. /
viii.[323]-426:
[323] LE / FANATISME, / OU / MAHOMET / LE PROPHETE, / *TRAGEDIE*. /
[324] blank; 325-329 Avis de l'Editeur; 330-37 A Sa Majesté le Roi de Prusse; 338 Lettre de Mr. de Voltaire au pape Benoît XIV; 339-40 Réponse du souverain pontife Benoît XIV à Mr. de Voltaire; 341-42 Lettre de remerciment de Monsieur de Voltaire au Pape; 342 Acteurs; [343]-426 Le Fanatisme, ou Mahomet le prophète, tragédie.
GB-Ld/U1.

W56 gives the final text of the 'Avis de l'éditeur' and of the letter to Frederick the Great. In the play itself it also introduces the definitive version of act I line 54 and corrects 'ce' to 'il' in act V line 184. On the other hand it substitutes the less correct 'des' for 'de' in act II line 127. In act II line 256, it reverts to the 1742 and definitive text. It still follows 43A3, W48D and 51B in act I line 195, act III 48, act IV lines 155, 287-290, act V lines 17, 85.

W57G1

[*half-title*] COLLECTION / COMPLETTE / DES / ŒUVRES / *de Mr. de VOLTAIRE,* / PREMIERE EDITION. / *TOME HUITIEME.* /
[*title-page (in black and red)*] OUVRAGES / DRAMATIQUES / AVEC / *LES PIECES RELATIVES A CHACUN.* / TOME SECOND / [*fleuron*] / [*thick-thin rule*] / MDCCLVII. /
viii.[323]-426:
[323] LE / FANATISME, / OU / MAHOMET / LE PROPHETE, / *TRAGÈDIE.* /
[324] blank; 325-29 Avis de l'Editeur; 330-337 A Sa Majesté le Roi de Prusse; 338 Lettre de Mr. de Voltaire au pape Benoît XIV; 339-40 Réponse du souverain pontife Benoît XIV à Mr. de Voltaire; 341-42 Lettre de remerciment de Monsieur de Voltaire au Pape; 342 Acteurs; [343]-426 Le Fanatisme, ou Mahomet le prophète, tragédie.
GB-Ox/U19: V1 1757 (8)

This is a resetting of W56. The text is as before, apart from correcting act I line 195 to 'pourrait' and act II line 127 to 'par de nouveaux efforts'. The *culs de lampe* are changed on pages 340, 352, 359, 365, 368, 380, 384, 395, 403, 414, 419, 426. New ones are added where there were none on pages 389 and 393.

W57P

ŒUVRES / DE / M. DE VOLTAIRE. / SECONDE EDITION, / Considérablement augmentée, / *Enrichie de Figures en taille-douce.* / TOME III. / Contenant ses piéces de Théâtre / [*ornament*] / [*double rule*] / M. DCC. LVII. / [*double rule*] /

iii.[193]-305:
[193] LE FANATISME, / *OU* / MAHOMET / LE PROPHETE, / TRAGEDIE, / Représentée pour la première fois le 9 / Août 1742. /
[194] blank; 195-200 Avis de l'éditeur en 1743; 201-10 A Sa Majesté le Roi de Prusse; 211 Lettera del signore di Voltaire alla santita di nostro signore Benedetto XIV; 212-13 Lettera del sommo pontefice al signore di Voltaire; 214-15 Lettera del signore di Voltaire alla sua santita per ringraziarla; 216 Lettre de Monsieur de Voltaire au pape Benoît XIV; 217-19 Lettre du souverain pontife Benoît XIV à Monsieur de Voltaire; 220-21 Lettre de remerciement de Monsieur de Voltaire au Pape; 222 Acteurs; [223]-297 Le Fanatisme, ou Mahomet le prophète, tragédie; [298]-305: De l'Alcoran et de Mahomet.
Frontispiece: 'LE FANATISME' (C. Eisen inv. Aliemet. Sculp.).
F-P/BnF: Z.24644.

W57P follows W56 with the final version of act I line 54, but does not change act V line 184. It has the same text as 43A3, W48D and 51B in act I line 195, act II line 256, act III line 48, act IV lines 155, 287-290, act V lines 17, 85, 184. There are a couple of printing errors in act III line 82 ('piont') and act V line 180 ('qàand'). Other particularities are found in act I lines 55 (having 'dans' for 'en'), 205 (with the meaningless 'loin de tant renommée'), 232 (having, like 42X1, a comma after 'insolent' and nothing after 'imposteur'), act III line 261 (giving 'ne [...] pas' rather than 'ne [...] point').

60B

MAHOMET, / *TRAGEDIE,* / PAR M. DE VOLTAIRE. / Représentée sur le Théâtre de la Comédie / Française à Paris. / *NOUVELLE EDITION.* / [*woodcut: in the middle a radiating sun with a face within a scalloped frame, and bearing the inscription* 'INDEXINENTER'] / A BRUXELLES, / [*triple rule*] / M. DCC. LX. /
8°. sig.A-E[4]; pag.48.
[1] title; [2] Acteurs; [3]-48 Mahomet, tragédie.
F-Vers.

Has the same post-script as 42B5 on p.48.

Based like 52B on the text of 42B5, it follows 52B in act I lines 91, 146, act II lines 136, 219, 272, act III line 52, act V lines 2, 60. There are a number of mistakes. See II.59 (a misprint: 'assemembIé'), 131 (has 'un' rather than 'ton'), 273 (has 'lieu' for 'lien'); IV.149 (omits 'frappons').

62B

Mahomet, Tragédie par M. de Voltaire. Représentée sur le Théâtre de la Comédie Française à Paris. Nouvelle Edition. Bruxelles, 1762 in-8° pag.48.
I-F/N (3903.129: copy destroyed in the floods of 1966).
I have not been able to see this edition, but it would appear to be yet another reissue of 42B5.

T62

[*within an ornamental border*] / *LE* / THEATRE / DE / M. DE VOLTAIRE. / *NOUVELLE EDITION*, / Qui contient un Recueïl complet de toutes / les Pièces de Théâtre que l'Auteur a / données jusqu'ici. / TOME SECOND. / [*woodcut*] / *A AMSTERDAM*, / Chez FRANÇOIS-CANUT RICHOFF. / près le Comptoir de Cologne. / [*thick-thin rule*] / M. DCC. LXII. /
ii.[283]-370:
[283] LE / FANATISME, / *OU* / MAHOMET / LE PROPHETE, / TRAGEDIE. /
[284] blank; 285-89 Avis de l'Editeur; 290-297 A Sa Majesté le Roi de Prusse; 298 Lettre de M. de Voltaire au pape Benoît XIV; 299-300 Réponse du souverain pontife Benoît XIV à M. de Voltaire; 301-302 Lettre de remerciement de M. de Voltaire au Pape; [302] Acteurs; 303-70 Le Fanatisme, ou Mahomet le prophète, tragédie
F-Qr; F-P/BnF: Rés.Z.Bengesco.123 (2).

T62 still has the text of 43A3, W48D, 51B, etc. in act III line 48, act IV lines 155, 287-290, act V lines 17, 85. Otherwise, it has the particularity of having the present participle rather than the third person plural in act II line 103 and 'pour' instead of 'de' in act II line 321. In act IV line 160, there is also 'vient-il' in place of 'veut-il' (cf. W64G, W70G, W70L).

T64A

LE / THEATRE / DE / M. DE VOLTAIRE. / *NOUVELLE EDITION.* / Qui contient un Recuëil complet de toutes / les Piéces de Théâtre que l'Auteur a / données jusqu'ici. / TOME SECOND. / [*woodcut*] / *A AMSTERDAM,* / Chez FRANÇOIS-CANUT RICHOFF, / près le comptoir de Cologne. / [*double rule*] / M. DCC. LXIV.
ii.[283]-371:
[283] LE / FANATISME, / *OU* / MAHOMET / LE PROPHETE, / *TRAGEDIE.* /
[284] blank; 285-89 Avis de l'Editeur; 290-96 A Sa Majesté le Roi de Prusse; 297 Lettre de M. de Voltaire au pape Benoît XIV; 298-99 Réponse du souverain pontife Benoît XIV à M. de Voltaire; 300-301 Lettre de remerciement de M. de Voltaire au Pape; [302] Acteurs; 303-71 Le Fanatisme, ou Mahomet le prophète, tragédie.
CH-178.

T64A follows T62 closely, with the same particular variants found in act II lines 103, 321, and act IV line 160. Like MS4 and 52B it has the less correct 'des' for 'de' in act I line 91. In act I line 314, 'murs' is replaced by 'mœurs'. In act IV line 164, T64A gives 'nos' for 'mes', and in act V line 128 there is the erroneous 'et qui venge'.

T64G

*LE* / THEATRE / DE MONSIEUR / *DE VOLTAIRE.* / NOUVELLE EDITION, / *Qui contient un Récueil complet de tou- / tes les Piéces que l'Auteur a données / jusqu'à ce jour.* / TOME SECOND / [*woodcut: two cherubs and suspended globe*] / A GENEVE, / Chez les Freres CRAMER, Libraires. / [*thick-thin rule, composed of three elements*] / M. DCC. LXIV. /
ii.[1]-90:

[1] LE / FANATISME, / *OU* / MAHOMET / LE PROPHETE, / *TRAGEDIE.* /
[2] blank; 1-4 Avis de l'Editeur; 5-9 A Sa Majesté le Roi de Prusse; 10 Lettre de Mr de Voltaire au pape Benoît XIV; 11-12 Réponse du souverain pontife Benoît XIV à M. de Voltaire; 13 Lettre de remerciement de M. de Voltaire au Pape; 41[=14] Acteurs; 15-85 Le Fanatisme, ou Mahomet le prophète. Tragédie; 86-90 De l'Alcoran et de Mahomet.
6 vol. in-12°.
F-P/Ar: Rf.14.092.

This tends to follow the text of W48D. Like T53, it has an oddity found in the 1742 Brussels editions: 'D'aucun ombre'. In the *Avis de l'Editeur* it has 'voulurent en avoir', thus partially anticipating Kehl. In act V line 145 it gives 'qui la suit' rather than 'qui me suit'.

T64P

OEUVRES / *DE* / THEATRE / *DE* / M. DE VOLTAIRE, / *De l'Académie Française, et celle de Berlin,* / *& de la Société Royale de Londres, &c.* / TOME SECOND / [*woodcut*] / A PARIS, / Chez DUCHESNE, Libraire, rue Saint Jacques, / au-dessous de la Fontaine Saint Benoît, / au Temple du Goût. / [*thick-thin rule*] / M. DCC. LXIV. / *Avec Approbation & Privilége du Roi.* /
[*half-title:*] THEATRE / *DE* / M. DE VOLTAIRE. / *TOME II.* /
ii.[181]-300:
[181] LE FANATISME, / *OU* / MAHOMET / LE PROPHETE, / *TRAGEDIE,* / EN CINQ ACTES, / *Représentée pour la première fois, par les* / *Comédiens Français ordinaires du Roi,* / *le* 9 *Août* 1742. / *Tome II.* / [182] blank; 183-188 Avis de l'éditeur en 1743; 183-88 Avis de l'éditeur en 1743; 189-98 A sa majesté le roi de Prusse; 199 Lettera del signore di Voltaire alla santita di nostro signore Benedetto XIV; 200-201 Lettera del sommo pontefice al signore di Voltaire; 202-203 Lettera del signore di Voltaire alla sua santita per ringraziarla; 204 Lettre

de monsieur de Voltaire au pape Benoist XIV; 205-207 Lettre du souverain pontife Benoist XIV à M. de Voltaire; 208-209 Lettre de remerciement de M. de Voltaire au pape; 210 Acteurs; [211]-286 Le Fanatisme, ou Mahomet le prophète, tragédie; 287-94 De l'Alcoran et de Mahomet; 295-300 Sur la police des spectacles.
5 vol. 12°.
Bengesco 311.
CH-16: B 2172 (2)

The text here owes something to W57P, which it follows exclusively in the prefatory material and in the play itself in act I lines 55 (with 'dans' for 'en'), 232 (with a comma between 'insolent' and 'imposteur'), and act III line 261 (with 'ne [...] pas' rather than 'ne [...] point'). Like W57P it has the same text as 43A3, W48D and 51B in act I line 195, act II line 256, act III line 48, act IV lines 155, 287-290, act V lines 17, 85 and 184.

W64R

COLLECTION / *COMPLETE* / DES ŒUVRES / *de Monsieur* / DE VOLTAIRE, / NOUVELLE EDITION, / *Augmentée de ses dernières Pièces de Théâtre,* / *et enrichie de 61 Figures en Taille-douce.* / TOME TROISIEME / *DEUXIEME PARTIE* / [*vignette*] / A AMSTERDAM, / *AUX DÉPENS DE LA COMPAGNIE.* / [*thick-thin rule*] / M. DCC.LIV. /
iii.2e.partie [3e.partie].1-128:
[1] LE / FANATISME, / OU / MAHOMET / LE / PROPHETE. / *TRAGÉDIE.* / [2] blank; 3-8 Avis de l'éditeur en 1743; 9-17 A Sa Majesté le Roi de Prusse; 18 Lettre de Mr. de Voltaire au Pape Benoît XIV; 19-20 Lettre du Souverain Pontife; 21 Lettre de remercîment de Mr de Voltaire au Pape; [22] Acteurs; [23]-120 Le Fanatisme ou Mahomet le prophète, tragédie; 121-28 De l'Alcoran et de Mahomet.
F-P/BnF: Rés.Z.Beuchot.26.

In the prefatory material, W64R gives the text of W48D and thus fails to include the notes on the *Avis de l'Editeur*. In the play itself, W64R follows 43A3, W48D, 51B, etc. in act I lines 54, 195, act II lines 161, 256, act III 48, act IV lines 155 and 287-290. It follows 43A3 in particular in act V lines 2 and 107. However, it gives the final versions of act I line 182, act II lines 7 and 172. It has the spelling 'Morade' in act II line 91.

W64G

[*half-title*] COLLECTION / COMPLETTE / DES / ŒUVRES / *de Mr. de VOLTAIRE.* / DERNIERE EDITION. / *TOME HUITIEME* /
[*title-page*] OUVRAGES / DRAMATIQUES, / *AVEC* / LES PIÉCES RELATIVES / A CHACUN / *TOME SECOND.* / [*woodcut*] / [*thick-thin rule*] / M. DCC. LXIV. /
viii.[313]-406:
[313] LE / FANATISME, / OU / MAHOMET / LE PRO-PHETE, / *TRAGÉDIE.* /
[314] blank; 315-19 Avis de l'éditeur; [320]-27 A Sa Majesté le Roi de Prusse; 328 Lettre de Mr. de Voltaire au pape Benoît XIV; 329-30 Réponse du souverain pontife Benoît XIV à Mr. de Voltaire; 331-32 Lettre de remerciment de Monsieur de Voltaire au Pape; 332 Acteurs; [333]-406 Le Fanatisme ou Mahomet le prophète, tragédie.
GB-Ox/U38: 36.f.10.

W64G still has the text of 43A3, W48D, 51B in act III line 48, act IV lines 155, 287-290, act V line 85. In act V line 17, it gives 'des' rather than 'de' as in 43A3 and W48D, but not 51B. In act IV line 160 – like T62 and T64 – it has 'vient-il' rather than 'veut-il'.

T66

[*within an ornamental border*] / LE / THEATRE / DE / M. DE VOLTAIRE. / *NOUVELLE EDITION.* / Qui contient un Recueil complet de toutes les Piéces de Théâtre que l'Auteur a / données jusqu'ici. / TOME SECOND. / [*woodcut*] / *A AMSTERDAM,* / Chez FRANÇOIS-CANUT RICHOFF, / près le Comptoir de Cologne. / [*thick-thin rule*] / M. DCC. LXVI.
ii.[285]-376:

[285] *LE* / FANATISME, / *OU* / MAHOMET / LE PROPHETE, / *TRAGEDIE.* /
[286] blank; 287-92 Avis de l'Editeur; 293-301 A Sa Majesté le Roi de Prusse; 203[=302]-303 Lettre de M. de Voltaire au pape Benoît XIV; 304-305 Réponse du souverain pontife Benoît XIV à M. de Voltaire; 306-307 Lettre de remerciment de M. de Voltaire au Pape; [308] Acteurs; 309-76 Le Fanatisme, ou Mahomet le prophète, tragédie
Frontispiece (facing p.309).
GB-Ad/U1: MH 84256 T ().

There are two obvious misprints: 'escavage' in act II line 19 and 'palmire' with a lower case 'p' in act IV line 98. Like W56, it has 'des' for 'de' in act II line 127. It also follows this edition as well as 43A3 and W48D in act III line 48, act IV lines 155, 287-290 and act V line 85. It follows these editions and not 51B in act V line 17.

T67

ŒUVRES / *DE THEATRE* / DE / M. DE VOLTAIRE, / Gentilhomme Ordinaire du Roi, de / l'Académie Française, / &c. &c. / *NOUVELLE EDITION,* / *Revûe & corrigée exactement sur l'Edition* / *de Genève in-4°.* / TOME SECOND. / [*ornament*] / *A PARIS,* / Chez la Veuve DUCHESNE, Libraire, rue Saint- / Jacques, au-dessous de la Fontaine Saint- / Benoît, au Temple du Goût. / [*double rule*] / M. DCC. LXVII. /
ii.[181]-300:
[181] LE / FANATISME, / *OU* / MAHOMET / LE PROPHETE, / *TRAGEDIE,* / EN CINQ ACTES, / *Représentée pour la première fois, par les* / *Comédiens Français ordinaires du Roi,* / *le 9 Août 1742.* /
[182] blank; 183-188 Avis de l'Editeur; 189-98 A Sa Majesté le Roi de Prusse; 199 Lettera del signore di Voltaire alla Santita di nostro signore Benedetto XIV; 200-201 Lettera del sommo pontifice al signore Voltaire; 202-203 Lettera del signore di Voltaire alla Sua Santita per ringraziarla; 204 Lettre de Monsieur de Voltaire au

pape Benoît XIV; 205-207 Lettre du souverain pontife Benoît XIV à M. de Voltaire; 208-209 Lettre de remerciement de M. de Voltaire au Pape; 210 Acteurs; [211]-286 Le Fanatisme, ou Mahomet le prophète, tragédie; 287-94 De l'Alcoran et de Mahomet; 295-300 Sur la police des spectacles.
Bengesco 312.
GB-Lo/N1: C 69 b 10 (4).

This is a reissue of T64P. After Voltaire's death, it was again reissued as the first play in tome XVI of the following collection:

BIBLIOTHEQUE DES THÉATRES, / *Composée de plus de 530 Tragédies, Comédies / Drames, Comédies-Lyriques, / Comédies- / Ballets, Pastorales, Opéras-Comiques, / Pièces à Vaudevilles, Divertissemens, / Parodies, Tragi-Comédies, Parades, tant / anciennes que nouvelles.* / RECUEIL AUSSI UTILE QU'AGRÉABLE. / On y a joint les Anecdotes concernant toutes les / Pièces qui ont été jouées tant à Paris qu'en Pro- / vince; les noms de tous les Auteurs, Poètes ou / Musiciens, qui ont travaillé pour nos Théâ- / tres, des Acteurs ou Actrices célèbres qui ont / joués à tous nos Spectacles, avec un Jugement / de leurs Ouvrages & de leurs talens. / Lettre F. / [*rule*] / TOME XVI. / [*rule*] / [*fleuron*] / A PARIS, / Chez la Veuve DUCHESNE, Libraire, / rue Saint-Jacques, au Temple du Goût. [*thick-thin rule*] / 1784 /
GB-MA/S: SC11313D.

67B

MAHOMET, / TRAGÉDIE, / PAR M. VOLTAIRE. / *Représentée sur le Théâtre de la Comédie / Françoise à Paris.* / NOUVELLE EDITION. / [*large ornament: sun radiating within a scalloped frame with the word* 'INDESINENTER' *at the top*] / *A BRUXELLES* / [*triple rule*] / M. DCC. LXVII. /
8°. sig.A-G4; pag.55.[i blank].
F-Lib: 4198 II 1.
[1] title; [2] Acteurs; [3]-55 Mahomet, tragédie.

Basically, this reproduces the text of 42B5 and has much in common with 52B, 60B and 78B (see I.91; II.131, 136; III.52; IV.149). It is more faithful to

42B5 than the latter in act I line 146, act II line 272, act V lines 2, 165. It differs in giving the more orthodox versions of act I line 160 ('de pleurs'), act IV line 197 ('je me meurs'), act V lines 107 ('même'), 166 ('je meurs'). It shares with 78B 'trompe la foi' in act I line 234.

67C

LE / FANATISME, / *OU* / MAHOMET / LE PROPHETE; / *TRAGEDIE*, / Par Mr. DE VOLTAIRE. / Corrigée sur les Manuſcrits de la Comédie Fran- / çaiſe à Paris, ſuivant l'Auteur./ *Repréſentée ſur le Théâtre de la Cour, par / les Comédiens François ordinaires du Roi, / le Nov.* 1767. / [*double rule*] / *A COPENHAGUE*, / Chez CL. PHILIBERT, / Imprimeur-Libraire. / [*thin rule*] / M DCC LXVII. / *Avec Permiſſion du ROI.* /
8°. sig.A-E$^{8}$, F$^{4}$; pag.87.[i blank].
[1] title; [2] Acteurs; [3]-6 Avis de l'éditeur; [7]-12 A Sa Majesté le Roi de Prusse; [13]-87 Le Fanatisme ou Mahomet le prophète, tragedie.
F-P/Ar: Rf.14.329.

As the title-page suggests, this edition is based on the actors' copy and has much in common with MS6 (see III.61, 87, 150-151, 198, 213-214, 229, 256, 278; IV.7, 18, 28, 177; V.165/166). Supplementary stage instructions are given at act IV lines 218/219, 224/225. The text is still that of 43A3, W48D, 51B, etc. in act III line 48, act IV line 155, act V line 85. In act V line 17 – like 43A3 and W48D, but not 51B – 67C still has 'des' rather than 'de'. 67C has two rather interesting otherwise unrecorded variants. In act I line 227 it inverts the word order in the first hemistich and then replaces 'conçois' with 'vois' in the second. The first hemistich of act IV line 160 reverts to the text of 42X1 (A*) with 'crime' in place of 'meurtre' and then, as in T64, W64G, W70G, etc., there is 'vient-il' rather than 'veut-il' in the second.

T68

*LE* / THEATRE / *DE* / M. DE VOLTAIRE. / *NOUVELLE EDITION*. / Qui contient un Recueil complet de toutes / les

Pieces de Théâtre que l'Auteur a / données jusqu'ici. / *TOME SECOND.* / [*woodcut*] / *A AMSTERDAM,* / Chez FRANÇOIS-CANUT RICHOFF, / près le Comptoir de Cologne. / [*double ornate rule*] / M. DCC. LXVIII. /
ii.[285]-376:
[285] *LE* / FANATISME, / *OU* / MAHOMET / LE PROPHETE, / *TRAGEDIE.* /
[286] blank; 287-92 Avis de l'Editeur; 293-301 A Sa Majesté le Roi de Prusse; 203[=302]-303 Lettre de M. de Voltaire au pape Benoît XIV; 304-305 Réponse du souverain pontife Benoît XIV à M. de Voltaire; 306-307 Lettre de remerciment de M. de Voltaire au Pape; [308] Acteurs; 309-76 Le Fanatisme, ou Mahomet le prophète, tragédie
Frontispiece (facing p.309).
Bengesco 311.
F-P/BnF: Yf.4261.

This is a reissue of T66, and the text is identical.

68P

MAHOMET, / *OU* / LE FANATISME, / *TRAGÉDIE.* / EN VERS, / *ET EN CINQ ACTES.* / Par M. DE VOLTAIRE. / [*woodcut: leaves and berries*] / A PARIS, / Chez CLAUDE HERISSANT, Imprimeur-Libraire, rue / Neuve Notre-Dame, à la Croix d'or. / [*double rule*] / M. DCC. LXVIII. / *Avec Approbation & Privilége du Roi.* /
8°. sig.A-F$^4$; G$^3$; pag.51[53].[i blank] (Pages 52-53 are misnumbered as 50-51 in some copies.)
[1] title; [2] Acteurs; [3]-51[53] Le Fanatisme ou Mahomet le prophète. Tragédie.
F-P/Ar: Rf.14.330; GB-Ox/U19 V3.M2.1768.

68P follows the text as printed in 43A3, W48D, 51B in act I lines 54 (thus ignoring the change brought in in W56), 195, act II lines 161, 256, act III 48, act IV lines 155, 287-290, act V lines 85, 184. In act V line 17 the text is as in 43A3, W48D, but not 51B ('des' for 'de'). In act I line 77 like W48D it has a comma after 'sais'. In common with W56 it has the rather less correct 'des' for 'de' in act II line 127. As in T64G, 68P has 'la' for 'me' in act V line 145. In places it reverts to earlier versions. In act II line 102 and act III line 32 it follows all the 1742 editions, just as in act III line 22 and act V line 3 it is faithful to the text of 42B1-42B5, and to 42B5 itself in act I line 206. Altogether it is a bit of a hotch-potch, and there are quite a few mistakes: see I.32 (adds partitive 'de', thus creating an extra syllable), 34 (like T66 prints 'escavage'), 44 (gives this line to Phanor), 315 (has meaningless 'suivons' for 'sauvons'); II.91 (like MS5, calls Morad 'Moad'), 296 (prints: 'en Prephète'); III.108 (by error has 'de' for 'des'), 200 (brings in a superfluous article), 262 (puts the first verb in the present, which is nonsense); IV.9-12: gives these lines to Omar).

(I*)

W68

[*half-title*] COLLECTION / Complette / DES / ŒUVRES / DE / MR. DE VOLTAIRE. / [*double rule*] / TOME TROISIÉME [QUATRIÉME]. / [*double rule*] /
[*title-page*] / THÉATRE / Complet / DE / *MR. DE VOLTAIRE.* / [*rule*] / TOME SECOND. / [*rule*] / *CONTENANT* [...] LE FANATISME [...] avec toutes les piéces rélatives à ces Drames / [*rule*] / *GENEVE.* / [*double rule*] / M. DCC. LXVIII. /
iii[iv]. [97]-184:
[97] LE / FANATISME, / OU / MAHOMET / LE PROPHÊTE, / *TRAGÉDIE.* /
98-101 Avis de l'éditeur; 102-107 A Sa Majesté le Roi de Prusse; 108 Lettre de Mr. de Voltaire au pape Benoît XIV; 109-10 Réponse du souverain pontife Benoît XIV à Mr. de Voltaire; 111 Lettre de remerciment de Mr. de Voltaire au Pape; [112] Acteurs; 113-84 Le Fanatisme, ou Mahomet le prophête, tragédie.
Frontispiece (facing p.[97]): 'Palmire, quel objet vient effrayer ma vue?' (Le Fanatisme, Act.IV sc.4; H. Gravelot inv. J. B. Simonet sculpsit.).
F-Dp; F-Qr; GB-Ox/U19.

'Palmire, quel objet vient effrayer ma vue?' Frontispiece to *Mahomet* in *Collection complette des œuvres de Mr. de Voltaire* (Genève 1768).

With w68 we reach the definitive stage of the text. It follows w56 and w64G in act II line 256, act IV line 155 and act V line 184, and still gives 'des' rather than 'de' in act V line 17. It introduces the final versions of act I line 161, act III line 48, act IV lines 287-290 and act V line 85. There is one mistake in act I line 233, where like T64G it has 'appas' for the more logical 'appât'.

T70

LE / THEATRE / *DE* / M. DE VOLTAIRE. / *NOUVELLE EDITION,* / Qui contient un Recueil complet de toutes / les Pieces de Théâtre que l'Auteur a don- / nées jusqu'ici. / *TOME SECOND.* / [*woodcut*] / *A AMSTERDAM,* / Chez FRANÇOIS CANUT RICHOFF, / près le Comptoir de Cologne. / [*double rule*] / M. DCC. LXX. /
ii.[285]-376:
[285] *LE* / FANATISME, / *OU* / MAHOMET / LE PRO-PHETE, / *TRAGEDIE.* /
[286] blank; 287-92 Avis de l'Editeur; 293-301 A Sa Majesté le Roi de Prusse; 302-303 Lettre de M. de Voltaire au pape Benoît XIV; 304-305 Réponse du souverain pontife Benoît XIV à M. de Voltaire; 306-307 Lettre de remerciment de M. de Voltaire au Pape; [308] Acteurs; 309-76 Le Fanatisme, ou Mahomet le prophète, tragédie.
Bengesco 313.
F-P/BnF: Yf.4267.

T70 has the same pagination as T66 and T68, but the text has been reset. It follows T66 and T68 in act II line 127, act III line 48, act IV lines 155, 287-290 – thus ignoring the change in w68 – act V lines 17, 85. It lacks act II line 184, omits 'et' in act III line 83, and has 'mêmes' in the plural in act III line 176.

W70G

[*half-title*] COLLECTION / COMPLETTE / DES / ŒUVRES / DE / MR. *de* VOLTAIRE. / DERNIERE EDITION. / TOME HUITIEME /

[*title-page*] OUVRAGES / DRAMATIQUES, / *AVEC* / LES PIÉCES RELATIVES / A CHACUN / *TOME SECOND.* / [*woodcut*] / [*thick-thin rule*] / M. DCC. LXX. /
viii.[313]-406:
[313] LE / FANATISME, / OU / MAHOMET / LE PROPHETE, / *TRAGÉDIE.* /
[314] blank; 315-19 Avis de l'éditeur; [320]-327 A Sa Majesté le Roi de Prusse; 328 Lettre de Mr. de Voltaire au pape Benoît XIV; 329-30 Réponse du souverain pontife Benoît XIV à Mr. de Voltaire; 331-32 Lettre de remerciment de Monsieur de Voltaire au Pape; 332 Acteurs; [333]-406 Le Fanatisme, ou Mahomet le prophète, tragédie.
F-P/BnF: Z.24751.

W70G reproduces with the same page-numbering the text of W64G, but with 'ma' for 'la' in act I line 286. The ornaments are also different.

70P

Le Fanatisme, ou Mahomet le prophète. Tragédie en cinq actes. Représentée pour la première fois, par les Comédiens français ordinaires du Roi le 9 août 1742. Par M. de Voltaire. Paris, Duchesne, 1770 in-8° pag.57.
D-185: Franz.Lit. 3.315 (destroyed in the Second World War).

I have not been able to see this edition, but presume that the text is similar to that of other editions from this publisher.

W70L

[*half-title*] *COLLECTION* / COMPLETTE / DES / ŒUVRES / DE M^R^. DE VOLTAIRE. / [*double ornate rule*] / *TOME QUINZIEME.* / [*double ornate rule*] /
[*title-page*] *THÉATRE* / COMPLET / *DE* / M^R^. DE VOLTAIRE. / LE TOUT REVUE ET CORRIGÉ / PAR L'AUTEUR MEME. / TOME SECOND, / *CONTENANT* / ZAYRE, ALZIRE, MÉROPE, / ET LE FANATISME. / [*woodcut*] / *A*

*LAUSANNE*, / CHEZ FRANÇ. GRASSET ET COMP. / [*double ornate rule*] / M. DCC. LXXII. /
xv.[275]-368:
[275] LE / FANATISME, / OU / MAHOMET / LE PROPHETE, / *TRAGÉDIE.* /
[276] blank; 277-281 Avis de l'éditeur; 282-289 A Sa Majesté le Roi de Prusse; 290 Lettre de Mr. de Voltaire au pape Benoît XIV; 291-292 Réponse du pape Benoît XIV à Mr. de Voltaire; 293-294 Lettre de remerciement de Monsieur de Voltaire au Pape; 294 Acteurs; 295-368 Le Fanatisme ou Mahomet le prophète, tragédie.
Bibl. publique d'Yverdon.

W70L adopts the text as given in W56, W64G and W70G rather than W68 in act III line 48, act IV lines 287-290, act V line 85, and follows most other editions with 'des' rather than 'de' in act V line 17.

71P1

*LE* / FANATISME, / *OU* / MAHOMET LE PROPHETE. / *TRAGEDIE.* / PAR Monsieur DE VOLTAIRE. / *NOUVELLE EDITION.* / [*fleuron: a basket full of flowers, etc.*] / A PARIS, / Par la Compagnie des Libraires associés. / [*triple rule*] / M. DCC. LXXI. /
8°. sig.A-E$^4$, F$^3$; pag.46.
[1] title; [2] Acteurs; [3]-46 Le Fanatisme, ou Mahomet le prophète, tragédie.
GB-Lo/N1: 11736.d.5 (1).

71P1 follows 51B (F*) rather than later editions most noticeably in act I lines 1, 54, act II lines 161, 256, act III line 48, act IV lines 287-290, act V lines 85, 184. See also the debt to 51B in act I lines 108, 122, 182, 214, 300, 305-308, 313, act II lines 21, 29, 61, 91, 247, act III lines 7, 111, 136, 172, act V lines 60 (the ominipresent erroneous 'suivre'), 42. We find the 1742 text in act III line 128, and that of 42X1, 42X2 (A*) in act II line 285 and act III line 108. It adopts the mistaken 'aucun' for 'aucune' found in 42B1-42B5 (B*) in act II line 35. In act IV line 231 it gives the final version of most of the line, but retains 'Hercide en expirant', as found in 42B1-42B5.

It brings in its own multitude of errors and small changes. See I.58 ('nos' for 'vos'), 91 (like MS4, 52B, T64 has the less correct 'des' for 'de'), 96 (gives 'Des derniers' instead of 'Ces derniers'), 231 (has 'des' rather than 'de'), 233 (puts 'appât' in the plural), 241 (puts 'fureur' into the plural), 262 ('Ta' becomes 'La'), 291 ('rentrer' is reduced to 'entrer'), 303 (has 'attacher' instead of 'arracher'); II.1 ('te' gives way to 'me'), 12 ('ma' is replaced by 'ta'), 17 ('mains' is put into the singular), 34 ('mouvement' is put into the plural), 54 ('nous' is replaced by 'me'), 59 (has 'Oui!' for 'Lui!'), 341 (puts 'seul' before the noun); III.32 (gives 'ce' for 'ceux'), 202 (has 'la' instead of 'sa'), 269 ('aussi bien' is replaced by 'de même'); IV.218 ('Ah! quel object' replacing 'Palmire'), 239 (has 'Nous!' for 'Vous!), 265 (gives 'lieux' in the singular), 281 (displaces the object pronoun), act V lines 107 ('mêmes' given in the plural), 114 (puts 'dangers' into the singular).

It lacks act III line 220, and there are a remarkable number of obvious misprints, especially in the second half of the play. It is almost as this were a proof copy, needing revision (see 72P2). See II.136 ('des plus grands'), 172/173 (prints the Roman 'V' in Scene v upside down), 184 ('nos cœur'), 253 ('venter' for 'vanter'); III.27 (has 'Publiant' for 'oubliant'), 45/46 (misumbers scenes ii and iii as iii and iv respectively), 53 ('les profonds respect'), 197 ('des vengeance suprêmes'), 206 ('sans arme,'), 290 ('mes sens déchiré'); IV (omits the words 'scène Première' after 'Acte IV'); 143 ('mes secrets sentiment'), 206 ('poignard d'homicide'), 216 ('plus que le tient'), 220 ('songlant'), 256 (lacks the agreement in 'retrouvé'); V.8 ('Nous ventons'; see above II.253), 20 ('les flanc' (71P2 will have the plural), 50 ('le destins'), 55 (prints 'veux' for 'vœux'), 67 ('les fureur'), 80 ('d'ypocrisie'), 111 ('le cris'), 123 ('je trihomphe'), 157 ('ce jours'), 162 ('de forfait'; in plural in 71P2).

### 71P2

Same title page (and same typographical ornaments) as 71P1.
8°. sig.A-F4; pag.48.
[1] title; [2] Acteurs; [3]-48 Le Fanatisme, ou Mahomet le Prophète, tragédie.
F-Nts: 91.910.

71P2 is based on the same source as 71P1. Initially, it appears to be have been revised and printed rather more carefully. For instance, it corrects a number of mistakes found in 71P1. See I.303; II.35, 136, 172/173, 184; III.45/46, 53, 197, 206, 220, 290; IV.1, 143, 206, 216, 218, 220; V.20, 50, 55, 60, 67, 80, 107, 123, 157, 162. On the other hand, it makes new mistakes, especially towards the end of the play. See II.131 (like 60B has 'un for 'ton'), 165 ('J'attirai' for 'J'attisai'), 304 ('ne [...] point' rather than 'ne [...] pas'); III.83 ('unit' instead of 'soumit'), 160 ('faut' in place of 'veut'), 183 ('le' for 'ce'), 204 ('ces' rather than 'ses'), 232 ('Ordonne' instead of 'Pardonne'), 250 ('on' for 'tu'), 274 ('ne [...] point' for 'ne [...] plus'); IV.21 (puts 'douter' into the plural), 45 (into singular with 'on' rather than 'ils'), 64 (for 'mes' has 'nos'), 220 ('nous' becomes 'vous'), 231/232 ('JALMIRE' for 'PALMIRE'), 247 (this line is missing.); IV.128 (puts first hemistich into second person singular), 185 (again putting the verb into the singular). 71P2 follows all 1742 editions with 'immoler' rather than 'm'immoler' in act IV line 40, and 'de' for 'du' in act IV line 272. In act II line 16, it follows 42B1-42B5 with 'où de carnage', etc. As in MS4 in act IV line 109, one finds here 'au meurtrier' rather than 'un meurtrier'), and in act IV line 223 'puis' instead of 'peux'. Like Lekain (42X1*), 71P2 replaces 'bonheur' with 'honneur' in act IV line 27. This may be significant, as the copy of this edition kept at Nantes has manuscript corrections, suggesting that it was used by actors.

W71

[*half-title*] COLLECTION / *COMPLETTE* / DES / *OEUVRES* / DE / M^R. DE VOLTAIRE. / [*double ornate rule*] / *TOME TROISIEME.* / [*double ornate rule*] /
[*title-page*] THEATRE / *COMPLET* / DE / *M. DE VOLTAIRE,* / [*rule*] / TOME SECOND / [*rule*] / *CONTENANT* / MEROPE, LE FANATISME, SEMIRAMIS, / ORESTE, CATILINA, avec toutes les piéces / rélatives à ces Drames. / [*fleuron*] / *GENEVE,* / [*double ornate rule*] / M. DCC. LXXII. /
iii.[81]-151:
[81] LE / FANATISME, / OU / MAHOMET, / LE PROPHETE, / *TRAGEDIE.* /
82-85 Avis de l'éditeur; 86-91 A Sa Majesté le Roi de Prusse; 92 Lettre de Mr. de Voltaire au pape Benoît XIV; 93-94 Réponse du souverain pontife Benoît XIV à Monsieur de Voltaire; 95 Lettre de

remerciement de Monsieur de Voltaire au Pape; 96 Acteurs; 97-151 Le Fanatisme, ou Mahomet le prophète, tragédie.
Frontispiece (hors texte, facing p.97): as in w68 (unsigned).
L-N: D.4.576.

Has the final text of w68.

W71P

[*half-title*] ŒUVRES / *DE* / THEATRE / *DE M. DE VOLTAIRE.* /
[*title-page*] ŒUVRES / DE / M. DE VOLTAIRE. / [*double ornate rule*] / *THEATRE.* / [*rule*] / TOME PREMIER. / [*rule*] / [*woodcut*] / *A NEUFCHATEL.* / [*double ornate rule*] / M.DCC. LXXXIII /
ii.[219]-293:
[219] LE FANATISME, / *OU* / MAHOMET / LE PROPHETE, / *TRAGEDIE.* /
[220] Personnages; [221]-293 Le Fanatisme, ou Mahomet le prophète, tragédie.
F-P/BnF: Z.24797.

w72P follows w68, by having the final versions of act II lines 161, 256, act III 48, act IV 155, 287-290, act V lines 85, 184. It also has the final version of act I line 54, but with 'carnage' instead of 'naufrage'. It has 'des' for 'de' as in all 1742 editions in act V line 11. In act II line 40, it adopts the variant found in 42X1, 42X2, and it adopts the text of 41B1-42B5 in act I lines 1, 160, and act V line 120, and like the earliest editions has the more correct 'de' in act V line 17. There are a number of oddities. See II.12 (has 'Tels périls' for 'Tes périls'), 14 (has 'ma' for 'la'), 80 ('voit' for 'voir'), 164 ('me' instead of 'se'), 251 ('La' for 'Ma'); III.206 ('armes' becomes 'amis'); IV.13 (has 'Réparons' instead of 'Préparons'), 116 (adds 'faire' after 'faut-il').

W72X

[*half-title*] COLLECTION / COMPLETTE / DES / ŒUVRES / DE / *M$^{R}$. DE VOLTAIRE.* / DERNIERE EDITION. / *TOME HUITIEME.* /

[*title-page*] OUVRAGES / DRAMATIQUES, / *AVEC* / LES PIECES RELATIVES / A CHACUN / TOME SECOND. / [*ornament*] / [*double ornate rule*] / M. DCC. LXXII. /
viii.[297]-387:
[297] LE / FANATISME, / OU / MAHOMET / LE PROPHETE, / *TRAGEDIE.* /
[298] blank; 299-303 Avis de l'éditeur; 304-10 A Sa Majesté le Roi de Prusse; 311 Lettre de Monsieur de Voltaire au pape Benoît XIV; 312-13 Réponse du souverain pontife Benoît XIV à Monsieur de Voltaire; 314-15 Lettre de remerciement de Monsieur de Voltaire au Pape; [316] Acteurs; [317]-87 Le Fanatisme, ou Mahomet le prophète, tragédie.
F-P/BnF: 16° Z.15081; S-S/N.

This edition ignores the changes in W68. It is based on W64G, and it follows W64G and W70G in act I line 286, act III line 48, act IV lines 160, 287-290, act V lines 17, 85. It has three errors. See I.109 (has 'partie errante' for 'errante patrie'); II.107 (has the meaningless 'Emprisonneriez-vous' instead of 'Empoisonneriez-vous'); III.274 (like 71P2, 74A, it has 'ne [...] pas' in place of 'ne [...] point').

T73A1

THEATRE / COMPLET / *DE* / M^R.^ DE VOLTAIRE. / LE TOUT REVU ET CORRIGÉ / PAR L'AUTEUR MEME. / TOME TROISIEME. / CONTENANT / MEROPE, LE FANATISME, / ET ADELAIDE DU GUESCLIN. / [*ornament*] / *A AMSTERDAM,* / Chez les LIBRAIRES ASSOCIÉS. / [*double ornate rule*] / M. DCC. LXXIII.
iii.[111]-212:
[111] LE / FANATISME, / *OU* / MAHOMET / LE PROPHETE, / *TRAGEDIE.* /
[112] blank; 113-18 Avis de l'éditeur; 119-27 A Sa Majesté le Roi de Prusse; 128 Lettre de monsieur de Voltaire au pape Benoît XIV; 129-30 Réponse du souverain pontife Benoît XIV à Monsieur de Voltaire; 131-32 Lettre de remerciement de monsieur de Voltaire

au Pape; 132 Acteurs; [133]-212 Le Fanatisme, ou Mahomet le prophète, tragédie.
CH-21: Qb.2566 (2); D-51.

Basically, we find here the final text of w68, etc., but there are a number of errors. T73A1 inverts act II lines 309-310. The object pronoun is placed before the modal verb in act II line 40. In act II line 266 'fasse' becomes 'passe'. Like 42X2, T73A1 has 'punit' for 'punir' in act IV line 273. In act IV line 227, like 42X1, 42X2, it puts the adjective after the noun, but, like MS5 and 42X1*, it has the verb in the plural. It follows 42B1-42B5 with 'des' rather than 'de' in act I line 160. There are a number of careless printing errors: see II.261 ('ttompe'); IV.19 ('rrépas'), 74 ('saus'), 239 ('Zopiae'), 259 ('pas' for 'par'); V.146 ('Dien').

T73A2

In tome ii (?) of
*Le Théâtre de M. de Voltaire*. Amsterdam: Richoff, 1773. 7 vol. 12°.
F-Beaune.

I have not been able to consult this edition, but presume that it is similar to T70, etc.

73P

MAHOMET / *OU* / LE FANATISME, / *TRAGEDIE* / EN CINQ ACTES ET EN VERS, / *PAR M. DE VOLTAIRE.* / [*ornate double rule*] / NOUVELLE EDITION. / [*ornate double rule*] [*ornament: delicate tracery forming a vertical diamond shape*] / *A PARIS,* / Chez DIDOT l'aîné, Libraire & Imprimeur, rue Pavée, / près du Quai des Augustins. / [*double ornate rule*] / M. DCC. LXXIII. / *Avec Approbation & Privilege du Roi.* /
8°. sig.A-F4, G2; pag.52.
[1] title; [2] Acteurs; [3]-52 Mahomet, tragédie.
F-P/BnF: 8°Fb.19266.

Although 73P noticeably incorporates the new version of Act III line 48 as given in w68, in act III lines 147, 172, act IV lines 155, and especially 287-290 it reverts to older variants in the text. It has the inevitable 'des' for 'de' in act V line 17. It shares a number of variants with 73M. See III.257 ('les dieux' are replaced by 'le ciel'); IV.218 (for 'vient effrayer ma vue', one has 'se présente à moi'); V.31 ('et' becomes 'ou'), 80 (has 'forfaits' instead of 'fureurs'). There are also errors and further oddities. See I.131 (puts 'égalité' into the plural), 200 ('vous' for 'nous'), 208 ('en' for 'dans'), 255 ('admiré' replaces 'admirable'), 338 ('des' is reduced to 'de'); II.286 ('des' is reduced to 'de'), 296 (prints 'prohète'); III.52 (omits 'même').

### 73M

MAHOMET / *OU* / LE FANATISME, / *TRAGÉDIE* / EN VERS ET EN CINQ ACTES. / *Par M. DE VOLTAIRE.* / [*single ornate rule*] / NOUVELLE EDITION. / *Revue ſur celle in-4°. de Geneve.* / [*single ornate rule*] / [*double ornate rule*] / Le Prix eſt de 12 ſols. / [*double ornate rule*] / [*ornament: a framed square cameo, surrounded by ornate tracery*] / A PARIS. / *Et ſe vend* A MARSEILLE, / Chez JEAN MOSSY, Imprimeur du Roi & de la / Marine, & Libraire, au Parc. / [*double ornate rule*] / M. DCC. LXXIII. /

8°. sig.A-F4; pag.48.

[1] title; [2] Acteurs; 3-48 Mahomet, tragédie.

F-P/Ar: Rf.14.331.

Despite the title-page, this edition has certain things in common with 73P, and like the latter adopts the older versions of act III lines 147, 172, act IV lines 155, 287-290, act V line 60. It also has the older versions of act I lines 290, 311, act IV line 86, act V line 11. It shares the same particular variants with 73P in act III line 257, act IV lines 64, 218, act V lines 31, 80. It has its own peculiarities. See I.91 (has 'ne [...] pas' in place of 'ne [...] point'), 140 ('point' again gives way to 'pas'), 177/178 (gives a differently worded stage instruction); II.132 ('père' is replaced by 'maître'), 175 (omits 'et'), 247 (prints 'au pieds'); III.274 (has 'point' instead of 'plus'), 292 ('dans' becomes 'à'); IV.23 (adds 'tout' before 'prêt'); V.9 ('à' is replaced by 'en'), 55 (has 'yeux' instead of 'vœux').

73X

[*title-page in an ornate frame*] *LE* / FANATISME, / *OU* / MAHOMET / *LE PROPHÈTE.* / *TRAGÉDIE.* / Par M. DE VOLTAIRE. / [*woodcut: a shield with leaves, etc.*] / [*ornate double rule*] / M. DCC. LXXIII.
8°. sig.A-D[8], E[7]; pag.78 [pag.76-77 misnumbered 66-67].
[1] title; [2] Acteurs; [3]-78 Le Fanatisme ou Mahomet le prophète, tragédie.
Bengesco 140.
B-Br; F-P/BnF: 8°Yth.6480.

Gives the final text of w68, except in act I line 160, where like 42B1-42B5 it has 'des' rather than 'de', and in act II line 264 where 'veut' becomes 'peut'.

74A

*LE* / FANATISME, / *OU* / MAHOMET LE PROPHÉTE. / *TRAGÉDIE.* / EN VERS ET EN CINQ ACTES, / *Par Monsieur de V*OLTAIRE. / [*double ornate rule*] / *NOUVELLE EDITION.* / [*double ornate rule*] / [*ornament: tracery in a vertical diamond shape, enclosing a horizontal rectangle with a star in the middle*] / *A AVIGNON,* / Chez LOUIS CHAMBEAU, Imprimeur-Libraire, / près le Collège. / [*double ornate rule*] / M. DCC. LXXIV. /
8°. sig.A-F[4]; pag.48.
[1] title; [2] Acteurs; 3-48 Le Fanatisme, ou Mahomet le Prophète. Tragédie.
GB-Ox/U19: Besterman 1973/50. V3.M2.1774.

74A follows 71P2 and only differs from it in two places. In act I line 96, it has 'Les derniers' for the normal 'Ces derniers', whereas 71P2, like 71P1, has 'Des derniers'. It begins act I line 171 with 'Non' rather than 'Moins'.

W75G

[*within an ornamental border*] LA / HENRIADE, / DIVERS AUTRES / *POËMES* / ET / TOUTES LES PIÉCES

RELATIVES / À L'ÉPOPÉE. [Genève, Cramer & Bardin], *M. DCC. LXXV*. 8°.
Volume iii:
[*within an ornamental border*] OUVRAGES / *DRAMATIQUES*, / PRÉCÉDÉS ET SUIVIS / DE TOUTES LES PIÉCES QUI LEUR / SONT RELATIFS. / [*rule*] / TOME SECOND / [*rule*] / *M. DCC. LXXV*.
ii.[307]-400 [*all within an ornamental border*]:
[307] LE / FANATISME, / OU / MAHOMET LE PROPHÉTE, / *TRAGÉDIE*. /
308-12 Avis de l'Editeur; 313-20 A Sa Majesté le Roi de Prusse; 321 Lettre de Mr. de Voltaire au pape Benoît XIV; 322-23 Réponse du souverain pontife Benoît XIV à Mr. de Voltaire; 324-25 Lettre de remerciement de Mr. de Voltaire au Pape; [326] Acteurs; 327-400 Le Fanatisme, ou Mahomet le prophète, tragédie.
Frontispiece (facing p.327): 'Palmire, quel objet vient effrayer ma vue?' (act IV sc.4).
F-Dp; GB-Ox/U19.

This is usually considered as the last edition to have been revised by Voltaire. It follows w68, even in act V line 17 with 'des' rather than 'de' (which we have not followed here). In act V line 113, by error it would seem, it also puts the imperative into the plural: 'Frappez' for 'Frappe'.

W75X

[*half-title*] [*within an ornamental border*] ŒUVRES / DE / *M*[R]. *DE VOLTAIRE* / [*rule*] / TOME SECOND. / [*rule*]
[*title-page*] [*within an ornamental border*] OUVRAGES / *DRAMATIQUES*, / PRÉCÉDÉS ET SUIVIS / *DE TOUTES LES PIECES QUI LEUR / SONT RELATIVES*. / [*rule*] / TOME SECOND. / [*rule*] / [*ornament*] / [*double ornate rule*] / *M. DCC. LXXV*. /
ii.[307]-400 [*all within an ornamental border*]:
[307] LE / FANATISME, / OU / MAHOMET LE PROPHETE, / *TRAGÉDIE*. /

308-12 Avis de l'Editeur; 313-20 A Sa Majesté le Roi de Prusse; 321 Lettre de M. de Voltaire au pape Benoît XIV; 322-23 Réponse du souverain pontife Benoît XIV à M. de Voltaire; 324-25 Lettre de remerciement de Monsieur de Voltaire au Pape; [326] Acteurs; 327-400 Le Fanatisme, ou Mahomet le prophête, tragédie.
Frontispiece (facing p.327): as in W75G.
F-P/BnF: Z.24882.

This is a pirated edition of W75G, and follows it to the point of having 'Frappez' in act V line 113. There are, however, further errors. It omits the first hemistich of act V line 93. Like 42B1-42B5, it leaves out 'me' in act IV line 197. In act I line 35 'portez' becomes 'partez', and in act III line 55 'Délivre-moi' is put into the plural.

T76X

THEATRE / COMPLET / DE MONSIEUR / DE VOLTAIRE. / TOME DEUXIEME. / *Contenant* ALZIRE *ou* LES AMÉRICAINS, / MÉROPE, LE FANATISME, *ou* / MAHOMET LE PROPHETE, / SEMIRAMIS, ORESTE, *avec* / *toutes les Pièces relatives à ces Drames.* / [*woodcut: spray of flowers*] / [*double ornate rule*] / M. DCC. LXXVI. /
[lines 1, 3, 5 and date are in red].
ii.[201]-298:
[201] LE / FANATISME, / *OU* / MAHOMET / *LE PROPHETE*, / TRAGÉDIE. /
[202]-207 Avis de l'Editeur; [208]-16 A Sa Majesté le Roi de Prusse; 217 Lettre de M. de Voltaire au pape Benoît XIV; 218-19 Réponse du souverain pontife Benoît XIV à M. de Voltaire; 220-21 Lettre de remerciment de M. de Voltaire au Pape; [222] Acteurs; [223]-98 Le Fanatisme, ou Mahomet le prophête, tragédie.
F-P/Ar: Rf.14.096.

This is a reissue of 73X in a collective edition, with the addition of the prefatory matter. Although the page numbering is different, with new signatures ([$N^5$-$N^8$], $O^8$-$S^8$, $T^5$), as far as the play itself is concerned, both editions have the same ornaments and layout. Both share the same harking back to 'des' rather than 'de' in act I line 160, and in both editions 'veut' becomes 'peut' in act II line 264.

T77

THEATRE / *COMPLET* / DE M. DE VOLTAIRE; / *NOUVELLE EDITION*, / *Revue & corrigée par l'AUTEUR*. / TOME TROISIEME, / CONTENANT / MEROPE, LE FANATISME OU MAHOMET / LE PROPHETE, ADELAIDE / DU GUESCLIN. / [*woodcut*] / *A AMSTERDAM*, / Chez les LIBRAIRES ASSOCIÉS. / [*double rule*] / M. DCC.LXXVII. /
iii.[111]-208:
[111] *LE FANATISME*, / *OU* / MAHOMET / LE PROPHETE, / *TRAGEDIE*. /
[112] blank; 113-17 Avis de l'Editeur; 118-25 A Sa Majesté le Roi de Prusse; 126 Lettre de M. de Voltaire au pape Benoît XIV; 127-28 Réponse du souverain pontife Benoît XIV à M. de Voltaire; 129-30 Lettre de remercîment de M. de Voltaire au Pape; 130 Acteurs; 131-208 Le Fanatisme, ou Mahomet le prophète, tragédie.
S-S/N: Litt.fr.Drama.

Basically this is a reissue of T73A1, which it follows in its oddities in act I line 160, act II lines 40, 266, 309-310, act IV lines 227, 273. It has even more obvious printing mistakes, but of which none coincides with those in T73A1. See here I.21 ('un troupe égarée'), 58 ('combats pas vous-même'), 77 ('cet infortunée'). Act II line 76 has 'graves' for 'braves', and in act III line 284 'du roi' is changed into 'd'un roi'. In act III line 167, in common with 42X1, 42X2, T77 puts 'ennemis' into the singular. Unlike T73A1 it has the more correct 'de' rather than 'des' in act V line 17.

77P1

MAHOMET / *OU* / LE FANATISME, / *TRAGÉDIE* / EN CINQ ACTES ET EN VERS, / *PAR M. DE VOLTAIRE*. / [*double ornate rule*] / NOUVELLE EDITION. / [*double ornate rule*] / [*woodcut: a lute, mask, quill and laurel leaves*] / *A PARIS*,

/ Chez N. B. DUCHESNE, Libraire, Rue S. Jacques, au- / deſſous de la Fontaine S. Bénoît, au Temple du Goût. / [*double ornate rule*] / M. DCC. LXXVII. /
8°. sig.; [A]-F$^4$ [sig.A is misnumbered as B]; pag.48.
[1] title; [2] Acteurs; [3]-48 Mahomet, tragédie.
p.48 (colophon): On trouve à Avignon, chez Jacques Garrigan, Imprimeur-Libraire, place Saint-Didier, un assortiment de Pièces de Théâtre, imprimées dans le même genre.
F-P/Ar: Rf.14.332.

77P1 is based on 73P and reproduces most of its oddities. However, it corrects the mistakes in act II lines 286, 296 and in act V line 17 has the more correct partitive 'de' instead of 'des'. Two other lines differ: in act I line 199 'ses' becomes 'tes', and act II line 127, as in W56, T66, 68P, T70, etc., 77P1 has 'des' rather the more correct 'de'.

### 77P2

*Mahomet, ou le Fanatisme, tragédie en vers et en cinq actes*. Par M. de Voltaire. Paris, Hérissant, 1777. in-8° pag.52.
GB-Ox/U19 (missing).

I have not been able to consult this edition, but presume that it is a reissue of 68P.

### 78B

MAHOMET, / *TRAGEDIE,* / PAR M. DE VOLTAIRE, / *Représentée sur le Théatre de la Comédie française,* / *à Paris.* / NOUVELLE EDITION. / [*woodcut: leaves, flowers and berries*] / A BRUXELLES. / [*double rule*] / M. DCC. LXXVIII. /
sig.A-G$^4$; pag.55.[i blank].
[1] title; [2] Acteurs; [3]-55 Mahomet, tragédie.
F-Nts: 28.767.

Despite its late date, this edition basically follows the text of 42B5 (C*), although like 42B3 it gives the correct 'aucune' in act II line 35. It also gives the final version of act II line 107. In act II line 67 it follows 42X1,

42X2 with 'mêmes' in the plural. There are other differences, and also a fair number of errors. See I.57 (as in 47A and W50 there is 'ces' for 'ses'), 191 (has 'examiner' for 'exterminer'), 234 ('tente' becomes 'trompe'), 292 (adds a spurious 'plus' before 'juste'), 298 (adds an unwanted 'à' after 'Tu penses'), 325 (gives the 41B1-42B5 version, but with 'J'y défendrai' rather than 'Je défendrai'); II.2 (reduces 'Te revois-je' to 'Te vois-je'), 6 (as 'de' and not 'du'), 131 (like 60B, 71P2, 74A, it has 'un' rather than 'ton'), 199 (omits 'Mais'), 328 ('te' becomes 'se'); III.100 (gives by error 'de' rather than 'à' after 's'empresse'), 119 ('ma' becomes 'sa'), 226 ('maison' becomes the meaningless 'raison'), 264 ('offre' is replaced by 'porte'); IV.95 ('ne [...] pas' rather than 'ne [...] point'), 222 (has the meaningless 'succède' for 'cède'), 247 (omits the first 'Rendez'); V.25 ('ses' becomes 'tes'), 84 (has 'ta' for 'la').

78P

MAHOMET / *OU* / LE FANATISME, *TRAGEDIE.* / EN CINQ ACTES, / *ET EN VERS.* / Par Monsieur DE VOLTAIRE. / [*double ornate rule*] / *NOUVELLE EDITION.* / [*double ornate rule*] / [*woodcut: various instruments (palette, etc.), heaped in a stone vase*] / *A PARIS,* / Chez DIDOT, l'aîné, Imprimeur / & Libraire, Rue Pavée. / [*ornate rule (two intertwined cords)*] / *M. DCC. LXXVIII.* /
8°. A-F4; pag.47.[i].
[1] title; [2] Acteurs; [3]-47 Mahomet, tragédie.
p.[48]: On trouve à Avignon, chez les frères Bonnet, Imprimeurs, Libraires, vis-à-vis le Puits des Bœufs, un assortiment de Pièces de Théâtre, imprimées dans le même goût.
GB-Lo/N1: 640.g.11 (1).

This edition owes quite a lot to 73P (see I.131, 255; IV.4, 286; III.52, 147, 172, 257; IV.218, 287-290; V.17, 60, 80. It contains a number of errors and odd changes. See I.78 ('ton' for 'mon'), 176 (omits 'vient'); II.67 (has an unwanted 'en'), 87 ('leur cris'), 91 ('Hammon' is written as 'Haumon'), 296 (omits 'et'); III.35 (through error has 'sous' for 'sans'), 51 (writes 'mahomet' with a lower case 'm'), 309 (has 'Au pied de' in the plural); IV.109 (follows MS4, 71P2, 74A with 'un' for 'au'), 169 ('les remords m'accable'), 170 (omits 'ou'). It omits 'Mahomet' before act V line 18, and thus inadvertently gives lines 18-20 to Omar. It is possibly again through inadvertence that 'Ministre' is given in the singular in act IV line 155.

K

OEUVRES / COMPLETES / DE / VOLTAIRE. / TOME TROISIEME. / [*swelled rule*] / DE L'IMPRIMERIE DE LA SOCIÉTÉ LITTÉRAIRE- / TYPOGRAPHIQUE. / 1784 [*or* 1785]. /
a) in-8°: iii.[117]-213:
[117] LE / FANATISME, / OU / MAHOMET LE PROPHETE, / *TRAGEDIE.* / Représentée, pour la première fois, le / 9 auguste 1742. /
[118] blank; [119]-20 Avertissement des éditeurs; [121]-25 Avis de l'Editeur; [126]-132 A Sa Majesté le Roi de Prusse; [133] Lettre de M. de Voltaire au pape Benoît XIV; [137] Traduction de la lettre précédente; [135]-36 Réponse du souverain pontife Benoît XIV à M. de Voltaire; 136-37 Traduction; [138] Lettre de remerciment de M. de Voltaire au Pape; [139] Traduction; [140] Personnages; [141]-211 Le Fanatisme, ou Mahomet le prophète, tragédie; [212] Variantes de Mahomet; [213] Notes.
F-Qr; GB-Ld/U1.
b) in-12°: iii.[129]-[238]:
[129] LE / FANATISME, / OU / MAHOMET LE PROPHETE, / *TRAGEDIE.* / Représentée, pour la première fois, le / 9 auguste 1742. /
[130] blank; [131]-32: Avertissement des éditeurs; [133]-38 Avis de l'Editeur; [139]-147 A Sa Majesté le Roi de Prusse; [148] Lettre de M. de Voltaire au pape Benoît XIV; [149] Traduction de la lettre précédente; [150]-51 Réponse du souverain pontife Benoît XIV à M. de Voltaire; 152-153 Traduction; [154]-55 Lettre de remerciment de M. de Voltaire au Pape; 156-57 Traduction; [158] Personnages; [159]-236 Le Fanatisme, ou Mahomet le prophète, tragédie; 237 Variantes de Mahomet; [238] Notes.
GB-Ld/U1.

The text of *Mahomet* is identical in both formats.

Basically Kehl gives the final version of the text, but with a few minor differences. It reverts to that of 1742 in general in act III lines 211-212, and to that of 42B1-42B5 in act I line 1, act II lines 263, 292, act V line 120. It differs also in two other lines: see III.235 ('des' for 'ses'), 310 ('les' for 'des'). It also has a different stage instruction at act IV line 183. There is a preface which we reproduce in Appendix III.

## Translations and adaptations

Sources include: Hans Fromm, *Bibliographie deutscher Übersetzungen aus dem Französischen, 1700-1948* (Baden-Baden 1950-1953), vi.275-76; V. S. Sopikov, Опытъ россійской библіографіи (Saint Petersburg 1905); Theodore Besterman's three bibliographies, 'A provisional bibliography of Italian editions and translations of Voltaire', *SVEC* 18 (1961), p.288-89, 'A provisional bibliography of Scandinavian and Finnish editions and translations of Voltaire', *SVEC* 47 (1966), p.74-75, 'Provisional bibliography of Portuguese editions of Voltaire', *SVEC* 66 (1970), p.27; Hywel Berwyn Evans, 'A provisional bibliography of English editions and translations of Voltaire', *SVEC* 8 (1959), p.83-86; Jeroom Vercruysse, 'Bibliographie provisoire des traductions néerlandaises et flamandes de Voltaire', *SVEC* 106 (1973), p.39-40; Francisco Lafarga, *Las traducciones españoles del teatro francés* (Barcelona 1983-1988), i.121-122, 124, ii.138; and Christopher Todd, 'A provisional bibliography of published Spanish translations of Voltaire', *SVEC* 166 (1976), p.108-10.

### Dutch

*Mahomet, treurspel. Gevolgd naar het Fransche van den Heere de Voltaire* [...] [*with a verse epistle by A. Hartsen*] Amsterdam, Izaak Duim, 1770. 8° pag.[xii].62.[ii].
(F-P/BnF: Yf.12141; F-P/Ar: Rf.14.352; USA-ICU, NN) (Vercruysse 77).

*De Dwepery, of Mahomet de Profeet, treurspel. Het Fransch gevolgt van den Hr. A. de Voltaire.* Te Leyden, C. Heyligert, 1770. 8° pag.[xiv].68.
(F-P/BnF: 8°Yth.67892) (Vercruysse 78).

*Mahomet, Treurspel. Gevoldt naar het Fransche.* Amsteldam, J. Helders en A. Mars, 1783. 8° pag.[xiv].62.
(F-P/Ar: Rf.14.353) (Vercruysse 79).

*De Profeét Mahomet treurspel in vyf deelen, uit het Fransch Stuk van den beruchten Heer De Voltaire, in Nederduitsche Verzen vertaeld.* Cortryk, P. Calewaert, 1783. 8° pag.68.
(B-G/U) (Vercruysse 80).

*De Profeét Mahomet treur-spel in vyf deelen, uit het Fransch Stuk van den beruchten Heer De Voltaire, in Nederduitsche Verzen vertaeld.* Gend [Ghent], J. F. Vander Scheuren [n.d.]. 4° pag.52.
(B-G/U) (Vercruysse 81).

English

*Mahomet, the Imposter, a tragedy [by James Miller and J. Hoadley] as it is acted at the Theatre Royal in Drury Lane, by His Majesty's servants.* London, J. Watts, 1744, 8° pag.[viii].70.[ii].
(F-P/BnF: 16°Yk.1124; GB-Ln/N1: 643.g.18 (2); GB-Ld/U; USA-DLC, MH, PU, CtY) (Evans 358).

*Mahomet, the Imposter, a tragedy [by James Miller and J. Hoadley] as it is acted at the Theatre Royal in Drury Lane, by His Majesty's servants. By a gentleman of Wadham-College. The Second Edition.* London, J. Watts, 1745, 8° pag.[viii]-70.[ii].
(GB-Lo/N1: 11735.e.44; USA-CLU-C, CtY, NN, ICU) (Evans 359).

*Mahomet, the Imposter, a tragedy [by James Miller and J. Hoadley] as it is acted at the Theatre Royal in Drury Lane, by His Majesty's servants.* Dublin, W. Smith, 1745, 8° pag.68.

(GB-Lo/N1: 11774.aaa.15 (3); USA-WU, ICU, DFo) (Evans 360).

*Mahomet, the Imposter. A tragedy. By Mons. Voltaire.* [*Translated by James Miller and J. Hoadley*]. Edinburgh, A. Donaldson, 1759, 8° pag.iv.57.[i].
(USA-CtY) (Evans 361).

*Mahomet. A Tragedy.* In: *Works of M. Voltaire* (1761-1770), xxv.21-108.
(USA-NBuG)

*Mahomet, the Imposter. A tragedy* [*by James Miller and J. Hoadley*]. *As it is now acted at the Theatre-Royal in Drury-lane.* London, T. Lowndes, 1765. 8° pag.[iv].64.[ii].
(USA-MH, OCU, IU, DFo, MdBP, TxU, InU) (Evans 362).

*Mahomet, the Imposter, a tragedy* [*by James Miller and J. Hoadley*] *as it is now acted at the Theatre Royal in Drury Lane. Fourth edition, with new improvements* [*by David Garrick*]. London, T. Lowndes, 1766, 8° pag.[xvi].64.
(GB-Lo/N1: 11740.n.58; GB-Ld/U; USA-NN, Oru, TxU, WU, CtY, IU) (Evans 363).

*Mahomet, the Imposter: a tragedy* [*adapted by James Miller and J. Hoadley*] *As it is acted at the Theatre-Royal in Drury-lane, by His Majesty's servants. By Mons. Voltaire.* Edinburgh: P. Williamson, 1773. 8° pag.[ii].[5]-59.[i].
(USA-DLC, PPL) (Evans 364).

*Mahomet the imposter; a tragedy from the French.* Edinburgh, J. Robertson, 1774. pag.59.
(USA-MF).

*Mahomet, the Imposter, a tragedy* [*by James Miller and J. Hoadley*] *as it is now acted at the Theatre Royal in Drury Lane. Fifth edition, with new improvements* [*by David Garrick*]. London, T. Lowndes, 1776, 8° pag.[vi].64.[ii].

(F-P/BnF: 8°Yth.60313; GB-Lo/N1: 643.i.7 (8); USA-CtY, InU, PPL, OU, DFo) (Evans 365).

*Bell's Edition. Mahomet, the Imposter, a tragedy, as written by the Rev, Mr. Miller. Distinguishing also the variations of the theatre, as performed at the Theatre-Royal in Drury-Lane. Regulated from the Prompt-Book, by Permission of the Managers, by Mr Hopkins, prompter.* London, John Bell; C. Etherington, 1776. 12° pag.54.[v]. (Bell's British theatre, vol.7 [no.3])
(F-P/BnF: Yk.1670; GB-Lo/N1: 82.d.11; USA-DFo, MH, NRU, MB, TxHU) (Evans 366).

*Mahomet, the Imposter, a tragedy [by James Miller and J. Hoadley]. Marked with the variations of the Manager's book, at the Theatre-Royal in Drury-Lane.* London, C. Bathurst, J. Rivington and sons, T. Longman, T. Lowdnes, T. Caslon, W. Nicoll, and S. Bladon, 1777. 12° pag.57. (The New English Theatre, vol. 8)
(F-P/BnF: 8°Yth.60315; GB-Lo/N1: 1342.n.3 (6); USA-DLC, CtY, MB, MH, NN, CtY) (Evans 367).

*Mahomet the imposter. A tragedy. Taken from the manager's book, at the Theatre Royal, Drury Lane.* London, Printed for R. Butters, no.79, Fleet-street; and sold by all Booksellers in Town and Country [n.d.] 8° pag.46.
(USA-FU).

*Mahomet, the Imposter, a tragedy. As it is acted at the Theatres-Royal in Drury-Lane and Covent-Garden. Written by the Rev. Mr. Miller.* London, J. Harrison, J.Wenman, 1778. 4° pag.16. (*Theatrical magazine*, vol.3).
(GB-Lo/N1: 11770.g.3 (12); GB-Ld/U; USA-MiU, TxU, CtY, DFo, IU, INU, NN) (Evans 368).

*Bell's Characteristical Edition. Mahomet the Imposter. A tragedy by the Rev. Mr. Miller. As performed at the Theatre-Royal Drury Lane. Regulated from the prompt-book by Mr Hopkins, prompter.*

[...] Edinburgh, the Apollo press; London, Bell, 1782. 12° pag.51. (British theatre, vol.7 [no.3]).
(F-P/BnF: Yk.3405; GB-Lo/N1: 1476.aa.38 (3); USA-IU, MH, CtY, NcD) (Evans 369).

*Mahomet. A Tragedy, by the Rev. Mr. Miller. Adapted for theatrical representation, as performed at the Theatre-Royal, Covent-Garden. Regulated from the prompt-book, by permission of the Manager.* [...] London, John Bell, 1795. 4° pag.v.[i].67.[i]. (Bell's British Theatre, vol.23, no.4).
(GB-Lo/N1: 2304.c.; GB-Ld/U; USA-DLC, PU, MB, MH, PHC, PNm, NN, ViU) (Evans 370).

*Mahomet. A Tragedy, by the Rev. Mr. Miller.* London, Bell, 1796. pag.67 (British theatre, vol.27).
(USA-PU) (Evans 371).

*Mahomet the imposter, a tragedy, marked with the variations of the manager's book at the Theatre-royal in Drury-lane.* London, Printed for W. Lowndes, 1796. pag.51[i].
(USA-NNC).

*Mahomet the imposter. By Miller.* in: *The British Drama; comprehending the best plays in the English language* (London 1804), vol.1, part 2, p.564-83.
(USA-NN, MH) (Evans 372).

*Mahomet, the imposter; a tragedy, in five acts; by the Rev. Mr. Miller. As performed at the Theatre Royal, Drury Lane, printed under the authority of the managers, from the prompt book. With remarks by Mrs. Inchbald.* London, Longman, Hurst, Rees, Orme, and Brown [1808]. 12° pp.57. (Mrs. Inchbald, *The British Theatre*, vol.13 [no.3]).
(F-P/BnF: Yk.4216; USA-DLC, USA-PU, NN) (Evans 373).

*Mahomet; a tragedy, in five acts. Translated from the French of M. Voltaire, by the Rev. Mr. Miller* [*altered by John Howard Payne*].

*As performed at the American theatres, with remarks.* New York, D. Longworth, 1809. 12° pag.72.
(GB-Lo/N1: 11735.aaa.42; USA-MH, CtY, PU, RPB, MH).

*Mahomet, the imposter. By Miller.* in: *The Modern British Drama* (London, 1811), vol.2 (Tragedies), p.187-206.
(GB-Lo/N1: 11783.bbb.41; GB-Ld/U) (Evans 374).

*Mahomet, the imposter. A tragedy. By the Rev. Mr. Miller. Correctly given, from copies used in the theatres, by Thomas Dibdin.* London, Printed at the Chiswick press for Whittington and Arliss, 1815. 12° pag.51.[i]. (T. J. Dibdin, *London theatre*, vol.8 [no.2]).
(USA-DLC, CU-BANC, InU, OC1, MB)

*Mahomet. A Tragedy, by the Rev. Mr. Miller.* 1824. (*British Theatre*, vol.12).
(Evans 375).

*Mahomet. A Tragedy, by the Rev. Mr. Miller.* London, Sherwood & Co. [1824] 4° pag.12. (*The London Stage*, vol.4).
(GB-Lo/N1: 2306.g.4; GB-Ld/U; USA-MB) (Evans 376).

*Mahomet, the Imposter; a tragedy in five acts.* London, printed for Longman, Hurst, Rees, and Orme [1824]. pag.57. (Mrs. E. S. Inchbald, *The British Theatre*).
(USA-MH-L).

*Mahomet, the imposter; a tragedy, in five acts. By the rev. Mr. Miller.* [1824-1827?] pag.12. (*The London Stage*, vol.4 [no.15]).
(USA-DLC, PU-F).

*Mahomet. A Tragedy, by the Rev. Mr. Miller.* in: *The British Drama* (London 1826), ix.[1466]-81.
(GB-Lo/N1: 11770.g.13; USA-NN) (Evans.378).

*Mahomet, the imposter: a tragedy in five acts. By the Rev. Mr. Miller. in: The British Drama* (Philadelphia 1850), ii.658-73.
(USA-DLC).

*Mahomet the imposter* [...] London, 1865.
(USA-TxU).

*Mahomet. A Tragedy, in five acts. By the Rev. Mr. Miller.* 1871. 8°.
(GB-Lo/N1: 11770.bbb.13 (35))

*Mahomet. A Tragedy, by the Rev. Mr. Miller.* [1875?] (Dick's standard plays, no.130).
(GB-Lo/N1: 11770.bbb.4) (Evans 379).

*Mahomet, translated by Oliver Leigh.* in: A. Bates, *The Drama* (London 1903), viii.229-79.
(USA-NN).

German

*Die Schwärmerey, oder Mahomet der Prophet. Ein Trauerspiel.* In: *Sechs Schauspiele. Übers.* Braunschweig. Hamburg 1748. No.2.
(Fromm 27061).

*Mahomet, der Lügen-Prophet. Ein Trauer-spiel, aus dem Französischen des Herrn von Voltaire Übersetzet Aufgefürt zu Wien* [...] *im Jahr 1749.* Wien, Gedrukt bey J. P. v. Ghelen [1749]. pag.57.
(USA-ICU) (Fromm 27062).

*Mahomet, der Prophet und die Scythen.* Leipzig, Heineck u. Faber, 1768. in-8° pp.154.
(F-P/BnF: 16°Yf.890) (Fromm 27063).

*Mahomet, der Prophet. Ein Trauerspiel in fünf Aufzügen. Aufgeführt im kaiserl.königl. Nationaltheater. Neue Übersetzung in Jamben.* [Translated by Johann Friedrich Löwen] Wien: Zu finden beym Logenmeister, 1778. 16° pag.76.
(USA-NN) (Fromm 27064).

*Mahomet der Prophet. Neue Übers. in Jamben v. L*** [Johann Friedrich Löwen] Wien, Gräff, 1783 (National aufgeführte Schauspiele, 2, 3).
(Fromm 27065).

*Mahomet, Trauerspiel in fünf Aufzügen nach Voltaire von [Johann Wolfgang von] Göthe*. Tübingen, der I. G. Cotta'schen Buchhandlung, 1802, in-12° pag.102.
(F-P/BnF: Rés.Z.Furstenberg.497 (2); GB-Lo/N1: 11735.e.4; USA-DLC, USA-MH, USA-MdBJ, USA-CU, USA-InU, USA-NjP) (Fromm 27066).

*Mahomet, Trauerspiel in fünf Aufzügen nach Voltaire von [Johann Wolfgang von] Göthe*. Tübingen, [Cotta], 1802. pag.87 (Neuste Theater Bibliothek, 1).
(USA-MH) (Fromm 27067).

*Mahomet, Trauerspiel in fünf Aufzügen nach Voltaire von [Johann Wolfgang v.] Göthe*. Tübingen 1802. 8° pag.94.
(USA-WU).

*Mahomet, Trauerspiel in 5 Aufzügen nach Voltaire von [Johann Wolfgang von] Göthe*. Mannheim 1803. pag.112.
(Fromm 27068).

*Le Fanatisme, ou Mahomet le prophète, tragédie en cinq actes – Die Schwärmerey oder Mahomet der Prophet, Trauerspiel in fünf Handlungen [...] uebersezt von Carl August Freiherrn von Perglas*. Augsburg, J. C. Würth, 1838, in-8° 75+75pp. (text + trans. in parallel).
(F-P/Ar: Rf.14.351).

*Mahomet, Trauerspiel in 5 Akten. Bearb. v. [Johann Wolfgang von] Goethe*. Stuttgart, Hoffmann [1869]. pag.vii.35. (Classische Theater-Bibliothek aller Nationen, 63).
(GB-Lo/N1: 11747.bb.63) (Fromm 27069).

*Mahomet, Trauerspiel in fünf Akten nach Voltaire von W. von Goethe*. Leipzig: P. Reclam jun. [1869]. 12° pag.56. (Reclam's Universal-Bibliothek, 122).
(Fromm 27070; Reissued in 1905: Fromm 27071).

*Mahomet, von Voltaire. Erklärt von dr. K. Sachs* [...] Berlin, Weidmann, 1884. 8° pag.40.
(USA-ICU, USA-RPB).

*Mahomet, Trauerspiel in funf Aufzügen nach Voltaire, uebersetzt von Goethe*. 1891. pag.360.
(USA-OU).

### Greek

Ho phanatismos, e Ho prophetes Moameth / tragodia eis pente praxeis tou Voltairou metaphrastheisa ek tou Gallikou hypo Ph. Th. Spathe. en Karlovasiois Samou: Ek tes typographias I. S. Pothetou Lekat, I. M. Garouphale, kai G. A. Kleanthous, 1832. 74 p; 40.
Bodleian: Vet. M6 c.1 (1).

*'Ο Φανατισμὸς, τραγω δία υ πὸ Γ. Σερονίου ή δη ποτὲ μεταφρασθει σα, καὶ τανυ ν πρω τον τύποις ϵ κδοθει σα.* Thermopylae 1848. 80. pag.118.

(GB-Lo/N1: 11735.g.3(2)).

For details of this translation by Giorgios Serouïos, see C. T. Dimaras, 'Notes sur la présence de Voltaire en Grèce', *SVEC* 55 (1967), p.444. The British Library also possesses it in manuscript (Cod. 10,078).

### Hungarian

A' hitetö Mahomet, avagy a' Fanaticismus, szomorú játék, mellyet magyarra forditott Zechenter A. [Introduction by Gy. Bessenyei]. Posonyban [1790?] 8° pag.93.
(GB-Lo/N1: 897.a.11 (4)).

### Italian

*Il Fanatismo o sia Maometto Profeta. Tragedia del Sig. de Voltaire. Tradotta dall'Abate Melchior Cesarotti*. [c.1750] 8° pag.[5]-90.

(I-F/N) (Besterman 118).

*Il Fanatismo, o sia Maometto il profeta, tragedia del Sig.di Voltaire, tradotta dal Signor Agostino Paradisi.* [n.p.n.d. (ante-1777)] 4° p.7-102.
(F-P/BnF: 8°Yf.1447 (1)).

*Il Fanatismo osia Maometto Profeta. Tragedia del Signor di Voltaire. Ridotta dal francese dall'Abate Melchior Cesarotti ad uso del teatro italiano.* Venezia, Giammaria Bassaglia, MDCC-LXXXVII[=1787]. 12° pag.82.
(I-F/N) (Besterman 119).

*Il Fanatismo, ossia Maometto il profeta, tragedia* [...] *da rappresentari nel carnovale dell'anno 1790 dalla compagnia comica de'signori cavalieri dilettante.* Napoli, F. Raimondi [s.d] 8° pag.15.
(F-P/Ar.: 14.347 (1)).

*Il Fanatismo ossia Maometto profeta. Tragedia di Voltaire. Traduzione dell'abate Melchior Cesarotti.* Venezia, Tipografia Pepoliana, presso Antonio Curti, 1796, in-16° pag. xxxi.126.
(F-P/Ar.: Rf.14.348; I-Mo; I-R/N) (Besterman 120).

*Il Fanatismo ossia Maometto profeta. Tragedia di Voltaire. Traduzione dell'abate Melchior Cesarotti.* Venezia, presso Antonio Rosa, 1809. 8° pp.80.
(GB-Lo/N1: 639.d.15) (Besterman 121).

*Maometto, tragedia* [*Melchior Cesarotti*] *Opere.* Firenze 1810, in-8°, vol.33. Versioni [...]
(F-P/BnF: Z.31585 (or: 1796: GB-Lo/N1: 639.d.15)).

*Maometto tragedia del signor di Voltaire. Tradotta dall'abate Melchior Cesarotti.* Milano, Nicoló Bettoni, 1829. 8° pag.84.
(Vicenza). (Besterman 122).

*Maometto, tragedia di Voltaire tradotta dall'abate Melchiorre Cesarotti.* Milano, Maria Visa, 1842. 8° pag.92.
(I-F/N, I-R/N) (Besterman 123).

*Il fanatismo ossia Maometto profeta. Tragedia in cinque atti di Voltaire liberamente tradotta in versi sciolti italiani e dedicata al chiarissimo signor conte Girolamo Dolfin da Elisa Zwonar*. Venezia, Clement, 1854. 4° pag.[5]-68.
(I-Pd, I-V) (Besterman 124).

*Biblioteca antica e moderna n.31-32. F. M. Arouet de Voltaire. Maometto. Tragedia. Traduzione di M. Cesarotti*. Torino, J. Meyer, [1884] 8° pag.84.
(I-R/N) (Besterman 125).

Polish

*Mahomet prorok; tragedya w piaciu aktach J. P. de Voltaire, z francuskiego przelozona po polsku przez J. D*[*ebour*]. Wilna 1788. pag.[v].96.
(USA-MiU).

Portuguese

*Traducção do Mafoma de Mr. de Voltaire*. Lisboa, Academia Real das Sciencias, 1785. 8° pag.112.
(CH-178) (Besterman 35).

Romanian

Fanatismul că Maxomet prooroRikul, tragedie in cinci akte, tpaduc de I. Eliad. Bukuresti, tip. lui Eliad, 1831. (Bukuresti, in tipografia lui Eliad, 1834 [1831]) 8° pag.87.
(F-P/BnF: Z.Bengesco 962).

According to the *Bibliothèque dramatique de m. de Soleinne*, iv.222, this translation by I. Eliad formed part of the latter's two volume *Théâtre valaque*.

Russian

*Магометъ въ 5 д. г. Вольмера* (translated by P. Potemkin); St Petersburg 1797. 8° pag.60. (Sopikov 11921).
*Магометъ въ 5 д. г. Вольмера* 1810 (Sopikov 11922).
*трагдія Магометъ* (translated by P. Potemkin); St Petersburg 1797. 8° pag.80. (Sopikov 2615).

Scandinavian

*Mahomet. Tragedi i Fem Akter, af Voltaire. Öfversättning af J. D. Valerius.* Stockholm, Carl Delen, 1806. 8° pag.79.
(CH-178; USA-ICU, NN) (Besterman 95).

*Mahomed. Sørgespil i 5 Acter ved Voltaire. Oversat ved Thomas Thaarup, Ridder af Dannebrogen.* Kjøbenhavn, J. F. Schultz, 1815. 8° pag.96.
(DK-C) (Besterman 96).

Spanish

*Mahoma, tragedia en 5. actos de Tomás de Iriarte*, fragment published in E. Cotarelo y Morí, *Iriarte y su época* (Madrid 1897), p.515-16, from the manuscript in the Biblioteca nacional, Madrid (ms.792222-[26]).
(Lafarga 40, Todd 199).

*Mohamned. Tragedia en cinco actos* [*de Dionisio Solís*].
(E-M/N1: ms.16186) (Lafarga 385).

*El Falso Profeta Mahoma. Tragedia en cinco actos, traducida del francés en verso castellano. Por El L.D.F.R. de L y V* [*Rodríguez de Ledesma*] Madrid, por la Viuda de D. Joaquín Ibarra, 1794. 8° pag.[viii].155.[i].
(E-M/N1) (Lafarga 268; Todd 200).

*Tragedia Heroica. El Falso Profeta Mahoma. En cinco actos,*

*traducida del francés en verso castellano por el L.D.F.R. de L y V* [*Rodríguez de Ledesma*] Barcelona, J. F. Piferrer, [n.d.]. 4° pag.32 (double column).
(GB-Lo/N1: 1342.f.2 (30)) (Lafarga 269; Todd 201).

*El Fanatismo. Tragedia en cinco actos, escrita en francés por Voltaire, traducida en castellano por D.T.B.y S.*[*?Tomás Betrán y Soler*] Barcelona, José Torner, 1821, 4° pag.30 (double column).
(Biblioteca nacional, Buenos Aires) (Lafarga 275; Todd 202).

*Mahoma ó el Fanatismo, tragedia en cinco actos, escrita en francés por Mr Voltaire, y traducida al castellano por José Palacios.* Cuzco, Juan Bautista Santa-Cruz, 1840. 8° pag.[iv].45.
(Todd 203).

*El Fanatismo. Tragedia en cinco actos, original de Voltaire, traducida libremente del francés por D. José Maria Heredia.* [1836]. Published in the *Revista de Cuba* 9 (1881), p.140-52, 229-42, 447-60, 559-74.
(Todd 204).

*El Fanatismo. Tragedia por Voltaire. Traducida al castellano por Jesús Echaiz.* Mexico, Ignacio Cumplido, 1871. 12° pag.120.
(Biblioteca nacional, Mexico) (Todd 205).

## 9. *The present edition*

We take as our base text of the play and of the prefatory matter that of the Cramer in-4° collective edition of 1768 (w68), which gives the text as finally revised by Voltaire. We choose this edition rather than the more usual 'édition encadrée' of 1775 (w75G). In the case of *Mahomet*, the text does not appear to have been revised in the latter edition, which even introduces some doubtful readings. We have also remained faithful to w68 in the case of act II lines 42 and 292, even though Kehl and Beuchot reverted to earlier variants for reasons that do not seem to us to be entirely justified. We feel sure that w68 gives us the text as Voltaire finally wanted it, whatever may have been his reasons for hesitating over it earlier. The only two places where we do not follow w68 are act I line 233, where it has 'appas' for 'appât', and act V line 17, where like other contemporary editions it misuses the partitive in 'des secrets chemins'. Finally, in act V we add the stage instruction 'A Omar' between lines 186 and 187.

Because of the importance of pirated and otherwise seemingly unauthorized editions in the development of the text, we include in the variants a number of obvious but repeated errors. They help us to identify families of editions. Some editions are obviously more important than others, and in our general bibliography the sigla of those editions which mark a new step in the nine major stages in the development of the printed text are preceded by the appropriate letter in brackets, ranging from A to I, followed by an asterisk, thus:

(A*) 42X1, (B*) 42B1, (C*) 42B5, (D*) 43A3, (E*) w48D, (F*) 51B, (G*) w52, (H*) w56, (I*) w68.

This means that while allowing for minor variants we can nevertheless identify families of editions, and show that many, despite their date, hark back to earlier versions:

(A*) 42X1, 42X2
(B*) 42B1-42B4, 43A1-43A2, 47A
(C*) 42B5, 52B, 60B, 62B, 67B, 68P, 77P2, 78B
(–) 42XX
(D*) 43A3, 45A, w50, 53A
(–) w46
(E*) w48D, T53, 54V, T64G, w64R
(F*) 51B
(–) w51
(–) T62, T64A
(–) w64G, w70G, w72X
(–) 71P1-71P2, 74A
(G*) w52
(H*) w56, w57G1, T66, T68, T70, T73A2

(–) w57P, T64P, T67, 70P
(–) 67C
(–) W70L
(I*) w68, w71, w72P
(–) T73A1, T77
(–) 73P, 73M, 77P1, 78P
(–) 73X, T76X
(–) w75G, w75X
(–) K.

## Modernisation of the basic text

The spelling of the names of persons and places in w68 has been respected, although we have added accents to: Cévennes, Salcède. The punctuation has been retained, except in act V line 103 of the play, where we have replaced a comma by a colon, as it precedes reported direct speech beginning with a capital letter. We have added the final s to the second person singular in the present tense of the verb 'arracher' in act IV line 225. We have respected the use of italics, except in the case of the *Avis de l'Editeur* and of the exchange of letters with the pope, which were entirely printed in italics. We also give the names of people in ordinary print.

The spelling and use of accents varies a great deal. The following aspects of orthography and grammar have been modified to conform to modern usage:

1. Consonants
- the consonant *d* was not used in: apprens, comprens, entens, prens, prétens, remors, rens, répons.
- the consonant *p* was not used in: longtems, tems.
- the consonant *t* was not used in the syllable endings *-ans* and *-ens*: ardens, brûlans, châtimens, commencemens, compatissans, déréglemens, différens, embrasemens, embrassemens, emportemens, enfans, errans, expirans, gémissans, innocens, languissans, méchans, moments, mourans, mouvemens, parens, penchans, pressentimens, ressentimens, sanglans, sentimens, sermens, surprenans, talens, touchans.
- double consonants were used in: allarmes, appaiser, appellé, appeller, infidelle, jettais, jetté.

- a single consonant was used in: apesanti, couroux, dévelopé, échapé, falu.
- the archaic form was used in: avanture, domter, entousiaste, étendarts, phrénésie, sheich, vuide. Even in prose one finds 'encor' and 'remercîment'. One also finds older forms in Spanish ('sanctos') and Italian ('honorarmi').

2. Vowels

- *y* was used in the place of *i* in: asyle, ayeux, croye, envoye, enyvré(e), joye, noye, paye, playe, proye, vraye(s)

3. Accents

The acute accent

- was used in place of the grave in: achévera, déréglement, élévera, piéce(s), siécle, siége, troisiéme.
- was only incompletely used in: societé

The grave accent

- was not used in: déja.

The circumflex accent

- was used in: accoûtumés, ajoûtez, ajoûter, assûrément, blasphême(s), interprête, lû, nâquit, ôtage, prophête, pû, toûjours, vû.
- was not used in: ame, chaine, connait, enchainer, entraine, grace, idolatrie, infame, maitre.
- was occasionally missing in the imperfect subjunctive: vint, n'entendit.

The dieresis

- was used in: abattuë, avouë, avouë, éperduë, étenduë, inconnuë, poëma, poëme, poësie, poëta, prévenuë, rompuë, ruïne, vuë.

4. Abbreviation

- Mr. now becomes M.

5. Capitalisation

- we have restored the capital letter in the first word of the title: sa Majesté.
- we have suppressed capitals in the following nouns: Agosto, Août, Dieux, Duc, Esclaves, Francese, Latino, Lieutenant, Magistrats, Ministres, Monarchi, Monarque, Pontifici, Prélats, Prince, Religion, Religione, Roi(s), Sanctos, Sénat, Sénateur, Shérif, Souverain,

Vicario. We keep the capital for 'Dieu' only when it is used in the singular and without an article. We do not follow the habit of printing some words in capitals throughout: VOTRE MAJESTÉ, DIEU, GRAND PRINCE, PADRE, DIO.

– initial capitals were attributed to adjectives denoting nationality: Espagnol, Française, Romain.

6. Points of grammar

– the final s was not used in the second person singular of the imperative: agi, appren, banni, conçoi, connai, croi, di, éclairci, fai, fui, pren, reçoi, répon, revien, soutien, vien, voi.
– the plural in -x was used in: loix.
– the inversion of the first person singular of *pouvoir* was written thus: puissai-je.
– the indefinite pronominal expression 'quoi que' is written like the conjunction 'quoique'.

7. Various

– the ampersand was used throughout, except at the beginning of sentences.
– the hyphen was used in: mal-entendus, non-seulement, sens-commun, tout-puissant, très-dangereux, très-nombreuse, très-sûr.

# LE FANATISME,
# OU
# MAHOMET LE PROPHÈTE,
# TRAGÉDIE

# AVIS DE L'ÉDITEUR[1]

J'ai cru rendre service aux amateurs des belles-lettres, de publier une tragédie du *Fanatisme*, si défigurée en France par deux éditions subreptices. Je sais très certainement qu'elle fut composée par l'auteur en 1736, et que dès-lors il en envoya une copie au Prince Royal, depuis roi de Prusse, qui cultivait les lettres avec 5 des succès surprenants, et qui en fait encore son délassement principal.

J'étais à Lille en 1741, quand Monsieur de Voltaire y vint passer quelques jours; il y avait la meilleure troupe d'acteurs qui ait jamais été en province. Elle représenta cet ouvrage d'une manière 10 qui satisfit beaucoup une très nombreuse assemblée; le Gouverneur de la province et l'Intendant y assistèrent plusieurs fois. On trouva que cette pièce était d'un goût si nouveau, et ce sujet si délicat parut traité avec tant de sagesse, que plusieurs prélats

a-107 42X1-43A2: [*absent*]

1 W52: de belles-lettres
11 W51: une nombreuse assemblée;

[1] This *Avis* first appeared in 1743 (see 43A3). There is little doubt that Voltaire was the author. Describing the Ledet 1743 edition of *Mahomet*, the *Bibliothèque française* said that the play was 'précédée d'un Avis d'un prétendu éditeur, qui n'est sans aucun doute que m. de Voltaire lui-même, qui s'efforce assez vainement de justifier l'horreur qu'a généralement causé une pièce où l'on ne voit qu'assassinat, que parricide et qu'inceste' (*Bibliothèque française*, 1743, xxxvi.178). In his comments on the Kehl edition Wagnière states that: 'L'avis de l'éditeur est de Mr. de V.' (Andrew Brown, 'Calendar of Voltaire manuscripts other than correspondence', *SVEC* 77, 1970, p.47).

voulurent en voir une représentation par les mêmes acteurs dans 15
une maison particulière.[2] Ils en jugèrent comme le public.

L'auteur fut encore assez heureux pour faire parvenir son manuscrit entre les mains d'un des premiers hommes de l'Europe et de l'Eglise, (*a*) qui soutenait le poids des affaires avec fermeté, et qui jugeait des ouvrages d'esprit avec un goût très sûr, dans un âge 20
où les hommes parviennent rarement, et où l'on conserve encore plus rarement son esprit et sa délicatesse. Il dit, que la pièce était écrite avec toute la circonspection convenable, et qu'on ne pouvait éviter plus sagement les écueils du sujet; mais que pour ce qui regardait la poésie, il y avait encore des choses à corriger. Je sais en 25
effet, que l'auteur les a retouchées avec beaucoup de soin. Ce fut aussi le sentiment d'un homme qui tient le même rang, et qui n'a pas moins de lumières.[3]

Enfin, l'ouvrage, approuvé d'ailleurs selon toutes les formes ordinaires, fut représenté à Paris le 9 d'août 1742. Il y avait une 30
loge entière remplie des premiers magistrats de cette ville; des ministres y furent présents. Ils pensèrent tous comme les hommes éclairés que j'ai déjà cités.

(*a*) Le cardinal de Fleury.

15 T64G: voulurent en avoir
K: voulurent avoir une représentation

19-20 43A3, 45A, W46, W48D, W50, W51, W52, 53A, T53, W57P, W64R, T64G, T64P, T67: soutient le poids des affaires avec fermeté, et qui juge des

30 K: le 9 d'auguste

32 43A3, 45A, W46, W48D, W51, 53A, T53, T64G, W64R, K: ministres même y furent

n.*a* 43A-W51 [*absent*]

[2] The fourth and last performance was given 'chez l'intendant m. de la Grandville, en son hôtel, rue Française. A cette dernière assistaient des personnalités de haut rang et même des chanoines de Saint-Pierre, qui avaient manifesté le désir de voir la pièce' (Lefèvre, *Histoire du théâtre de Lille*, i.235).

[3] No doubt cardinal Tencin, see D2643.

Il se trouva (*b*) à cette première représentation quelques personnes qui ne furent pas de ce sentiment unanime. Soit que dans la rapidité de la représentation ils n'eussent pas suivi assez le fil de l'ouvrage, soit qu'ils fussent peu accoutumés au théâtre, ils furent blessés que Mahomet ordonnât un meurtre, et se servît de sa religion pour encourager à l'assassinat un jeune homme qu'il fait l'instrument de son crime. Ces personnes, frappées de cette atrocité, ne firent pas assez réflexion qu'elle est donnée dans la pièce comme le plus horrible de tous les crimes, et que même il est moralement impossible qu'elle puisse être donnée autrement. En un mot, ils ne virent qu'un côté; ce qui est la manière la plus ordinaire de se tromper. Ils avaient raison assurément d'être scandalisés, en ne considérant que ce côté qui les révoltait. Un peu plus d'attention les aurait aisément ramenés. Mais, dans la première chaleur de leur zèle ils dirent, que la pièce était un ouvrage très dangereux, fait pour former des Ravaillac et des Jacques Clément.

On est bien surpris d'un tel jugement, et ces Messieurs l'ont désavoué sans doute. Ce serait dire qu'Hermione enseigne à assassiner un roi, qu'Electre apprend à tuer sa mère, que Cléopâtre et Médée montrent à tuer leurs enfants. Ce serait dire que Harpagon forme des avares, le Joueur des joueurs, Tartuffe des hypocrites. L'injustice même contre *Mahomet* serait bien plus grande que contre toutes ces pièces; car le crime du faux prophète y est mis dans un jour beaucoup plus odieux, que ne l'est aucun des

(*b*) Le fait est que l'abbé Desfontaines et quelques hommes aussi méchants que lui dénoncèrent cet ouvrage comme scandaleux et impie; et cela fit tant de bruit, que le cardinal de Fleury, premier ministre, qui avait lu et approuvé la pièce, fut obligé de conseiller à l'auteur de la retirer.

37 W50, W51: ils ne fussent pas accoutumés
W75G: qu'ils fussent accoutumés
54 W57P, T64P, T67: joueurs, le Tartuffe des
56-57 W51: prophète est mis
n.*b* 43A3-W51: [*absent*]
W57P, T64P, T67: que des gens mal intentionnés dénoncèrent

vices et des dérèglements que toutes ces pièces représentent. C'est précisément contre les Ravaillac et les Jacques Clément que la pièce est composée; ce qui a fait dire à un homme de beaucoup 60 d'esprit, que si *Mahomet* avait été écrit du temps de Henri III et de Henri IV cet ouvrage leur aurait sauvé la vie.[4] Est-il possible, qu'on ait pu faire un tel reproche à l'auteur de *la Henriade*; lui qui a élevé sa voix si souvent dans ce poème et ailleurs, je ne dis pas seulement contre de tels attentats, mais contre toutes les maximes 65 qui peuvent y conduire?

J'avoue, que plus j'ai lu les ouvrages de cet écrivain, plus je les ai trouvés caractérisés par l'amour du bien public; il inspire partout l'horreur contre les emportements de la rébellion, de la persécution et du fanatisme. Y a-t-il un bon citoyen qui n'adopte toutes les 70 maximes de *la Henriade*? Ce poème ne fait-il pas aimer la véritable vertu? Mahomet me paraît écrit entièrement dans le même esprit, et je suis persuadé que ses plus grands ennemis en conviendront.

Il vit bientôt, qu'il se formait contre lui une cabale dangereuse; les plus ardents avaient parlé à des hommes en place, qui ne 75 pouvant voir la représentation de la pièce, devaient les en croire. L'illustre Molière, la gloire de la France, s'était trouvé autrefois à peu-près dans le même cas, lorsqu'on joua le *Tartuffe*; il eut recours directement à Louis le Grand, dont il était connu et aimé. L'autorité de ce monarque dissipa bientôt les interprétations 80 sinistres qu'on donnait au *Tartuffe*. Mais les temps sont différents; la protection qu'on accorde à des arts tout nouveaux, ne peut pas être toujours la même, après que ces arts ont été longtemps cultivés. D'ailleurs, tel artiste n'est pas à portée d'obtenir ce qu'un autre a eu aisément. Il eût fallu des mouvements, des discussions, 85 un nouvel examen. L'auteur jugea plus à propos de retirer sa pièce lui-même, après la troisième représentation, attendant que le

82 W46, W48D, W50, W51, W52, T53, T64G, W64R: tous nouveaux

[4] Fontenelle – the usual source of such witticisms – said that the play was 'horriblement beau' (Clément and La Porte, *Anecdotes*, i.504).

temps adoucît quelques esprits prévenus ce qui ne peut manquer d'arriver dans une nation aussi spirituelle et aussi éclairée que la française.(*c*) On mit dans les nouvelles publiques que la tragédie de *Mahomet* avait été défendue par le gouvernement. Je puis assurer, qu'il n'y a rien de plus faux. Non seulement il n'y a pas eu le moindre ordre donné à ce sujet, mais il s'en faut beaucoup que les premières têtes de l'Etat, qui virent la représentation, aient varié un moment sur la sagesse qui règne dans cet ouvrage.

Quelques personnes ayant transcrit à la hâte plusieurs scènes aux représentations, et ayant eu un ou deux rôles des acteurs, en ont fabriqué les éditions qu'on a faites clandestinement. Il est aisé de voir à quel point elles diffèrent du véritable ouvrage que je donne ici. Cette tragédie est précédée de plusieurs pièces intéressantes, dont une des plus curieuses, à mon gré, est la lettre que l'auteur écrivit à Sa Majesté le roi de Prusse, lorsqu'il repassa par la Hollande, après être allé rendre ses respects à ce monarque. C'est dans de telles lettres, qui ne sont pas d'abord destinées à être publiques, qu'on voit les véritables sentiments des hommes. J'espère qu'elles feront aux véritables philosophes le même plaisir qu'elles m'ont fait.

(*c*) Ce que l'éditeur semblait espérer en 1742 est arrivé en 1751. La pièce fut représentée alors avec un prodigieux concours. Les cabales et les persécutions cédèrent au cri public, d'autant plus qu'on commençait à sentir quelque honte d'avoir forcé à quitter sa patrie un homme qui travaillait pour elle.

99-101 43A3, 45A, W46, W48D, W50, W51, W52, 53A, T53, W57P, T64G, T64P, W64R, T67: véritable ouvrage que je tiens de la main d'un homme irréprochable, ainsi que les autres pièces que je donne dans l'Edition présente. La plus curieuse, à mon gré,

105-107 43A3, 45A, W46, W48D, W50, W51, W52, 53A, T53, W57P, T64G, T64P, W64R, T67: hommes. Celle que j'ai eue encore d'un ami de feu Mr de Sgravesende est de ce genre. J'espère qu'elle fera aux véritables philosophes le même plaisir qu'elle m'a fait.

*A Amsterdam, le 18 de novembre 1742.*

*P.D.L.M.*

n.*c* 43A3-W51: [*absent*]

## À SA MAJESTÉ LE ROI DE PRUSSE[1]

A Rotterdam 20 janvier 1742.

SIRE,

Je ressemble à présent aux pèlerins de la Mecque, qui tournent leurs yeux vers cette ville après l'avoir quittée: je tourne les miens vers votre cour. Mon cœur, pénétré des bontés de Votre Majesté, ne connaît que la douleur de ne pouvoir vivre auprès d'elle. Je prends la liberté de lui envoyer une nouvelle copie de cette tragédie de *Mahomet*, dont elle a bien voulu, il y a déjà longtemps, voir les premières esquisses. C'est un tribut que je paie à l'amateur des arts, au juge éclairé, surtout au philosophe, beaucoup plus qu'au souverain.

Votre Majesté sait quel esprit m'animait en composant cet ouvrage. L'amour du genre humain et l'horreur du fanatisme, deux vertus qui sont faites pour être toujours auprès de votre trône, ont conduit ma plume. J'ai toujours pensé que la tragédie ne doit pas être un simple spectacle, qui touche le cœur sans le corriger. Qu'importe au genre humain les passions et les malheurs d'un héros de l'antiquité, s'ils ne servent pas à nous instruire? On avoue que la comédie de *Tartuffe*, ce chef-d'œuvre qu'aucune

a-170 42X1-43A2: [*absent*]
6 51B, W51: de vous envoyer

[1] This letter first appears in 43A3. Voltaire wrote to d'Argental in November 1742: 'Il n'y a point d'épitre dédicatoire au roy de Prusse, mais on imprime une lettre que je luy avois écritte il y a deux ans en luy envoiant un exemplaire manuscrit de la pièce' (D2683). This account would place the letter in 1740, and it can be supposed that the date of January 1742 was added by Voltaire at the time of printing. Th. Besterman prints the letter from a manuscript copy headed in Voltaire's hand 'Copie d'une lettre écritte au roy de Prusse' (Copenhagen, Kongelige Bibliothek, Ny kgl. Saml. 580, 4°); variants from the base text are minor.

nation n'a égalé, a fait beaucoup de bien aux hommes, en montrant l'hypocrisie dans toute sa laideur. Ne peut-on pas essayer d'attaquer dans une tragédie, cette espèce d'imposture qui met en œuvre à la fois l'hypocrisie des uns et la fureur des autres? Ne peut-on pas remonter jusqu'à ces anciens scélérats, fondateurs illustres de la superstition et du fanatisme, qui les premiers ont pris le couteau sur l'autel pour faire des victimes de ceux qui refusaient d'être leurs disciples?

Ceux qui diront que les temps de ces crimes sont passés, qu'on ne verra plus de Barcochebas, de Mahomets, de Jeans de Leyde, etc. que les flammes des guerres de religion sont éteintes, font, ce me semble, trop d'honneur à la nature humaine. Le même poison subsiste encore, quoique moins développé: cette peste, qui semble étouffée, reproduit de temps en temps des germes capables d'infecter la terre. N'a-t-on pas vu de nos jours les prophètes des Cévennes tuer au nom de Dieu ceux de leur secte qui n'étaient pas assez soumis?

L'action, que j'ai peinte, est atroce; et je ne sais, si l'horreur a été plus loin sur aucun théâtre. C'est un jeune homme né avec de la vertu, qui séduit par son fanatisme, assassine un vieillard qui l'aime, et qui dans l'idée de servir Dieu, se rend coupable, sans le savoir, d'un parricide; c'est un imposteur qui ordonne ce meurtre, et qui promet à l'assassin un inceste pour récompense. J'avoue, que c'est mettre l'horreur sur le théâtre; et Votre Majesté est bien persuadée, qu'il ne faut pas que la tragédie consiste uniquement dans une déclaration d'amour, une jalousie et un mariage.

Nos historiens même nous apprennent des actions plus atroces que celle que j'ai inventée. Seïde ne sait pas du moins que celui qu'il assassine est son père; et quand il a porté le coup, il éprouve un repentir aussi grand que son crime. Mais Mézerai rapporte, qu'à Melun un père tua son fils de sa main pour sa religion, et n'en eut

24 51B: illustres des superstitions et du
27 T64A: diront que le temps
32 W52: temps de germes

aucun repentir.[2] On connaît l'aventure des deux frères Diaz, dont l'un était à Rome, et l'autre en Allemagne, dans les commencements des troubles excités par Luther. Barthelemi Diaz apprenant à Rome, que son frère donnait dans les opinions de Luther à Francfort, part de Rome dans le dessein de l'assassiner, arrive et l'assassine.[3] J'ai lu dans Herrera,[4] auteur espagnol, que ce *Barthelemi Diaz risquait beaucoup par cette action; mais que rien n'ébranle un homme d'honneur quand la probité le conduit.* Herrera, dans une religion toute sainte et toute ennemie de la cruauté, dans une religion qui enseigne à souffrir et non à se venger, était donc persuadé que la probité peut conduire à l'assassinat et au parricide! Et on ne s'élèvera pas de tous côtés contre ces maximes infernales!

Ce sont ces maximes qui mirent le poignard à la main du monstre qui priva la France de Henri le Grand: voilà ce qui plaça le portrait de Jacques Clément sur l'autel, et son nom parmi les bienheureux: c'est ce qui coûta la vie à Guillaume prince d'Orange, fondateur de la liberté et de la grandeur des Hollandais. D'abord Salcede le blessa au front d'un coup de pistolet:[5] et

66 w50: et la grandeur

[2] I have not been able to locate the source of this story. For the other examples of fanaticism described here see Mézeray's *Histoire de France* (1643-1651), ii.898-901, iii.649-52, 736-37, 1055-56, 1112-14. At his death Voltaire possessed two editions of Mézeray's *Abrégé chronologique de l'histoire de France* (BV2443-2444).

[3] 'Mais m. de V. plus familiarisé avec Melpomène qu'avec Clio, et aussi peu heureux ici en fait d'histoire que dans son *Essai sur les guerres civiles de France*, n'a pas pris garde que ce prétendu Barthélemy Diaz se nommait Alfonse, et commit son assassinat à Neubourg et non point à Francfort' (*Bibliothèque française*, 1743, xxxvi.179). For a similar passage on the same murder, see the beginning of the article 'Fanatisme' in the *Dictionnaire philosophique*, *OC*, vol.36, p.105-106.

[4] *Comentarios de los hechos de los Españoles, Franceses y Venecianos en Italia y de otras repúblicas* (Madrid 1624).

[5] 'Ce fut Jaurigny, et non point Salcède, qui *blessa le prince d'Orange d'un coup de pistolet*, non *au front*, mais *aux deux joues* qu'il traversa de part en part, sans toutefois offenser les dents, la langue ni le palais, ainsi que s'en explique le *Journal de Henri III*, ou bien une ou deux dents près, comme le prétend Strada' (*Bibliothèque française*, 1743, xxxvi.179). For a more accurate rendition by Voltaire himself, see *Essai sur les mœurs*, ii.447

Strada[6] raconte que *Salcede* (ce sont ces propres mots) n'osa entreprendre cette action qu'après avoir purifié son âme par la confession aux pieds d'un Dominicain, et l'avoir fortifiée par le pain céleste. Herrera dit quelque chose de plus insensé et de plus atroce: *Estando firme con el exemplo de nuestro Salvador Jesu Christo y de sus santos*. Balthazar Gérard, qui ôta enfin la vie à ce grand homme, en usa de même que Salcède. 70

Je remarque, que tous ceux qui ont commis de bonne foi de pareils crimes étaient de jeunes gens comme Seïde. Balthazar Gérard avait environ vingt ans. Quatre Espagnols, qui avaient fait avec lui serment de tuer le prince, étaient de même âge. Le monstre qui tua Henri III[7] n'avait que vingt-quatre ans. Poltrot, qui assassina le grand duc de Guise, en avait vingt-cinq; c'est le temps de la séduction et de la fureur. J'ai été presque témoin en Angleterre de ce que peut sur une imagination jeune et faible la force du fanatisme. Un enfant de seize ans, nommé Shepherd,[8] se chargea d'assassiner le roi George I, votre aïeul maternel. Quelle était la cause qui le portait à cette frénésie? C'était uniquement que 75 80 85

72 43A3, 45A, W46, W48D, W50, W51, W52, 53A, T53, W57P, T64G, T64P, W64R, T66, T67, T68, T70: Salvadore

76 51B, K: étaient des jeunes gens

77 43A3, 45A, W46, W48D, W50, W51, 51B, 53A, T53, W64R: avait environ vingt années.

78 T64P, T67, K: étaient du même âge

78-79 43A3, 45A, W46, 53A: de même âge. Le monstre de Henri III

[6] Famiano Strada, *De bello belgico* (Romæ 1632). Voltaire quotes the Latin in the Notebooks, *OC*, vol.81, p.401, vol.82, p.610.

[7] The *Bibliothèque française* commented as follows on the original published version of this passage: 'Quant au *monstre de Henri III* [...], on ne sait d'abord ce que veut signifier une expression si extraordinaire; et ce n'est qu'après quelques efforts de réflexion, qu'on reconnaît enfin que m. de V. aussi néologique en cela qu'aucun de ceux contre lesquels il s'élève quelquefois si dédaigneusement, a prétendu parler de l'exécrable Jacques Clément, assassin de Henri III, à qui cette expression aussi équivoque qu'hétéroclite est beaucoup moins injurieuse qu'à ce malheureux prince' (*Bibliothèque française*, xxxvi.179).

[8] Cf. the Notebooks, *OC*, vol.81, p.402.

Shepherd n'était pas de la même religion que le roi. On eut pitié de sa jeunesse, on lui offrit sa grâce, on le sollicita longtemps au repentir; il persista toujours à dire, qu'il valait mieux obéir à Dieu qu'aux hommes, et que s'il était libre, le premier usage qu'il ferait de sa liberté serait de tuer son prince. Ainsi on fut obligé de l'envoyer au supplice comme un monstre qu'on désespérait d'apprivoiser. 90

J'ose dire, que quiconque a un peu vécu avec les hommes, a pu voir quelquefois combien aisément on est prêt à sacrifier la nature à la superstition. Que de pères ont détesté et déshérité leurs enfants! que de frères ont poursuivi leurs frères par ce funeste principe! J'en ai vu des exemples dans plus d'une famille. 95

Si la superstition ne se signale pas toujours par ces excès qui sont comptés dans l'histoire des crimes, elle fait dans la société tous les petits maux innombrables et journaliers qu'elle peut faire. Elle désunit les amis, elle divise les parents; elle persécute le sage, qui n'est qu'homme de bien, par la main du fou qui est enthousiaste. Elle ne donne pas toujours de la ciguë à Socrate, mais elle bannit Descartes d'une ville[9] qui devait être l'asile de la liberté; elle donne à Jurieu, qui faisait le prophète, assez de crédit pour réduire à la pauvreté le savant et le philosophe Bayle. Elle bannit, elle arrache à une florissante jeunesse qui court à ses leçons, le successeur du grand Leibnitz;[10] et il faut pour le rétablir que le ciel fasse naître un roi philosophe; vrai miracle qu'il fait bien rarement. En vain la raison humaine se perfectionne par la philosophie qui fait tant de progrès en Europe; en vain, vous surtout, Grand Prince, vous efforcez-vous de pratiquer et d'inspirer cette philosophie si hu- 100 105 110

106 43A3, 45A, W46, W48D, W51, 53A, T53, T64G, W64R: les savants et le philosophe
W50: le savant, le philosophe
T76X, K: le savant et philosophe Bayle
111 T64P, T67: vous efforcerez-vous

[9] Amsterdam.
[10] Wolff.

maine; on voit dans ce même siècle, où la raison élève son trône d'un côté, le plus absurde fanatisme dresser encore ses autels de l'autre.

On pourra me reprocher que, donnant trop à mon zèle je fais commettre dans cette pièce un crime à Mahomet, dont en effet il ne fut point coupable. 115

M. le comte de Boulainvilliers écrivit, il y a quelques années, la vie de ce prophète.[11] Il essaya de le faire passer pour un grand homme, que la Providence avait choisi pour punir les Chrétiens, et pour changer la face d'une partie du monde. M. Sale, qui nous a donné une excellente version de l'Alcoran en Anglais,[12] veut faire regarder Mahomet comme un Numa et comme un Thésée. J'avoue, qu'il faudrait le respecter si, né prince légitime, ou appelé au gouvernement par le suffrage des siens, il avait donné des lois paisibles comme Numa, ou défendu ses compatriotes, comme on le dit de Thésée. Mais qu'un marchand de chameaux excite une sédition dans sa bourgade; qu'associé à quelques malheureux Coracites, il leur persuade, qu'il s'entretient avec l'ange Gabriel; qu'il se vante d'avoir été ravi au ciel, et d'y avoir reçu une partie de ce livre inintelligible, qui fait frémir le sens commun à chaque page; que pour faire respecter ce livre il porte dans sa patrie le fer et la flamme; qu'il égorge les pères; qu'il ravisse les filles; qu'il donne aux vaincus le choix de sa religion ou de la mort; c'est assurément ce que nul homme ne peut excuser, à moins qu'il ne soit né Turc, et que la superstition n'étouffe en lui toute lumière naturelle. 120 125 130 135

Je sais que Mahomet n'a pas tramé précisément l'espèce de trahison qui fait le sujet de cette tragédie. L'histoire dit seulement qu'il enleva la femme de Seïde, l'un de ses disciples, et qu'il 140

118 W52, W56, W57P, T64P, T67: le comte Boulanvilliers
124 51B: Mais j'avoue
132-133 T64A: porte sa patrie

[11] Voltaire's debt to Boulainvilliers is discussed in the introduction, p.9-17.
[12] London 1734. BV1786. Voltaire had read it by 1738 (D1588).

persécuta Abusosian, que je nomme Zopire; mais quiconque fait la guerre à son pays, et ose la faire au nom de Dieu, n'est-il pas capable de tout? Je n'ai pas prétendu mettre seulement une action vraie sur la scène, mais des mœurs vraies, faire penser les hommes comme ils pensent dans les circonstances où ils se trouvent, et représenter enfin ce que la fourberie peut inventer de plus atroce, et ce que le fanatisme peut exécuter de plus horrible. Mahomet n'est ici autre chose que Tartuffe les armes à la main.

Je me croirai bien récompensé de mon travail, si quelqu'une de ces âmes faibles, toujours prêtes à recevoir les impressions d'une fureur étrangère qui n'est pas au fond de leur cœur, peut s'affermir contre ces funestes séductions par la lecture de cet ouvrage; si après avoir eu en horreur la malheureuse obéissance de Seïde, elle se dit à elle même: pourquoi obéirais-je en aveugle à des aveugles qui me crient: Haïssez, persécutez, perdez celui qui est assez téméraire pour n'être pas de notre avis sur des choses même indifférentes que nous n'entendons pas? Que ne puis-je servir à déraciner de tels sentiments chez les hommes! L'esprit d'indulgence ferait des frères, celui d'intolérance peut former des monstres.

C'est ainsi que pense Votre Majesté. Ce serait pour moi la plus grande des consolations de vivre auprès de ce roi philosophe. Mon attachement est égal à mes regrets; et si d'autres devoirs m'entraînent, ils n'effaceront jamais de mon cœur les sentiments que je dois à ce prince, qui pense et qui parle en homme; qui fuit cette fausse gravité sous laquelle se cachent toujours la petitesse et l'ignorance; qui se communique avec liberté, parce qu'il ne craint point d'être pénétré; qui veut toujours s'instruire, et qui peut instruire les plus éclairés.

Je serai toute ma vie avec le plus profond respect et la plus vive reconnaissance, &c.

144 W52: mais de mœurs
159 43A3, 45A: former de monstres.
170 43A3, 45A, W46, 53A: reconnaissance, Sire, de Votre Majesté le très humble et très obéissant serviteur, VOLTAIRE.
A Rotterdam, ce 20 de Janvier 1742.

# LETTRE DE M. DE VOLTAIRE AU PAPE BENOIT XIV[1]

Bmo. Padre,

La Santità Vostra perdonerà l'ardire che prende uno de' più infimi fedeli, ma uno de' maggiori ammiratori della virtù, di sottomettere al capo della vera religione questa opera contro il fondatore d'una falsa e barbara setta. 5

A chi potrei più convenevolmente dedicare la satira della crudeltà e degli errori d'un falso profeta, che al vicario ed imitatore d'un Dio di verità e di mansuetudine?

Vostra Santità mi conceda dunque di poter mettere a i suoi piedi il libretto e l'autore, e di domandare umilmente la sua protezzione 10 per l'uno, e le sue benedizioni per l'altro. In tanto profundissimamente m'inchino, e le baccio i sacri piedi.

Parigi, 17 agosto 1745.

a-13 42X1-47A: [*absent*]
1-13 W57P, T64P and T67 [*with translation*]:
Très-Saint Père, ¶Si je suis un des moins élevés des fidèles, je suis un des plus grands admirateurs de votre vertu. J'espère donc que Sa Sainteté voudra bien pardonner la liberté que je prends de soumettre au chef de la vraie religion un ouvrage fait contre le fondateur d'une secte fausse et barbare. ¶A qui, mieux qu'au vicaire et qu'à l'imitateur d'un Dieu de paix et de vérité, pourrais-je dédier cette satire de la cruauté et des erreurs d'un faux prophète? ¶Que Votre Sainteté veuille donc bien permettre que, mettant à ses pieds et l'ouvrage et l'auteur, je lui demande sa protection pour l'un et sa bénédiction pour l'autre. C'est dans ces sentiments de la plus profonde humilité que je m'abaisse devant Elle, et que je lui baise les pieds. ¶*A Paris le 17 Août 1745.*
[*The translation in* K *differs*]
4 K: contra

[1] Prospero Lambertini, pope 1740-1758.

# RÉPONSE DU SOUVERAIN PONTIFE BENOÎT XIV À M. DE VOLTAIRE

*BENEDICTUS P.P. XIV, dilecto filio Salutem et Apostolicam benedictionem.*

Settimane sono ci fu presentato da sua parte la sua bellissima tragedia di *Mahomet*, la quale leggemmo con sommo piacere. [1] Poi

a-31 42X1-47A: [*absent*]

1-31 W57P, T64P and T67 [*with translation*]:

*BENOÎT XIV, Pape, à son cher fils, salut et bénédiction apostolique.* ¶On nous présenta de votre part, il y a quelques semaines, votre belle tragédie de *Mahomet*, à la lecture de laquelle nous prîmes un grand plaisir. Le Cardinal Passioneï nous a présenté depuis, en votre nom, votre excellent poème de *Fontenoy*. Monseigneur Leprotti nous a encore donné le distique, que vous avez fait pour être mis au bas de notre portrait. Hier matin enfin, le Cardinal Valentini nous présenta votre lettre datée du 17 août. Sensible à cette continuité d'attentions, nous y voyons mille choses, de chacune desquelles nous nous reconnaissons obligés de vous remercier en particulier. Nous vous en remercions en général, et, vous rendant les grâces qui vous sont dues pour votre bonté singulière envers nous, nous vous assurons de notre estime pour votre mérite justement applaudi. ¶Le distique dont nous avons parlé ci-dessus (*), ayant été rendu public à Rome, on nous a rapporté qu'un homme de lettres de votre pays avait trouvé une faute de quantité dans le second vers, prétendant que le mot hic que vous avez fait bref, doit toujours être long. ¶Notre réponse a été qu'il se trompait, que ce mot pouvait être long ou bref, d'après les exemples qu'on en voit dans les poètes, et que Virgile, qui l'avait employé comme bref dans le vers suivant, ¶*Solus hic inflexit sensus, animumque labantem*, ¶ l'avait employé comme long dans celui-ci: ¶*Hic finis Priami fatorum, hic exitus illum.* ¶Il nous semble avoir répondu bien à propos, y ayant surtout plus de cinquante ans que nous n'avons lu Virgile. Quoique l'objet de la dispute vous regarde personnellement, nous avons une si bonne idée de votre sincérité et de votre droiture, que nous vous laissons décider qui a tort sur le point dont il s'agit, de nous ou de votre censeur. Nous finissons en vous donnant notre bénédiction apostolique. ¶*Donné à Rome à Sainte Marie Majeure, le 17* [*sic*] *septembre 1745, et de notre Pontificat le sixième.*'

[*The translation in* K *differs*]

1-2 W48D, W50, 51B, W51, W52, T53, 54V, W57P, T64P, W64R, T67: salutem apostolicam et benedictionem

[1] Voltaire forged the reference to *Mahomet*; see the notes to D3210, and

ci presentò il Cardinal Passionei in di lei nome il suo eccelente poema di *Fontenoy*[2] ... Monsignor Leprotti ci diede poscia il distico fatto da lei sotto il nostro ritratto.[3] Ieri mattina il Cardinal Valenti ci presentò la di lei lettera del 17 agosto. In questa serie d'azzioni si contengono molti capi per ciascheduno de' quali ci reconosciamo in obbligo di ringraziarla. Noi gli uniamo tutti assieme, e rendiamo a lei le dovute grazie per cosi singolare bontà verso di noi, assicurandola che abbiamo tutta la dovuta stima del suo tanto applaudito merito.

Publicato in Roma il di lei distico (*a*) sopradetto, ci su riserito esservi stato un suo pæsano letterato che in una publica conversazione aveva detto peccare in una sillaba, avendo fatta la parola *hic* breve, quando sempre deve esser longa.

Rispondemmo che sbagliava, potendo essere la parola e breve e longa, conforme vuole il poeta, avendola Virgilio fatta breve in quel verso:

(*a*) Voici le distique:

Lambertinus hic est, Romæ decus et pater orbis,
Qui mundum scriptis docuit, virtutibus ornat.

5 K: il cardinale Passionei
7 K: il cardinale Valenti
14 W48D, 54V, W64R: sopra detto, ei su

R. Pomeau, *Voltaire en son temps*, 2nd edn (Oxford and Paris 1995), i.470-72. On how Voltaire prepared the ground before writing to the pope, see Pierre Martino, 'L'interdiction du *Mahomet* de Voltaire et la dédicace au pape (1742-1745)', in *Mémorial Henri Basset* (Paris 1928), ii.89-103. On angry reaction to the pope's apparent patronage for *Mahomet* from François Philibert Louzeau, see Pierre Martino, 'Un réquisitoire contre Voltaire (1746)', *Rhl* 35 (1928), p.563-67. The views of the *Nouvelles ecclésiastiques* concerning this 'hypocritical subterfuge' (17 April 1746, p.61, 1 May 1746, p.69) are considered by John Pappas in *Berthier's Journal de Trévoux et les philosophes*, *SVEC* 3 (1957), p.91.

[2] Librarian of the Vatican; for this letter see D3195.

[3] The pope's doctor; for this letter, which contains the couplet referred to below, see D3194.

*Solus hic inflexit sensus animumque labantem:*[4]

Avendola fatta longa in un altro:

*Hic finis Priami fatorum, hic exitus illum.*[5]

Ci sembra d'aver risposto ben espresso, ancor che siano più di cinquanta anni che non abbiamo letto Virgilio. Benche la causa sia propria della sua persona, abbiamo tanta buona idea della sua sincerità e probità che facciamo la stessa giudice sopra il punto della ragione a chi assista, se a noi o al suo oppositore, ed in tanto restiamo col dare a lei l'apostolica benedizione.

*Datum Romæ apud Sanctam Mariam majorem die 19 Sept. 1745. Pontificatus nostri anno sexto.*

[4] Virgil, *Aeneid*, iv.22.

[5] *Aeneid*, ii.5554-55; the first 'hic' should read 'hæc'.

# LETTRE DE REMERCIEMENT DE M. DE VOLTAIRE AU PAPE

Non vengono tanto meglio figurate le fatezze di Vostra Beatitudine su i medaglioni che ho ricevuti dalla sua singolare benignità, di quello che si vedono espressi l'ingegno e l'animo suo nella lettera della quale s'è degnata d'onorarmi; ne pongo a i suoi piedi le più vive ed umilissime grazie. 5

Veramente sono in obbligo di riconoscere la sua infallibilità nelle decisioni di letteratura, si come nelle altre cose più riverende: V.S. è più prattica del latino che quel francese il di cui sbaglio s'è degnato di corregere: mi maraviglio come si ricordi cosi appuntino

a-23 42X1-47A: [*absent*]
1-23 W57P, T64P and T67 [*with translation*]:
J'ai reçu les médailles dont votre bienveillance singulière m'a favorisé. Si les traits de Votre Sainteté y sont bien représentés, on ne voit pas moins paraître son esprit et son caractère dans la lettre dont Elle a daigné m'honorer, et pour laquelle je lui rends les plus vives et les plus humbles actions de grâces. ¶Je suis certainement obligé de reconnaître son infaillibilité dans les décisions de littérature, comme je la reconnais sur d'autres points plus respectables. Votre Sainteté connaît mieux la langue latine, que ne la connaît le Français dont Elle a daigné relever l'erreur. Je suis étonné comment Elle peut se rappeler si à propos son Virgile. Les Souverains Pontifes se sont toujours distingués dans les plus grandes monarchies, mais je ne crois pas qu'il y en ait jamais eu aucun parmi eux qui ait joint tant de science, à tant de littérature: ¶*Agnosco rerum dominos gentemque togatam.* ¶Si le Français qui s'est trompé sur la quantité du mot hic, avait eu son Virgile aussi présente que l'a Votre Sainteté, il aurait pu citer un vers qui serait venu bien à propos, où le mot hic se trouve employé et comme bref et comme long. Ce beau vers semblait m'offrir un présage des faveurs dont votre bienveillance m'a comblé. Le voici: ¶*Hic vir, hic est, tibi quem promitti sæpius audis.* ¶C'est de ce vers que Rome a dû retentir l'exaltation de Benoît XIV. C'est avec le plus profond respect et la plus parfaite reconnaissance que je baise les pieds de Votre Sainteté, &c.
[*The translation in* K *differs*]
4 W48D, W50, 51B, W51, W52, T53, 54V, W57P, T64G, T64P, W64R, T67: ne porgo a

del suo Virgilio. Tra i più letterati monarchi furono sempre segnalati i summi pontifici; ma tra loro, credo che non se ne trovasse mai uno che adornasse tanta dottrina di tanti fregi di bella letteratura; 10

*Agnosco rerum dominos gentemque togatam.*[1]

Se il francese che sbagliò nel riprendere questo *hic*, avesse tenuto a mente Virgilio come sa Vostra Beatitudine, avrebbe potuto citare un bene adatto verso dove *hic* è breve e longo insieme. Questo bel verso mi pareva un presagio de i favori à me conferiti dalla sua beneficenza. Eccolo. 15

*Hic vir hic est tibi quem promitti sæpius audis.*[2] 20

Cosi Roma doveva gridare quando Bened. XIV fù esaltato. In tanto baccio con somma riverenza e gratitudine i suoi sacri piedi; &c.

10 W48D, 51B, T53, T64G, T64P, W64R, T67: monarche
22 W48D, T53, W57P, T64G, T64P, W64R, T67: somma rivenza e gratitudine

[1] Virgil, *Aeneid*, i.282; for 'Agnosco' read 'Romanos'.
[2] *Aeneid*, iv.791.

# LE FANATISME, OU MAHOMET LE PROPHÈTE, TRAGÉDIE

a-c MS4: Mahomet I
MS5, 42X1-43A2, 67B, 78B, 78P: Mahomet, tragédie
MS6: Mahomet Premier
68P, 73P, 73M, 77P1, 77P2: Mahomet ou le fanatisme, tragédie

# ACTEURS[1]

MAHOMET
ZOPIRE, cheikh ou shérif de la Mecque
OMAR, lieutenant de Mahomet
SEÏDE, PALMIRE, esclaves de Mahomet
PHANOR, sénateur de la Mecque 5
Troupe de Mecquois
Troupe de Musulmans
*La scène est à la Mecque.*[2]

1 MS4, MS5, 42X1: MAHOMET, faux prophète
3 MS4, MS5, 42X1: OMAR, disciple et confident de Mahomet
42B1: OMAR, général de Mahomet
4 MS4, MS5, 42X1: SÉÏDE, fils inconnu de Zopire, frère et amant de Palmire
42B1: SÉÏDE, PALMIRE, enfants de Zopire élevés secrètement dans le camp de Mahomet.
5 MS4, MS5, 42B1, 42X1: PHANOR, confident de Zopire
6-7 MS4, MS5, 42X1: PALMIRE, fille inconnue de Zopire, sœur et amante de Séide
Suite de Mahomet
Peuple [MS5: Peuple de la Mecque]
8 MS4: *La scène est à la Mecque, dans le palais de Zopire.*
42B1: *dans le temple des faux dieux de Zopire.*

[1] MS Lekain shows how the various 'troupes' are to be managed: 'Quatre officiers supérieurs de la Suite de Mahomet, Vingt soldats arabes de la Suite de Mahomet*, Trente hommes du peuple de la Mecque. *Nota: Il y a quatorze hommes de cette troupe que l'on peut faire servir pour le peuple mecquois au cinquième acte; ainsi il n'y a vraiment que 40 hommes d'employés.'

[2] 'Le théâtre doit représenter un lieu vaste décoré de différents portiques, sous celui du fond, l'on découvre un autel antique éclairé par deux lampadaires suspendus à la coupole. Les parties latérales de l'avant-scène sont également décorées de portiques auxquels on parvient par trois degrés. La droite du théâtre, en deçà du petit temple domestique de Zopire, conduit à la résidence de Zopire et de Palmire, la gauche mène au palais de Mahomet' (MS Lekain).

# ACTE PREMIER

## *SCÈNE PREMIÈRE*

## ZOPIRE, PHANOR

ZOPIRE

Qui moi, baisser les yeux devant ses faux prodiges?
Moi de ce fanatique encenser les prestiges?
L'honorer dans la Mecque après l'avoir banni!
Non. Que des justes dieux Zopire soit puni,
Si tu vois cette main, jusqu'ici libre et pure, 5
Caresser la révolte et flatter l'imposture!

PHANOR

Nous chérissons en vous ce zèle paternel
Du chef auguste et saint du sénat d'Ismaël;
Mais ce zèle est funeste; et tant de résistance,
Sans lasser Mahomet, irrite sa vengeance. 10
Contre ses attentats vous pouviez autrefois
Lever impunément le fer sacré des lois,
Et des embrasements d'une guerre immortelle
Etouffer[1] sous vos pieds la première étincelle.

1 MS5, 42B1-42B5, 43A, 47A, 51B, W51, 52B, 60B, 67B, 71P1, 71P2, W71P, 74A, 78B, K: prodiges!
42B5*: →β

7 MS4, MS5, 43A2*, 42X1, 42X2, 42XX: vous le zèle
42X1*: →β

11 MS4, 42X1, 42X2: [*absent*]
42X1*, 42X2 errata: →β

14 42B1-42B5, 43A1, 43A2, 47A, 52B, 60B, 67B, 78B: sous les pieds
42B5*: →β

[1] 'Je ne sais si l'usage veut qu'on dise *écraser des étincelles*; j'ai cru qu'il fallait dire *éteindre* ou *étouffer* des étincelles' (D2072; to Frederick, 9 September 1739).

Mahomet citoyen ne parut à vos yeux 15
Qu'un novateur obscur, un vil séditieux:
Aujourd'hui c'est un prince: il triomphe, il domine;
Imposteur à la Mecque, et prophète à Médine,
Il sait faire adorer à trente nations
Tous ces mêmes forfaits qu'ici nous détestons. 20
Que dis-je? en ces murs même une troupe égarée,
Des poisons de l'erreur avec zèle enivrée,
De ces miracles faux soutient l'illusion,
Répand le fanatisme et la sédition,
Appelle son armée, et croit qu'un dieu terrible 25
L'inspire, le conduit, et le rend invincible.
Tous nos vrais citoyens avec vous sont unis;
Mais les meilleurs conseils sont-ils toujours suivis?
L'amour des nouveautés, le faux zèle, la crainte,
De la Mecque alarmée ont désolé l'enceinte; 30
Et ce peuple, en tout temps chargé de vos bienfaits,
Crie encore à son père,[2] et demande la paix.

15 MS4: V↑citoyen
MS4, 42X1,42X2: à nos yeux.
20 MS4: V↑forfaits
MS4, 42X1, 42X2: Tous les mêmes
42X1*: →β
24 MS4: Reprend le fanatisme et l'illusion
42X1, 42X2: fanatisme et l'irréligion,
27 42B5, 43A1, 52B, 60B, 67B, 78B: avec nous sont
29 42B1-42B5, 42XX, 43A1, 43A2, 47A, 52B, 60B, 67B, 78B: zèle, et la crainte
31 43A1: de nos bienfaits,
32 68P: demande de la paix.

[2] Cideville seems to have suggested an alternative reading here. Voltaire replied: '*Crie encor à son père* me paraît aussi je vous l'avoue bien supérieur à *invoque encor son père*. L'un peint et donne une idée précise, l'autre est vague' (D2515; 19 July 1741).

ZOPIRE

La paix avec ce traître? Ah! peuple sans courage,
N'en attendez jamais qu'un horrible esclavage.
Allez, portez en pompe, et servez à genoux 35
L'idole dont le poids va vous écraser tous.
Moi, je garde à ce fourbe une haine éternelle;[3]
De mon cœur ulcéré la plaie est trop cruelle;
Lui-même a contre moi trop de ressentiments.
Le cruel fit périr ma femme et mes enfants; 40
Et moi jusqu'en son camp j'ai porté le carnage;
La mort de son fils même honora mon courage.
Les flambeaux de la haine entre nous allumés,
Jamais des mains du temps ne seront consumés.[4]

34-35 MS1:
Vous qui craignez / [redoutez] la mort et cherchez l'esclavage
Portez d'une main faible, encensez à genoux
35 MS4: Allez, parlez en
W75X: Allez, partez en
36 MS5: vous accabler tous.
37 MS1: Je garde aux tyrans une haine immortelle;
42B1-42B5, 42XX, 43A1, 43A2, 47A, 52B, 60B, 67B, 78B: haine immortelle;
43A2*: →β
40 42X1, 42X2: Ce cruel
41 MS4: jusqu'en son cain, j'ai
42 MS5: La mort de < mon > fils
44 68P: [*gives this line to Phanor*]

[3] The 1742 variant of this hemistich more closely echoes lines in other plays, such as: 'Rome n'a point pour eu une haine immortelle' (*Brutus*, act III line 317); see also Appendix IV.

[4] 'La métaphore des flambeaux de la haine consumés des mains du temps me paraît encore très exact. Le temps consume un flambeau précisément et physiquement comme il consume du marbre, en enlevant les parties *insensibles*' (D2515; to Cideville, 19 July 1741).

PHANOR

Ne les éteignez point: mais cachez-en la flamme: 45
Immolez au public les douleurs de votre âme.
Quand vous verrez ces lieux par ses mains ravagés,
Vos malheureux enfants seront-ils mieux vengés?
Vous avez tout perdu, fils, frère, épouse, fille:
Ne perdez point l'Etat; c'est là votre famille. 50

ZOPIRE

On ne perd les Etats que par timidité.

PHANOR

On périt quelquefois par trop de fermeté.

ZOPIRE

Périssons, s'il le faut.

PHANOR

Ah! quel triste courage,
Quand vous touchez au port, vous expose au naufrage?[5]

47 MS5: ↑lieux détruits et ravagés,
48 MS4: enfants en seront-ils
42X2: enfants seraient-ils mieux
53 MS4, MS5, 42X1, 42X2, 42B1-42B5, 43A1, 43A2, 47A, 52B, 60B, 67B, 78B:
ZOPHIRE
On périt avec gloire.
43A2*: β
54 MS4, MS5, MS6↑β, 42X1, 42X2, 42B1-42B5, 42XX, 43A1-43A3, W46, 47A, W48D, W50, 51B, W51, 52B, T53, 54V, 60B, T64G, W64R, 67B, 68P, 71P2, 74A, 78B: Vous fait si près du port exposer au naufrage?
W71P: au carnage?

[5] Cf. 'Cherchent un port tranquille après tant de naufrages' (*Adélaïde*, act II line 326); and see Appendix IV.

Le ciel, vous le voyez, a remis en vos mains 55
De quoi fléchir encor ce tyran des humains.
Cette jeune Palmire en ses camps élevée,
Dans vos derniers combats par vous-même enlevée,
Semble un ange de paix descendu parmi nous,
Qui peut de Mahomet apaiser le courroux. 60
Déjà par ses hérauts il l'a redemandée.

ZOPIRE

Tu veux qu'à ce barbare elle soit accordée?
Tu veux que d'un si cher et si noble trésor
Ses criminelles mains s'enrichissent encor?
Quoi! lorsqu'il nous apporte et la fraude et la guerre, 65
Lorsque son bras enchaîne et ravage la terre,
Les plus tendres appas brigueront sa faveur,
Et la beauté sera le prix de la fureur?
Ce n'est pas qu'à mon âge, aux bornes de ma vie,

55 W57P, T64P, T67: remis dans vos
56 MS4, 42X1, 42X2: encor le tyran
57 MS4, 42X1, 42X2: en son camp
47A, W50, 78B: en ces camps
42X1*: →β
58 42B1-42B5, 43A1, 43A2, 47A, 52B, 60B, 67B, 71P1, 71P2, 74A, 78B: Dans nos derniers
MS4, MS5, 42X1, 42X2, 42B1-42B5, 42XX, 43A1-43A3, W46, 47A, 52B, 60B, 67B, 78B: par vos mains enleveé,
43A2*: →β
65 MS5, 42B1-42B5, 42XX, 43A1, 43A2, 47A, 52B, 60B, 67B, 78B: Qui, lorsqu'il nous apporte et l'erreur [MS5: <la fraude>] et la guerre,
42B5*, 43A2*: →β
68 MS5, 42B1-42B5, 42XX, 43A1, 43A2, 47A, 52B, 60B, 67B, 78B: sa fureur.
42B5*: →β
69 MS5↑, 42B1-42B4, 42XX, 43A1, 43A2, 47A: âge, vers la fin de ma vie,
42B5, 52B, 60B, 67B, 78B: Non qu'à l'âge où je suis, vers la fin de ma vie
42B5*, 43A2*: →β

Je porte à Mahomet une honteuse envie; 70
Ce cœur triste et flétri, que les ans ont glacé,
Ne peut sentir les feux d'un désir insensé;
Mais soit qu'en tous les temps un objet né pour plaire,
Arrache de nos vœux l'hommage involontaire;
Soit que privé d'enfants je cherche à dissiper 75
Cette nuit de douleurs qui vient m'envelopper;
Je ne sais quel penchant pour cette infortunée
Remplit le vide affreux de mon âme étonnée.
Soit faiblesse ou raison, je ne puis sans horreur
La voir aux mains d'un monstre, artisan de l'erreur. 80
Je voudrais qu'à mes vœux heureusement docile,
Elle-même en secret pût chérir cet asile;
Je voudrais que son cœur, sensible à mes bienfaits,
Détestât Mahomet autant que je le hais.
Elle veut me parler sous ces sacrés portiques, 85
Non loin de cet autel de nos dieux domestiques;[6]

70 42B5, 52B, 60B, 67B, 78B: une mortelle envie,
42B5*: →β
77 W48D, W52, T53, 54V, 68P: sais, quel
78 42B2, 43A1, 43A2, 47A: Rempli le
78P: de ton âme
81 42B1-42B5, 42XX, 43A1, 43A2, 47A, 52B, 60B, 67B, 78B: qu'à mes yeux heureusement
42B5*, 43A2*: →β
84 MS4: détesta Mahomet autant que la hais
85 MS4: sous ses sacrés

[6] This expression surely rings truer in a Roman setting. See, for instance: 'Rome n'a pu vous rendre à vos dieux domestiques' (*Brutus*, act III line 254); see also Appendix IV.

Elle vient, et son front, siège de la candeur,
Annonce en rougissant les vertus de son cœur.

## *SCÈNE II*

### ZOPIRE, PALMIRE

ZOPIRE

Jeune et charmant objet, dont le sort de la guerre,
Propice à ma vieillesse, honora cette terre, 90
Vous n'êtes point tombée en de barbares mains;
Tout respecte avec moi vos malheureux destins,
Votre âge, vos beautés, votre aimable innocence:
Parlez; et s'il me reste encore quelque puissance,
De vos justes désirs si je remplis les vœux, 95
Ces derniers de mes jours seront des jours heureux.

PALMIRE

Seigneur, depuis deux mois sous vos lois prisonnière,
Je dus à mes destins pardonner ma misère:
Vos généreuses mains s'empressent d'effacer

87 MS4: vient en son
42B1-42B5, 42XX, 43A1, 43A2, 47A, 52B, 60B, 67B, 78B: Elle approche, et
43A2*: →β
91 MS4, 52B, 60B, T64, 67B, 71P1, 71P2, 74A, 78B: en des barbares mains,
42X2: tombée en barbares
73M: n'êtes pas tombée
96 MS4, MS5, 42X1, 42X2, 42B1-42B5, 42XX, 43A1, 43A2, 47A, 52B, 60B, 67B, 74A, 78B: Les [MS4, MS5, MS6, 42X1: Ces] derniers de mes jours seront les plus heureux.
MS6, 42X1*: →β
71P1, 71P2: Des derniers
74A: Les derniers
98 MS4, 42X1, 42X2: Je dois à
99 MS6: < s'empresseront >

Les larmes que le ciel me condamne à verser. 100
Par vous, par vos bienfaits, à parler enhardie,
C'est de vous que j'attends le bonheur de ma vie.[7]
Aux vœux de Mahomet j'ose ajouter les miens.
Il vous a demandé de briser mes liens;
Puissiez-vous l'écouter, et puissé-je lui dire 105
Qu'après le ciel et lui je dois tout à Zopire!

ZOPIRE

Ainsi de Mahomet vous regrettez les fers,
Ce tumulte des camps, ces horreurs des déserts,
Cette patrie errante au trouble abandonnée.

PALMIRE

La patrie est aux lieux où l'âme est enchaînée. 110
Mahomet a formé mes premiers sentiments,
Et ses femmes en paix guidaient mes faibles ans;
Leur demeure est un temple, où ces femmes sacrées
Lèvent au ciel des mains de leur maître adorées.
Le jour de mon malheur, hélas, fut le seul jour, 115

101 MS4: bienfaits, en parler
108 MS4: Le tumulte des camps, les horreurs, les déserts
MS5, 42X1, 42X2: Ce tumulte [MS5: Ces tumultes], ces camps, ces horreurs, ces déserts,
42X1*: →β
51B, W51, 71P1, 71P2, 74A: Ces tumultes des camps,
109 42B1-42B5, 42XX, 43A1, 43A2, 47A, 52B, 60B, 67B, 78B: Cette errante patrie au
43A2*: →β
W72X: Cette partie errante
113 53A: où ses femmes

[7] The same line appears in *Alzire*, I.i.141. Voltaire also uses the second hemistich in *Zaïre*: 'Tout est prêt: commencez le bonheur de ma vie' (*Zaïre*, act III line 230). See also Appendix IV.

Où le sort des combats a troublé leur séjour.
Seigneur, ayez pitié d'une âme déchirée,
Toujours présente aux lieux dont je suis séparée.

ZOPIRE

J'entends: vous espérez partager quelque jour
De ce maître orgueilleux et la main et l'amour. 120

PALMIRE

Seigneur, je le révère, et mon âme tremblante
Croit voir dans Mahomet un dieu qui m'épouvante.
Non, d'un si grand hymen mon cœur n'est point flatté;
Tant d'éclat convient mal à tant d'obscurité.

ZOPIRE

Ah! qui que vous soyez, il n'est point né peut-être 125
Pour être votre époux, encor moins votre maître;
Et vous semblez d'un sang fait pour donner des lois
A l'Arabe insolent[8] qui marche égal aux rois.

PALMIRE

Nous ne connaissons point l'orgueil de la naissance.

116 MS4, MS5, 42X1, 42X2, 42B1-42B5, 42XX, 43A1, 43A2, 47A, 52B, 60B, 67B, 78B: Où le sort de la guerre a troublé

118 MS6, 43A2*<β>: dont elle est séparée
42B5, 52B, 60B, 67B, 78B: lieux d'où je suis

121 42B1-42B5, 42XX, 43A1, 43A2, 47A, 52B, 60B, 67B, 78B: le respecte, et
43A2*: →β

122 42B1-42B5, 42XX, 43A1, 43A2, 47A, 51B, W51, 52B, 60B, 67B, 71P1, 71P2, 74A, 78B: voir en Mahomet

125 42B1-42B5, 43A1, 43A2, 47A, 52B, 60B, 67B, 78B: n'est pas né

128 MS4: < marchent >

129 W46: ne connaissions point

[8] Voltaire uses the same adjective to describe the Arabs in *Tancrède*, II.iii: 'Et l'insolent Arabe a pu le voir puni'.

Sans parents, sans patrie, esclaves dès l'enfance, 130
Dans notre égalité nous chérissons nos fers;
Tout nous est étranger, hors le dieu que je sers.

ZOPIRE

Tout vous est étranger! cet état peut-il plaire?
Quoi! vous servez un maître, et n'avez point de père?
Dans mon triste palais, seul et privé d'enfants, 135
J'aurais pu voir en vous l'appui de mes vieux ans.
Le soin de vous former des destins plus propices[9]
Eût adouci des miens les longues injustices.
Mais non, vous abhorrez ma patrie et ma loi.

PALMIRE

Comment puis-je être à vous? je ne suis point à moi. 140
Vous aurez mes regrets, votre bonté m'est chère.
Mais enfin Mahomet m'a tenu lieu de père.

130 43A3: parents, sans, patrie,
42B1-42B4, 42XX, 43A1, 43A2, 47A: esclave
43A2*: →β
131 73P, 77P1, 78P: Dans nos égalités nous
42B1-42B5, 42XX, 43A1, 43A2, 47A, 52B, 60B, 67B, 78B: chérissons les fers,
137 MS4: destins plus < heureux >
138 MS4, 42X1, 42X2: Ont adouci
138-139 MS1:
Adoucirait des miens les longues injustices.
Les héros que la Mecque enferme en son sein
Brigueraient à l'envi l'honneur de votre main.
139 42B1-42B5, 42XX, 43A1, 43A2, 47A, 52B, 60B, 67B, 78B: vous détestez ma
140 MS4: être à < moi >
73M: suis pas à
141 MS5: votre amitié m'est chère,

[9] 'Pouvait lui préparer des destins plus propices' (*Adélaïde*, act II line 289).

ZOPIRE

Quel père! justes dieux! lui? ce monstre imposteur?

PALMIRE

Ah! quels noms inouïs lui donnez-vous, Seigneur?
Lui dans qui tant d'Etats adorent leur prophète? 145
Lui, l'envoyé du ciel, et son seul interprète?

ZOPIRE

Etrange aveuglement des malheureux mortels!
Tout m'abandonne ici, pour dresser des autels
A ce coupable heureux qu'épargna ma justice,
Et qui courut au trône, échappé du supplice. 150

PALMIRE

Vous me faites frémir, Seigneur, et de mes jours
Je n'avais entendu ces horribles discours.
Mon penchant, je l'avoue, et ma reconnaissance,[10]

143 MS4, 42X1, 42X2: le monstre
42X1*: →β
144 MS4↑, MS5V↑, 42B1-42B5, 42XX, 43A1, 43A2, 47A, 52B, 60B, 67B, 78B: noms odieux lui
43A2*: →β
145 MS6, 43A2*<β>: d'Etats révèrent leur Prophète!
146 42B1-42B5, 42XX, 43A1, 43A2, 47A, 67B: l'envoyé de Dieu, et
42B5*: Lui, envoyé de Dieu, son
51B, 60B, 78B: Lui, envoyé de Dieu, et
43A2*: →β
150 43A3: échappé de supplice.

[10] 'Mais malgré son service et ma reconnaissance' (*Adélaïde*, act I line 115); see also Appendix IV.

Vous donnaient sur mon cœur une juste puissance;
Vos blasphèmes affreux contre mon protecteur, 155
A ce penchant si doux font succéder l'horreur.

ZOPIRE

O superstition! tes rigueurs inflexibles
Privent d'humanité les cœurs les plus sensibles.
Que je vous plains, Palmire, et que sur vos erreurs
Ma pitié malgré moi me fait verser de pleurs! 160

PALMIRE

Et vous me refusez!

ZOPIRE

Oui. Je ne puis vous rendre
Au tyran qui trompa ce cœur flexible et tendre.
Oui, je crois voir en vous un bien trop précieux,
Qui me rend Mahomet encor plus odieux.

154 MS6: Tous donnaient sur
MS6, 43A2*<β>: mon âme une
156 MS4: Au penchant si
157 43A3: les rigueurs
158 MS5: ↑Privent du peuple humain les
159-160 42X1*:
Hélas, que je vous plains! qu'il est dur à mon cœur
De voir tant de vertus dans les bras de l'erreur.
160 MS5: ↑m'a fait verser
MS4, MS5, MS6, 42B1-42B5, 42XX, 43A1, 43A2, 47A, 52B, 60B, W71P, T73A1, 73X, T76X, T77: des pleurs.
161 MS4, MS5, 42X1, 42X2, 42B1-42B5, 42XX, 43A1, 43A2, 47A, 52B, 60B, 67B, 78B:
refusez!

ZOPHIRE

Ah! Je
42X1*, 43A2*: →β
163 MS4, MS5, 42X1, 42X2, 42B1-42B5, 42XX, 43A1, 43A2, 47A, 52B, 60B, 67B, 78B: Non, je crois voir
42X1*, 43A2*: →β

## *SCÈNE III*

ZOPIRE, PALMIRE, PHANOR

ZOPIRE

Que voulez-vous, Phanor?

PHANOR

Aux portes de la ville 165

D'où l'on voit de Moad[11] la campagne fertile,[12]

Omar est arrivé.

ZOPIRE

Qui? ce farouche Omar,

Que l'erreur aujourd'hui conduit après son char,

Qui combattit longtemps le tyran qu'il adore,[13]

Qui vengea son pays?

PHANOR

Peut-être il l'aime encore. 170

Moins terrible à nos yeux, cet insolent guerrier,

165 MS4: [*absent*]

166 42B1-42B5, 42XX, 43A1, 43A2, 47A, 52B, 60B, 67B, 78B: voit de Morad la
45A, 53A: Moab

167 MS4: Qui? le farouche

169 MS4, MS5, 42X1, 42X2: Qui combattit jadis un tyran

171 74A: Non terrible

[11] Cf. act II line 91, and notes.

[12] 'La situation de la ville de la Mecque se trouve dans un terrain mêlé de cailloutage et de petits rochers dispersées dans la campagne' (Boulainvilliers, p.51).

[13] 'Omar, après avoir été longtemps ennemi du prophète, en devint l'appui, ou le protecteur le plus illustre, puisqu'il a été l'organe, et l'auteur des plus importantes conquêtes des Musulmans' (Boulainvilliers, p.189). See also Gagnier, i.125-30.

Portant entre ses mains le glaive et l'olivier,[14]
De la paix à nos chefs a présenté le gage.
On lui parle, il demande, il reçoit un otage.
Seïde est avec lui.

PALMIRE

Grand Dieu! destin plus doux! 175

Quoi? Seïde?

PHANOR

Omar vient, il s'avance vers vous.

ZOPIRE

Il le faut écouter. Allez, jeune Palmire.

(*Palmire sort.*)

Omar devant mes yeux! qu'osera-t-il me dire?

173-175 MS4, MS5, 42X1, 42X2, 42B1-42B5, 42XX, 43A1, 43A2, 47A, 52B, 60B, 67B, 78B:

De la paix à nos chefs représente [MS4, MS5, 42X1, 42X2: a présenté] le gage,
Un guerrier qui le suit, s'est offert en otage,
On le nomme Seïde.

PALMIRE

O Ciel! O [MS4, MS5, 42X1, 42X2: quel] sort plus doux!

43A2*: →β

174-175 42X1*:
On l'écoute, il demande, il reçoit en otage,
Seïde est avec lui.

PALMIRE

Seïde quel sort plus doux!

175 MS6: dieu! < quel > destin
43A2*: Dieux! quel destin

176 78P: Omar s'il avance

176a MS4, MS6, 42X1, 42X2: (*Elle s'en va.*)
73M: *Elle se retire.*
42B1-42B5, 42XX, 43A1, 43A2, 47A, 52B, 60B, 67B, 78B: [*stage direction for Palmire absent; scene iv starts here*]

[14] Humbert: 'L'olivier symbole de la paix chez les Grecs [...] ne l'était point chez les arabes.'

O dieux de mon pays, qui depuis trois mille ans
Protégiez d'Ismaël les généreux enfants; 180
Soleil, sacrés flambeaux, qui dans votre carrière,
Images de ces dieux, nous prêtez leur lumière,
Voyez et soutenez la juste fermeté
Que j'opposai toujours contre l'iniquité.

## *SCÈNE IV*

### ZOPIRE, OMAR, PHANOR, *SUITE*[15]

ZOPIRE

Eh bien, après six ans tu revois ta patrie, 185
Que ton bras défendit, que ton cœur a trahie.
Ces murs sont encore pleins de tes premiers exploits.
Déserteur de nos dieux, déserteur de nos lois,
Persécuteur nouveau de cette cité sainte,
D'où vient que ton audace en profane l'enceinte? 190

180 MS4, 42X1, 42X2, 42B1-42B5, 42XX, 43A1, 43A2, 47A, 52B, 60B, 67B, 78B: Protégez

181 MS4, 42X1, 42X2, 42B1-42B5, 42XX, 43A1, 43A2, 47A, 52B, 60B, 67B, 78B: sacré flambeau,

182 MS4, 42X1, 42X2, 42B1-42B5, 42XX, 43A1, 43A2, 47A, 51B, 52B, 60B, 67B, 71P1, 71P2, 74A, 78B: Image de

184 MS4, 42X1, 42X2: j'oppose
42X1*: →β

185 MS4, MS5, 42X1, 42X2: après dix ans

187 MS5: encor teints de

[15] 'Quatre des soldats arabes suivent Omar, et vont se placer, deux à droite, et deux à gauche, sous l'un des portiques, en deçà du petit temple de Zopire' (MS Lekain, instructions for the *commandant des assistants*).

Ministre d'un brigand qu'on dût exterminer,
Parle; que me veux-tu?

OMAR

Je veux te pardonner.
Le prophète d'un dieu, par pitié pour ton âge,
Pour tes malheurs passés, surtout pour ton courage,
Te présente une main qui pourrait t'écraser, 195
Et j'apporte la paix qu'il daigne proposer.

ZOPIRE

Un vil séditieux prétend avec audace
Nous accorder la paix, et non demander grâce!
Souffrirez-vous, grands dieux, qu'au gré de ses forfaits
Mahomet nous ravisse ou nous rende la paix? 200
Et vous, qui vous chargez des volontés d'un traître,
Ne rougissez-vous point de servir un tel maître?
Ne l'avez-vous pas vu, sans honneur et sans biens,
Ramper au dernier rang des derniers citoyens?
Qu'alors il était loin de tant de renommée! 205

191 MS6, 43A2*<β>: qu'on doit exterminer,
78B: dût examiner,

195 43A3, W46, W48D, W50, 51B, W51, W52, T53, 54V, W56, W57P, T64G, W64R, T67, 68P: qui pouvait t'écraser,

196 MS4, MS5, 42X1, 42X2: Et t'apporte
42X1*: →β

198 MS4, MS5, 42X1, 42X2, 42B1-42B5, 42XX, 43A1, 43A2, 47A, 52B, 60B, 67B, 78B: Me proposer la paix, et

199 77P1: de tes forfaits

200 73P, 77P1: Mahomet vous ravisse
42B1-42B5, 43A1, 43A2, 47A, 52B, 60B, 67B, 78B: nous donne la paix?
43A2*: →β

205 W57P: loin de tant renommée!

OMAR

A tes viles grandeurs ton âme accoutumée
Juge ainsi du mérite, et pèse les humains
Au poids que la fortune avait mis dans tes mains.
Ne sais-tu pas encore, homme faible et superbe,
Que l'insecte insensible[16] enseveli sous l'herbe,[17] 210
Et l'aigle impérieux, qui plane au haut du ciel,
Rentrent dans le néant aux yeux de l'Eternel?
Les mortels sont égaux; ce n'est point la naissance,[18]
C'est la seule vertu qui fait leur différence.
Il est de ces esprits favorisés des cieux, 215
Qui sont tout par eux-mêmes, et rien par leurs aïeux.[19]

206 42B5, 52B, 60B, 68P, 67B, 78B: A ces viles
208 MS4: fortune a remis dans leurs mains.
73P, 77P1: mis en tes
214 51B, 71P1, 71P2, 74A: fait la différence.
215 42B1: favorisés des dieux,

[16] 'L'insecte *insensible* n'est pas l'insecte qui ne sent pas, mais qui n'est pas senti' (D2515; to Cideville, 19 July 1739).

[17] 'Voudront-ils que leur temple enseveli sous l'herbe [...]' (Racine, *Athalie*, III.iii.903); 'Celui devant qui le superbe / Paraît plus bas dans sa grandeur / Que l'insecte caché sous l'herbe' (J.-B. Rousseau, *Ode première, tirée du Psaume XIV*, lines 19-22). In his *Lettre à M. de V*** sur la tragédie de Mahomet*, Villaret found these lines no more than a 'commentaire louche de ces vers de Rousseau'.

[18] Lines 213 and 214 also appear in *Eriphyle*, act II lines 53-54, and are followed by two lines expressing the same idea as in lines 215-216 here: 'Les mortels sont égaux; ce n'est point la naissance, / C'est la seule vertu qui fait leur différence. / C'est elle qui met l'homme au rang des demi-dieux / Et qui sert son pays n'a pas besoin d'aïeux'. A similar theme also occurs in *Mérope*, act I lines 175-176: 'Le premier qui fut roi, fut un soldat heureux; / Qui sert bien son pays n'a pas besoin d'aïeux'.

[19] Commenting on act I lines 215-216, the abbé Le Blanc wrote: 'Pour la versification elle est fort inégale et les rimes en sont négligées à son ordinaire: dans ses plus beaux morceaux l'auteur même ne respecte pas toujours la langue' (D2635).

Tel est l'homme en un mot que j'ai choisi pour maître;
Lui seul dans l'univers a mérité de l'être.
Tout mortel à sa loi doit un jour obéir,
Et j'ai donné l'exemple aux siècles à venir.[20] 220

ZOPIRE

Je te connais, Omar; en vain ta politique
Vient m'étaler ici ce tableau fanatique.
En vain tu peux ailleurs éblouir les esprits,
Ce que ton peuple adore excite mes mépris.
Bannis toute imposture, et d'un coup d'œil plus sage 225
Regarde ce prophète à qui tu rends hommage.
Vois l'homme en Mahomet, conçois par quel degré
Tu fais monter aux cieux ton fantôme adoré.

220-220a MS7, 42B1-42B5, 42XX, 43A1, 43A2, 47A, 52B, 60B, 67B, 78B [*add after line 20*]:

Dieu maître de son choix ne doit rien à personne,
Il éclaire, il aveugle, il condamne, il pardonne;
C'est lui qui par ma voix daigne ici te parler,
Au nom de Mahomet, qu'on apprenne à trembler.

43A2*: [*these four lines suppressed*]

221-224 MS4-MS7, 42X1, 42X2, 42B1-42B5, 42XX, 43A1, 43A2, 47A, 52B, 60B, 67B, 78B:

Je te connais Omar, en vain ta politique
Vient ici m'étaler ce tableau fanatique;
Il peut des Musulmans éblouir les esprits,
Mais l'erreur qu'on adore excite mes mépris

[MS6, 42X1*, 43A2*: →β]

224 MS6: Ce que ton < temple > adore

226 MS4: tu dois hommage;

227 MS5, 42X1, 42X2: Mahomet, connais par

42X1*: →β

67C: En Mahomet vois l'homme, et vois par tel degré,

[20] 'Pour étendre sa gloire aux siècles à venir' (*Sémiramis*, III.vi); see also Appendix IV.

Enthousiaste ou fourbe, il faut cesser de l'être;
Sers-toi de ta raison, juge avec moi ton maître. 230
Tu verras de chameaux un grossier conducteur,
Chez sa première épouse insolent imposteur,
Qui sous le vain appât d'un songe ridicule,
Des plus vils des humains tente la foi crédule,
Comme un séditieux à mes pieds amené, 235
Par quarante vieillards à l'exil condamné;
Trop léger châtiment qui l'enhardit au crime.
De caverne en caverne il fuit avec Fatime.[21]
Ses disciples errants de cités en déserts,
Proscrits, persécutés, bannis, chargés de fers, 240
Promènent leur fureur qu'ils appellent divine.
De leurs venins bientôt ils infectent Médine.
Toi-même alors, toi-même, écoutant la raison,
Tu voulus dans sa source arrêter le poison.
Je te vis plus heureux, et plus juste, et plus brave, 245

229-230 MS1:
Enthousiaste ou fourbe, apprends à le connaître,
Sers-toi de ta raison, sois juge de ton maître.
231 71P1, 71P2, 74A: verras des chameaux
42B5, 52B, 60B, 67B, 78B: un ancien conducteur,
232 42X1, 42X2, W57P, T64P, T67: insolent, imposteur
233 T64G, W68: le vain appas
71P1, 71P2, 74A: les vains appas
234 67B, 78B: trompe la foi
236 43A3: Pas quarante
239 MS5: de cités en < cités >,
241 MS4, MS5, MS6, 42X1, 42X2: Des débris de leur secte étendent la ruine,
42B1-42B5, 42XX, 43A1, 43A2, 47A, 52B, 60B, 78B: Vont de leur secte impie étendre la ruine,
43A2*: →β
71P1, 71P2, 74A: leurs fureurs
243 MS6: toi-même, < vomissant > la raison,
244 MS6, 43A2*: arrêter ce poison.

[21] Fatima was Mohammed's daughter, not one of his wives (see Boulainvilliers, p.369). She married Ali (Gagnier, i.315-16).

Attaquer le tyran dont je te vois l'esclave.
S'il est un vrai prophète, osas-tu le punir?
S'il est un imposteur, oses-tu le servir?

OMAR

Je voulus le punir, quand mon peu de lumière
Méconnut ce grand homme entré dans la carrière. 250
Mais enfin quand j'ai vu que Mahomet est né
Pour changer l'univers à ses pieds consterné;
Quand mes yeux éclairés du feu de son génie,
Le virent s'élever dans sa course infinie,
Eloquent, intrépide, admirable en tout lieu, 255
Agir, parler, punir, ou pardonner en dieu,
J'associai ma vie à ses travaux immenses;
Des trônes, des autels en sont les récompenses.[22]
Je fus, je te l'avoue, aveugle comme toi.
Ouvre les yeux, Zopire, et change ainsi que moi: 260
Et sans plus me vanter les fureurs de ton zèle,

247 MS5: ↑S'il fut un vrai un vrai prophète, osas-tu [*on own line*: oses-tu] le
W46: oses-tu

250 MS4, MS5, 42X1, 42X2, 42B1-42B5, 42XX, 43A1, 43A2, 47A, 52B, 60B, 67B, 78B: Ne me fit voir en lui rien qu'un homme ordinaire,
42X1*, 43A2*: →β

254 MS4, MS5, 42X1, 42X2, 42B1-42B5, 42XX, 43A1, 43A2, 47A, 52B, 60B, 67B, 78B: Le virent commencer sa carrière infinie,
42X1*, 43A2*: →β

255 73P, 77P1, 78P: intrépide admiré en

258 MS6: sont la récompense.

259 42X1, 42X2: aveuglé

261 42X1*: Et loin de me vanter

261-266 MS4, MS5, 42X1, 42X2, 42B1-42B5, 42XX, 43A1, 43A2, 47A, 52B, 60B, 67B, 78B:

Reconnais une loi qui s'étend par la guerre,
Tu me vois après lui le premier de la terre,
43A2*: →β

[22] 'Des trônes renversés en sont les récompenses; ils sont alors, dites-vous, de peu de valeur. Non, non, les morceaux en sont bons' (D2515; to Cideville, 19 July 1741).

Ta persécution, si vaine et si cruelle,
Nos frères gémissants, notre dieu blasphémé,
Tombe aux pieds d'un héros par toi-même opprimé.
Viens baiser cette main qui porte le tonnerre. 265
Tu me vois après lui le premier de la terre;[23]
Le poste qui te reste est encore assez beau,
Pour fléchir noblement sous ce maître nouveau.
Vois ce que nous étions, et vois ce que nous sommes.
Le peuple aveugle et faible est né pour les grands hommes, 270
Pour admirer, pour croire, et pour nous obéir.
Viens régner avec nous, si tu crains de servir;
Partage nos grandeurs, au lieu de t'y soustraire,
Et las de l'imiter, fais trembler le vulgaire.

ZOPIRE

Ce n'est qu'à Mahomet, à ses pareils, à toi, 275
Que je prétends, Omar, inspirer quelque effroi.
Tu veux que du sénat le shérif[24] infidèle
Encense un imposteur, et couronne un rebelle!

262 71P1, 71P2, 74A: La persécution
264 42X1*: pieds du héros
272 42B1-42B5, 43A1, 43A2, 47A, 52B, 60B, 67B, 78B: régner avec moi si
274 MS5: ↑Lassé de l'imiter,
278 MS4: Encense un < infidel[e] >

[23] 'Veux-tu vivre en effet le premier de la terre' (*La Mort de César*, act III line 165).

[24] Humbert: '*Shérif* en Arabe signifie *noble, élevé en naissance* ou *en dignité*; c'est le titre que prennent ceux qui descendent de Mahomet par Ali son gendre et Fatime sa fille. *Shérif* est aussi le titre que portèrent plus tard, sous le règne des Ayoubites, les gouverneurs de la Mecque et de Médine.'

Je ne te nierai point que ce fier séducteur
N'ait beaucoup de prudence et beaucoup de valeur. 280
Je connais comme toi les talents de ton maître;
S'il était vertueux, c'est un héros peut-être:
Mais ce héros, Omar, est un traître, un cruel,
Et de tous les tyrans c'est le plus criminel.
Cesse de m'annoncer sa trompeuse clémence; 285
Le grand art qu'il possède est l'art de la vengeance.
Dans le cours de la guerre un funeste destin
Le priva de son fils, que fit périr ma main;
Mon bras perça le fils, ma voix bannit le père;
Ma haine est inflexible, ainsi que sa colère; 290
Pour rentrer dans la Mecque il doit m'exterminer,
Et le juste aux méchants ne doit point pardonner.

OMAR

Eh bien, pour te montrer que Mahomet pardonne,
Pour te faire embrasser l'exemple qu'il te donne,
Partage avec lui-même, et donne à tes tribus 295

279 MS4, 42X1, 42X2: te dirai point
42X1*: →β [*underlined*]

279-280 MS5:
↑J'aperçois, il est vrai, [*other variants crossed out and illegible*] dans ce fier séducteur,
Tous les vastes projets [<les projets ingénieux>?] d'un grand législateur

285 MS4, MS5, 42X1, 42X2, 42B1-42B5, 42XX, 43A1, 43A2, 47A, 52B, 60B, 67B, 78B: Tu me vantes en vain sa trompeuse clémence,
42X1*, 43A2*: →β

286 W70G, W72X: de ma vengeance

290 42B1-42B5, 42XX, 43A1, 43A2, 47A, 52B, 60B, 67B, 73M, 78B: que ma colère,
43A2*: →β

291 71P1, 71P2, 74A: Pour entrer dans

292 78B: Le plus juste
MS4, MS5, 42X1, 42X2, 42B1-42B5, 42XX, 43A1, 43A2, 47A, 52B, 60B, 67B, 78B: ne sait point
43A2*: →β

Les dépouilles des rois que nous avons vaincus.
Mets un prix à la paix, mets un prix à Palmire;
Nos trésors sont à toi.

ZOPIRE

Tu penses me séduire,
Me vendre ici ma honte et marchander la paix,
Par ses trésors honteux, le prix de ses forfaits? 300
Tu veux que sous ses lois Palmire se remette?
Elle a trop de vertus pour être sa sujette;
Et je veux l'arracher aux tyrans imposteurs,
Qui renversent les lois, et corrompent les mœurs.

OMAR

Tu me parles toujours comme un juge implacable, 305
Qui sur son tribunal intimide un coupable.
Pense et parle en ministre, agis, traite avec moi,
Comme avec l'envoyé d'un grand homme et d'un roi.

ZOPIRE

Qui l'a fait roi? qui l'a couronné?

OMAR

La victoire.
Ménage sa puissance et respecte sa gloire. 310
Aux noms de conquérant et de triomphateur,

298 78B: penses à me
300 MS5: honteux, acquis par ses forfaits, < le prix de >
51B, W51, 71P1, 71P2, 74A: de tes forfaits?
301 MS5: ↑Palmire je remette
303 71P1: l'attacher aux
304a-308 71P1, 71P2, 74A: [*give these lines to Zopire*]
306 MS4, MS5, 42X1, 42X2: tribunal interroge un coupable.
307 42X2: ministre, agis avec
311 42B1-42B5, 43A1, 43A2, 47A, 52B, 60B, 67B, 73M, 78B: Au nom de
43A2*: →β

Il veut joindre le nom de pacificateur.
Son armée est encore aux bords du Saïbare;[25]
Des murs où je suis né le siège se prépare.
Sauvons, si tu m'en crois, le sang qui va couler; 315
Mahomet veut ici te voir et te parler.

ZOPIRE

Lui! Mahomet?

OMAR

Lui-même, il t'en conjure.

ZOPIRE

Traître!
Si de ces lieux sacrés j'étais l'unique maître,
C'est en te punissant que j'aurais répondu.

OMAR

Zopire, j'ai pitié de ta fausse vertu.[26] 320
Mais puisqu'un vil sénat insolemment partage

312 42B1-42B5, 42XX, 43A1, 43A2, 47A, 52B, 60B, 67B, 78B: joindre celui de
43A2*: →β
313 51B, 71P1, 71P2, 74A: encore au bord du
314 T64: Des mœurs où
315 68P: Suivons, si
321 MS4, MS5, 42X1, 42X2, 42B1-42B5, 42XX, 43A1, 43A2, 47a, 52B, 60B, 67B, 78B: puisque ton sénat
MS5: ↑un vil sénat
43A2*: →β

[25] 'La Mecque située au 63 degré de longtitude et de 23 de latitude septentrionale, placée sur la rivière Chaïbar, à 20 lieues de son embouchure' (Boulainvilliers, p.50). The source of this reference is not clear.

[26] 'Cet orgueil insultant de ta fausse vertu' (*Brutus*, II.iv.282).

De ton gouvernement le fragile avantage,[27]
Puisqu'il règne avec toi, je cours m'y présenter.

ZOPIRE

Je t'y suis: nous verrons, qui l'on doit écouter.
Je défendrai mes lois, mes dieux et ma patrie; 325
Viens-y contre ma voix prêter ta voix impie
Au dieu persécuteur, effroi du genre humain,
Qu'un fourbe ose annoncer les armes à la main.[28]
(*à Phanor*)
Toi, viens m'aider, Phanor, à repousser un traître;
Le souffrir parmi nous, et l'épargner, c'est l'être. 330
Renversons ses desseins, confondons son orgueil,

322 MS4, MS5, 42X1, 42X2: De ce [MS5: ↑β] gouvernement
MS6, 42B1-42B5, 42XX, 43A1, 43A2, 47A, 52B, 60B, 67B, 78B: De ce gouvernement le frivole avantage,
323 MS4, MS5, 42X1, 42X2: toi, je vais m'y
324 MS4, MS5, 42X1, 42X2: Je te suis
MS5: β
325 MS4, MS5↑, 42X1, 42X2, 42XX, 67B, 78B: J'y défendrai
42B1-42B5, 42XX, 43A1, 43A2, 47A, 52B, 60B, 67B, 78B: défendrai mes dieux, mes lois et ma patrie
43A2*: →β
327 43A3: Au dieu persécuté,
328a MS4 (V↑Phanor), MS5↑, 42X1, 42X2, 42B1-42B5, 42XX, 43A1, 43A2, 47A, 52B, 60B, 67B, 78B:

SCENE VI
ZOPHIRE, PHANOR
Toi, Phanor, viens m'aider [MS4, 42X1, 42X2: Toi, viens m'aider, Phanor,] à repousser ce traître,

328-334 MS6, 43A2*, Nantes copy of 71P2: à la main.// [*remainder crossed out*]
330 MS4, MS5, 42X1, 42X2: Le souffrir en ces lieux, lui pardonner, c'est l'être,
MS5: ↑β

[27] The 1742 version of this line echoes a hemistich from *Œdipe*, act IV line 170: 'Des vains honneurs du pas le frivole avantage'.

[28] 'Met à tous les Français, les armes à la main' (*La Henriade*, II line 4); 'Mais je te l'apprendrai les armes à la main' (*Tancrède*, III.vi); 'Qui toujours contre moi, les armes à la main' (*La Mort de César*, act I line 79); see also Appendix IV.

Préparons son supplice, ou creusons mon cercueil.
Je vais, si le sénat m'écoute et me seconde,
élivrer d'un tyran ma patrie et le monde.

*Fin du premier acte.*[29]

332 MS5, 42X2: creusons son cercueil.
MS5: ↑β

333-334 MS4, MS5, 42X1, 42X2, 42B1-42B5, 42XX, 43A1-43A3, W46, 47A, 52B, 60B, 67B, 78B:

De lui seul ennemi, pour lui seul implacable,
L'amour de la vertu me rend inexorable.
*Fin du premier acte.*

[29] 'Les quatre soldats arabes suivent Omar à deux de hauteur, par la gauche du théâtre' (MS Lekain, instructions for the *commandant des assistants*).

# ACTE SECOND

## *SCÈNE PREMIÈRE*

### SEÏDE, PALMIRE

PALMIRE

Dans ma prison cruelle est-ce un dieu qui te guide?
Mes maux sont-ils finis? te revois-je, Seïde?

SEÏDE

O charme de ma vie, et de tous mes malheurs!
Palmire, unique objet qui m'a coûté des pleurs;
Depuis ce jour de sang, qu'un ennemi barbare, 5
Près des camps du prophète, aux bords du Saïbare,
Vint arracher sa proie à mes bras tout sanglants,
Qu'étendu loin de toi sur des corps expirants,
Mes cris mal entendus sur cette infâme rive,
Invoquèrent la mort sourde à ma voix plaintive! 10
O ma chère Palmire, en quel gouffre d'horreur

1 MS1: Dans cette ville impie est-ce
MS5[↑], 42B1-42B5, 42XX, 43A1, 43A2, 47A, 52B, 60B, 67B, 78B: prison affreuse,
43A2*: →β
71P1, 71P2, 74A: qui me guide,
2 43A3: finis? je revois Seïde.
45A, 53A: je te revois,
78B: Te vois-je,
3 W48D, 54V: & des tous
4 73P, 77P1, 78P: coûté de pleurs.
6 78B: bords de Saïbare,
7 W71P: Vint m'arracher sa proie

Tes périls et ma perte ont abîmé mon cœur!
Que mes feux, que ma crainte, et mon impatience,
Accusaient la lenteur des jours de la vengeance!
Que je hâtais l'assaut si longtemps différé, 15
Cette heure de carnage, où de sang enivré[1]
Je devais de mes mains brûler la ville impie,
Où Palmire a pleuré sa liberté ravie!
Enfin de Mahomet les sublimes desseins,
Que n'ose approfondir l'humble esprit des humains, 20
Ont fait entrer Omar en ce lieu d'esclavage;
Je l'apprends, et j'y vole. On demande un otage;
J'entre, je me présente, on accepte ma foi;
Et je me rends captif, ou je meurs avec toi.

PALMIRE

Seïde, au moment même, avant que ta présence 25
Vînt de mon désespoir calmer la violence,
Je me jetais aux pieds de mon fier ravisseur.

12 MS4, MS5, MS6 ↑β, 42X1, 42X2, 42B1-42B5, 42XX, 43A1, 43A2, 47A, 52B, 60B, 67B, 78B: et ta perte
W71P: Tels périls
71P1, 71P2, 74A: Tes périls et ma vie ont
14 W71P: jours de ma vengeance!
16 42B1-42B5, 42XX, 43A1, 43A2, 47A, 50B, 60B, 67B, 71P2, 74A, 78B: Cette heure, où de carnage et de sang enivré,
43A2*: →β
17 71P1, 71P2, 74A: de ma main brûler
18 MS4: sa liberté, sa vie,
19 MS4: La fin de Mahomet les
21 MS4, 42B1-42B5, 42XX, 43A1, 43A2, 47A, 51B, 52B, 60B, 67B, 71P1, 71P2, 74A, 78B: Omar dans ce lieu

[1] 'Sans raison, sans justice, et de sang enivré' (*Adélaïde*, act I line 62); 'Fatigués de carnage et de sang enivrés' (*Alzire*, act IV line 119).

Vous voyez, ai-je dit, les secrets de mon cœur:[2]
Ma vie est dans les camps dont vous m'avez tirée;
Rendez-moi le seul bien dont je suis séparée. 30
Mes pleurs, en lui parlant, ont arrosé ses pieds;
Ses refus ont saisi mes esprits effrayés.
J'ai senti dans mes yeux la lumière obscurcie;
Mon cœur sans mouvement, sans chaleur et sans vie,
D'aucune ombre d'espoir n'était plus secouru; 35
Tout finissait pour moi quand Seïde a paru.

SEÏDE

Quel est donc ce mortel insensible à tes larmes?

PALMIRE

C'est Zopire; il semblait touché de mes alarmes;
Mais le cruel enfin vient de me déclarer,
Que des lieux où je suis rien ne peut me tirer.[3] 40

SEÏDE

Le barbare se trompe, et Mahomet mon maître,

29 42B1-42B5, 42XX, 43A1, 43A2, 47A, 52B, 60B, 67B, 78B: dans le camp
MS5, 42X1, 42X2, 51B, W51, 71P1, 71P2, 74A: camps d'où vous
31 MS6↑β, 43A2*<β>: ont inondé ses pieds
34 71P1, 71P2, 74A: sans mouvements,
35 MS5, 42B1-42B2, 42B4-42B5, 42XX, 43A1, 43A2, 47A, 52B, T53, 60B, 67B, T64G: D'aucun ombre
37 MS5, 42X1, 42X2: mortel inflexible à
37-40 MS4: [*absent*]
39 42B1-42B5, 42XX, 43A1, 43A2, 47A, 52B, 60B, 67B, 78B: Mais! hélas le cruel vient
43A2*: →β
40 MS5, 42X1, 42X2, 42XX, T73A1, T77, W71P: rien ne me peut tirer

[2] 'Ne veut-on qu'arracher les secrets de mon cœur?' (*Brutus*, act III line 116).
[3] 'Je sais que du sérail rien ne peut me tirer' (*Zaïre*, act V line 52).

Et l'invincible Omar,[4] et ton amant peut-être,
(Car j'ose me nommer après ces noms fameux,
Pardonne à ton amant cet espoir orgueilleux)
Nous briserons ta chaîne, et tarirons tes larmes. 45
Le dieu de Mahomet, protecteur de nos armes,
Le dieu dont j'ai porté les sacrés étendards,
Le dieu, qui de Médine a détruit les remparts,
Renversera la Mecque à nos pieds abattue.
Omar est dans la ville, et le peuple à sa vue 50
N'a point fait éclater ce trouble et cette horreur
Qu'inspire aux ennemis un ennemi vainqueur.
Au nom de Mahomet un grand dessein l'amène.

PALMIRE

Mahomet nous chérit; il briserait ma chaîne;
Il unirait nos cœurs; nos cœurs lui sont offerts; 55
Mais il est loin de nous, et nous sommes aux fers.

42 42B1-42B5, 42XX, 43A1, 43A2, 47A, 52B, 60B, 67B, 78B: et moi-même peut-être,
MS6: ↑Omar, et Séïde peut-être
43 42B2, 42B4, 42XX, 43A1: Ca j'ose
43A2, 47A: Si j'ose
47 MS4, 42B1-42B5, 42XX, 43A1, 43A2, 47A, 52B, 60B, 67B, 78B: Ce Dieu
43A2*: →β
48 MS4, MS5, 42X1, 42X2, 42B1-42B5, 42XX, 43A1, 43A2, 47A, 52B, 60B, 67B, 78B: Ce Dieu
43A2*: →β
49 42B1-42B5, 43A1, 43A2, 47A, 52B, 60B, 67B, 78B: Mecque à nos yeux abattus.
51 MS4, MS5, 42X1, 42X2: trouble, cette horreur
42X1*: →β
54 71P1, 71P2, 74A: Mahomet me chérit,

[4] Voltaire wrote to Cideville: 'Je ne sais ce que vous voulez dire d'un *à l'invincible Omar*. Il y a et l'invincible Omar *et* ton amant *peut-être*. Ce *peut-être* me paraît un correctif nécessaire pour un jeune homme qui se fait de fête avec Mahomet et Omar' (D2515; 19 July 1741).

## *SCÈNE II*

### PALMIRE, SEÏDE, OMAR

OMAR

Vos fers seront brisés, soyez pleins d'espérance.
Le ciel vous favorise, et Mahomet s'avance.

SEÏDE

Lui!

PALMIRE

Notre auguste père!

OMAR

Au conseil assemblé
L'esprit de Mahomet par ma bouche a parlé. 60
'Ce favori du dieu, qui préside aux batailles,
Ce grand homme, ai-je dit, est né dans vos murailles.
Il s'est rendu des rois le maître et le soutien,
Et vous lui refusez le rang de citoyen!
Vient-il vous enchaîner, vous perdre, vous détruire? 65
Il vient vous protéger, mais surtout vous instruire.
Il vient dans vos cœurs même établir son pouvoir.'

58 MS6, 42B1-42B5, 42XX, 43A1, 43A2, 47A, 52B, 60B, 67B, 78B: Le ciel nous favorise,
59 71P1, 71P2, 74A: Oui!
61 51B, 71P2, 74A: favori de Dieu qui
62 42X1, 42X2: est tué dans vos murailles,
42X1*: →β
42B1-42B5, 43A1, 43A2, 47A, 52B, 60B, 67B, 78B: nos murailles,
43A2*: →β
67 MS5 →β, 42X1, 42X2, 42XX, 78B: cœurs mêmes
42X1*: →β
MS6, 43A2*: ↑dans nos cœurs même
78P: établir en son pouvoir

Plus d'un juge à ma voix a paru s'émouvoir;
Les esprits s'ébranlaient: l'inflexible Zopire,
Qui craint de la raison l'inévitable empire, 70
Veut convoquer le peuple, et s'en faire un appui.
On l'assemble, j'y cours, et j'arrive avec lui.
Je parle aux citoyens, j'intimide, j'exhorte;
J'obtiens qu'à Mahomet on ouvre enfin la porte.
Après quinze ans d'exil[5] il revoit ses foyers; 75
Il entre accompagné des plus braves guerriers,
D'Ali, d'Hammon, d'Hercide, et de sa noble élite;
Il entre, et sur ses pas chacun se précipite.
Chacun porte un regard comme un cœur différent;
L'un croit voir un héros, l'autre voir un tyran. 80
Celui-ci le blasphème, et le menace encore;
Cet autre est à ses pieds, les embrasse et l'adore.
Nous faisons retentir à ce peuple agité
Les noms sacrés de Dieu, de paix, de liberté.
De Zopire éperdu la cabale impuissante 85
Vomit en vain les feux de sa rage expirante.
Au milieu de leurs cris, le front calme et serein,
Mahomet marche en maître, et l'olive à la main:
La trêve est publiée; et le voici lui-même.

76 42B1-42B5, 42XX, 43A1, 43A2, 47A, 52B, 60B, 67B, 78B: Il vient accompagné
43A2*: →β
T77: des plus graves guerriers
78 42X2: sur ces pas
80 W71P: , l'autre voit un tyran
83 MS4: faisons retenti au peuple
86 MS4, MS5, 42X1, 42X2, 42B1-42B5, 42XX, 43A1, 43A2, 47A, 52B, 60B, 67B, 78B: Nous importune en vain de sa rage expirante,
42X1*, 43A2*: →β
88 43A1: maître, l'olive

[5] 'Hélas! après quinze ans d'exil et de misère' (*Mérope*, act III line 21).

## *SCÈNE III.*

### MAHOMET, OMAR, ALI, HERCIDE,[6] *etc.*, SEÏDE, PALMIRE, *SUITE*[7]

MAHOMET

Invincibles soutiens de mon pouvoir suprême,[8] 90
Noble et sublime Ali,[9] Morad,[10] Hercide, Hammon,

89b MS4: [*omits Hercide among those present in scene iii*]
90 42B1-42B5, 42XX, 43A1, 43A2, 47A, 52B, 60B, 67B, 78B: de ma grandeur suprême,
91 MS4$^{V\uparrow}$β: Ali, Moad, <Alcide,> Ammon.
MS5, 68P: Ali, Moad,
43A1, 51B, W51, W64R, 71P1, 71P2, 74A: Ali, Morade,

[6] Ali and Hercide are non-speaking parts.

[7] 'Les quatre officiers arabes et les vingt soldats de la suite de Mahomet décrivent autour de lui un grand demi-cercle; Savoir douze hommes en quart de cercle à sa droite et douze autres à sa gauche; Mahomet est au centre du demi cercle, et les officiers aux deux extrémités' (MS Lekain, instructions for the *commandant des assistants*).

[8] 'J'attendais encor moins de mon pouvoir suprème' (*Alzire*, act I line 297). See also Appendix IV. The 1742 version of this hemistich is reminiscent of others elswhere: 'Toi, dont le sort dépend de ma grandeur suprême' (*Mérope*, act I line 298).

[9] 'Enfin le troisième prosélyte fut Ali, qui fut depuis gendre de Mahomed, qui l'aimait autant que si c'eût été son fils, [...] à cause de sa docilité à se soumettre à la justice et à la raison, malgré l'impétuosité de son tempérament. On a dit de lui qu'il était aussi véritable et aussi juste qu'il était courageux' (Boulainvilliers, p.274). See also Gagnier, i.110-11; and cf. Humbert: 'Ali, gendre de Mahomet, fut le quatrième calife. – Morad, Hercide, Ammon sont des personnages fictifs; les noms d'Hercide et d'Ammon ne sont pas même orientaux.'

[10] Although the remaining names in this line seem to be inventions, two at least are reminiscent of real ones. Judging from the variants here Morad possibly echoes either the biblical Moab (Genesis, xix.37), Mohammed's missionary to the Ansarians, Mosa'ab (Boulainvilliers, p.358; Gagnier, i.268-71), Maad whom Mohammed sent to Mecca to instruct the people (Boulainvilliers, p.397), or even

Retournez vers ce peuple, instruisez-le en mon nom.
Promettez, menacez, que la vérité règne;
Qu'on adore mon dieu, mais surtout qu'on le craigne.
Vous, Seïde, en ces lieux!

SEÏDE

O mon père! ô mon roi! 95
Le dieu qui vous inspire a marché devant moi.
Prêt à mourir pour vous, prêt à tout entreprendre,
J'ai prévenu votre ordre.

MAHOMET

Il eût fallu l'attendre.
Qui fait plus qu'il ne doit, ne sait point me servir.
J'obéis à mon dieu; vous, sachez m'obéir. 100

PALMIRE

Ah! Seigneur, pardonnez à son impatience.
Elevés près de vous dans notre tendre enfance,

92 MS4, MS5, MS6, 43A2*, 42X1, 42X2, 42XX: Retournez à ce peuple,
MS5<β>, 42B1-42B5, 43A1, 43A2, 47A, 52B, 60B, 67B, 78B: instruisez en mon nom;
43A2*: →β
94/95 MS8: [*with stage direction*: (*Il fait signe à sa suite de se retirer.*)]
98 43A1: Il fallut l'attendre.
100 MS4$^{V\uparrow}$β: sachez < me servir >
102 MS4, MS6, MS5, 42X1, 42X2, 42B1-42B5, 42XX, 43A1, 43A2, 47A, 52B, 60B, 67B, 68P, 78B: vous dès notre

---

Ma'ad, the eleventh son of Ismael (Gagnier, i.27-28). Ammon could similarly be based on Moab's brother, Ben-ammi (Genesis, xix.38). It is also the name given to Jupiter in Libya (Ovid, *Metamorphoses*, xv.310). In the abbé Pellegrin's opera *Jephté* (Brenner 9840), we find another Ammon 'fils du roi des Ammonites dans Maspha': see *Mercure* (March 1732), p.577-88; (March 1733), p.564-66; (April 1737), p.789-94. Voltaire himself had also already used the name for Sohême's confidant in *Mariamne*.

Les mêmes sentiments nous animent tous deux.
Hélas! mes tristes jours sont assez malheureux.
Loin de vous, loin de lui, j'ai langui prisonnière; 105
Mes yeux de pleurs noyés s'ouvraient à la lumière.
Empoisonneriez-vous l'instant de mon bonheur?

MAHOMET

Palmire, c'est assez; je lis dans votre cœur;
Que rien ne vous alarme, et rien ne vous étonne.
Allez; malgré les soins de l'autel et du trône, 110
Mes yeux sur vos destins seront toujours ouverts;
Je veillerai sur vous comme sur l'univers.

(*à Seïde*)

Vous, suivez mes guerriers;[11] et vous, jeune Palmire,
En servant votre dieu ne craignez que Zopire.

103 T62, T64: nous animant tous deux
106 MS5: yeux noyés de pleurs s'ouvraient
MS4, 42X1, 42X2: s'ouvrent
107 42B1-42B5, 42XX, 43A1, 43A2, 47A, 52B, 60B: M'empoisonneriez-vous
43A2*: →β
W72X: Emprisonneriez-vous l'instant
109 MS5: Ne vous alarmez point, que rien
MS5: < Que rien ne vous alarme, que/et >
113 42X1, 42X2:
(*à Seïde*) (*à Palmire*)
Vous suivez mes guerriers; et vous, jeune Palmire,
114 MS4β$^{V\uparrow}$, MS5: craignez point Zopire

[11] 'Toute la troupe précédée par ses officiers se replie à quatre hommes de hauteur et sort par la gauche du théâtre' (MS Lekain, instructions for the *commandant des assistants*).

## *SCÈNE IV*

### MAHOMET, OMAR

MAHOMET

Toi, reste, brave Omar; il est temps que mon cœur 115
De ses derniers replis t'ouvre la profondeur.
D'un siège encore douteux la lenteur ordinaire[12]
Peut retarder ma course, et borner ma carrière.
Ne donnons point le temps aux mortels détrompés,
De rassurer leurs yeux de tant d'éclat frappés. 120
Les préjugés, ami, sont les rois du vulgaire.
Tu connais quel oracle, et quel bruit populaire
Ont promis l'univers à l'envoyé d'un dieu,
Qui, reçu dans la Mecque, et vainqueur en tout lieu,
Entrerait dans ces murs en écartant la guerre; 125
Je viens mettre à profit les erreurs de la terre:
Mais tandis que les miens, par de nouveaux efforts,
De ce peuple inconstant font mouvoir les ressorts,
De quel œil revois-tu Palmire avec Seïde?

OMAR

Parmi tous ces enfants enlevés par Hercide, 130

116 43A1: replis trouve la
117 42B1-42B5, 42XX, 43A1, 43A2, 47A, 52B, 60B, 67B, 78B: douteux la longueur ordinaire,
43A2*: →β
120 MS1: yeux de mon éclat
125 43A1: Entrerait en ces murs
126 MS4: les horreurs de la terre
127 W56, T66, T68, 68P, T70, 77P1: par des nouveaux
130 MS4, MS5, 42X1, 42X2: tous les enfants

[12] 'De mes secrets agents la lenteur ordinaire' (*La Henriade*, I line 126).

Qui, formés sous ton joug, et nourris dans ta loi,
N'ont de dieu que le tien, n'ont de père que toi,
Aucun ne te servit avec moins de scrupule,
N'eut un cœur plus docile, un esprit plus crédule;
De tous tes Musulmans ce sont les plus soumis. 135

MAHOMET

Cher Omar, je n'ai point de plus grands ennemis.
Ils s'aiment; c'est assez.

OMAR

Blâmes-tu leurs tendresses?

MAHOMET

Ah! connais mes fureurs, et toutes mes faiblesses.

OMAR

Comment?

MAHOMET

Tu sais assez quel sentiment vainqueur
Parmi mes passions règne au fond de mon cœur. 140
Chargé du soin du monde, environné d'alarmes,
Je porte l'encensoir, et le sceptre, et les armes:
Ma vie est un combat,[13] et ma frugalité

131 43A1: Que formés
60B, 67B, 71P2, 74A, 78B: sous un joug
132 73M: n'ont de maître que
135 MS4, MS6, MS5, 42X1, 42X2, 42B1-42B5, 42XX, 43A1, 43A2, 47A, 52B, 60B, 67B, 78B: tous les Musulmans
136 52B, 60B, 67B, 78B: je n'ai pas de
71P1: point des plus
137 MS4, MS5, 42X1, 42X2: Ils s'aiment, tu le vois.
138 MS4: et toutes mes tendresses

[13] '"Ma vie est un combat". On sait que Beaumarchais prit cet hémistiche pour devise' (Georges Avenel).

Asservit la nature à mon austérité.
J'ai banni loin de moi cette liqueur traîtresse 145
Qui nourrit des humains la brutale mollesse:
Dans des sables brûlants, sur des rochers déserts,
Je supporte avec toi l'inclémence des airs.
L'amour seul me console; il est ma récompense,
L'objet de mes travaux, l'idole que j'encense, 150
Le dieu de Mahomet; et cette passion
Est égale aux fureurs de mon ambition.
Je préfère en secret Palmire à mes épouses.
Conçois-tu bien l'excès de mes fureurs jalouses,
Quand Palmire à mes pieds, par un aveu fatal, 155
Insulte à Mahomet, et lui donne un rival?

OMAR

Et tu n'es pas vengé?

MAHOMET

Juge, si je dois l'être.

148 42B5, 52B, 60B, 67B, 78B: avec moi l'inclémence

150-151 42B1-42B5, 42XX, 43A1, 43A2, 47A, 52B, 60B, 67B, 78B:
Le fruit de mes travaux, l'idole que j'encense,
Le seul Dieu qui me parle, et cette passion
MS1: [β *for line 150, but this version of line 151*]
43A2*: [*this version of line 150, but* β *for line 151*]

153 42XX Je préfère un secret

154 MS4, 42X1, 42X2: Connais-tu bien
42X1*: →β
MS8: bien l'objet de mon fatal amour, [*see line* 343]

156-158 MS1:
Donne ici devant moi son cœur à mon rival.
OMAR
Ce rival doit périr.
MAHOMET
Il périra, le traître.
Pour le mieux condamner apprends à le connaître.

Pour le mieux détester apprends à le connaître.
De mes deux ennemis apprends tous les forfaits:
Tous deux sont nés ici du tyran que je hais. 160

OMAR

Quoi! Zopire...

MAHOMET

Est leur père. Hercide en ma puissance
Remit depuis quinze ans leur malheureuse enfance.
J'ai nourri dans mon sein ces serpents dangereux;
Déjà sans se connaître ils m'outragent tous deux.
J'attisai de mes mains leurs feux illégitimes. 165
Le ciel voulut ici rassembler tous les crimes.

158 MS8: Pour les mieux détester, apprends à les connaître,
159 42B1-42B3, 42B5, 42XX, 43A, 52B, 60B, 67B, 78B: De mes dieux ennemis
160 MS1: Il sont nés en ces lieux du tyran
161 MS1, MS5<β>, 43A2*<β>, 43A3, W46, W48D, W50, 51B, W51, T53, 54V, T64G, W64R, 68P, 71P1, 71P2, 74A:

OMAR

Quoi! Zopire est leur père?

MAHOMET

Hercide en ma puissance

164 W71P: sans me connaître.
165 MS4, MS5, MS6<β>, 42X1, 42X2, 42B1-42B5, 42XX, 43A1, 43A2, 47A, 52B, 60B, 67B, 78B: J'attisais
43A2*: →β
71P2, 74A: J'attirai de mes mains
166 MS1:

Le ciel voulut ici rassembler tous les crimes,
Et mon fier ennemi retrouve entre ses bras
Ses coupables enfants qu'il ne reconnais pas.
Je puis me servir d'eux, mais pour punir leur père
Ce sont des instruments de haine et de colère
Qui conduits par mes mains vont peut-être aujourd'hui
Ou m'asservir Zopire, ou me venger de lui.

MS6, 43A2*<β>: tous leurs crimes

Je veux... Leur père vient, ses yeux lancent vers nous
Les regards de la haine et les traits du courroux.
Observe tout, Omar, et qu'avec son escorte
Le vigilant Hercide assiège cette porte. 170
Reviens me rendre compte, et voir s'il faut hâter,
Ou retenir les coups que je dois lui porter.

## *SCÈNE V*[14]

## ZOPIRE, MAHOMET

ZOPIRE

Ah! quel fardeau cruel à ma douleur profonde![15]
Moi, recevoir ici cet ennemi du monde!

167 D2411: Je veux... Zopire vient. Ses yeux
MS6, 42B1-42B5, 42XX, 43A1, 43A2, 47A, 52B, 60B, 67B, 78B: lancent sur nous
169 MS1: Va, tu peux nous laisser, mais qu'avec ton escorte
171 42B1-42B5, 42XX, 43A1, 43A2, 47A, 52B, 60B, 67B, 78B: s'il faut lancer
43A2*: →β
MS4: compte, et s'il faut hâter
172 MS6, 43A2*<β>: Ou suspendre les coups
174 MS4, 43A1: Moi! revoir ici

[14] This scene 'est conduite avec tant d'art', writes J.-J. Rousseau, 'que Mahomet, sans se démentir, sans rien perdre de la supériorité qui lui est propre, est pourtant éclipsé par le simple bon sens et l'intrépide vertu de Zopire. Il faloit un Auteur qui sentît bien sa force pour oser mettre vis à vis l'un de l'autre deux pareils interlocuteurs. Je n'ai jamais ouï faire de cette scène en particulier tout l'éloge dont elle me paroît digne; mais je n'en connois pas une au théatre françois, où la main d'un grand maître soit plus sensiblement empreinte, et où le sacré caractère de la vertu l'emporte plus sensiblement sur l'elévation du génie' (*Lettre à d'Alembert sur les spectacles*, in *Œuvres complètes*, v.28). This scene is parodied in the form of a dialogue between Voltaire and Le Franc de Pompignan in *Les Nouveaux Si et Pourquoi, suivis d'un dialogue en vers* (Montauban 1760).

[15] 'O mort, toujours présente à ma douleur profonde' (*Mérope*, act I line 62); see also Appendix IV.

MAHOMET

Approche, et puisqu'enfin le ciel veut nous unir, 175
Vois Mahomet sans crainte, et parle sans rougir.

ZOPIRE

Je rougis pour toi seul, pour toi dont l'artifice
A traîné ta patrie au bord du précipice;[16]
Pour toi, de qui la main sème ici les forfaits,
Et fait naître la guerre au milieu de la paix. 180
Ton nom seul parmi nous divise les familles,
Les époux, les parents, les mères et les filles
Et la trêve pour toi n'est qu'un moyen nouveau,
Pour venir dans nos cœurs enfoncer le couteau.
La discorde civile est partout sur ta trace; 185
Assemblage inouï de mensonge et d'audace,
Tyran de ton pays, est-ce ainsi qu'en ce lieu
Tu viens donner la paix, et m'annoncer un dieu?

MAHOMET

Si j'avais à répondre à d'autres qu'à Zopire,
Je ne ferais parler que le dieu qui m'inspire. 190
Le glaive et l'Alcoran dans mes sanglantes mains,

175 73M: Approche, puisqu'enfin
42X1, 42X2: veut vous unir,
176a 42X1, 42X2: [*adds stage direction*: (*Ils s'asseyent.*)]
180 42B1-42B5, 43A1, 43A2, 47A, 52B, 60B, 67B, 78B: Et fit naître
183 MS4: toi est un moyen
184 T70: [*absent*]
190 MS8: ferais jamais parler que

[16] A typical line-filling cliché: 'Il faut qu'on le retienne au bord du précipice' (*Adélaïde*, act IV line 214); 'Au bord du précipice où le sénat l'a mis' (*Brutus*, act II line 98); see also Appendix IV. The expression frequently appears in slightly different forms: 'Tranquille, il s'endormait au bord des précipices' (*La Henriade*, III line 108); 'Nous suscite un secours aux bords du précipice' (*Adelaïde*, act IV line 14); see also Appendix IV.

Imposeraient silence au reste des humains.[17]
Ma voix ferait sur eux les effets du tonnerre,
Et je verrais leurs fronts attachés à la terre:
Mais je te parle en homme, et sans rien déguiser: 195
Je me sens assez grand pour ne pas t'abuser.
Vois quel est Mahomet; nous sommes seuls, écoute:
Je suis ambitieux; tout homme l'est sans doute;
Mais jamais roi, pontife, ou chef, ou citoyen,
Ne conçut un projet aussi grand que le mien. 200
Chaque peuple à son tour a brillé sur la terre,
Par les lois, par les arts, et surtout par la guerre.
Le temps de l'Arabie est à la fin venu.
Ce peuple généreux, trop longtemps inconnu,
Laissait dans ses déserts ensevelir sa gloire; 205
Voici les jours nouveaux marqués pour la victoire.[18]

192 42X2: Imposerais silence
195 42B3: Mais je parle
199 78B: Jamais roi,
203 43A2: l'Arabie et à
203-204 MS5:
↑Le temps de l'Arabie est enfin arrivé:
Ce peuple généreux, trop longtemps ignoré,
205 43A3, W46: ensevelir la gloire,
206 42B1-42B5, 43A1, 43A2, 47A, 52B, 60B, 67B, 78B: marqués par la victoire,
43A2*: →β

[17] 'Ces fers qu'ils destinaient au reste des humains' (*Brutus*, act I line 242); see also Appendix IV.

[18] The source of these lines 206-216 on future conquests over the weakened Persians and others would appear to be Boulainvilliers, p.210-11, but there is a rather similar passage in La Noue, *Mahomet II* (1739), p.70. The Aga talks to Mahomet about his glory rather than that of a nation, but the lines show the same triumph over decadence in a whole catalogue of nations (V.ii): 'Depuis que tes aïeux, du fond de la Scythie, / Fiers enfants de la guerre, ont inondé l'Asie, / Aucun d'eux n'a régné, tous ils ont triomphé. / Vois par eux des Soudans le pouvoir étouffé; / Par eux l'Asirien chassé de Babylone; / L'efféminé Persan renversé de son trône; / Le Caraman vaincu; le Bulgare asservi; / Le Hongrois abaissé; le Thrace anéanti. / Ils régnaient tous ces rois que leur valeur écrase: / De leur trône abattu l'équité fut la

Vois du Nord au Midi l'univers désolé,
La Perse encor sanglante, et son trône ébranlé,
L'Inde esclave et timide, et l'Egypte abaissée,
Des murs de Constantin la splendeur éclipsée; 210
Vois l'empire romain tombant de toutes parts,
Ce grand corps déchiré, dont les membres épars
Languissent dispersés sans honneur et sans vie;
Sur ces débris du monde élevons l'Arabie.
Il faut un nouveau culte, il faut de nouveaux fers; 215
Il faut un nouveau dieu pour l'aveugle univers.
En Egypte Osiris,[19] Zoroastre[20] en Asie,
Chez les Crétois Minos,[21] Numa[22] dans l'Italie,
A des peuples sans mœurs, et sans culte et sans rois,
Donnèrent aisément d'insuffisantes lois. 220
Je viens après mille ans changer ces lois grossières.
J'apporte un joug plus noble aux nations entières.

210 42B1-42B5, 43A1, 43A2, 47A, 52B, 60B, 67B, 78B: la grandeur éclipsée,
43A2*: →β
215 42B1-42B5, 42XX, 43A1, 43A2, 47A, 52B, 60B, 67B, 78B: faut de nouveaux cultes,
43A2*: →β
219 52B, 60B: peuples sans murs et
221 42B1-42B5, 42XX, 43A1, 43A2, 47A, 52B, 60B, 67B, 78B: ans chasser ces
43A2*: →β

---

base. / L'amour ainsi qu'au tien, siégeant à leur côté, / Leur mollesse usurpait le nom de majesté, / Ah! lorsque dans ces murs, théâtre de la gloire, / Ton intrépidité conduisit la victoire, / Lorsque ton bras puissant foudroyant ces remparts, / Abattit et saisit le sceptre des Césars: / Ah! tu régnais alors; et si j'ose le dire, / Plus que tous tes aïeux tu méritais l'Empire. / L'univers consterné présageant ta grandeur, / Déjà tendait les mains aux fers de son vainqueur.'

[19] See *La Philosophie de l'histoire*, *OC*, vol.59, p.185.

[20] See *Essai sur les moeurs*, i.247-53.

[21] See *La Philosophie de l'histoire*, *OC*, vol.59, p.176, 216; *Notebooks*, *OC*, vol.82, p.487.

[22] See *Notebooks*, *OC*, vol.81, p.113; vol.82, p.533, 545.

J'abolis les faux dieux, et mon culte épuré
De ma grandeur naissante est le premier degré.
Ne me reproche point de tromper ma patrie; 225
Je détruis sa faiblesse et son idolâtrie.
Sous un roi, sous un dieu, je viens la réunir;
Et, pour la rendre illustre, il la faut asservir.

ZOPIRE

Voilà donc tes desseins! c'est donc toi dont l'audace
De la terre à ton gré prétend changer la face! 230
Tu veux, en apportant le carnage et l'effroi,[23]
Commander aux humains de penser comme toi?
Tu ravages le monde, et tu prétends l'instruire?
Ah! si par des erreurs il s'est laissé séduire,
Si la nuit du mensonge a pu nous égarer, 235
Par quels flambeaux affreux veux-tu nous éclairer?
Quel droit as-tu reçu d'enseigner, de prédire,
De porter l'encensoir, et d'affecter l'empire?

MAHOMET

Le droit qu'un esprit vaste, et ferme en ses desseins,
A sur l'esprit grossier des vulgaires humains.[24] 240

223 MS8: J'abolis ces faux débris,
227 MS5: Sous un dieu, sous un roi je

[23] 'Rapporter à son tour le carnage et l'effroi' (*La Henriade*, VIII line 60).
[24] Kehl note: 'C'est le mot de la maréchale d'Ancre à un de ses juges, qui lui demandait de quel charme elle s'était servie pour captiver l'esprit de la reine: de l'ascendant que les âmes fortes ont sur les esprits faibles.' Cf. 'Mon sortilège a été le pouvoir que les âmes fortes doivent avoir sur les esprits faibles' (*Essai sur les mœurs*, ii.574).

ZOPIRE

Eh quoi! tout factieux, qui pense avec courage,
Doit donner aux mortels un nouvel esclavage?
Il a droit de tromper, s'il trompe avec grandeur?

MAHOMET

Oui; je connais ton peuple, il a besoin d'erreur;
Ou véritable ou faux, mon culte est nécessaire. 245
Que t'ont produit tes dieux? quel bien t'ont-ils pu faire?
Quels lauriers vois-tu croître au pied de leurs autels?[25]
Ta secte obscure et basse avilit les mortels,
Enerve le courage, et rend l'homme stupide;
La mienne élève l'âme, et la rend intrépide. 250
Ma loi fait des héros.

ZOPIRE

Dis plutôt des brigands.
Porte ailleurs tes leçons, l'école des tyrans.
Va vanter l'imposture à Médine où tu règnes,

241 MS5↑, MS6, 42B1-42B5, 42XX, 43A1, 43A2, 47A, 52B, 60B, 67B, 78B: Ainsi tout scélérat qui pense
MS4: qu'il pense
43A2*, MS8: Ainsi tout factieux qui pense
243 MS8: A droit de tromper,
245 MS1: [*two variants with the comment in the margin*: 'Si vous voulez...ou...']
Tu crois mon culte faux, mais il est nécessaire.
Ma secte fausse ou vraie est enfin nécessaire.
246 MS4: V↑bien
247 MS5: ↑lauriers voit-on croître
MS5, MS8, 42X1, 42X2, 42B1-42B5, 42XX, 43A1, 43A2, 47A, 51B, 52B, 60B, 67B, 71P1, 71P2, 74A, 78B: aux pieds de
73M: au pieds
251 W71P: La loi

[25] A strange cliché to find in a play dealing with Islam. It frequently appears in slightly different forms: 'Répondez: ce matin aux pieds de vos autels' (*Sémiramis*, III.ii); see also Appendix IV.

Où tes maîtres séduits marchent sous tes enseignes,
Où tu vois tes égaux à tes pieds abattus. 255

MAHOMET

Des égaux, dès longtemps Mahomet n'en a plus.
Je fais trembler la Mecque, et je règne à Médine;
Crois-moi, reçois la paix, si tu crains ta ruine.

ZOPIRE

La paix est dans ta bouche, et ton cœur en est loin:
Penses-tu me tromper?

MAHOMET

Je n'en ai pas besoin. 260
C'est le faible qui trompe, et le puissant commande.
Demain j'ordonnerai ce que je te demande;
Demain je peux te voir[26] à mon joug asservi:
Aujourd'hui Mahomet veut être ton ami.

ZOPIRE

Nous amis! nous? cruel! ah quel nouveau prestige! 265
Connais-tu quelque dieu qui fasse un tel prodige?

254 MS4: sous tes < lois >.
256 43A3, W46, W48D, W50, 51B, W51, W52, T53, 54V, W57P, T64G, T64P, W64R, T67, 68P, 71P1, 71P2, 74A: Des égaux! de longtemps
259 42B1-42B4, 43A1, 43A2, 47A: bouche, mais ton cœur
43A2*: →β
261 MS8: trompe, mais le puissant commande,
263 MS4, 42X1, 42X2: Demain je peux t'avoir
42B1-42B5, 42XX, 43A1, 43A2, 47A, 52B, 60B, 67B, 78B, K: Demain je puis te voir
264 73X, T76X: Mahomet peut être
266 T73A1, T77: qui passe un tel prodige?

[26] This correction from the early editions was made by de Missy (D2689).

'Dessiné d'après nature par Whirsker', *Les Métamorphoses de Melpomène et de Thalie ou caractères dramatiques des comédies française et italienne* (Paris n.d. [*c*.1780]). II, 5, lines 259-260, misquoted. (*British Museum*)

Voltaire and Lekain acting in *Mahomet* at Ferney. Engraver unknown.

MAHOMET

J'en connais un puissant, et toujours écouté,
Qui te parle avec moi.

ZOPIRE

Qui?

MAHOMET

La nécessité,
Ton intérêt.

ZOPIRE

Avant qu'un tel nœud nous rassemble,
Les enfers et les cieux seront unis ensemble. 270
L'intérêt est ton dieu, le mien est l'équité;
Entre ces ennemis il n'est point de traité.
Quel serait le ciment,[27] réponds-moi, si tu l'oses,
De l'horrible amitié qu'ici tu me proposes?
Réponds; est-ce ton fils que mon bras te ravit? 275
Est-ce le sang des miens que ta main répandit?

269 MS4, MS5, 42X1, 42X2: nous assemble,
272 MS5, 42X1, 42X2: Entre ses ennemis
42X1*: →β
42B1-42B5, 42XX, 43A1, 43A2, 47A, 67B: Contre ces ennemis
43A2*: →β
52B, 60B, 78B: Contre ses ennemis
273 MS4, MS5, 42X1, 42X2: Quel sera le ciment?
42B1-42B5, 42XX, 43A1, 43A2, 47A, 52B, 67B, 78B: serait le lien, réponds-moi
43A2*: →β
60B: serait le lieu
274 MS4: que tu me proposes?
275 42X1, 42X2, 42XX: que ton bras me ravit

[27] 'Je ne trouve point le mot de *ciment* de l'amitié bas' (D2515; to Cideville, 19 July 1741). In fact the word 'ciment' had already been used figuratively by Rotrou (*Cosroès*, V.v.1634): 'Ma tête n'est la base et mon sang le ciment'.

MAHOMET

Oui, ce sont tes fils même. Oui, connais un mystère,
Dont seul dans l'univers je suis dépositaire:
Tu pleures tes enfants, ils respirent tous deux.

ZOPIRE

Ils vivraient! qu'as-tu dit? ô ciel! ô jour heureux! 280
Ils vivraient! c'est de toi qu'il faut que je l'apprenne!

MAHOMET

Elevés dans mon camp tous deux sont dans ma chaîne.

ZOPIRE

Mes enfants dans tes fers! ils pourraient te servir!

MAHOMET

Mes bienfaisantes mains ont daigné les nourrir.

ZOPIRE

Quoi! tu n'as point sur eux étendu ta colère? 285

MAHOMET

Je ne les punis point des fautes de leur père.

277 MS6: ↑tes enfants même
283 MS4: Enfants dans les fers,
284 MS4, MS5, 42X1, 42X2: Mes bienfaits en mes mains
42X1*: →β
285 MS4, MS5, 42X1, 42X2, 71P1, 71P2, 74A: Quoi, tu n'as pas sur eux
42B1-42B5, 42XX, 43A1, 43A2, 47A, 52B, 60B, 67B, 78B: Quoi! sur eux tu n'as point étendu
MS6: ↑Et, tu n'as point
43A2*: →β
286 MS8: punis des
73P, 78P: point de fautes

ZOPIRE

Achève, éclaircis-moi, parle, quel est leur sort?

MAHOMET

Je tiens entre mes mains et leur vie et leur mort;
Tu n'as qu'à dire un mot, et je t'en fais l'arbitre.

ZOPIRE

Moi, je puis les sauver! à quel prix? à quel titre? 290
Faut-il donner mon sang? faut-il porter leurs fers?

MAHOMET

Non. Mais il faut m'aider à dompter l'univers.
Il faut rendre la Mecque, abandonner ton temple,
De la crédulité donner à tous l'exemple,
Annoncer l'Alcoran aux peuples effrayés, 295
Me servir en prophète, et tomber à mes pieds:
Je te rendrai ton fils, et je serai ton gendre.

ZOPIRE

Mahomet, je suis père, et je porte un cœur tendre.
Après quinze ans d'ennuis retrouver mes enfants,
Les revoir, et mourir dans leurs embrassements, 300
C'est le premier des biens pour mon âme attendrie:
Mais s'il faut à ton culte asservir ma patrie,
Ou de ma propre main les immoler tous deux,

292 MS5, 42B1-42B5, 43A1, 43A2, 47A, 52B, 60B, 67B, 78B, K: à tromper l'univers.

293 MS4, 42X1, 42X2: abandonner son temple

296 MS4: [*absent*]

78P: prophète, tomber

299 MS4: ans d'ennui, je trouve mes

302 42B1-42B5, 42XX, 43A1, 43A2, 47A, 52B, 60B, 67B, 78B: Mais s'il faut à l'erreur asservir ma

43A2*: →β

Connais-moi, Mahomet, mon choix n'est pas douteux.
Adieu.

MAHOMET *seul.*

Fier citoyen, vieillard inexorable, 305
Je serai plus que toi, cruel, impitoyable.

## *SCÈNE VI*

### MAHOMET, OMAR

OMAR

Mahomet, il faut l'être, ou nous sommes perdus.
Les secrets des tyrans me sont déjà vendus.
Demain la trêve expire, et demain l'on t'arrête;
Demain Zopire est maître, et fait tomber ta tête. 310
La moitié du sénat vient de te condamner;
N'osant pas te combattre, on t'ose assassiner.
Ce meurtre d'un héros, ils le nomment supplice,
Et ce complot obscur, ils l'appellent justice.[28]

304 71P2, 74A: choix n'est point douteux.
71P1: β

308 MS4, 42X1, 42X2, 42B1-42B5, 42XX, 43A1, 43A2, 47A, 52B, 60B, 67B, 78B: secrets du tyran me
MS5: déjà rendus,

309-310 T73A1, T77: [*invert these lines*]

313 42B1-42B5, 42XX, 43A1, 43A2, 47A, 52B, 60B, 67B, 78B: Le meurtre

314 42B1-42B5, 42XX, 43A1, 43A2, 47A, 52B, 60B, 67B, 78B: Et cet affreux complot, ils le nomment justice.
43A2*: Et cet complot obscur, ils le nomment justice.

[28] Voltaire further reworked this scene, notably shortening Mahomet's first speech, on advice from Cideville in August 1741 (D2521): 'Votre nouvelle scène 6 du second acte et qui le termine entre Mahomet et Omar, me paraît infiniment mieux, en ce qu'elle explique le pourquoi Mahomet choisit plutôt Seïde qu'un autre pour assassiner Zopire, mais l'explique t'elle encore assez? Cette scène est dans le

MAHOMET

Ils sentiront la mienne. Ils verront ma fureur. 315
La persécution fit toujours ma grandeur.
Zopire périra.

OMAR

Cette tête funeste,

316 42B1-42B5, 43A1, 43A2, 47A, 52B, 60B, 67B, 78B: persécution fut toujours
43A2*: →β

317 MS4, MS5, 42X1, 42X2, 42B1-42B5, 42XX, 43A1, 43A2, 47A, 52B, 60B, 67B, 78B: Zophire va périr.

---

genre délibératif. Quelques raisons de plus pour le déterminer seraient à mon gré des beautés, en ce qu'elles satisferaient davantage le spectateur. Les raisons entassées et auxquelles il n'y plus de réplique sont les beautés de ces sortes de scènes, il faut dans ces cas que les acteurs se fassent toutes les objections que pourraient faire les critiques. Le fonds y est bien dans votre scène mais peut-être n'est-il pas assez dévélopé ni assez bien tourné. Il est de la politique de Mahomet qu'il veuille un bras obscur pour commettre cette horrible action afin qu'il reste dans l'oubli et qu'on ne puisse lui en imputer la faute, et en ce que ce n'est pas lui qui nomme Seïde vous lui sauvez le ridicule d'en vouloir à Seïde comme à son rival, mais ne doit-il point balancer sur le peu qu'on doit se fier à un homme de cette trempe et de cet âge pour l'exécution d'un meurtre si important? et c'est là qu'Omar doit, ce me semble, peindre le pouvoir qu'a le fanatisme sur les hommes que de lâches et faibles il rend capables de tout oser, et de plus il doit encore rassurer pleinement Mahomet en lui disant qu'il ne perdra pas Seïde de vue et en lui jurant que si Seïde balance il immolera Zopire lui-même et Seïde après. Tout ceci ne doit pas être long mais il me paraît trop court et trop peu dévelopé, il n'y a de long que ce qui est inutile.

J'ai trouvé de l'obscurité dans La première tirade de Mahomet,

Et moi dès cette nuit assurant son trépas
Je le plonge au tombeau qu'il ouvre sous nos pas.
Quel bras servira mieux mon culte et ma vengeance?

Ce second vers ne veut-il pas dire que Mahomet veut ne s'en fier qu'à lui-même pour tuer Zopire, surtout quand il dit au dernier vers – quel bras servira mieux mon culte et ma vengeance que le mien sans doute.

Si c'est là le sens de ce vers, il y a contradiction avec ce que Mahomet dit ensuite:

Je veux un bras obscur &c.
Si je n'ai pas pris le vrai sens il y a obscurité.'

En tombant à tes pieds, fera fléchir le reste.
Mais ne perds point de temps.

MAHOMET

Mais, malgré mon courroux,
Je dois cacher la main qui va lancer les coups, 320
Et détourner de moi les soupçons du vulgaire.

OMAR

Il est trop méprisable.

MAHOMET

Il faut pourtant lui plaire:
Et j'ai besoin d'un bras, qui par ma voix conduit,
Soit seul chargé du meurtre, et m'en laisse le fruit.

OMAR

Pour un tel attentat je réponds de Seïde. 325

MAHOMET

De lui?

OMAR

C'est l'instrument d'un pareil homicide.
Otage de Zopire, il peut seul aujourd'hui

319 MS8: perds pas de
319-320 42B1-42B5, 42XX, 43A1, 43A2, 47A, 52A, 60B, 67B, 78B:
MAHOMET
Malgré tout mon courroux, [42XX: Mais malgré mon courroux]
Je veux cacher le bras d'où partiront [43A1: porteront] les coups,
320 MS4, MS5, 42X1, 42X2: Je veux cacher la main qui va porter les coups,
MS6: ↑main qui a porté <d'où partira> les coups
43A2*: Je dois cacher la main qui doit porter les coups,
MS8: lancer ces coups,
321 T62, T64: Et détourner pour moi
MS8: ces soupçons du vulgaire

L'aborder en secret, et te venger de lui.
Tes autres favoris, zélés avec prudence,
Pour s'exposer à tout ont trop d'expérience; 330
Ils sont tous dans cet âge, où la maturité
Fait tomber le bandeau de la crédulité.
Il faut un cœur plus simple, aveugle avec courage,
Un esprit amoureux de son propre esclavage.
La jeunesse est le temps de ces illusions; 335
Seïde est tout en proie aux superstitions;
C'est un lion docile à la voix qui le guide.

MAHOMET

Le frère de Palmire?

OMAR

Oui, lui-même. Oui, Seïde,
De ton fier ennemi le fils audacieux,
De son maître offensé rival incestueux. 340

MAHOMET

Je déteste Seïde, et son nom seul m'offense.

328 78B: et se venger de lui.
329 MS4: Les autres favoris
MS5, 42X1, 42X2: Des autres
331 47A: sont dans cet
336-337 MS4, MS5, 42X1, 42X2, 42B1-42B5, 42XX, 43A1, 43A2, 47A, 52B, 60B, 67B, 78B:
Et Seïde enivré de superstitions,
Est un lion docile à la voix [MS4: voie] qui le guide.
MS8, 43A2*: →β
338 42B1-42B5, 42XX, 43A1, 43A2, 47A, 52B, 60B, 67B, 78B:
OMAR
Oui, lui-même, Seïde,
339 42B1-42B4, 42XX, 43A1, 43A2, 47A: ennemi fils audacieux,
340 42B1-42B3, 42XX, 43A1: De ton maître
42B5, 52B, 60B, 67B, 78B: De mon maître
341 71P1, 71P2, 74A: et son seul nom m'offense:

La cendre de mon fils me crie encor vengeance.
Mais tu connais l'objet de mon fatal amour;
Tu connais dans quel sang elle a puisé le jour.
Tu vois, que dans ces lieux environnés d'abîmes, 345
Je viens chercher un trône, un autel, des victimes;
Qu'il faut d'un peuple fier enchanter les esprits,
Qu'il faut perdre Zopire, et perdre encor son fils.
Allons, consultons bien mon intérêt, ma haine,
L'amour, l'indigne amour, qui malgré moi m'entraîne, 350
Et la religion, à qui tout est soumis,
Et la nécessité, par qui tout est permis.

*Fin du second acte.*[29]

349 MS8: mon intérêt, < l'amour > ma haine,

[29] 'A la fin du second et du quatrième acte, il faut faire déshabiller quatorze hommes de ceux qui sont à la suite de Mahomet, et les revêtir d'habits mecquois pour la suite de Seide [...]. Ils sont armés de sabres' (MS Lekain, instructions for the *tailleur magasinier*).

# ACTE III

## *SCÈNE PREMIÈRE*

### SEÏDE, PALMIRE

PALMIRE

Demeure. Quel est donc ce secret sacrifice?[1]

c-10 MS4, MS5, 42X1, 42X2, 42B1-42B5, 42XX, 43A1, 43A2, 47A, 52B, 60B, 67B, 78B:

SEÏDE, PALMIRE

SEÏDE

Quoi! Zopire en secret demande à nous [MS4, MS5, 42X1, 42X2: vous] parler;
Dans quel temps, dans quels lieux, [MS4, MS5, 42X1, 42X2: quel lieu] qu'a-t-il à révéler?
Le temps presse, dit-il,

PALMIRE

Ah! demeure Seïde;
Crains les complots sanglants d'un sénat homicide;
Zopire nous trahit, on s'arme, on va frapper,
Le Pontife l'a dit, il ne peut nous tromper,
Garde-toi de Zopire, évite sa présence: [42B1: *gives this line to Seïde*]

SEÏDE

Je verrais ce vieillard avec pleine assurance:
Mais mon devoir m'appelle, il lui faut obéir,

[1] The 1742 version of this hemistich is closer to others found elsewhere: 'Avait fait à nos dieux un secret sacrifice' (*Œdipe*, act II line 114); 'Ninias vous révère. Un secret sacrifice' (*Sémiramis*, V.i); 'J'offris sur ses autels un secret sacrifice' (Racine, *Iphigénie*, I.i.54). The act also began with a line reminiscent of the opening of act II, scene 3 in Racine's *Bérénice* (553): 'Bérénice, Seigneur, demande à vous parler'. Similarly, the initial version of Palmire's first speech in this act ended with another Racinian-sounding line: 'Garde-toi de Zopire, évite sa présence'. See: 'Autant que je le puis, j'évite sa présence' (Racine, *Athalie*, I.ii.192).

Quel sang a demandé l'éternelle justice?[2]
Ne m'abandonne pas.

SEÏDE

Dieu daigne m'appeler.
Mon bras doit le servir, mon cœur va lui parler.
Omar veut à l'instant, par un serment terrible, 5
M'attacher de plus près à ce maître invincible.
Je vais jurer à Dieu de mourir pour sa loi,
Et mes seconds serments ne seront que pour toi.

PALMIRE

D'où vient qu'à ce serment je ne suis point présente?
Si je t'accompagnais, j'aurais moins d'épouvante. 10
Omar, ce même Omar, loin de me consoler,

---

Je m'arrache à moi-même, et c'est pour t'obtenir.
Omar offre pour nous un secret sacrifice,
J'y vais parler à Dieu, réclamer sa justice,
Lui [MS4, MS5, 42X1, 42X2: Et] jurer de mourir pour défendre sa loi,
Et mes serments [MS4, MS5, 42X1, 42X2: mes seconds serments; 42B5, 52B, 60B, 67B, 78B: mes serments enfin ne; 47A: Palmire, et mes serments] ne seront que pour toi.

PALMIRE

D'où vient qu'à ces serments je ne suis pas présente [MS4, MS5, 42X1, 42X2, 42XX: point présenté!]
Si je l'accompagnais [42B5, MS9→β, 60B, 67B, 78B: t'accompagnais] 42X1*, 43A2*: →β

5 42X1*: serment < fidèle >
6 42X1*: plus à
7 51B, W51, 71P1, 71P2, 74A: mourir sous sa
11 MS4, MS5, 42X1, 42X2: de nous consoler

[2] 'Mon fils apaisera l'éternelle justice' (*Sémiramis*, V.ii).

Parle de trahison, de sang prêt à couler,
Des fureurs du sénat, des complots de Zopire.
Les feux sont allumés, bientôt la trêve expire.
Le fer cruel est prêt, on s'arme, on va frapper; 15
Le prophète l'a dit, il ne peut nous tromper.
Je crains tout de Zopire, et je crains pour Seïde.

SEÏDE

Croirai-je que Zopire ait un cœur si perfide?
Ce matin, comme otage à ses yeux présenté,
J'admirais sa noblesse et son humanité. 20
Je sentais qu'en secret une force inconnue
Enlevait jusqu'à lui mon âme prévenue.
Soit respect pour son nom, soit qu'un dehors heureux
Me cachât de son cœur les replis dangereux;
Soit que dans ces moments où je t'ai rencontrée, 25
Mon âme tout entière à son bonheur livrée,
Oubliant ses douleurs, et chassant tout effroi,
Ne connût, n'entendît, ne vît plus rien que toi.

12-14 42X1*:
Ne parle que de sang déjà prêt à couler,
Des fureurs du Sénat, des complots de Zopire,
Les feux sont allumés, demain la trêve expire.

12-17 MS4, MS5, 42X1, 42X2, 42B1-42B5, 42XX, 43A1, 43A2, 47A, 52B, 60B, 67B, 78B:
Ne parle que de sang déjà prêt à couler,
Il m'avertit surtout de craindre pour Seïde.

16 MS1, MS6, 42X1, 43A2*, 43A3, W46: Le Pontife l'a

17 42X1*: < Garde-toi de Zopire >

18 MS4, MS5, 42X1, 42X2: Zopire est un

22 42B1-42B5, 42XX, 43A1, 43A2, 47A, 52B, 60B, 68P, 67B, 78B: Elevait jusqu'à

24 42B2, 43A1: Ne cachât

25 42B1-42B5, 42XX, 43A1, 43A2, 47A, 52B, 60B, 67B, 78B: ces moments [42X2, 52B, 60, 67B, 78B: ce moment] que je t'ai [43A1: j'ai] rencontrée,

27 71P1, 71P2, 74A: Publiant ses douleurs;

Je me trouvais heureux d'être auprès de Zopire.
Je le hais d'autant plus,[3] qu'il m'avait su séduire; 30
Mais, malgré le courroux dont je dois m'animer,
Qu'il est dur de haïr ceux qu'on voulait aimer!

PALMIRE

Ah! que le ciel en tout a joint nos destinées!
Qu'il a pris soin d'unir nos âmes enchaînées!
Hélas! sans mon amour, sans ce tendre lien, 35
Sans cet instinct charmant qui joint mon cœur au tien,
Sans la religion que Mahomet m'inspire,
J'aurais eu des remords en accusant Zopire.

SEÏDE

Laissons ces vains remords, et nous abandonnons
A la voix de ce dieu qu'à l'envi nous servons. 40

30 MS4, MS5, MS6, 42X1, 42X2, 42B1-42B5, 42XX, 43A1, 43A2, 47A, 52B, 60B, 67B, 78B: qu'il a su me séduire,

32 MS4, MS5, MS6, 42X1, 42X2, 42B1-42B5, 42XX, 43A1, 43A2, 47A, 52B, 60B, 68P, 67B, 78B: qu'on voudrait aimer.

71P1, 71P2, 74A: haïr ce qu'on

33 MS4: tout < unit > nos

35 78P: , sous ce

35-36 MS4, MS5, 42X1, 42X2, 42B1-42B5, 42XX, 43A1, 43A2, 47A, 52B, 60B, 67B, 78B:

Sans toi, sans mon [42B1, 41B2: cet] amour, sans ce tendre lien,
Sans cet instinct puissant [42X1*: charmant] qui joint mon cœur au tien [MS4, D2699, 42X1, 42X2: ton cœur au mien],

43A2*: →β

40 42B1-42B5, 42XX, 43A1, 43A2, 47A, 52B, 60B, 67B, 78B: ce dieu que tous deux nous

43A2* →β

[3] A common expression with the verb *haïr*: 'Je le hais d'autant plus qu'il sait se faire aimer' (*Eriphyle*, III i.52); see also Appendix IV.

Je sors. Il faut prêter ce serment redoutable;
Le dieu qui m'entendra nous sera favorable;
Et le pontife roi, qui veille sur nos jours,
Bénira de ses mains de si chastes amours.
Adieu. Pour être à toi, je vais tout entreprendre. 45

## *SCÈNE II*

PALMIRE *seule.*

D'un noir pressentiment je ne puis me défendre.
Cet amour dont l'idée avait fait mon bonheur,
Ce jour tant souhaité n'est qu'un jour de terreur.
Quel est donc ce serment qu'on attend de Seïde?
Tout m'est suspect ici; Zopire m'intimide. 50
J'invoque Mahomet, et cependant mon cœur
Eprouve à son nom même une secrète horreur.

41 MS4, MS5β↑, 42X1, 42X2, 42B1-42B5, 42XX, 43A1, 43A2, 47A, 52B, 60B, 67B, 78B: Je vais prêter, Palmire, un serment redoutable.
43A2*: →β
42 42B1-42B5, 42XX, 43A1, 43A2, 47A, 52B, 60B, 67B, 78B: m'entendra, me sera
43A2*: →β
43 42B1-42B5, 42XX, 43A1, 43A2, 47A, 52B, 60B, 67B, 78B: le prophète roi
43-45 MS1:

SEÏDE

Il me protège, il t'aime, il chérit l'innocence.

PALMIRE

Sois sûr qu'il s'intéresse à nos chastes ardeurs.

48 MS4, MS5, 42X1, 42X2, 42B1-42B5, 42XX, 43A1, 43A2, 47A, 52B, 60B, 67B, 78B: Ce jour si [MS4, MS5: tant] souhaité, n'est-il qu'un jour d'horreur?
MS6, 43A2*, 43A3, W46, W48D, W50, 51B, W51, 54V, W52, T53, W56, W57P, T62, T64A, T64G, T64P, W64R, W64G, T66, T67, 67B, 67C, 68P, T68, T70, W70G, W70L, W72X, 71P1, 71P2, 74A: Ce jour tant souhaité me semble un jour d'horreur.
52 MS4: Eprouve en son
52B, 60B, 78B: à ce nom
73P, 77P1, 78P: nom une

Dans les profonds respects que ce héros m'inspire,
Je sens que je le crains presque autant que Zopire.
Délivre-moi, grand Dieu, de ce trouble où je suis. 55
Craintive je te sers, aveugle je te suis;
Hélas! daigne essuyer les pleurs où je me noie.

## SCÈNE III[4]

### MAHOMET, PALMIRE

PALMIRE

C'est vous qu'à mon secours un dieu propice envoie,
Seigneur, Seïde...

54 MS4: crains < tout > autant
55 W75X: Délivrez-moi
58 MS4, MS5$\beta^{\uparrow}$, 42X1, 42X2, 42B1-42B5, 42XX, 43A1, 43A2, 47A, 52B, 60B, 67B, 78B: C'est Mahomet, c'est lui, qu'un dieu puissant m'envoie: [MS4, MS5, 42X1, 42X2: dieu propice envoie:]
59 42B1-42B4, 43A1, 43A2, 47A:
Seigneur, sauvez Seïde.
MAHOMET
Quel est donc cet effroi?
43A2*: $\rightarrow\beta$
MS4, MS5$\beta^{\uparrow}$, 42X1, 42X2, 42B5, 43A3, W46, 52B, 60B, 67B, 78B:
PALMIRE
Seigneur. Sauvez Seïde. [*line* 58 *absent*]
MAHOMET
Eh [MS4, MS5, 42X1, 42X2: Ah!] quel est cet effroi?

[4] 'Il y a une scène qui m'embarrasse infiniment. C'est celle de Palmire et de Mahomet au 3ème acte. Vous sentez bien que Mahomet après avoir envoyé Séide recevoir les derniers ordres pour un parricide, tout rempli d'un attentat d'un intérêt si grand, peut avoir bien mauvaise grâce à parler longtemps d'amour avec une jeune innocente. Cette scène doit être très courte. Si Mahomet y joue trop le rôle de Tartuffe et d'amant, le ridicule est bien près. Il faut courir vite dans cet endroit-là, c'est de la cendre brûlante' (Voltaire to d'Argental, D2404; 19 January 1741).

MAHOMET

Eh bien, d'où vous vient cet effroi?
Et que craint-on pour lui quand on est près de moi? 60

PALMIRE

O ciel! vous redoublez la douleur qui m'agite.
Quel prodige inouï! votre âme est interdite;
Mahomet est troublé pour la première fois.[5]

MAHOMET

Je devrais l'être au moins du trouble où je vous vois.
Est-ce ainsi qu'à mes yeux votre simple innocence 65
Ose avouer un feu qui peut-être m'offense?
Votre cœur a-t-il pu, sans être épouvanté,
Avoir un sentiment que je n'ai pas dicté?
Ce cœur que j'ai formé n'est-il plus qu'un rebelle,
Ingrat à mes bienfaits, à mes lois infidèle? 70

PALMIRE

Que dites-vous? surprise et tremblante à vos pieds,
Je baisse en frémissant mes regards effrayés.
Eh quoi, n'avez-vous pas daigné, dans ce lieu même,

60 MS4, 42X1, 42X2, 42B1-42B5, 42XX, 43A1, 43A2, 47A, 52B, 60B, 67B, 78B: quand il est près de moi.

61 MS4, MS5, MS6, 42X1, 42X2, 42B1-42B5, 42XX, 43A1, 43A2, 47A, 52B, 60B, 67B, 67C, 78B: la terreur [MS6: < douleur >] qui m'agite,

43A2*: →β

62 42B1-42B5, 42XX, 43A1, 43A2, 47A, 52B, 60B, 67B, 78B: Seigneur, en me parlant, votre

43A2*: →β

65 43A1: yeux notre simple

68 MS4, MS5β↑, 42X1, 42X2: n'ai point dicté

[5] A much used line-filler: 'Marchait sous nos drapeaux pour la première fois' (*La Henriade*, VI line 269); see also Appendix IV.

Vous rendre à nos souhaits, et consentir qu'il m'aime?
Ces nœuds, ces chastes nœuds, que Dieu formait en nous, 75
Sont un lien de plus qui nous attache à vous.[6]

MAHOMET

Redoutez des liens formés par l'imprudence.
Le crime quelquefois suit de près l'innocence.
Le cœur peut se tromper; l'amour et ses douceurs

74 MS6, 42B1-42B5, 42XX, 43A1, 43A2, 47A, 52B, 60B, 67B, 78B: Justifier son choix, et

76 MS5β↑, 42X1, 42X2: Font un
MS8: qui vous attache à nous

76a-82 MS1 [*SCÈNE III*]

PALMIRE

Daignez les protéger.

MAHOMET

Ah! c'en est trop, ingrate...

PALMIRE

Quoi, Seigneur!

MAHOMET

Ecoutez... quelque espoir qui vous flatte,
Je crains de cet amour les trompeuses douceurs.
Tremblez qu'il ne nous coûte, et du sang, et des pleurs.

PALMIRE

Si je perdais Seïde, ils couleraient sans doute.
Vous préviendrez nos maux, votre cœur les redoute.
Seïde vous doit tout, et vos bienfaits passés

79-89 MS4, MS5β↑, 42X1, 42X2, 42B1-42B5, 42XX, 43A1, 43A2, 47A, 52B, 60B, 67B, 78B:

A d'étranges erreurs le cœur peut se livrer.

PALMIRE

Non, en aimant Seïde, il ne peut s'égarer.

MAHOMET

Il vous charme à ce point.

[6] De Missy, pondering his London edition, seems to have been responsible for the final wording here: 'je n'ose choisir entre *Font* et *Sont*' (D2689).

Pourront coûter, Palmire, et du sang et des pleurs. 80

PALMIRE

N'en doutez pas, mon sang coulerait pour Seïde.

MAHOMET

Vous l'aimez à ce point?

PALMIRE

Depuis le jour qu'Hercide
Nous soumit l'un et l'autre à votre joug sacré,
Cet instinct tout puissant, de nous-mêmes ignoré,
Devançant la raison, croissant avec notre âge, 85
Du ciel, qui conduit tout, fut le secret ouvrage.
Nos penchants, dites-vous, ne viennent que de lui.
Dieu ne saurait changer; pourrait-il aujourd'hui
Réprouver un amour, que lui-même il fit naître?
Ce qui fut innocent peut-il cesser de l'être? 90

---

PALMIRE

Seigneur, je le confesse,
J'ai pensé que Dieu même approuvait ma tendresse.
Nos penchants, disiez-vous [MS4, MS5, 42X1, 42X2: dites-vous], ne viennent que de lui,
Il ne saurait changer: voudrait-il [MS4, MS5, 42X1, 42X2: changer; pourrait-il] aujourd'hui
Réprouver un amour, que sans doute [MS4, MS5, 42X1, 42X2: que lui-même] il fit naître?
42X1*: →β
43A2*: →β [*except for part of line* 88 *(see below)*]

81 42X1*: doutez point,
82 W57P: piont
83 71P2, 74A: Nous unit l'un
T70: l'un l'autre
87 MS6< β >, 67C: penchants, disiez-vous,
88 42X1*: Il ne
43A2*: [*leaves unchanged* voudrait-il aujourd'hui (*see variant to lines* 79-89)]
89 MS6: lui-même a fait naître

Pourrais-je être coupable?

MAHOMET

Oui. Vous devez trembler.
Attendez les secrets que je dois révéler;
Attendez que ma voix veuille enfin vous apprendre
Ce qu'on peut approuver, ce qu'on doit se défendre.
Ne croyez que moi seul.

PALMIRE

Et qui croire que vous? 95
Esclave de vos lois, soumise à vos genoux,
Mon cœur d'un saint respect ne perd point l'habitude.

MAHOMET

Trop de respect souvent mène à l'ingratitude.

PALMIRE

Non, si de vos bienfaits je perds le souvenir,
Que Seïde à vos yeux s'empresse à m'en punir! 100

91 MS6: < Pourrai-je >

91-99 MS4, MS5β↑, 42X1, 42X2, 42B1-42B5, 42XX, 43A1, 43A2, 47A, 52B, 60B, 67B, 78B:

Oui, vous l'êtes pour moi,
Vous, sous mes yeux nourrie à l'ombre de la foi [MS4, MS5, 42X1, 42X2: de ma loi],
Des enfants de tribut [67B: tribu], vous toujours distinguée,
Vous à qui ma tendresse est encor prodiguée,
Vous qu'un profane enfin commence à me ravir.

PALMIRE

Non, Seigneur, près de vous il veut vivre et mourir.
Rien ne m'arrache à vous, non, vos bontés passées
Ne s'effaceront pas du fond de nos pensées.
Seigneur, si j'en perdais le sacré souvenir,

42X1*, 43A2*: →β

92 MS6<↑>, MS8: Attendez des secrets

98 42X1*: Le respect bien souvent

100 42X1*: vos pieds s'empresse

78B: s'empresse de m'en punir.

MAHOMET

Seïde!

PALMIRE

Ah! quel courroux arme votre œil sévère?

MAHOMET

Allez, rassurez-vous, je n'ai point de colère.
C'est éprouver assez vos sentiments secrets;
Reposez-vous sur moi de vos vrais intérêts.
Je suis digne du moins de votre confiance; 105
Vos destins dépendront de votre obéissance.[7]
Si j'eus soin de vos jours, si vous m'appartenez,
Méritez des bienfaits qui vous sont déstinés.

101 MS5: courroux a sur votre
101-117 MS1:

MAHOMET

... il est temps que je règne.

PALMIRE

Ah! n'y régnez vous pas, vous, notre unique appui.
[...] vous pourrai-je offenser?

MAHOMET

Sujet à quelle honte il faut donc m'abaisser.
Il suffit, et je vois quelle est votre constance.
Allez. Tout dépendra de votre obéissance.
Vous pouvez mériter un hymen glorieux
Et les bienfaits d'un père, et les faveurs des cieux.
Quoique leur voix terrible ordonne de Seïde;
Affermissez ses pas où son devoir le guide,
Qu'il garde ses serments, et soit digne de vous.

PALMIRE

N'en doutez point, Seigneur, il les remplira tous.
Je cours à vous servir encourager son âme.

104 MS4, MS5, 42X1, 42X2: de tous vos intérêts.
108 MS4, 42X1, 42X2, 42XX, 71P1, 71P2, 74A: Méritez les bienfaits
68P: Méritez de bienfaits

[7] 'Veut s'assurer ici de votre obéissance' (*Eriphyle*, II.iii.102); see Appendix IV.

Quoique la voix du ciel ordonne de Seïde,
Affermissez ses pas où son devoir le guide: 110
Qu'il garde ses serments, qu'il soit digne de vous.

PALMIRE

N'en doutez point, mon père,[8] il les remplira tous.
Je réponds de son cœur, ainsi que de moi-même.
Seïde vous adore encor plus qu'il ne m'aime.
Il voit en vous son roi, son père, son appui; 115
J'en atteste à vos pieds l'amour que j'ai pour lui.
Je cours à vous servir encourager son âme.

## *SCÈNE IV*

MAHOMET *seul.*

Quoi! je suis malgré moi confident de sa flamme?

109 42X1, 42X2: ciel l'ordonne
110 MS6, 42B1-42B5, 42XX, 43A1, 43A2, 47A, 52B, 60B, 67B, 78B: Affermissez les pas
111 47A, 51B, W51, 71P1, 71P2, 74A: garde les serments
112 MS4, MS5, 42X1, 42X2, 42B1-42B5, 42XX, 43A2, 47A, 52B, 60B, 67B, 78B: doutez pas,
43A1: Ne doutez pas,
114 MS4, MS5, 42X1, 42X2: vous chérit encore plus
42B1-42B5, 42XX, 43A1, 43A2, 47A, 52B, 60B, 67B, 78B: Il vous chérit encore beaucoup plus
43A2*: →β
117 42X1: Je course
42X2: Je courre
42X1*: →β
118-119 MS1

MAHOMET

Que leur intelligence irrite mes fureurs.
Contresignons-nous surtout...

[8] By replacing the earlier 'Seigneur' of 1742 with 'mon père', Voltaire moves away only slightly from a stock Racinian phrase; see Appendix IV.

Quoi! sa naïveté, confondant ma fureur,
Enfonce innocemment le poignard dans mon cœur?[9] 120
Père, enfants, destinés au malheur de ma vie,[10]
Race toujours funeste, et toujours ennemie,
Vous allez éprouver, dans cet horrible jour,
Ce que peut à la fois ma haine et mon amour.[11]

## *SCÈNE V*

### MAHOMET, OMAR

OMAR

Enfin, voici le temps, et de ravir Palmire, 125
Et d'envahir la Mecque, et de punir Zopire.

119 42B5*, 78B: confondant sa fureur

120 42B1-42B5, 42XX, 43A1, 43A2, 47A, 52B, 60B, 67B, 78B: M'enfonce innocemment le poignard dans le cœur.

43A2*: →β

124 MS5: ↑β la fin ma haine, et

125-126 MS1: ↑β

[9] Another reading prompted by de Missy: 'Je balance un peu moins entre les deux leçons, *Enfonce innocemment le poignard dans mon sein*, et *M'enfonce innocemment le poignard dans le sein*: Mais c'est à vous à fixer mon choix' (D2689).

[10] 'C'est lui qui met le comble au malheur de ma vie' (*Brutus*, II.i.92); see also Appendix IV.

[11] A commonly used antithesis: 'Toujours troublé, toujours plein de haine et d'amour' (*Mariamne*, III.iv); 'Et celle qui commande et la haine et l'amour' (*Tancrède*, II.i); see also Appendix IV.

Sa mort seule à tes pieds mettra nos citoyens;
Tout est désespéré, si tu ne le préviens.
Le seul Seïde ici te peut servir sans doute;
Il voit souvent Zopire, il lui parle, il l'écoute. 130
Tu vois cette retraite, et cet obscur détour,
Qui peut de ton palais conduire à son séjour.
Là, cette nuit Zopire à ses dieux fantastiques

127 42B1-42B4, 42XX, 43A1: à vos pieds mettra ses citoyens,
MS5, 42B5, 43A2, 47A, 52B, 60B, 67B, 78B: mettra ses citoyens,
127-138 MS1 [*cf. act II lines* 321-332]:
nos citoyens:
Nous sommes prévenus si tu ne les préviens,
Ton seul rival ici te peut servir sans doute.
Il voit souvent Zopire, il lui parle, il l'écoute,
Et non loin de ces lieux sans tumulte et sans bruit
Seul il peut l'immoler dans l'ombre de la nuit.[12]
MAHOMET
Vengeons-nous, mais cachons ma vengeance au vulgaire.
Je méprise le peuple et je cherche à lui plaire.
128 MS4, MS5, MS6, 42X1* [*underlined*], 42X1, 42X2, 42B1-42B5, 42XX, 43A1, 43A2, 47A, 52B, 60B, 67B, 71P1, 71P2, 74A, 78B: ne les préviens.
129 42B1-42B4, 42XX, 43A1, 43A2, 47A: ici peut le servir, sans
42B5, 52B, 60B, 67B, 78B: Seïde ici peut te servir, sans
130 MS6, 42B1-42B5, 42XX, 43A1, 43A2, 47A, 52B, 60B, 67B, 78B: Lui seul il voit Zopire,
131 MS5: Près de cette
132 MS5: de ce palais
133 MS8: Où... Zopire
W46: à ces dieux
133-136 MS4, MS5↑β, 42X1, 42X2, 42B1-42B5, 42XX, 43A1, 43A2, 47A, 52B, 60B, 67B, 78B:
Là, cette nuit Zophire à ses dieux chimériques
Offre un encens frivole, et des vœux fanatiques;
Là, Seïde enivré du zèle de la [MS4, MS5, 42X1, 42X2: ta] loi,
Peut [MS4, MS5, 42X1, 42X2: Va] l'immoler au Dieu qui lui parle par [MS5↑: pour] toi.
43A2*: →β

[12] Cf. *La Henriade*, IV line 38: 'A la clarté des cieux, dans l'ombre de la nuit'.

Offre un encens frivole, et des vœux chimériques.
Là, Seïde, enivré du zèle de ta loi, 135
Va l'immoler au dieu qui lui parle par toi.

MAHOMET

Qu'il l'immole, il le faut, il est né pour le crime.
Qu'il en soit l'instrument, qu'il en soit la victime.
Ma vengeance, mes feux, ma loi, ma sûreté,
L'irrévocable arrêt de la fatalité, 140
Tout le veut: mais crois-tu que son jeune courage,
Nourri du fanatisme, en ait toute la rage?

OMAR

Lui seul était formé pour remplir ton dessein.
Palmire à te servir excite encor sa main.
L'amour, le fanatisme, aveuglent sa jeunesse; 145
Il sera furieux par excès de faiblesse.

MAHOMET

Par les nœuds des serments as-tu lié son cœur?

136 MS8, 51B, W51, 71P1, 71P2, 74A: parle pour toi.

137-138 MS5:
↑Qu'il l'immole, il le faut, né l'instrument du crime,
Qu'il en devienne, Omar, la première victime.

139 MS6, 42B1-42B5, 42XX, 43A1, 43A2, 47A, 52B, 60B, 67B, 78B: Ma vengeance, ma [MS8: mes] loi, mes feux, ma sûreté,

143 42B1-42B5, 42XX, 43A1, 43A2, 47A, 52B, 60B, 67B, 78B: seul semble formé
43A2*: →β

145 MS4, 42X1, 42X2: aveugle

146 MS4, MS5, 42X1, 42X2, 42B1-42B5, 42XX, 43A, 43A3, 47A, W46, 52B, 60B, 67B, 78B: furieux à force de
43A2*: →β

147 MS4, 42X1, 42X2, 42B1-42B5, 42XX, 43A1, 43A2, 47A, 52B, 60B, 67B, 73M, 73P, 77P1, 78B, 78P: nœuds du serment as-tu

OMAR

Du plus saint appareil la ténébreuse horreur,
Les autels, les serments, tout enchaîne Seïde.
J'ai mis un fer sacré dans sa main parricide, 150
Et la religion le remplit de fureur.
Il vient.

## SCÈNE VI

### MAHOMET, OMAR, SEÏDE

MAHOMET

Enfant d'un dieu qui parle à votre cœur,
Ecoutez par ma voix sa volonté suprême;
Il faut venger son culte, il faut venger Dieu même.

SEÏDE

Roi, pontife et prophète, à qui je suis voué, 155
Maître des nations, par le ciel avoué,
Vous avez sur mon être une entière puissance;
Eclairez seulement ma docile ignorance.
Un mortel venger Dieu!

MAHOMET

C'est par vos faibles mains

150-151 MS6<β>, 67C, 71P2, F-Nts copy, ms corrections:
Arme d'un fer sacré cette main parricide,
Que la religion l'enflamme [71P2, F-Nts copy: redouble] de fureur.
MS1: [*see act IV lines* 6-112]

152 43A1: Enfin d'un
MS4, 42X1, 42X2:
MAHOMET
Venez, enfant d'un dieu

156 43A1: [*absent*]

157 42B1-42B5, 43A1, 43A2, 47A, 52B, 60B, 67B, 78B: mon cœur une

159 W46: C'est en vos

Qu'il veut épouvanter les profanes humains. 160

SEÏDE

Ah! sans doute ce dieu, dont vous êtes l'image,
Va d'un combat illustre honorer mon courage.

MAHOMET

Faites ce qu'il ordonne, il n'est point d'autre honneur.
De ses décrets divins aveugle exécuteur,
Adorez, et frappez; vos mains seront armées 165
Par l'ange de la mort, et le dieu des armées.

SEÏDE

Parlez: quels ennemis vous faut-il immoler?
Quel tyran faut-il perdre, et quel sang doit couler?

MAHOMET

Le sang du meurtrier que Mahomet abhorre,
Qui nous persécuta, qui nous poursuit encore, 170
Qui combattit mon dieu, qui massacra mon fils;

160 71P2, 74A: Qu'il faut épouvanter
161 MS4, 42X1, 42X2: doute le dieu,
163 MS8: n'est pas d'autre
165 43A1: frappez, nos mains
166-202 MS1 [*still scene ii*]:
Par l'ange de la mort et le dieu des armées.
Allez, et d'un esprit et d'un cœur captivés,
Songez quel dieu commande, et quel roi vous servez.
Allez et sans pitié, teint du sang d'un impie,
Méritez par sa mort une immortelle vie.
Vengez Dieu, Mahomet, mes lois et mon pays.
167 MS4, MS5, 42X1, 42X2, T77: quel ennemi
42B1-42B5, 42XX, 43A1, 43A2, 47A, 52B, 60B, 67B, 78B: ennemis faut-il vous immoler?
169 MS6<β>, MS8, 42B1-42B5, 42XX, 43A1, 43A2, 47A, 52B, 60B, 67B, 78B: sang d'un meurtrier
43A2*: →β
170 MS4: nous persécute,

Le sang du plus cruel de tous nos ennemis,
De Zopire.

SEÏDE

De lui! quoi mon bras!

MAHOMET

Téméraire,
On devient sacrilège alors qu'on délibère.
Loin de moi les mortels assez audacieux 175
Pour juger par eux-mêmes, et pour voir par leurs yeux.
Quiconque ose penser n'est pas né pour me croire.
Obéir en silence est votre seule gloire.
Savez-vous qui je suis? Savez-vous en quels lieux
Ma voix vous a chargé des volontés des cieux? 180
Si, malgré ses erreurs et son idolâtrie,
Des peuples d'Orient la Mecque est la patrie;[13]
Si ce temple du monde est promis à ma loi,
Si Dieu m'en a créé le pontife et le roi;

172 42B1-42B5, 43A1, 43A2, 47A, 51B, 52B, 60B, 67B, 71P1, 71P2, 73M, 73P, 74A, 77P1, 78B, 78P: tous mes ennemis,

174 MS5: <β>On devient criminel, lorsque l'on délibère.
MS4, 42X1, 42X2: L'on devient

175 MS4, MS8, 42X1, 42X2: moi ces mortels

176 MS5, 42X1, 42X2, T70: eux-mêmes et voir
42X1*: →β

178 MS4: V↑β

179 MS4, MS5, 42X1, 42X2, 42B1-42B5, 42XX, 43A1, 43A2, 47A, 52B, 60B, 67B, 78B: Songez-vous qui je suis, songez-vous qu'en ces lieux,
43A2*: songez-vous en quels lieux,

183 71P2, 74A: Si le temple

[13] See Humbert: 'C'est un anachronisme. A l'époque dont il s'agit, la Mecque n'était pas encore la *patrie des peuples de l'Orient*; depuis Mahomet cela fut vrai. Cependant bien des siècles auparavant, la Mecque était déjà une ville importante pour les Arabes, mais pour eux seuls, et non pour les *peuples de l'Orient*. C'est près de la Mecque que se trouvait ce fameux puits Zemzem, que l'ange découvrit à Agar dans le désert.'

Si la Mecque est sacrée, en savez-vous la cause? 185
Ibrahim y naquit, et sa cendre y repose (*a*):
Ibrahim, dont le bras docile à l'Eternel
Traîna son fils unique aux marches de l'autel,
Etouffant pour son dieu les cris de la nature.
Et quand ce dieu par vous veut venger son injure, 190
Quand je demande un sang à lui seul adressé,
Quand Dieu vous a choisi, vous avez balancé![14]
Allez, vil idolâtre, et né pour toujours l'être,
Indigne Musulman, cherchez un autre maître.
Le prix était tout prêt, Palmire était à vous; 195
Mais vous bravez Palmire et le ciel en courroux.
Lâche et faible instrument des vengeances suprêmes,
Les traits que vous portez vont tomber sur vous-mêmes;

(*a*) Les Musulmans croient avoir à la Mecque le tombeau d'Abraham.[15]

186-187 MS4: Abraham
198 MS4, MS5, MS6, MS8, 42X1, 42X2, 42B1-42B5, 42XX, 43A1, 43A2, 47A, 52B, 60B, 67B, 67C, 78B: portiez

[14] 'L'art de la déclamation théâtrale n'a peut-être jamais rien offert de plus frappant, de plus vrai, de plus sublime, que tout ce couplet, dans la bouche du célèbre Le Kain. Aucun de ceux qui ont pu l'entendre ne démentirait ce témoignage. Le spectateur, partageant en ce moment l'illusion du jeune Séide, était tenté de s'écrier, comme lui: *Je crois entendre Dieu*' (La Harpe, *Commentaire*, p.208n).

[15] This is the only note by Voltaire on the play itself; it first appears in 43A3. Kehl develops it. 'Les Musulmans croyaient avoir à la Mecque le tombeau d'Abraham. Le sacrifice d'Isaac est le premier assassinat ordonné par Dieu, dans nos livres. On se contenta de la bonne volonté pour cette seule fois; mais c'était le premier pas, et cette tradition, une fois établie, donna aux fanatiques un prétexte pour obtenir davantage. Ils savaient bien que lorsqu'ils auraient déterminé un furieux à lever le poignard, un ange ne viendrait pas lui arrêter le bras.' It is not clear why Voltaire wrote what he wrote here. According to tradition the tomb is that of Abraham's concubine Hagar; see Gagnier, *La Vie de Mahomet*, i.23.

Fuyez, servez, rampez sous mes fiers ennemis.

SEÏDE

Je crois entendre Dieu; tu parles; j'obéis. 200

MAHOMET

Obéissez, frappez: teint du sang d'un impie,
Méritez par sa mort une éternelle vie.
(*à Omar*)
Ne l'abandonne pas; et, non loin de ces lieux,
Sur tous ses mouvements ouvre toujours les yeux.

## *SCÈNE VII*

SEÏDE *seul.*

Immoler un vieillard, de qui je suis l'otage, 205
Sans armes, sans défense,[16] appesanti par l'âge!
N'importe; une victime amenée à l'autel,
Y tombe sans défense, et son sang plaît au ciel.
Enfin, Dieu m'a choisi pour ce grand sacrifice;

199 MS4, MS5, 42X1, 42X2: sous vos fiers
42X1*, 42B1-42B5, 42XX, 43A1, 43A2, 47A, 52B, 60B, 67B, 78B: sous nos fiers
199a 43A2*: [*with stage direction*:] (*à part*)
200 68P: entendre un Dieu;
200a MS4, MS5, 42X1, 42X2: [*with stage direction*:] *en s'en allant.*
202 71P1, 71P2, 74A: par la mort
204 71P2, 74A: tous ces mouvements
206 W71P: Sans amis, sans défense,
208 MS5: < Qui > tombe
MS4: défense, son
209 MS6↑, 42B1-42B5, 42XX, 43A1, 43A2, 47A, 52B, 60B, 67B, 78B: Dieu m'a daigné choisir pour ce grand sacrifice,
43A2*: →β

[16] 'Le héros malheureux, sans armes, sans défense' (*La Henriade*, II line 197); see also Appendix IV.

J'en ai fait le serment, il faut qu'il s'accomplisse. 210
Venez à mon secours, ô vous, de qui les bras
Aux tyrans de la terre ont donné le trépas;
Ajoutez vos fureurs à mon zèle intrépide,
Affermissez ma main saintement homicide.[17]
Ange de Mahomet, ange exterminateur,[18] 215
Mets ta férocité dans le fond de mon cœur.[19]
Ah! que vois-je?

211 MS4, MS5, 42X1, 42X2, 42B1-42B5, 42XX, 43A1, 43A2, 47A, 52B, 60B, 67B, 78B, K: qui le bras

212 MS4, MS5, 42X1, 42X2, 42B1-42B5, 42XX, 43A1, 43A2, 47A, 52B, 60B, 67B, 78B, K: Aux tyrans de la terre a donné

213 42X1*: Vous, inflexible Aod, vous, idole intrépide

213-214 MS4, MS6↑, MS5, MS7, 42X1, 42X2, 67C:
Venez, remplissez-moi de votre âme intrépide;
Affermissez ma main saintement homicide,
MS5↓, MS6, MS7, 42B1-42B5, 42XX, 43A1, 43A2, 47A, 52B, 60B, 67B, 78B:
Ajoutez vos fureurs au zèle qui me presse,
Otez-moi ma pitié, ce n'est qu'une faiblesse,

216 MS4, MS6<β>, 42B1-42B5, 43A1, 43A2, 47A, 52B, 60B, 67B, 78B: Mets la férocité
43A2*: →β

[17] Kehl has the following comment here: 'On trouve dans le quatrième acte [line 54]: "Mes pleurs baignent tes mains saintement homicides" / Cette expression est de Racine: De leurs plus chers parents saintement homicides, dit-il, en parlant de vingt mille juifs égorgés pour un veau, par la main des lévites. Mais Racine, dans *Athalie*, employait son génie à consacrer ces saintes horreurs.'

[18] 'Fais marcher devant toi l'ange exterminateur' (*La Henriade*, V line 72); 'Ange exterminateur, âme de ces combats' (*La Henriade*, VI line 282); 'Ce glaive dont s'arma l'ange exterminateur' (*La Henriade*, X line 84); see Appendix IV.

[19] 'Ta' rather than 'la' in the base text was proposed by de Missy (D2689). The second part of the line is a traditional line-filler: 'Qu'il n'eût jamais trouvés dans le fond de son cœur' (*Brutus*, I.iii.230); see also Appendix IV.

## *SCÈNE VIII*

### ZOPIRE, SEÏDE

ZOPIRE

A mes yeux tu te troubles, Seïde!
Vois d'un œil[20] plus content le dessein qui me guide;
Otage infortuné, que le sort m'a remis,
Je te vois à regret parmi mes ennemis. 220
La trêve a suspendu le moment du carnage;
Ce torrent retenu peut s'ouvrir un passage:
Je ne t'en dis pas plus; mais mon cœur malgré moi,
A frémi des dangers assemblés près de toi.
Cher Seïde, en un mot, dans cette horreur publique, 225
Souffre que ma maison soit ton asile unique.
Je réponds de tes jours, ils me sont précieux;
Ne me refuse pas.

SEÏDE

O mon devoir! ô cieux!
Ah! Zopire, est-ce vous qui n'avez d'autre envie

217 MS5: troubles, < Zopire! >
218 MS4, MS5, 42X1, 42X2, 42XX: d'un cœur plus
219 MS4: le ciel m'a
220 MS4, MS5, MS6, 42X1, 42X2, 42B1-42B5, 42XX, 43A1, 43A2, 47A, 52B, 60B, 67B, 78B: parmi nos ennemis
221 42B1-42B5, 42XX, 43A1, 43A2, 47A, 52B, 60B, 67B, 78B: les moments
222 42B1-42B5, 42XX, 43A1, 43A2, 47A, 52B, 60B, 67B, 78B: torrent suspendu peut
42B5*, 43A2*: →β
223 MS6: Je < n'en > dis
MS4: V↑mon cœur
MS4, MS5, 42X1, 42X2: malgré soi,
226 67B, 78B: ma raison soit
229 MS6, 42B1-42B5, 42XX, 43A1, 43A2, 47A, 52B, 60B, 67B, 67C, 78B: Quoi, Zophire est-ce

[20] 'Œil' rather than 'cœur' is from de Missy (D2689).

Que de me protéger, de veiller sur ma vie? 230
Prêt à verser son sang, qu'ai-je ouï? qu'ai-je vu?
Pardonne, Mahomet, tout mon cœur s'est ému.

ZOPIRE

De ma pitié pour toi tu t'étonnes peut-être;
Mais enfin je suis homme,[21] et c'est assez de l'être,
Pour aimer à donner ses soins compatissants 235
A des cœurs malheureux que l'on croit innocents.
Exterminez, grands dieux de la terre où nous sommes,
Quiconque avec plaisir répand le sang des hommes![22]

SEÏDE

Que ce langage est cher à mon cœur combattu!
L'ennemi de mon dieu connaît donc la vertu! 240

231 MS6: < Tout > prêt à
MS4, MS5, 42X1, 42X2, 42B1-42B5, 42XX, 43A1, 43A2, 47A, 52B, 60B, 67B, 67B, 78B:
(*à part*)
Tout prêt à le frapper, qu'ai-je ouï, qu'ai-je vu?
43A2*: →β
232 71P2, 74A: Ordonne, Mahomet,
MS4, MS5, 42X1, 42X2: cœur est ému.
234 42B3: homme, c'est assez
235 K: donner des soins

[21] 'J'ai le cœur aussi bon, mais enfin je suis homme' (Corneille, *Horace*, II.iii.468). Corneille expresses a similar idea in *Sertorius*, IV.i.1194: 'Ah! pour être Romain, je n'en suis pas moins homme', a line which was famously parodied by Molière: 'Ah! pour être dévot, je n'en suis pas moins homme' (*Tartuffe*, III.iii.966).

[22] Under the Terror these two lines were suppressed; see A.-L.-D. Martainville and C.-G. Etienne, *Histoire du Théâtre français, depuis le commencement de la Révolution jusqu'à la réunion générale* (Paris 1802), iii.143. After Thermidor the play was first staged at the Théâtre de l'Egalité on 5 vendémiaire an III (26 September 1794).

ZOPIRE

Tu la connais bien peu, puisque tu t'en étonnes.
Mon fils, à quelle erreur hélas tu t'abandonnes!
Ton esprit fasciné par les lois d'un tyran,
Pense que tout est crime hors d'être Musulman.
Cruellement docile aux leçons de ton maître, 245
Tu m'avais en horreur avant de me connaître;
Avec un joug de fer, un affreux préjugé
Tient ton cœur innocent dans le piège engagé.
Je pardonne aux erreurs où Mahomet t'entraîne.
Mais peux-tu croire un dieu qui commande la haine?[23] 250

SEÏDE

Ah! je sens qu'à ce dieu je vais désobéir;
Non, Seigneur, non, mon cœur ne saurait vous haïr.

ZOPIRE

Hélas! plus je lui parle, et plus il m'intéresse;

241, 243-246 MS1: [*adds these lines, omits line* 242]
245-258 MS6: [*absent*]
247 43A1: Avec le joug
248 MS4, MS5, 42X1, 42X2: le crime engagé.
249 MS5, 42X1, 42X2: aux horreurs où
250 71P2, 74A: Mais peut-on croire
253-254 MS1: [*added*]

[23] Kehl note: 'C'est la seule bonne réponse à tous ceux qui croient, ou font semblant de croire qu'il n'y a de vertu que parmi les hommes qui pensent comme eux. Ce vers renferme un sens profond. Un homme, en effet, qui pense que pour avoir de la justice, de l'humanité, de la générosité, il faut croire une telle opinion spéculative, imaginer que dans un autre monde on sera payé; un tel homme regarde nécessairement la vertu comme une chose peu naturelle à l'espèce humaine, ne connaît pas les véritables motifs qui inspirent les actions vertueuses aux âmes nées pour la vertu. Enfin, les bonnes actions qu'il a pu faire n'ont été inspirées que par des motifs étrangers, ou bien il n'a pas su démêler le principe de ses propres actions. Tel est le sens de ce vers, le plus philosophique peut-être, et le plus vrai de la pièce.'

Son âge, sa candeur, ont surpris ma tendresse.
Se peut-il qu'un soldat de ce monstre imposteur 255
Ait trouvé malgré lui le chemin de mon cœur?[24]
Quel es-tu? de quel sang les dieux t'ont-ils fait naître?

SEÏDE

Je n'ai point de parents, seigneur, je n'ai qu'un maître,
Que jusqu'à ce moment j'avais toujours servi,
Mais qu'en vous écoutant ma faiblesse a trahi. 260

ZOPIRE

Quoi, tu ne connais point de qui tu tiens la vie?

SEÏDE

Son camp fut mon berceau,[25] son temple est ma patrie;
Je n'en connais point d'autre; et parmi ces enfants,
Qu'en tribut à mon maître on offre tous les ans,
Nul n'a plus que Seïde éprouvé sa clémence. 265

254 MS1: Son âge et sa candeur
256 MS6, 43A2*, 67C: malgré moi le
257 73M, 73P, 77P1, 78P: sang le ciel t'a-il fait
259 MS4: Qui jusqu'à
261 W57P, T64P, T67: connais pas de
262 68P: camp est mon
MS5, MS4, 42X1, 42X2, 42B1-42B5, 42XX, 43A1, 43A2, 47A, 52B, 60B, 67B, 78B: temple ma patrie:
43A2*: →β
263 MS6: parmi < des > enfants
264 78B: on porte tous

[24] 'Ah! que vous saviez bien le chemin de mon cœur' (*Adélaïde*, act I line 326); 'Un traître avait surpris le chemin de mon cœur' (*Eriphyle*, I.iii.line 162).

[25] 'Son camp fut mon berceau; là, parmi les guerriers' (*La Henriade*, II line 95).

ZOPIRE

Je ne puis le blâmer de sa reconnaissance.[26]
Oui, les bienfaits, Seïde, ont des droits sur un cœur.
Ciel! pourquoi Mahomet fut-il son bienfaiteur?
Il t'a servi de père, aussi bien qu'à Palmire;
D'où vient que tu frémis, et que ton cœur soupire? 270
Tu détournes de moi ton regard égaré;
De quelque grand remords tu sembles déchiré.

SEÏDE

Eh, qui n'en aurait pas dans ce jour effroyable!

ZOPIRE

Si tes remords sont vrais, ton cœur n'est plus coupable.
Viens, le sang va couler, je veux sauver le tien 275

SEÏDE

Juste ciel! et c'est moi qui répandrais le sien!
O serments! ô Palmire! ô vous, Dieu des vengeances!

ZOPIRE

Remets-toi dans mes mains, tremble, si tu balances;

266 MS4, MS6<β>, 42X1, 42X2, 42B1-42B5, 42XX, 43A1, 43A2, 47A, 52B, 60B, 67B, 78B: Je ne puis te blâmer de ta reconnaissance.
42X1*, 43A2*: →β
268 MS6<β>, 42B1-42B5, 43A1, 43A2, 47A, 52B, 60B, 67B, 78B: ton bienfaiteur
43A2*: →β
269 71P1, 71P2, 74A: père de même qu'à
273 MS5: aurait point dans
274 71P2, W72X, 74A: n'est pas coupable.
73M: n'est point coupable.
278 MS6<β>, 67C: mes bras,
278-314 MS4, MS5, 42X1, 42X2, 42B1-42B5, 42XX, 43A1, 43A2, 47A, 52B, 60B, 67B, 78B: [*see Appendix I*]

[26] 'Vous ait rien dérobé de sa reconnaissance' (*Mariamne*, III.i); see Appendix IV.

Pour la dernière fois,[27] viens, ton sort en dépend.

## *SCÈNE IX*

### ZOPIRE, SEÏDE, OMAR, *SUITE*

OMAR *entrant avec précipitation.*

Traître, que faites-vous, Mahomet vous attend. 280

SEÏDE

Où suis-je! ô ciel! où suis-je? et que dois-je résoudre?
D'un et d'autre côté je vois tomber la foudre.
Où courir? où porter un trouble si cruel?
Où fuir?

OMAR

Aux pieds du roi qu'a choisi l'Eternel.

279-280 MS1: (*sur la fin de la scène*)
Hercide... qu'ai-je lu? dieux, votre providence
Voudrait-elle adoucir soixante ans de souffrance?
Suis-moi.

SEÏDE

Seigneur, hélas!

ZOPIRE

Viens, ton sort en dépend.

OMAR

Traître que faites-vous? Mahomet vous attend.

282 MS6: je < suis frappé du > foudre.

284 T77: d'un roi qui a

[27] Just as Voltaire had 'pour la première fois' as a line-filler in act III line 63, so here and in act IV line 136 he employs 'pour la dernière fois': 'Pour la dernière fois le sort guida vos pas (*Œdipe*, I.i.29); 'Pour la dernière fois il paraisse à mes yeux' (*Œdipe*, III.i.2); 'Pour la dernière fois je vais l'entretenir' (*Eriphyle*, II.ii.96); see also Appendix IV.

SEÏDE

Oui, j'y cours abjurer un serment que j'abhorre. 285

## *SCÈNE X*

ZOPIRE *seul.*

Ah! Seïde, où vas-tu? Mais il me fuit encore.
Il sort désespéré, frappé d'un sombre effroi,
Et mon cœur qui le suit s'échappe loin de moi.
Ses remords, ma pitié, son aspect, son absence,
A mes sens déchirés font trop de violence. 290
Suivons ses pas.

## *SCÈNE XI*

ZOPIRE, PHANOR

PHANOR

Lisez ce billet important,
Qu'un Arabe en secret m'a donné dans l'instant.

ZOPIRE

Hercide! qu'ai-je lu? Grands dieux! votre clémence
Répare-t-elle enfin soixante ans de souffrance?
Hercide veut me voir! lui, dont le bras cruel 295

287-291 MS6: [Bon *written against these words in the margin*]
289 42X1*: < Seïde! > ses remords
43A2*: Seïde... cet écrit, ton aspect, ton absence.
292 73M: donné à l'instant.
293-294 42X1*:
Hercide! ah! qu'ai-je lu! dieux, votre providence
Adoucit-elle enfin soixante ans de souffrance?

Arracha mes enfants à ce sein paternel!
Ils vivent! Mahomet les tient sous sa puissance,
Et Seïde et Palmire ignorent leur naissance?
Mes enfants! tendre espoir, que je n'ose écouter;
Je suis trop malheureux, je crains de me flatter.[28] 300
Pressentiments confus, faut-il que je vous croie?
O mon sang, où porter mes larmes et ma joie?
Mon cœur ne peut suffire à tant de mouvements;
Je cours, et je suis prêt d'embrasser mes enfants.
Je m'arrête, j'hésite, et ma douleur craintive 305
Prête à la voix du sang une oreille attentive.
Allons. Voyons Hercide au milieu de la nuit;[29]
Qu'il soit sous cette voûte en secret introduit,
Au pied de cet autel,[30] où les pleurs de ton maître
Ont fatigué des dieux qui s'apaisent peut-être. 310
Dieux, rendez-moi mes fils; dieux, rendez aux vertus
Deux cœurs nés généreux, qu'un traître a corrompus.

296 43A2*: enfants au sein
297 43A2*: tient en sa
303-306 MS6, 43A2*: [*absent*]
309 42X1*: Auprès de
78P: Aux pieds de
310 K: fatigué les dieux
311 42X1*: fils, et rendez

[28] In the first published version of the end of act III, Zopire said 'J'embrasse aveuglement de flatteuses erreurs'. This line has definite Cornelian overtones: 'Que ma douleur séduite embrasse aveuglement' (Corneille, *Cinna*, I.i.4). Left alone at the end of the act, the old man cries out: 'O ciel! ayez pitié d'un destin que j'ignore'. There is an echo here of *Adélaïde du Guesclin*, act I line 227: 'Ah! qui m'éclaircira d'un destin que j'ignore?'

[29] 'Tout sera prêt, seigneur, au milieu de la nuit' (*Brutus*, III .i.11); 'Qu'on doit attaquer Rome au milieu de la nuit' (*Brutus*, IV.iv.160); see also Appendix IV.

[30] 'Aux pieds de cet autel il demande à s'instruire' (*La Henriade*, V line 115).

S'ils ne sont point à moi, si telle est ma misère,
Je les veux adopter; je veux être leur père. 315

*Fin du troisième acte.*[31]

314 42X1*: Je veux les adopter,

[31] 'Entre le troisième et le quatrième acte, le théâtre n'est qu'à demi éclairé' (MS Lekain, instructions for the *décorateur machiniste*).

# ACTE IV

## *SCÈNE PREMIÈRE*

### MAHOMET, OMAR

OMAR

Oui, de ce grand secret la trame est découverte;[1]
Ta gloire est en danger, ta tombe est entr'ouverte.
Seïde obéira: mais avant que son cœur,
Raffermi par ta voix, eût repris sa fureur,
Seïde a révélé cet horrible mystère. 5

MAHOMET

O ciel!

a-b MS6, in margin: *Nuit.*

1 MS4, MS5, 42X1, 42X2, 42B1-42B5, 42XX, 43A1, 43A2, 47A, 52B, 60B, 67B, 78B: De ton [MS4, MS5, 42X1, 42X2: De cet; 42X1*: →β] affreux secret

2 42B1-42B5, 42XX, 43A1, 43A2, 47A, 52B, 60B, 67B, 78B: Ta gloire est profanée et la tombe entr'ouverte:

MS4, MS5, 42X1, 42X2: danger, et ta tombe est ouverte [42X1, 42X2: entr'ouverte].

43A2*: et la tombe

3 MS4, MS5, 42X1, 42X2, 42B1-42B5, 42XX, 43A1, 43A2, 47A, 52B, 60B, 67B, 78B Seïde est rassuré; mais

4 47A: repris la fureur.

6 47A: Hercine

MS4: l'aime, et lui

6-112 MS1 [*and placed at III.v.150*]:

MAHOMET

A qui?

OMAR

Tu sais qu'Hercide éleva son enfance.

[1] 'Ou, si de nos desseins la trame est découverte' (*Brutus*, I.iv.307).

OMAR

Hercide l'aime: il lui tient lieu de père.

MAHOMET

Eh bien, que pense Hercide?

OMAR

Il paraît effrayé;

Il semble pour Zopire avoir quelque pitié.

MAHOMET

Hercide est faible; ami, le faible est bientôt traître.

Qu'il tremble, il est chargé du secret de son maître. 10

Je sais comme on écarte un témoin dangereux.

Suis-je en tout obéi?

OMAR

J'ai fait ce que tu veux.

---

MAHOMET

Ciel!

OMAR

Hercide sait tout, et paraît effrayé;

MAHOMET

Ah! je connais Hercide et sa fausse pitié.
Il est faible. Il suffit, le faible est bientôt traître.
Qu'il tremble; il est chargé du secret de son maître.
Je sais comme on écarte un dangereux témoin.
Toi veille sur Seïde.

7 MS4, MS5, MS6<β>, 42X1, 42X2, 42B1-42B5, 42XX, 43A1, 43A2, 47A, 52B, 60B, 67B, 67C, 78B: Que dit, que pense Hercide?
43A2*: →β

8 MS4: Et semble

9-12 68P: [*gives these lines to Omar*]

10 MS4, MS5, 42X1, 42X2, 42B1-42B5, 42XX, 43A1, 43A2, 47A, 52B, 60B, 67B, 78B: Il n'aura pas longtemps le secret
43A2*: →β

MAHOMET

Préparons donc le reste. Il faut que dans une heure
On nous traîne au supplice, ou que Zopire meure.
S'il meurt, c'en est assez; tout ce peuple éperdu 15
Adorera mon dieu, qui m'aura défendu.
Voilà le premier pas; mais sitôt que Seïde
Aura rougi ses mains de ce grand homicide,
Réponds-tu qu'au trépas Seïde soit livré?
Réponds-tu du poison qui lui fut préparé? 20

OMAR

N'en doute point.

MAHOMET

Il faut que nos mystères sombres
Soient cachés dans la mort, et couverts de ses ombres.

13 W71P: Réparons donc

15 42B1-42B4, 42XX, 43A1: c'est assez:

16 MS4, MS5, 42X1, 42X2, 42B1-42B3, 42XX, 43A1, 43A2, 47A, 52B, 60B, 67B, 78B: Craindra du moins le dieu qui m'aura défendu,

43A2*: →β

18 MS6→β, 67C: grand parricide,

MS8: sa main

18-29 MS4, MS5, 42X1, 42X2, 42B1-42B5, 42XX, 43A1, 43A2, 47A, 52B, 60B, 67B, 78B:

Aura rougi ses mains [MS4, 42X1, 42X2: sa main] de [43A1: dans] ce grand parricide [MS4: sang homicide; 42X1, 42X2: grand homicide],
Que dans son propre sang ce [MS4, MS5, 42X1, 42X2: son] secret soit noyé,
Que délivré d'eux tous, je sois justifié;
Qu'aveugle [MS5: Qu'aveuglé] pour jamais ce peuple m'applaudisse,
Et jusqu'en mes fureurs adore ma justice,
Qu'on remette à l'instant Palmire entre nos mains,
Epaississons la nuit qui couvre ses [67B: ces] desseins [MS4, 42X1, 42X2, 42B2, 42B5*: destins].
Elle naquit en vain de ce sang que j'abhorre,

42X1*, 43A2*: →β

21 71P2, 74A: doutez point,

Mais tout prêt à frapper, prêt à percer le flanc,
Dont Palmire a tiré la source de son sang,
Prends soin de redoubler son heureuse ignorance: 25
Epaississons la nuit qui voile sa naissance,
Pour son propre intérêt, pour moi, pour mon bonheur.
Mon triomphe en tout temps est fondé sur l'erreur.
Elle naquit en vain de ce sang que j'abhorre.
On n'a point de parents, alors qu'on les ignore. 30
Les cris du sang, sa force et ses impressions,
Des cœurs toujours trompés sont les illusions.
La nature à mes yeux n'est rien que l'habitude;[2]
Celle de m'obéir fit son unique étude:
Je lui tiens lieu de tout. Qu'elle passe en mes bras, 35
Sur la cendre des siens qu'elle ne connaît pas.
Son cœur même en secret, ambitieux peut-être,
Sentira quelque orgueil à captiver son maître.
Mais déjà l'heure approche où Seïde en ces lieux
Doit m'immoler son père à l'aspect de ses dieux. 40

23 73M: frapper, tout prêt
25 42X1*: < Il faut amuser > [?]
26 42X1*: qui couvre sa
27 42X1*: pour < son > bonheur
MS8, 71P2, 74A: mon honneur.
28 MS6<→β>, 67C: temps fut fondé
30 MS4: parents, lorsqu'on
32 42B1-42B5, 42XX, 43A1, 43A2, 47A, 52B, 60B, 67B, 78B: cœurs souvent trompés
33 MS4, MS5, 42X1, 42X2, 42B1-42B5, 42XX, 43A1, 43A2, 47A, 52B, 60B, 67B, 78B: nature, crois-moi, n'est
42X1*: →β
40 MS4, MS5, MS6, 42X1, 42X2, 42B1-42B5, 42XX, 43A1, 43A2, 47A, 52B, 60B, 67B, 71P2, 74A, 78B: Doit immoler

[2] 'L'on est surpris qu'on ait permis la représentation de cette pièce, où il y a des traits hardis et pour la religion et pour la politique; celui qui envisage les préjugés de la nature comme une habitude a révolté' ([Mouhy] 'Journal de police', Barbier, viii.149).

Retirons-nous.

OMAR

Tu vois sa démarche égarée:
De l'ardeur d'obéir son âme est dévorée.

## *SCÈNE II*

MAHOMET, OMAR, *sur le devant, mais retirés de côté*;
SEÏDE, *dans le fond.*[3]

SEÏDE

Il le faut donc remplir ce terrible devoir?

41-42 MS4, MS5, 42X1, 42X2, 42B1-42B5, 42XX, 43A1, 43A2, 47A, 52B, 60B, 67B, 78B:

OMAR

Il vient, sa démarche égarée
Marque une âme inquiète et de zèle enivrée.
43A2*: →β

42a MS1:

*SCÈNE III*

Dans laquelle on devrait voir une colonnade en péristyle avancée sur le théatre, l'autel dans un [ ] entre colonnes, les deux enfants cachés aux yeux du père par des colonnes, et vus des spectateurs, comme cela se pratiquait dans l'ancienne Rome, et même encore en Italie, mais chez nous dont les salles de spectacles tiennent encore à la barbarie on fera comme on pourra. On est obligé de supporter les actions théâtrales qu'on ne peut exécuter sur notre trop ridicule théâtre.

42b 42X1, 42X2: MAHOMET, OMAR *sur le devant du théâtre, mais de côte*
42B1-42B5, 42XX, 43A1, 43A2, 47A, 52B, 60B, 78B: MAHOMET, OMAR *d'un côté*

[3] '[Préparer] deux flambeaux des lampadaires du petit temple de Zopire que l'on n'allume qu'à la scène seconde du quatrième acte' (MS Lekain, instructions for the *premier garçon de théâtre*).

MAHOMET

Viens, et par d'autres coups assurons mon pouvoir.[4]
(*Il sort avec Omar.*)

SEÏDE, *seul.*

A tout ce qu'ils m'ont dit je n'ai rien à répondre. 45
Un mot de Mahomet suffit pour me confondre.
Mais quand il m'accablait de cette sainte horreur,
La persuasion n'a point rempli mon cœur.
Si le ciel a parlé, j'obéirai sans doute.
Mais quelle obéissance! ô ciel! et qu'il en coûte! 50

## *SCÈNE III*

SEÏDE, PALMIRE

SEÏDE

Palmire, que veux-tu? Quel funeste transport!

45 71P2, 74A: ce qu'on m'a dit,

45-50 42B1-42B5, 42XX, 43A1, 43A2, 47A, 52B, 60B, 78B: [*these lines given as* SCENE III, *with consequent renumbering*]

47-48 42B1-42B5, 42XX, 43A1, 43A2, 47A, 52B, 60B, 67B, 78B:
Mais quand il m'a rempli de cette sainte horreur,
La persuasion n'entrait pas dans mon cœur.
43A2*: →β

50 42B1-42B5, 42XX, 43A1, 43A2, 47A, 52B, 60B, 67B, 78B: obéissance, hélas, et qu'il m'en

43A2*: obéissance, ô ciel, et qu'il m'en

[4] 'Réplique pour augmenter l'obscurité et allumer les lampadaires du petit temple de Zopire' (MS Lekain, instructions for the *décorateur machiniste*).

Qui t'amène en ces lieux[5] consacrés à la mort?

PALMIRE

Seïde, la frayeur et l'amour sont mes guides;
Mes pleurs baignent tes mains saintement homicides.
Quel sacrifice horrible hélas! faut-il offrir? 55
A Mahomet, à Dieu, tu va donc obéir?

SEÏDE

O de mes sentiments souveraine adorée,
Parlez, déterminez ma fureur égarée!
Eclairez mon esprit, et conduisez mon bras;
Tenez-moi lieu d'un dieu que je ne comprends pas. 60
Pourquoi m'a-t-il choisi? Ce terrible prophète
D'un ordre irrévocable est-il donc l'interprète?

PALMIRE

Tremblons d'examiner. Mahomet voit nos cœurs,

52 MS5: en des lieux
MS4: T'amène en
42X1, 42X2: T'amène dans ces lieux consacrer
42B1-42B5, 42XX, 43A1, 43A2, 47A, 52B, 60B, 67B, 78B: Te conduit en
MS6<β>: en des lieux
42X1*, 43A2*: →β
53 MS5<β>, 42B1-42B5, 42XX, 43A1, 43A2, 47A, 52B, 60B, 67B, 78B: La frayeur, cher Seïde, et l'amour, sont
43A2*: →β
57 MS4: $^{V\uparrow}\beta$ souveraine < égarée >!
58 42B1-42B5, 42XX, 43A1, 43A2, 47A, 52B, 60B, 67B, 78B: ma raison égarée,
43A2*: →β

[5] The 1742 version of this hemistich was nearer Racine: 'Mais un heureux destin le conduit en ces lieux' (Racine, *Andromaque*, II.iii.603). See also 'Qui t'amène en des lieux où l'on fuit ta présence (Racine, *Andromaque*, V.iii.1554). See act III line 214 for a hemistich that is identical in sound and the discussion of a Racinian echo.

Il entend nos soupirs, il observe mes pleurs.
Chacun redoute en lui la divinité même. 65
C'est tout ce que je sais, le doute est un blasphème;
Et le dieu qu'il annonce avec tant de hauteur,
Seïde, est le vrai dieu, puisqu'il le rend vainqueur.

SEÏDE

Il l'est, puisque Palmire et le croit et l'adore.
Mais mon esprit confus ne conçoit point encore, 70
Comment ce dieu si bon, ce père des humains,
Pour un meurtre effroyable a réservé mes mains.
Je ne le sais que trop que mon doute est un crime,
Qu'un prêtre sans remords égorge sa victime,
Que par la voix du ciel Zopire est condamné, 75
Qu'à soutenir ma loi j'étais prédestiné.
Mahomet s'expliquait, il a fallu me taire;
Et tout fier de servir la céleste colère,
Sur l'ennemi de Dieu je portais le trépas:

64 T64, 71P2, 73M, 74A: observe nos pleurs.

64-66 MS4, MS5, 42X1, 42X2, 42B1-42B5, 42XX, 43A1, 43A2, 47A, 52B, 60B, 67B, 78B:

Il entend nos discours, il observe nos [MS5, 42X1, 42X2: mes] pleurs;
Chacun révère en lui la divinité même:
C'est tout ce que j'en sais, [MS4, MS5, 42X1, 42X2, 42XX, Ghent: je sais] le doute est un blasphème;
43A2*: →β [*for* lines 64 *and* 66 *only*]

66 MS6: j'en sais,

71 MS4, MS5, 42X1, 42X2: bon, et père
42X1*: →β

72-77 42B1-42B5, 42XX, 43A1, 43A2, 47A, 52B, 60B, 67B, 78B:

Pour un meurtre effroyable a réservé mes mains?
Sa voix s'est fait entendre, il a fallu se taire,

43A2*:

Pour un meurtre effroyable a réservé mes mains?
Mahomet s'expliquait, il a fallu se taire,

[43A2* *adds* β *for lines* 73-76]

73 MS4, MS5, 42X1, 42X2: Je le sais comme vous, que le doute

75 MS4: la voix du ciel < la voix >

Un autre dieu, peut-être, a retenu mon bras. 80
Du moins, lorsque j'ai vu ce malheureux Zopire,
De ma religion j'ai senti moins l'empire.
Vainement mon devoir au meurtre m'appelait;
A mon cœur éperdu l'humanité parlait.
Mais avec quel courroux, avec quelle tendresse, 85
Mahomet de mes sens accuse la faiblesse!
Avec quelle grandeur, et quelle autorité,
Sa voix vient d'endurcir ma sensibilité!
Que la religion est terrible et puissante!
J'ai senti la fureur en mon cœur renaissante; 90
Palmire, je suis faible, et du meurtre effrayé:
De ces saintes fureurs je passe à la pitié;
De sentiments confus une foule m'assiège;
Je crains d'être barbare ou d'être sacrilège.
Je ne me sens point fait pour être un assassin. 95
Mais quoi! Dieu me l'ordonne, et j'ai promis ma main;
J'en verse encor des pleurs de douleur et de rage.[6]
Vous me voyez, Palmire, en proie à cet orage,
Nageant dans le reflux des contrariétés,
Qui pousse et qui retient mes faibles volontés. 100

82 42B1-42B5, 42XX, 43A1, 43A2, 47A, 52B, 60B, 67B, 78B: j'ai moins senti l'empire,

43A2*: →β

84 MS4, MS5, 42X1, 42X2: cœur attendri l'humanité

85-101 MS6: [*added on a slip*]

86 MS4, MS5, MS6, 42X1, 42X2, 73M: accusait

87 MS6: grandeur et quelle majesté,

94 MS4, MS5, 42X1, 42X2: d'être un barbare, ou d'être un sacrilège.

95 78B: sens pas fait

96 MS4, MS5, MS6, 42X1, 42X2, 42B1-42B5, 42XX, 43A1, 43A2, 47A, 52B, 60B, 67B, 78B: Mais c'est un dieu qui parle, et

99 MS5: <β>dans un reflux de contrariétés

[6] 'Mais vous avez prévu la douleur et la rage' (*Sémiramis*, III.i); see also Appendix IV.

C'est à vous de fixer mes fureurs incertaines;
Nos cœurs sont réunis par les plus fortes chaînes:
Mais sans ce sacrifice à mes mains imposé,
Le nœud qui nous unit est à jamais brisé.
Ce n'est qu'à ce seul prix que j'obtiendrai Palmire. 105

PALMIRE

Je suis le prix du sang du malheureux Zopire!

SEÏDE

Le ciel et Mahomet ainsi l'ont arrêté.

PALMIRE

L'amour est-il donc fait pour tant de cruauté?

SEÏDE

Ce n'est qu'au meurtrier que Mahomet te donne.

PALMIRE

Quelle effroyable dot!

SEÏDE

Mais si le ciel l'ordonne, 110
Si je sers et l'amour et la religion?

PALMIRE

Hélas!

SEÏDE

Vous connaissez la malédiction

107 MS4, 42X1, 42X2: l'ont ainsi arrêté
42X1*: →β
MS6, 42B1-42B5, 42XX, 43A1, 43A2, 47A, 52B, 60B, 67B, 78B: l'ont ordonné.
109 MS4, 71P2, 74A, 78P: qu'un meurtrier
110 MS5: ↑β Quel effroyable don!
MS4, 42X1, 42X2: effroyable loi!
42X1*: →β
111-221 MS4: [*added at end*]

Qui punit à jamais la désobéissance.

PALMIRE

Si Dieu même en tes mains a remis sa vengeance,
S'il exige le sang que ta bouche a promis? 115

SEÏDE

Eh bien, pour être à toi que faut-il?

PALMIRE

Je frémis.

SEÏDE

Je t'entends, son arrêt est parti de ta bouche.

PALMIRE

Qui moi?

SEÏDE

Tu l'as voulu.

PALMIRE

Dieu, quel arrêt farouche!

Que t'ai-je dit?

116 MS6: J'en frémis.W71P: toi, que faut-il faire?
117 42B1-42B5, 42XX, 43A1, 43A2, 47A, 52B, 60B, 67B, 78B: est sorti de
43A2*: →β
119 42B1, 42B2, 43A1 Que t'ai-je.
42B5, 52B, 60B, 67B, 78B Qu'entends-je?
MS5, MS7, 42B1-42B5, 42XX, 43A1, 43A2, 47A, 52B, 60B, 67B, 78B: ciel a parlé par ta voix.
42X1*, 43A2*: →β
119-121 MS4, MS7, 42X1, 42X2:
Pour un si tendre hymen quel augure odieux!
SEÏDE.
Vois l'autel domestique, élevé dans ces lieux;
Voici l'heure où Zopire, à cet autel funeste,
MS5 →β

SEÏDE

Le ciel vient d'emprunter ta voix;
C'est son dernier oracle, et j'accomplis ses lois. 120
Voici l'heure où Zopire à cet autel funeste
Doit prier en secret des dieux que je déteste.
Palmire, éloigne-toi.

PALMIRE

Je ne puis te quitter.

SEÏDE

Ne vois point l'attentat qui va s'exécuter:
Ces moments sont affreux. Va, fui, cette retraite 125
Est voisine des lieux qu'habite le prophète.
Va, dis-je.

PALMIRE

Ce vieillard va donc être immolé!

SEÏDE

De ce grand sacrifice ainsi l'ordre est réglé.
Il le faut de ma main traîner sur la poussière,
De trois coups dans le sein lui ravir la lumière, 130
Renverser dans son sang cet autel dispersé.

122 MS4, 42X1, 42X2, 42XX: secret les dieux
MS5, 42B1-42B5, 43A1, 43A2, 47A, 52B, 60B, 67B, 78B: secret ses dieux
43A2*: →β

123 MS4: Je ne te puis quitter.

124 MS5 ↓, 42B1-42B5, 42XX, 43A1, 43A2, 47A, 52B, 60B, 67B, 78B: Crains le spectacle affreux que Dieu va présenter,
43A2*: →β

125 MS4, 42X1, 42X2: Les moments
MS5↑, 43A2*↑β, 42B1-42B5, 42XX, 43A1, 43A2, 47A, 52B, 60B, 67B, 78B: moments sont cruels, va

129 42B1-42B5, 43A1, 43A2, 47A, 52B, 60B, 67B, 78B: traîner dans la
43A2*: →β

PALMIRE

Lui mourir par tes mains! tout mon sang s'est glacé.
Le voici. Juste ciel...
(*Le fond du théâtre s'ouvre. On voit un autel.*)

## *SCÈNE IV*

ZOPIRE, SEÏDE, PALMIRE *sur le devant.*

ZOPIRE *près de l'autel.*

O dieux de ma patrie![7]
Dieux prêts à succomber sous une secte impie,
C'est pour vous-même ici que ma débile voix 135
Vous implore aujourd'hui pour la dernière fois.[8]
La guerre va renaître, et ses mains meurtrières
De cette faible paix vont briser les barrières.
Dieux! si d'un scélérat vous respectez le sort...

132 MS4, 42X1, 42X2: sang est glacé
133 MS4, MS5, 42X1, 42X2:
*SCÈNE IV* [*SCÈNE III*]
*Le fond du théâtre s'ouvre, et laisse voir un autel.*
ZOPIRE, *près de l'autel.* SEIDE, PALMIRE *sur le devant du théâtre.*
MS6, 42B1-42B5, 42XX, 43A1, 43A2, 47A, 52B, 60B, 67B, 78B:
(*Le fond du théâtre s'ouvre, et on voit un autel.*)
*SCÈNE V*
SEIDE, PALMIRE, ZOPIRE
137 MS1, MS4, MS5, 42X1, 42X2, 42B1-42B5, 42XX, 43A1, 43A2, 47A, 52B, 60B, 67B, 78B: La guerre est à la porte, et des [MS1, MS4, MS5, 42X1, 42X2: ses] mains meurtrières,
42X1*, 43A2*: →β

[7] 'J'y cours. O dieux de Rome! ô dieux de ma patrie!' (*Brutus*, III.viii.350).
[8] Whereas the expression 'pour la dernière fois' occupies the first hemistich in act III line 279, here it comes last: 'En un mot, parlez-lui pour la dernière fois' (*Alzire*, I.i.151); 'Sauvez ma gloire au moins pour la dernière fois' (*Zulime*, III.iii); see also Appendix IV.

SEÏDE *à Palmire.*

Tu l'entends qui blasphème?[9]

ZOPIRE

Accordez-moi la mort; 140

Mais rendez-moi mes fils à mon heure dernière;
Que j'expire en leurs bras, qu'ils ferment ma paupière.
Hélas! si j'en croyais mes secrets sentiments,
Si vos mains en ces lieux ont conduit mes enfants...

PALMIRE *à Seïde.*

Que dit-il? ses enfants?

ZOPIRE

O mes dieux que j'adore! 145

Je mourrais du plaisir de les revoir encore.
Arbitre des destins, daignez veiller sur eux;
Qu'ils pensent comme moi, mais qu'ils soient plus heureux!

SEÏDE

Il court à ses faux dieux! frappons.
(*Il tire son poignard.*)

142 42B1-42B4, 42XX, 43A1: Que j'expire entre leurs bras,
144 MS4, MS5, 42X1, 42X2, 42XX: mains dans ces
43A3, W46: Vos mains en
148a-149 60B, 67B, 78B:

SEÏDE *tirant son poignard.*

Il court à ses faux dieux.

PALMIRE

Que vas-tu faire?

[9] 'Pour la scène du quatrième acte, il est aisé de supposer que les deux enfants entendent ce que dit Zopire. Cela est même plus théâtral et augmente la terreur. Je pousserais la hardiesse jusqu'à leur faire écouter attentivement Zopire' (Voltaire to d'Argental, D2404; 19 January 1741).

PALMIRE

Que vas-tu faire?

Hélas!

SEÏDE

Servir le ciel, te mériter, te plaire. 150

Ce glaive à notre dieu vient d'être consacré.
Que l'ennemi de Dieu soit par lui massacré!
Marchons. Ne vois-tu pas dans ces demeures sombres
Ces traits de sang, ce spectre, et ces errantes ombres?

PALMIRE

Que dis-tu?

SEÏDE

Je vous suis, ministre du trépas; 155

Vous me montrez l'autel, vous conduisez mon bras.
Allons.

PALMIRE

Non, trop d'horreur entre nous deux s'assemble.

Demeure.

151 MS4: Le glaive
153-156 MS6: [*adds these lines on a slip*]
153-157 43A2*:
Marchons.

PALMIRE

Non,

154 MS4, 42X1, 42X2: ce sceptre, et les errantes
42X1*: ce sceptre,

155 MS5, 42X1, 42X2, 42B1-42B5, 42XX, 43A1, 43A2, 43A3, 47A, W48D, W50, 51B, W51, W52, 52B, T53, 54V, W56, W57P, 60B, T62, T64A, T64G, T64P, W64R, W64G, T66, 67B, 67C, T67, 68P, T68, T70, 71P1, 71P2, 73M, 73P, 74A, 77P1, 78B: ministres

156 MS4, MS5, 42X1, 42X2: conduisez mes pas;
42B1-42B5, 42XX, 43A1, 43A2, 47A, 52B, 60B, 67B, 78B: montrez le lieu, vous conduisez mes pas:

SEÏDE

Il n'est plus temps, avançons; l'autel tremble.

PALMIRE

Le ciel se manifeste, il n'en faut pas douter.[10]

SEÏDE

Me pousse-t-il au meurtre, ou veut-il m'arrêter? 160
Du prophète de Dieu la voix se fait entendre;
Il me reproche un cœur trop flexible et trop tendre,
Palmire!

PALMIRE

Eh bien?

SEÏDE

Au ciel adressez tous vos vœux.
Je vais frapper.

(*Il sort, et va derrière l'autel où est Zopire.*)

159 MS4, MS5, 42X1, 42X2, 42B1-42B5, 42XX, 43A1, 43A2, 47A, 52B, 60B, 67B, 78B: faut point douter
160 MS4, MS5, 42X1, 42X2, 67C: au crime,
42X1*: →β
W64G, W70G, W70L, W72X, T62, T64, 67C: ou vient-il
162 MS5, 42X1, 42X2: flexible, trop tendre.
163-165 MS6<β>, 42B1-42B5, 42XX, 43A1, 43A2, 47A, 52B, 60B, 67B, 78B:
Chère Palmire au ciel adressez tous vos vœux,
Je vais frapper.
(*Il sort et va derrière l'autel où est Zophire.*)
PALMIRE *seule.*
O ciel! ô moments douloureux!
Quelle effrayante [42XX: effroyable] voix dans mon âme s'élève!
43A2*: →β

[10] The earlier version of this hemistich with 'point' rather than 'pas' was more in line with an often used line-filler: see Appendix IV.

PALMIRE

Je meurs. O moment douloureux !
Quelle effroyable voix dans mon âme s'élève? 165
D'où vient que tout mon sang malgré moi se soulève?
Si le ciel veut un meurtre, est-ce à moi d'en juger?
Est-ce à moi de m'en plaindre, et de l'interroger?
J'obéis. D'où vient donc que le remords m'accable?
Ah! quel cœur sait jamais s'il est juste ou coupable? 170
Je me trompe, ou les coups sont portés cette fois;
J'entends les cris plaintifs d'une mourante voix.
Seïde... hélas!...

SEÏDE *revient d'un air égaré.*

Où suis-je? et quelle voix m'appelle?
Je ne vois point Palmire; un dieu m'a privé d'elle.

PALMIRE

Eh quoi! méconnais-tu celle qui vit pour toi? 175

SEÏDE

Où sommes-nous?

PALMIRE

Eh bien, cette effroyable loi,

164 MS4: V↑vais
45A: Je me meurs
166 MS4: V↑où
168 42X2, 42B1-42B5, 42XX, 43A1, 43A2, 47A, 52B, 60B, 67B, 78B: de me plaindre
MS4, MS5, 42X1, 42X2: plaindre, ou de
170 78P: juste coupable?
175 MS4, MS5, 42X1, 42X2: Eh quoi! tu méconnais celle
176 MS4, 42X1, 42X2, 42XX: bien, quelle effroyable loi
42X1*: →β

Cette triste promesse est-elle enfin remplie?

SEÏDE

Que me dis-tu?

PALMIRE

Zopire a-t-il perdu la vie?

SEÏDE

Qui? Zopire?

PALMIRE

Ah grand Dieu! Dieu de sang altéré,
Ne persécutez point son esprit égaré. 180
Fuyons d'ici.

SEÏDE

Je sens que mes genoux s'affaissent.
(*Il s'assied.*)
Ah! je revois le jour, et mes forces renaissent.
Quoi! c'est vous?

177 MS4: Cette terrible promesse
MS5, MS6<β>, 42X1, 42X2, 42B1-42B5, 42XX, 43A1, 43A2, 47A, 52B, 60B, 67B, 67C, 78B: Cette horrible promesse
43A2*: →β

181 42B1-42B5, 42XX, 43A1, 43A2, 47A, 52B, 60B, 67B, 78B: genoux s'abaissent,
43A2*: →β

181a-182 MS5, 42X1, 42X2: (*Il se relève*) (*à Palmire*)
MS4: O! je vois le jour
MS6: [<β> *gives two variants:*]
MS6↑:

PALMIRE

Seïde, ah! ciel! Seïde!

SEÏDE

Ah! mes forces renaissent.

MS6 [*on a slip*]:

PALMIRE

Qu'as-tu fait?

SEÏDE

(*Il se relève.*)

Moi! je viens d'obéir...

D'un bras désespéré je viens de le saisir.

Par ses cheveux blanchis j'ai traîné ma victime. 185

O ciel! tu l'as voulu, peux-tu vouloir un crime?

Tremblant, saisi d'effroi, j'ai plongé dans son flanc

Ce glaive consacré qui dut verser son sang.

J'ai voulu redoubler: ce vieillard vénérable

A jeté dans mes bras un cri si lamentable; 190

La nature a tracé dans ses regards mourants,

Un si grand caractère, et des traits si touchants!...

De tendresse et d'effroi mon âme s'est remplie,

Et plus mourant que lui je déteste ma vie.

---

SEÏDE *il tombe.*

Je sens... que mes genoux... Palmire?

(*sans la voir*)

PALMIRE

Seïde, ô ciel, Seïde?

SEÏDE *répétant le cri de Zopire.*

Ah! je l'entends ...

ZOPIRE *jetant les yeux sur Palmire.*

Quoi, c'est vous?

186 42B1-42B5, 42XX, 43A1, 43A2, 47A, 52B, 60B, 67B, 78B: Grand Dieu tu l'as voulu,

43A2*: →β

188 MS4, MS5, MS6<β>, 42X1, 42X2: Le glaive

42B1-42B5, 42XX, 43A1, 43A2, 47A, 52B, 60B, 67B, 78B: Ce glaive destiné à répandre son sang.

42B5*: destiné pour répandre

43A2*: →β

PALMIRE

Fuyons vers Mahomet, qui doit nous protéger: 195
Près de ce corps sanglant vous êtes en danger.
Suivez-moi.

SEÏDE

Je ne puis. Je me meurs. Ah! Palmire!

PALMIRE

Quel trouble épouvantable à mes yeux le déchire?

SEÏDE *en pleurant.*

Ah! si tu l'avais vu, le poignard dans le sein,[11]
S'attendrir à l'aspect de son lâche assassin! 200
Je fuyais. Croirais-tu que sa voix affaiblie,
Pour m'appeler encore a ranimé sa vie?

195-211 MS1:

SEÏDE.

Qu'avons-nous fait?

PALMIRE.

Peut-être un crime épouvantable.
Ah! cours à Mahomet, innocent ou coupable.
Viens.

SEÏDE.

Laisse-moi, pourquoi ton amour malheureux

196 42B1-42B5, 42XX, 43A1, 43A2, 47A, 52B, 60B, 67B, 78B: sanglant nous sommes en danger,

197 MS5, 42X1, 42X2: (*Il s'assied.*)
42X1*: →β
42B1-42B5, 42XX, 43A1, 43A2, 47A, 52B, 60B, 67B, 78B: (*Seïde s'assied.*) (*Il se relève.*)
42X2: Suis-moi.
42B1-42B5, 42XX, 43A1, W75X: je meurs...

198 MS4, MS5, 42X1, 42X2: yeux te déchire
42X1*: →β

200 42X2: S'attendrir dans le cœur de

[11] A tragic cliché: see Appendix IV.

Il retirait ce fer de ses flancs malheureux.
Hélas! il m'observait d'un regard douloureux.
Cher Seïde, a-t-il dit, infortuné Seïde! 205
Cette voix, ces regards, ce poignard homicide,
Ce vieillard attendri, tout sanglant à mes pieds,
Poursuivent devant toi mes regards effrayés.
Qu'avons-nous fait?

PALMIRE

On vient, je tremble pour ta vie.
Fuis au nom de l'amour et du nœud qui nous lie. 210

SEÏDE

Va, laisse-moi. Pourquoi cet amour malheureux[12]
M'a-t-il pu commander ce sacrifice affreux?
Non, cruelle, sans toi, sans ton ordre suprême,
Je n'aurais pu jamais obéir au ciel même.

PALMIRE

De quel reproche horrible oses-tu m'accabler? 215

206 MS5, 42X1, 42X2: voix, ses regards, ce
42B1-42B5, 42XX, 43A1, 43A2, 47A, 52B, 60B, 67B, 78B: voix, ce regard, ce
71P1: poignard d'homicide
208 MS4, MS5, MS6, 43A2*, 42X1, 42X2: toi mes esprits effrayés
42B1-42B5, 42XX, 43A1, 43A2, 47A, 52B, 60B, 67B, 78B: toi nos regards effrayés,
210 MS4, MS5, 42X1, 42X2, 42XX: amour, et du Dieu qui
211 MS5: Va, laisse, mais pourquoi
214 42B1-42B5, 43A1, 43A2, 47A, 52B, 60B, 67B, 78B: Je n'aurais jamais pu obéir
43A2*: →β
215 42B5, 52B, 60B, 67B, 78B: reproche affreux oses-tu

[12] 'Etouffe dans mon sang cet amour malheureux' (*Eriphyle*, IV.v.231).

Hélas! plus que le tien mon cœur se sent troubler.
Cher amant, prends pitié de Palmire éperdue!

SEÏDE

Palmire! quel objet vient effrayer ma vue?
(*Zopire paraît appuyé sur l'autel, après s'être relevé derrière cet autel où il a reçu le coup.*)

PALMIRE

C'est cet infortuné luttant contre la mort,
Qui vers nous tout sanglant se traîne avec effort. 220

SEÏDE

Eh quoi! tu vas à lui?

PALMIRE

De remords dévorée,
Je cède à la pitié dont je suis déchirée.
Je n'y puis résister, elle entraîne mes sens.

218a 67C: (*Zopire apparaît, appuyé sur une colonne du temple, et se traînant avec effort.*)
71P2, 74A: (*après s'être retiré derrière cet autel*)
42B1-42B5, 42XX, 43A1, 43A2, 47A, 52B, 60B, 67B, 78B:
vient s'offrir à ma vue?
(*Zopire s'appuie sur l'autel.*)
73M, 73P, 77P2, 78P: objet se présente à ma vue?
71P1: Ah! quel objet
219 MS4: V↑< β > luttant < avec > la mort,
220 71P2, 74A: Qui vers vous tout
222 78B: Je succède à la pitié,
223 MS4, 71P2, 74A: Je ne puis
42B1-42B5, 42XX, 43A1, 43A2, 47A, 52B, 60B, 67B, 78B: résister; elle a vaincu mes
43A2*: →β

ZOPIRE *avançant et soutenu par elle.*

Hélas! servez de guide à mes pas languissants.
(*Il s'assied.*)
Seïde, ingrat! c'est toi qui m'arrache la vie! 225
Tu pleures! ta pitié succède à ta furie![13]

## *SCÈNE V*

## ZOPIRE, SEÏDE, PALMIRE, PHANOR

PHANOR

Ciel! quels affreux objets se présentent à moi!

ZOPIRE

Si je voyais Hercide!...Ah, Phanor, est-ce toi?

223a MS4, MS5, 42X1, 42X2: ZOPIRE *avançant et soutenu par Palmire.*
42B1-42B5, 42XX, 43A1, 43A2, 47A, 52B, 60B, 67B, 78B: ZOPIRE *soutenu par Palmire.*

224 42B1-42B5, 42XX, 43A1, 43A2, 47A, 52B, 60B, 67B, 78B: mes pas chancelants, 43A2*: ↑β

224a 67C: (*Assis sur les marches du temple.*)

225 42B1-42B5, 42XX, 43A1, 43A2, 47A, 52B, 60B, 67B, 78B: Seïde, [42B5, 52B, 60B, 67B, 78B: Ah! Seïde] (*Il s'assied.*) C'est toi

226 42B1-42B5, 42XX, 43A1, 43A2, 47A, 52B, 60B, 67B, 78B: Tu pleures, la pitié succède à la furie.

227 MS4, 42X1, 42X2: Ciel, quel objet affreux se présente
MS5, 42X1*, T73A1, T77: Ciel, quels objets affreux se

[13] 'Aisément sa pitié succède à sa furie' (*La Henriade*, III line 7).

Voilà mon assassin.

PHANOR

O crime! affreux mystère!

Assassin malheureux, connaissez votre père.[14] 230

SEÏDE

Qui?

229-231 MS2:

Pardonne à l'assassin.

PHANOR

O crime! affreux mystère!

Seïde... malheureux... connaissez votre père.

SEÏDE

Lui!

ZOPIRE

Dieux!

SEÏDE

Mon père, vous.

231 42B1-42B5, 42XX, 43A1, 43A2, 47A, 52B, 60B, 67B, 78B:

PALMIRE

Qui, lui?

SEÏDE

Mon père!

ZOPHIRE

O ciel!

PHANOR

Hercide en [42XX: est] expirant

43A2*:

SEÏDE

Qui?

PALMIRE

Lui!

71P1, 71P2, 74A: Hercide en expirant

[14] On Voltaire's debt here to George Lillo's *The London Merchant*, see above p.38-39.

PALMIRE

Lui?

SEÏDE

Mon père?

ZOPIRE

O ciel!

PHANOR

Hercide est expirant,
Il me voit, il m'appelle, il s'écrie en mourant:
S'il en est encor temps, préviens un parricide:
Cours arracher ce fer à la main de Seïde:
Malheureux confident d'un horrible secret, 235
Je suis puni, je meurs des mains de Mahomet:
Cours, hâte-toi d'apprendre au malheureux Zopire,
Que Seïde est son fils, et frère de Palmire.

SEÏDE

Vous!

233 MS4, 42X1, 42X2: S'il est encor temps,
MS6, 42B1-42B5, 42XX, 43A1, 43A2, 47A, 52B, 60B, 67B, 78B: S'il en est temps encor, préviens

234 MS4, MS6, MS5, 42X1, 42X2, 42B1-42B5, 42XX, 43A1, 43A2, 47A, 52B, 60B, 67B, 78B: arracher le fer

235 42B1-42B5, 42XX, 43A1, 43A2, 47A, 52B, 60B, 67B, 78B: confident de cet affreux secret,
43A2*: →β

239 42B1-42B5, 42XX, 43A1, 43A2, 47A, 52B, 60B, 67B, 78B:

PALMIRE

Vous, mon frère.

ZOPIRE

O mes fils! ô nature! ô mes dieux!

43A2*: →β
MS4 V↑, MS5: O mon fils!
71P1, 71P2, 74A:

SEÏDE

Nous!

PALMIRE

Mon frère?

ZOPIRE

O mes fils! ô nature! ô mes dieux!
Vous ne me trompiez pas, quand vous parliez pour eux. 240
Vous m'éclairiez sans doute. Ah! malheureux Seïde!
Qui t'a pu commander cet affreux homicide?

SEÏDE *se jetant à genoux.*

L'amour de mon devoir et de ma nation,
Et ma reconnaissance, et ma religion,
Tout ce que les humains ont de plus respectable 245
M'inspira des forfaits le plus abominable.
Rendez, rendez ce fer à ma barbare main.

240 MS4, MS5, 42X1, 42X2: trompiez point quand

241 MS4, MS5, 42X1, 42X2, 42B1-42B5, 42XX, 43A1-43A3, 47A, 52B, 60B, 67B, 78B:

Vous préveniez mon cœur, ah! malheureux Seïde,

43A2*: →β

W48D, T53, T64G: Vous m'éclairez sans doute.

242 42B1-42B5, 42XX, 43A1, 43A2, 47A, 52B, 60B, 67B, 78B: commander un si noir parricide!

43A2*: →β

242a MS4, MS5, 42X1, 42X2: SEÏDE *se jetant aux pieds de Zopire.*

42B1-42B5, 42XX, 43A1, 43A2, 47A, 52B, 60B, 67B, 78B: SEÏDE *aux pieds de Zopire.*

243 MS5: de la nation,

244 MS6<β>: Et la reconnaissance

42B5: [*absent*]

245 MS2: Tout ce que les mortels ont

246 MS4: forfaits les plus abominables.

W52: forfaits de plus abominables.

247 MS5: Donnez, rendez ce fer

MS4, 42X1, 42X2: Rendez ce fer cruel à

42B1-42B5, 42XX, 43A1, 43A2, 47A, 52B, 60B, 67B: Rendez, rendez le fer

43A2*: →β

78B: Rendez le fer à

71P2, 74A: [*absent*]

PALMIRE *à genoux arrêtant le bras de Seïde.*

Ah! mon père, ah! Seigneur, plongez-le dans mon sein.
J'ai seule à ce grand crime encouragé Seïde;
L'inceste était pour nous le prix du parricide. 250

SEÏDE

Le ciel n'a point pour nous d'assez grands châtiments.
Frappez vos assassins.

ZOPIRE *en les embrassant.*

J'embrasse mes enfants.[15]

247-248 MS2:

Rends ce fer.

PALMIRE *se jetant entre eux.*

Arrêtez.

SEÏDE

Non, laissez-moi périr.

*SCÈNE IV*

ZOPIRE, PALMIRE, SEIDE, PHANOR.

PHANOR

Que vois-je, ô ciel? que vois-je?

ZOPIRE

Ami, je vais mourir.

247a 42B1-42B5, 42XX, 43A1, 43A2, 47A, 52B, 60B, 67B, 78B: PALMIRE *aux genoux de Zopire.*

43A2*: PALMIRE *arrêtant le bras de Seïde.*

[15] La Harpe compares and contrasts this act with the fifth act of Corneille's *Rodogune* and gives the advantage to Voltaire: 'On pourrait donner de très bonnes raisons pour le quatrième acte de *Mahomet*: il n'est fondé sur aucune vraisemblance, au lieu que la situation d'Antiochus est achetée tout ce qu'elle peut valoir; l'on n'est qu'effrayé de l'incertitude terrible où est Antiochus entre sa mère et sa maîtresse; on est profondément affligé, étouffé de sanglots, en voyant Zopire et ses enfants sacrifiés aux artifices d'un scélérat. Joignez à cela la grande moralité qui résulte de *Mahomet*, au lieu qu'il ne résulte rien de *Rodogune*' (La Harpe, *Commentaire*, p.214; see also La Harpe, *Lycée*, ix.148).

Le ciel voulut mêler, dans les maux qu'il m'envoie,
Le comble des horreurs au comble de la joie.
Je bénis mon destin, je meurs; mais vous vivez. 255
O vous, qu'en expirant mon cœur a retrouvés,
Seïde, et vous Palmire, au nom de la nature,[16]
Par ce reste de sang qui sort de ma blessure,
Par ce sang paternel, par vous, par mon trépas,
Vengez-vous, vengez-moi, mais ne vous perdez pas. 260
L'heure approche, mon fils, où la trêve rompue
Laissait à mes desseins une libre étendue:
Les dieux de tant de maux ont pris quelque pitié;
Le crime de tes mains n'est commis qu'à moitié.
Le peuple avec le jour en ces lieux va paraître; 265
Mon sang va les conduire; ils vont punir un traître.
Attendons ces moments.

253-256, 261-264 MS6: [*absent*]
254 MS4, 42X1, 42X2, 42XX: des honneurs au
42X1*: →β
258 MS4: $^{V\uparrow}$β sort de < la Nature >
260 MS4, MS5, 42X1, 42X2, 42B1-42B5, 42XX, 43A1, 43A2, 47A, 52B, 60B, 67B, 78B: Vengez-moi, vengez-vous, mais.
43A2*: →β
261 42B1-42B5, 42XX, 43A1, 43A2, 47A, 52B, 60B, 67B, 78B: fils, et la trêve
262 MS4, MS5, 42X1, 42X2: Laissant à
42X1*: →β
263 MS4, MS5, 42X1, 42X2: maux prendront quelque pitié!
42X1*: →β
265 71P1, 71P2, 74A: en ce lieu va
266 42B1-42B5, 42XX, 43A1, 43A2, 47A, 52B, 60B, 67B, 78B: conduire, ils puniront un traître,.
43A2*: →β
267 MS4, MS5, 42X1, 42X2: Attendons ce moment.

[16] 'Au nom de la nature, au nom de ma tendresse' (*Alzire*, act I, line 278).

SEÏDE

Ah! je cours de ce pas
Vous immoler ce monstre et hâter mon trépas;[17]
Me punir, vous venger.

## SCÈNE VI

ZOPIRE, SEÏDE, PALMIRE, PHANOR, OMAR, *SUITE*[18]

OMAR

Qu'on arrête Seïde.
Secourez tous Zopire, enchaînez l'homicide. 270
Mahomet n'est venu que pour venger les lois.

ZOPIRE

Ciel, quel comble du crime! et qu'est-ce que je vois?

268 MS5: hâter son trépas,
269 MS4: punir et vous venger
43A3: [*omits* PHANOR *from list of characters at beginning of scene vi*]
270 MS4, 42X1, 42X2: Zopire, entraînez l'homicide
42X1*: →β
272 42X1, 42X2, 42B1-42B5, 42XX, 43A1, 43A2, 47A, 52B, 60B, 67B, 71P2, 74A, 78B: comble de crime
43A2*: →β

[17] 'Moi, je vais fuir la honte, et hâter mon trépas' (*Zulime*, I.iv).

[18] 'Préparer deux flambeaux pour les soldats arabes, à la scène sixième du quatrième acte' (MS Lekain, instructions for the *premier garçon de théâtre*). The instructions for the Suite on stage are precise: 'Des douze soldats arabes commandés par deux officiers de Mahomet, les deux premiers qui portent des flambeaux se postent l'un à la droite et l'autre à la gauche du portique qui précède le petit temple de Zopire. Quatre autres se rangent derrière Seide ayant un officier à leur tête qui enchaîne le jeune arabe. Quatre autres également précédés par un officier, se placent à deux hommes de hauteur derrière l'estrade sur laquelle Zopire est étendu. Et les deux autres se tiennent au milieu du théâtre derrière Omar.'

SEÏDE

Mahomet me punir?

PALMIRE

Eh quoi! tyran farouche,
Après ce meurtre horrible ordonné par ta bouche!

OMAR

On n'a rien ordonné.

SEÏDE

Va; j'ai bien mérité 275
Cet exécrable prix de ma crédulité.

OMAR

Soldats, obéissez.[19]

PALMIRE

Non. Arrêtez. Perfide!

273 42X2, T73A1, T77: me punit!

274 42B1-42B5, 42XX, 43A1, 43A2, 47A, 52B, 60B, 67B, 78B: Après cet attentat ordonné

43A2*: →β

MS5 ↑: par sa bouche!

275 MS5<β>: Il n'a rien ordonné.

276 MS4: de ma < naïveté >.

MS5: de ma témérité.

277 MS4, MS5, 42X1, 42X2: Qu'on l'enlève, soldats.

42B1-42B5, 42XX, 43A1, 43A2, 47A, 52B, 60B, 67B, 78B: Qu'on l'emmène, soldats!

43A2*: →β

[19] 'Les quatre soldats qui gardent Seide entraînent ce dernier hors de la scène par la gauche du théâtre, l'officier les précède' (MS Lekain, instructions for the *premier garçon de théâtre*).

OMAR

Madame, obéissez, si vous aimez Seïde.
Mahomet vous protège, et son juste courroux,
Prêt à tout foudroyer, peut s'arrêter par vous. 280
Auprès de votre roi, Madame, il faut me suivre.[20]

PALMIRE

Grand Dieu! de tant d'horreurs que la mort me délivre!
(*On emmène Palmire et Seïde.*)

ZOPIRE *à Phanor*

On les enlève? ô ciel! ô père malheureux!
Le coup qui m'assassine est cent fois moins affreux.

280 MS4, MS5, 42X1, 42X2: Prêt à vous foudroyer,
42X1*: →β
42B1-42B5, 42XX, 43A1, 43A2, 47A, 52B, 60B, 67B, 78B: s'arrêter sur vous,
281 MS4, 42X1, 42X2: Auprès de notre Roi
71P1, 71P2, 74A: , il me faut suivre.
282a-283 42X1, 42X2: (*On mène Seïde et Palmire.*)
42B1-42B5, 42XX, 43A1, 43A2, 47A, 52B, 60B, 67B, 78B: [*stage direction concerning Seïde and Palmire absent*]
*SCÈNE VIII*
ZOPIRE, PHANOR, *le peuple qui s'avance.*
283 42B1-42B5, 42XX, 43A1, 43A2, 47A, 52B, 60B, 67B, 78B: enlève, Ciel! ô père
283-290 72P2, F-Nts copy: [*these lines cut out;* fin d'acte *in the margin against line* 282]
284-285 MS4, MS5, 42X1, 42X2: (*Le peuple arrive.*)
284-290 MS6, 43A2*:
Le coup qui m'assassine est cent fois moins affreux.
Mais allons, s'il se peut, sauver de leur furie
Ces deux enfants que j'aime, et qui m'ôtent la vie.
*Fin du quatrième acte.*

[20] 'Réplique pour faire revenir le jour par degrés insensibles' (MS Lekain, instructions for the *décorateur machiniste*).

PHANOR

Déjà le jour renaît, tout le peuple s'avance; 285
On s'arme, on vient à vous, on prend votre défense.

ZOPIRE

Quoi! Seïde est mon fils!

PHANOR

N'en doutez point.

ZOPIRE

Hélas!
O forfaits! ô nature!... allons, soutiens mes pas,
Je meurs. Sauvez, grands dieux, de tant de barbarie,
Mes deux enfants que j'aime et qui m'ôtent la vie.[21] 290

*Fin du quatrième acte.*

285 MS4, MS5, 42X1, 42X2, 42B1-42B5, 42XX, 43A1, 43A2, 47A, 52B, 60B, 67B, 78B: Enfin le jour renaît,

286 MS4$^{V\uparrow}$β: < tout le peuple s'avance >

287-290 MS4, MS5, 42X1, 42X2, 42B1-42B5, 42XX, 43A1-43A3, W46, 47A, W48D, W50, 51B, W51, W52, 52B, T53, 54V, W56, W57P, 60B, T62, T64A, T64G, T64P, W64R, W64G, T66, T67, 67B, 67C, 68P, T68, T70, W70G, W70L, 71P1, 71P2, W72X, 73M, 73P, 74A, 77P1, 78B, 78P:

ZOPIRE

Soutiens mes pas, allons; j'espère encor punir
L'hypocrite assassin qui m'ose secourir;
Ou du moins, en mourant, sauver de sa furie
Ces deux enfants que j'aime, et qui m'ôtent la vie.
*Fin du quatrième acte.*

[21] 'Les deux soldats portant des flambeaux précèdent Omar et Palmire qui sortent par la gauche du théâtre. Les deux soldats restés au milieu de la scène les suivent' (MS Lekain, instructions for the *commandant des assistants*).

# ACTE V

## *SCÈNE PREMIÈRE*

MAHOMET, OMAR, *SUITE dans le fond.*

OMAR

Zopire est expirant, et ce peuple éperdu
Levait déjà son front dans la poudre abattu.
Tes prophètes et moi, que ton esprit inspire,
Nous désavouons tous le meurtre de Zopire.
Ici, nous l'annonçons à ce peuple en fureur, 5
Comme un coup du Très-Haut qui s'arme en ta faveur.
Là, nous en gémissons, nous promettons vengeance;
Nous vantons ta justice, ainsi que ta clémence.
Partout on nous écoute, on fléchit à ton nom;
Et ce reste importun de la sédition 10
N'est qu'un bruit passager de flots après l'orage,
Dont le courroux mourant frappe encor le rivage,
Quand la sérénité règne aux plaines du ciel.

2 MS5, 42X1, 42X2: Le voit déjà sans front
42X1*: →β
MS5, 42B1-42B5, 42XX, 43A1, 43A2, 47A, 67B: Se voit déjà sans front
42B5*, 43A2*: →β
52B, 60B, 78B: Se voit déjà son front
43A3, W46, W48D, W50, 54V, W64R: Le voit déjà son front

3 MS6<β>, 42B1-42B5, 42XX, 43A1, 43A2, 47A, 52B, T53, 60B, 67B, 68P, 78B: Les prophètes

5-57 MS3: [*see appendix* II]

9 73M: fléchit en ton nom;

11 MS4, MS5, MS6→β, MS8, 42X1, 42B1-42B5, 43A1, 43A2, 47A, 52B, 60B, 67B, W71P, 73M, 78B: passager des flots

12 MS4: De ce courroux mourant

13 42B3: Quand ta sérénité

MAHOMET

Imposons à ces flots un silence éternel.
As-tu fait des remparts approcher mon armée? 15

OMAR

Elle a marché la nuit vers la ville alarmée:
Osman[1] la conduisait par de secrets chemins.

MAHOMET

Faut-il toujours combattre, ou tromper les humains?
Seïde ne sait point qu'aveugle en sa furie,
Il vient d'ouvrir le flanc dont il reçut la vie? 20

OMAR

Qui pourrait l'en instruire? un éternel oubli
Tient avec ce secret Hercide enseveli:[2]
Seïde va le suivre, et son trépas commence.

17 42B5, 42XX, 43A3, W46, W48D, W52, 52B, T53, 54V, W57P, 60B, W56, T62, T64A, T64G, T64P, W64G, T66, 67B, 67C, T67, W68, T68, 68P, W70G, W70L, T70, W71, 71P1, 71P2, W72X, 73M, 73P, T73A1, 73X, 74A, W75G, W75X, T76X, 78B, 78P: par des secrets

18 MS5: combattre, et tromper

19 MS8: ne sait pas qu'aveugle

20 42B1-42B5, 42XX, 43A1, 43A2, 47A, 52B, 60B, 67B, 78B: Il a versé le sang qui lui donna la vie.

43A2* →β

71P2, 74A: d'ouvrir les flancs dont

71P1: les flanc

22 MS4, MS5, 42X1, 42X2, 42B1-42B5, 42XX, 43A1, 43A2, 47A, 52B, 60B, 67B, 78B: avec le secret

42X1*: →β

[1] Humbert notes that Osman is the Turkish spelling of the Arabic Othman or Uthman. The name was also used by Voltaire during the first run of *Zulime* for an 'Espagnol de la suite de Ramire' (see *Mercure*, June 1740, p.1418-24).

[2] For a detailed suggestion on how to make 'la catastrophe [...] beaucoup plus nette' and more in keeping with Mahomet's character from this point on, see D2642; La Place to Voltaire).

J'ai détruit l'instrument qu'employa ta vengeance.
Tu sais que dans son sang[3] ses mains ont fait couler 25
Le poison qu'en sa coupe on avait su mêler.
Le châtiment sur lui tombait avant le crime;
Et tandis qu'à l'autel il traînait sa victime,
Tandis qu'au sein d'un père il enfonçait son bras,
Dans ses veines lui-même il portait son trépas. 30
Il est dans la prison, et bientôt il expire:
Cependant en ces lieux j'ai fait garder Palmire.
Palmire à tes desseins va même encor servir;
Croyant sauver Seïde, elle va t'obéir.
Je lui fais espérer la grâce de Seïde. 35
Le silence est encor sur sa bouche timide:
Son cœur toujours docile, et fait pour t'adorer,
En secret seulement n'osera murmurer.
Législateur, prophète, et roi dans ta patrie,
Palmire achèvera le bonheur de ta vie. 40
Tremblante, inanimée, on l'amène à tes yeux.

25 78B: sang tes mains

27 MS4, 42X1, 42X2, 42B1-42B5, 42XX, 43A1, 43A2, 47A, 52B, 60B, 67B, 78B: tombait avec le crime,

42X1*: →β

31 73M, 73P, 77P1: prison où bientôt

37 42X1, 42X2, 42XX: Le cœur

42X1*: →β

MS4, MS5, 42B1-42B5, 43A1, 43A2, 47A, 52B, 60B, 67B, 78B: Ce cœur

39 MS5: < ton pays >

[3] MS1 reads (see Appendix II): 'Dans son sang odieux lui-même a fait couler', which has a Racinian ring: 'Dans leur sang odieux, j'au pu tremper mes mains' (Racine, *Mithridate*, V.v.1665). In the same manuscript, Mahomet says in a much longer speech at the end of the scene: 'M'attache avec fureur au sang que je déteste'. This too is Racinian: 'Tout me retrace enfin un sang que je déteste' (Racine, *Athalie*, V.vi.1772).

MAHOMET

Va rassembler mes chefs, et revole en ces lieux.

## *SCÈNE II*

MAHOMET, PALMIRE, *SUITE de Palmire et de Mahomet*

PALMIRE

Ciel! où suis-je? ah grand Dieu!

MAHOMET

Soyez moins consternée;
J'ai du peuple et de vous pesé la destinée.
Le grand événement qui vous remplit d'effroi 45
Palmire, est un mystère entre le ciel et moi.
De vos indignes fers à jamais dégagée,
Vous êtes en ces lieux, libre, heureuse et vengée.
Ne pleurez point Seïde; et laissez à mes mains
Le soin de balancer le destin des humains. 50
Ne songez plus qu'au vôtre: et si vous m'êtes chère,
Si Mahomet sur vous jeta des yeux de père,
Sachez qu'un sort plus noble, un titre encore plus grand,
Si vous le méritez, peut-être vous attend.

42 51B, W51, 71P1, 71P2, 74A: rassembler les chefs

44 42B1-42B5, 43A1, 43A2, 47A, 52B, 60B, 67B, 78B: de vous pressé la destinée, 43A2*: →β

45 MS5, MS6, 42B1-42B5, 43A1, 43A2, 47A, 52B, 60B, 67B, 78B: Ce grand événement

46 42B1-42B5, 42XX, 43A1, 43A2, 47A, 52B, 60B, 67B, 78B: un secret entre

47 42B1-42B5, 42XX, 43A1, 43A2, 47A, 52B, 60B, 67B, 78B: fers par mes mains dégagée,

49 MS8: Ne pleurez pas Seïde,

50 MS5, 42X1, 42X2, 43A3: balancer les destins des

52 42B1-42B5, 43A1, 43A2, 47A, 52B, 60B, 67B, 78B: Mahomet jeta sur vous des

Portez vos vœux hardis au faîte de la gloire; 55
De Seïde et du reste étouffez la mémoire;
Vos premiers sentiments[4] doivent tous s'effacer,
A l'aspect des grandeurs où vous n'osiez penser.
Il faut que votre cœur à mes bontés réponde,
Et suive en tout mes lois, lorsque j'en donne au monde. 60

PALMIRE

Qu'entends-je? quelles lois, ô ciel, et quels bienfaits!
Imposteur teint de sang, que j'abjure à jamais,
Bourreau de tous les miens, va; ce dernier outrage
Manquait à ma misère,[5] et manquait à ta rage.
Le voilà donc, grand Dieu! ce prophète sacré, 65
Ce roi que je servis, ce dieu que j'adorai?
Monstre, dont les fureurs et les complots perfides
De deux cœurs innocents ont fait deux parricides:
De ma faible jeunesse infâme séducteur,
Tout souillé de mon sang, tu prétends à mon cœur! 70
Mais tu n'as pas encore assuré ta conquête;
Le voile est déchiré,[6] la vengeance s'apprête.

55 73M: vos yeux hardis
58 42B1-42B5, 42XX, 43A1, 43A2, 47A, 52B, 60B, 67B, 78B: n'osiez monter,
59-60 MS3:
Que votre cœur docile à mes bienfaits réponde,
Et chérissez mes lois lorsque j'en donne au monde.
60 MS4, MS5, 42X1, 42X2, 42B1, 42B2, 42B4, 42B5, 42XX, 43A1, 43A2, 47A, 51B, W51, 71P1, 73M, 73P, 77P1, 78P: Et suivre
42X1*: →β
62 42B1-42B5, 42XX, 43A1, 43A2, 47A, 52B, 60B, 67B, 78B: teint du sang
MS5: ↑sang; je t'abjure à jamais;
63 MS5↑, 42B1-42B5, 43A1, 43A2, 47A, 52B, 60B, 67B, 78B: va, ce cruel outrage,
43A2*: →β
68 MS4, MS5↑β, 42X1, 42X2, 42XX: fait des parricides;

[4] 'Nos cœurs se soit appris leurs premiers sentiments' (*Adélaïde*, V.i.38).
[5] 'Cruel, et vos soupçons manquaient à ma misère' (*Adélaïde*, III.ii.84).
[6] 'Le voile est déchiré, je m'étais mal connu' (*Adélaïde*, V.ii.73).

Entends-tu ces clameurs? entends-tu ces éclats?
Mon père te poursuit des ombres du trépas.[7]
Le peuple se soulève, on s'arme en ma défense; 75
Leurs bras vont à ta rage arracher l'innocence.
Puissé-je de mes mains te déchirer le flanc,[8]
Voir mourir tous les tiens, et nager dans leur sang!
Puissent la Mecque ensemble, et Médine, et l'Asie,
Punir tant de fureur et tant d'hypocrisie! 80
Que le monde par toi séduit et ravagé,
Rougisse de ses fers, les brise et soit vengé!
Que ta religion, que fonda l'imposture,
Soit l'éternel mépris de la race future!
Que l'enfer, dont tes cris menaçaient tant de fois 85

73 MS4: Entends-tu les clameurs, entends-tu les éclats?
75 MS4, MS5, 42X1, 42X2: Sans doute on se soulève,
MS5↑, 42B1-42B5, 42XX, 43A1, 43A2, 47A, 52B, 60B, 67B, 78B: Je vois qu'on se soulève,
43A2*: →β
76 MS4, MS5, 42X1, 42X2, 42B1-42B4, 42XX, 43A1, 43A2, 47A: Le ciel veut à ta rage
43A2*: →β
42B5, 52B, 60B, 67B, 78B: Le ciel vient à ta rage
77 MS4: V↑β de < tes > mains
79 MS4, MS5↑β, 42X1, 42X2: la Mecque en cendre, et
80 73M, 73P, 77P1, 78P: Punir tant de forfaits, et tant
T53: fureurs
82 MS5(↑β), 42B1-42B5, 42XX, 43A1, 43A2, 47A, 52B, 60B, 67B, 78B: de tes fers,
43A2*: →β
83 42B1-42B5, 43A1, 43A2, 47A, 52B, 60B, 67B, 78B: Que la religion
43A2*: →β
84 MS6: < Que > l'éternel
78B: de ta race
85 42B1-42B5, 42XX, 43A1-43A3, W46, 47A, W48D, W50, 51B, W51, 52B, 54V, W52, T53, W56, W57P, 60B, 67C, T62, T64A, T64G, T64P, W64G, T66, T67, 67B, 68P, T68, W70G, W70L, T70, 71P1, 71P2, W72X, 74A, 78B: dont les cris
43A2*: →β

[7] 'Pâle, et déjà couvert des ombres du trépas' (*La Henriade*, III, line 214).

[8] The model for Palmire's outburst against Mahomet is obviously Camille's outburst in Corneille's *Horace*, IV.v.1305-18.

Quiconque osait douter de tes indignes lois,
Que l'enfer, que ces lieux de douleur et de rage,
Pour toi seul préparés, soient ton juste partage![9]
Voilà les sentiments[10] qu'on doit à tes bienfaits,
L'hommage, les serments, et les vœux que je fais! 90

MAHOMET

Je vois qu'on m'a trahi; mais quoiqu'il en puisse être,
Et qui que vous soyez, fléchissez sous un maître.
Apprenez que mon cœur...

90-93 MS3:
Le sort que je demande et les vœux que je fais!
MAHOMET
Je pardonne à votre âge un excès d'imprudence
Que dans tout autre esclave eût puni ma vengeance.
Mais si vous résistez ...
SCENE 3
MAHOMET, PALMIRE, MORAD, ALI, *SUITE*
OMAR
On sait tout Mahomet:

90a-91 43A3, W46:
MAHOMET
Je pardonne à votre âge cet excès d'imprudence.
Je vois qu'on m'a trahi,//

93 W75X: [*first hemistich absent*]

[9] Voltaire wrote to Cideville on 19 July 1741: 'L'indigne partage me paraît aussi mauvais qu'à vous' (D2515).

[10] 'Voilà les sentiments que mon sang a tracés' (*Adélaïde*, II.v.175).

## *SCÈNE III*

### MAHOMET, PALMIRE, OMAR, ALI, *SUITE*

OMAR

On sait tout, Mahomet;
Hercide en expirant révéla ton secret.
Le peuple en est instruit, la prison est forcée; 95
Tout s'arme, tout s'émeut; une foule insensée,
Elevant contre toi ses hurlements affreux,[11]
Porte le corps sanglant de son chef malheureux.
Seïde est à leur tête, et d'une voix funeste
Les excite à venger ce déplorable reste. 100
Ce corps souillé de sang est l'horrible signal,
Qui fait courir le peuple à ce combat fatal.
Il s'écrie en pleurant, Je suis un parricide;
La douleur le ranime, et la rage le guide.
Il semble respirer pour se venger de toi; 105
On déteste ton dieu, tes prophètes, ta loi.

95 MS3: < Tout s'arme > le peuple en

97 MS5↑, 42B1-42B5, 42XX, 43A1, 43A2, 47A, 52B, 60B, 67B, 78B: toi des hurlements

101 MS4: Le corps

103 MS3: Seïde annonce à tous son affreux parricide,
MS4, MS5, 42X1, 42X2, 42B1-42B5, 42XX, 43A1, 43A2, 47A, 52B, 60B, 67B, 78B: Son fils crie en tout lieu, je suis un parricide,
43A2*: →β

105 MS4, MS5, 42X1, 42X2, 42B1-42B5, 42XX, 43A1, 43A2, 47A, 52B, 60B, 67B, 78B: Il respire à demi pour se venger de toi,
43A2*: →β

106 MS4, MS5↑, 42X1, 42X2: Il déteste ton dieu,
42X1*: →β

[11] The 1742 variant of this hemistich echoes even more closely other lines: 'Alors on entendit des hurlements affreux' (*La Henriade*, X, line 215); see also Appendix IV.

Ceux même qui devaient dans la Mecque alarmée
Faire ouvrir cette nuit la porte à ton armée,
De la fureur commune avec zèle enivrés,
Viennent lever sur toi leurs bras désespérés. 110
On n'entend que les cris de mort et de vengeance.

PALMIRE

Achève, juste ciel! et soutiens l'innocence.[12]
Frappe.

MAHOMET *à Omar.*

Eh bien, que crains-tu?

OMAR

Tu vois quelques amis,
Qui contre les dangers comme moi raffermis,
Mais vainement armés contre un pareil orage, 115
Viennent tous à tes pieds mourir avec courage.

107 42B1-42B5, 42XX, 43A1, 43A2, 47A, 52B, 60B, 71P1, 78B: Ceux mêmes qui
43A3, W46, W48D, W50, W64R: qui devraient
108 MS4: nuit sa porte
109-111 MS3: [*partially struck out*]
110 MS3: < Viennent porter sur toi leurs corps désespérés. >
MS4: $^{V\uparrow}$lever [...] bras
111 71P1, 71P2, 74A: que le cris
113 W75G, W75X: Frappez.
114 MS4, 42X1, 42X2, 42XX: dangers comme moi affermis;
42B1-42B4, 43A1, 43A2, 47A: dangers contre moi raffermis;
42B5, 52B, 60B, 67B, 78B: dangers avec moi raffermis;
71P1, 71P2, 74A: le danger

[12] 'Achève ton ouvrage, et soutiens l'innocence' (*Mérope*, V.vi.246).

MAHOMET

Seul je les défendrai. Rangez-vous près de moi,
Et connaissez enfin qui vous avez pour roi.

## *SCÈNE IV*

MAHOMET, OMAR, *sa suite d'un côté*, SEÏDE, *et le peuple de l'autre*, PALMIRE, *au milieu.*

SEÏDE *un poignard à la main, mais déjà affaibli par le poison.*

Peuple, vengez mon père, et courez à ce traître.

MAHOMET

Peuples, nés pour me suivre, écoutez votre maître. 120

SEÏDE

N'écoutez point ce monstre, et suivez-moi...Grands dieux!
Quel nuage épaissi se répand sur mes yeux!
(*Il avance, il chancelle.*)

117 MS4, MS5, 42X1, 42X2: Je me défendrai

118b-d MS4, MS5, 42X1, 42X2:

MAHOMET ET OMAR *SUITE, de Mahomet d'un côté, SEIDE, Le peuple de l'autre côté*, PALMIRE

SEÏDE *au milieu du peuple, un poignard à la main.*

MS6, 42B1-42B5, 42XX, 43A1, 43A2, 47A, 52B, 60B, 67B, 78B:

MAHOMET, OMAR, *et sa SUITE les armes à la main.*

PALMIRE, SEIDE, PHANOR *et le peuple, les armes à la main.*

SEÏDE *un poignard à la main*

43A3, W46:

MAHOMET, OMAR, *sa* SUITE *d'un côté*, SEIDE *et le peuple de l'autre.*

SEÏDE *au milieu*

118d 42X1*: [*adds*:] *mais affaibli déjà par l'effet du poison.*

119 43A1: père, courez

120 42B1-42B5, 42XX, 43A1, 43A2, 47A, 52B, 60B, 67B, W71P, 78B, K: Peuple né pour

Frappons...Ciel! je me meurs.

MAHOMET

Je triomphe.

PALMIRE *courant à lui.*

Ah! mon frère;

N'auras-tu pu verser que le sang de ton père?

SEÏDE

Avançons. Je ne puis... Quel dieu vient m'accabler? 125

(*Il tombe entre les bras des siens.*)

123 MS5, 42X1, 42X2, 42B1-42B5, 42XX, 43A1, 43A2, 47A, 52B, 60B, 67B, 78B: [*stage direction for Palmire absent*]

123-125 MS3:

Frappons... soutenez-moi!

PALMIRE

Seïde, indigne frère!

Ton bras n'est-il armé pour tuer son père?

SEÏDE

Ciel, où suis-je? ah! ma sœur, quel dieu vient m'accabler.

(*Il tombe entre les bras des siens.*)

123-148 MS1:

PALMIRE

Seïde, indigne frère,

N'auras-tu pas pu verser que le sang de ton père.

MAHOMET.

Dieu qui m'a confié sa parole et sa foudre, [β *line* 131]

Si je me veux venger, va vous réduire en poudre. [β *line* 132]

SEÏDE

Toi, tremble, scélérat, puisque le ciel punit.

PALMIRE

Ah! le poison sans doute.

MAHOMET.

Apprenez, infidèles, [β *line* 147]

A former désormais des trames criminelles.

124a-125 MS4, MS5, 42X1, 42X2:

SEÏDE *Il tombe entre les mains des siens.*

Avançons...

MS6, 42B1-42B5, 42XX, 43A1, 43A2, 47A, 52B, 60B, 67B, 78B:

SEÏDE *tombe* [MS6: *tombant*] *entre les bras de Phanor.*

Avançons...

MAHOMET

Ainsi tout téméraire à mes yeux doit trembler.
Incrédules esprits, qu'un zèle aveugle inspire,
Qui m'osez blasphémer, et qui vengez Zopire,
Ce seul bras que la terre apprit à redouter,
Ce bras peut vous punir d'avoir osé douter. 130
Dieu, qui m'a confié sa parole et sa foudre,
Si je me veux venger, va vous réduire en poudre.
Malheureux! connaissez son prophète et sa loi;
Et que ce dieu soit juge entre Seïde et moi.
De nous deux, à l'instant, que le coupable expire! 135

PALMIRE

Mon frère! eh, quoi! sur eux ce monstre a tant d'empire!
Ils demeurent glacés, ils tremblent à sa voix.

126-127 MS4, MS5, 42X1, 42X2, 42B1-42B5, 42XX, 43A1, 43A2, 47A, 52B, 60B, 67B, 78B:

Ainsi tout sacrilège à mes yeux doit trembler.
Mortels séditieux qu'un zèle aveugle inspire,
43A2*: < séditeux > téméraire
MS6: β↑Mortels séditieux

128 71P2, 74A: Qui m'oses blasphémer,
T64: et qui venge

130 MS5: < bras pour vous punir >

132 MS3: Si je vous veux punir, va
MS4, MS6, MS5, MS8, 42X1, 42X2, 42B1-42B5, 42XX, 43A1, 43A2, 47A, 52B, 60B, 67B, 78B: Si je veux me venger, va

135 MS4, MS5, 42X1, 42X2, 42B1-42B5, 42XX, 43A1, 43A2, 47A, 52B, 60B, 67B, 78B: De nous deux devant vous que le coupable expire.
43A2*: →β

Mahomet, comme un dieu, leur dicte encor ses lois.
Et toi, Seïde, aussi!

SEÏDE *entre les bras des siens.*

Le ciel punit ton frère.
Mon crime était horrible, autant qu'involontaire. 140
En vain la vertu même habitait dans mon cœur.
Toi, tremble, scélérat, si Dieu punit l'erreur.
Vois quel foudre il prépare aux artisans des crimes:
Tremble; son bras s'essaie à frapper ses victimes.

138 MS3: leur donne ici des lois,
MS4, MS5, 42X1, 42X2: encor des lois!
MS5↑, 42B1-42B5, 42XX, 43A1, 43A2, 47A, 52B, 60B, 67B, 78B: dicte ici des lois,

139-147 MS3:

SEÏDE

Le ciel venge mon père,
Palmire c'en est fait, vous n'avez plus de frère.
Le ciel poursuit sur moi ce crime détesté,
Commis par l'innocence avec crédulité.
Il punit mon erreur encor qu'involontaire.
Ma sœur, puisse mon sang suffise à sa colère.
Adieu, ce jour horrible à mes yeux s'obscurcit.
Toi ... tremble, scélérat, puisque le ciel punit.
(*Il se relève.*)
Ce poison ...

MAHOMET *au peuple.*

Il expire, apprenez, infidèles,

139a MS6, 42B1-42B5, 42XX, 43A1, 43A2, 47A, 52B, 60B, 67B, 78B: [*stage directions absent*]

140 42B1-42B5, 42XX, 43A1, 43A2, 47A, 52B, 60B, 67B, 78B: Mon crime est détestable autant qu'involontaire.
43A2*: →β

143 MS5: < quels foudres >
MS4, MS5<β>, 42X1, 42X2: artisans du crime;

144 MS5: < Tremblez >
MS4, MS5<β>, 42X1, 42X2: frapper sa victime.
42B1-42B5, 42XX, 43A1, 43A2, 47A, 52B, 60B, 67B, 78B: Tremblez, son bras s'essaie à frapper des victimes;
43A2*: →β

Détournez d'elle, ô Dieu, cette mort qui me suit! 145

PALMIRE

Non, peuple, ce n'est point un dieu qui le poursuit.<br>
Non; le poison sans doute...

MAHOMET *en l'interrompant, et s'adressant au peuple.*

Apprenez, infidèles,<br>
A former contre moi des trames criminelles;<br>
Aux vengeances des cieux reconnaissez mes droits.<br>
La nature et la mort ont entendu ma voix. 150<br>
La mort, qui m'obéit, qui, prenant ma défense,<br>
Sur ce front pâlissant a tracé ma vengeance,<br>
La mort est à vos yeux, prête à fondre sur vous.

145 68P, T64G: qui la suit?

147 42B1-42B5, 42XX, 43A1, 43A2, 47A, 52B, 60B, 67B, 78B:<br>
Non, ce traître sans doute...<br>
MAHOMET *au peuple.*

148 MS4, MS8, 42X1, 42X2, 42B1-42B5, 42XX, 43A1, 43A2, 47A, 52B, 60B, 67B, 78B: A former désormais des [MS5$^{\uparrow}$: des] trames criminelles;<br>
MS5: A former désormais ces trames criminelles;<br>
43A2*: →β

149 MS5: < O vengeances des cieux >

149-154 MS3:<br>
Apprenez à douter, à blasphémer mes droits,<br>
Voyez si la nature obéit à ma voix.<br>
Regardez sur ce front la mort pale et livide,<br>
Observez dans ses traits les crimes du perfide.<br>
Ce n'est en ma faveur qu'un miracle de plus.<br>
Ainsi mes ennemis seront tous confondus;

150-155 42B1-42B5, 42XX, 43A1, 43A2, 47A, 52B, 60B, 67B, 78B:<br>
La nature et la mort ont entendu ma voix.<br>
Ainsi je punirai les erreurs insensées [42XX: encensées],

151 MS4: m'obéit, en prenant

Ainsi mes ennemis sentiront mon courroux;[13]
Ainsi je punirai les erreurs insensées, 155
Les révoltes du cœur, et les moindres pensées.
Si ce jour luit pour vous, ingrats, si vous vivez,
Rendez grâce au pontife à qui vous le devez.
Fuyez, courez au temple apaiser ma colère.

(*Le peuple se retire.*)[14]

154 MS4: $^{V\uparrow}$mes ennemis

154-156 MS4, MS5, MS7<β>, 42X1, 42X2:

mon courroux,
Ainsi mes ennemis seront tous confondus,
Ce n'est en ma faveur qu'un miracle de plus.[100]
Si ce jour

157-161 MS3:

Ainsi le ciel s'explique et décide entre nous.

PALMIRE

Hélas, les malheureux tombent à ses genoux.
O ciel, de Mahomet serais-tu le complice!
Et monstre...

MAHOMET

Allez, ingrats, et craignez ma justice,
Tremblez qu'un même sort, et que les mêmes coups
Ne partent à ma voix, et ne fondent sur vous.
De mon Dieu dans le temple apaisez la colère.

(*Le peuple se retire.*)

PALMIRE

Tu meurs empoisonné, cher et coupable frère;
Monstre, ainsi son trépas t'aura justifié!

159a 42X1, 42X2: [*stage direction absent*]

42B1-42B5, 42XX, 43A1, 43A2, 47A, 52B, 60B, 67B, 78B: (*Le peuple s'en va.*)

[13] MS7, 42X1 and 42X2 tell us that the two extra lines were spoken at the first performance.

[14] 'Ils se retirent tous, pêle-mêle et sans ordre par toutes les issues quelconques' (MS Lekain, instructions for the *commandant des assistants*).

PALMIRE *revenant à elle.*

Arrêtez. Le barbare empoisonna mon frère, 160
Monstre, ainsi son trépas t'aura justifié;
A force de forfaits[15] tu t'es déifié.
Malheureux assassin de ma famille entière,
Ote-moi de tes mains ce reste de lumière.[16]
O frère! ô triste objet d'un amour plein d'horreurs! 165

159b 42B1-42B5, 42XX, 43A1, 43A2, 47A, 52B, 60B, 67B, 78B: [*stage direction for Palmire absent*]

159-161 MS1:

PALMIRE

O ciel, de Mahomet, serais-tu le complice.
Peuple, écoutez.

MAHOMET

Ingrats, redoutez ma justice.
Tremblez qu'un même sort, et que les mêmes coups
Ne partent à ma voix et ne tombent sur vous.
Fuyez et dans le temple apaisez ma colère.

PALMIRE *revenant à elle.*

Arrêtez, le barbare empoisonna mon frère.
Monstre, ainsi son trépas

160 MS3: Tu meurs empoisonné, cher et coupable frère,
42B1: barbare empoisonne mon frère.

162 47A: [*absent*]

164 MS4: mains le reste

165 MS3: objet de mes tendres erreurs.
42B5, 67B: horreur!
42B5*: →β
W48D: amour pleins

[15] 'Réparer ma faiblesse à force de forfaits' (*Mérope*, IV.iv.202).

[16] 'Ses yeux ne voyant plus qu'un reste de lumière' (*La Henriade*, V, line 334); see also Appendix IV.

Que je te suive au moins.
(*Elle se jette sur le poignard de son frère.*)

MAHOMET

Qu'on l'arrête!

PALMIRE

Je meurs.
Je cesse de te voir, imposteur exécrable.
Je me flatte, en mourant, qu'un dieu plus équitable
Réserve un avenir pour les cœurs innocents.
Tu dois régner; le monde est fait pour les tyrans. 170

MAHOMET

Elle m'est enlevée...[17] Ah! trop chère victime!

166 42B1-42B5, 42XX, 43A1, 43A2, 47A, 52B, 60B, 67B, 78B:
au moins.
(*Elle se jette sur le poignard de Seïde, et s'en frappe.*)
MS4, MS5, 42X1, 42X2:

MAHOMET

l'arrête!
PALMIRE *tombant aux pieds* [42X1*: *près*] *de Seïde dans les bras des siens.*
42B1-42B5, 42XX, 43A1, 43A2, 47A, 52B, 60B, 67B, 78B: *tombant dans les bras des siens.*

Je meurs.

42B5*: →β
167 MS3: Je ne te verrai plus, imposteur exécrable
170 MS3: Régne en ces lieux; ce monde
MS1, MS5, MS6, 42B1-42B5, 42XX, 43A1, 43A2, 47A, 52B, 60B, 67B, 78B: régner, ce monde

[17] 'Au premier hémistiche de cette réplique, Omar donne l'ordre tacite aux suivants de Mahomet de se retirer, ce qu'ils exécutent par la gauche du théâtre' (MS Lekain, instructions for the *commandant des assistants*).

Je me vois arracher le seul prix de mon crime.
De ses jours pleins d'appas détestable ennemi,
Vainqueur et tout puissant, c'est moi qui suis puni.
Il est donc des remords![18] ô fureur! ô justice! 175
Mes forfaits dans mon cœur ont donc mis mon supplice!
Dieu que j'ai fait servir aux malheur des humains,
Adorable instrument de mes affreux desseins,
Toi que j'ai blasphémé, mais que je crains encore,
Je me sens condamné, quand l'univers m'adore. 180
Je brave en vain les traits dont je me sens frapper.
J'ai trompé les mortels, et ne puis me tromper.

172 MS4, MS5, 42X1, 42X2, 42B1-42B5, 42XX, 43A1, 43A2, 47A, 52B, 60B, 67B, 78B: arracher le prix d'un si grand crime;

43A2*: →β

173 MS3: D'elle et du monde entier, de moi-même haï,

MS4, MS5, 42X1, 42X2, 42B1-42B5, 42XX, 43A1, 43A2, 47A, 52B, 60B, 67B, 78B: tes jours malheureux détestable

MS6, 43A2*: De ses divins appas détestable

175 MS3, MS4, 42X1, 42X2: remords! ô douleur! ô justice!

MS5: remords? Ah! douleur! ô justice!

179-180 43A1: Toi que j'ai blasphémé, quand l'univers m'adore

182 42B1-42B5, 42XX, 43A1, 43A2, 47A, 52B, 60B, 67B, 78B: mortels, et je puis me tromper.

43A2*: →β

[18] 'Le jeune élève joua successivement devant son maître les rôles de Séide et de Mahomet. J'ai ouï dire plusieurs fois à m. de Voltaire, qu'un des moments où l'on dût concevoir la plus grande idée de son disciple, fut celui où dans le cinquième acte de *Mahomet*, il prononça cet hémistiche sublime: *Il est donc des remords!* Lekain, lui-même, avouait qu'il n'avait jamais pu le retrouver depuis' (*Œuvres de La Harpe* (1820), iv.452-453). Not everybody admired Lekain's handling of the role: 'Bien différent de ces acteurs qui varient leur action selon le caractère du personnage; qu'il joue *Hippolyte*, *Tancrède*, *Lyncée*, *Rhadamiste*, *Zamore*, *Mahomet*, *Cinna*, c'est toujours m. Lekain avec ses gestes étudiés, ses attitudes académiques, ses regards distraits, ses chutes nombreuses; on ne peut pas le perdre un moment de vue, et il semble prendre autant de peine à montrer l'acteur sur la scène qu'il en faudrait à un comédien médiocre pour le faire oublier' (*Al*, 1777, v.123). For a general discussion of the subject, see *Le Journal des théâtres* (1778), iii.361-372.

Père, enfants malheureux, immolés à ma rage,[19]
Vengez la terre et vous, et le ciel que j'outrage.
Arrachez-moi ce jour, et ce perfide cœur, 185
Ce cœur né pour haïr, qui brûle avec fureur.
Et toi, de tant de honte étouffe la mémoire;

183-190 MS3:
Père, enfants malheureux, sanglant objet que j'aime,
Vous êtes tous vengés, je me connais moi-même.
Tombe le trône affreux par le sang émeuté,
Périsse mon empire, il est trop acheté,
Et périsse avec moi ma funeste mémoire.
OMAR
Amis, veillez sur lui, je tremble pour sa gloire.
Gardez et laissez voir aux mortels curieux,
Que celui qui les dompte est un homme comme eux.
Cachons l'égarement où son grand cœur s'abaisse,
Que les siècles futurs ignorent sa faiblesse.
Il doit régir en Dieu l'univers prévenu;
Notre empire est détruit, si l'homme est reconnu.//

184 MS6, MS8, 42B1-42B5, 42XX, 43A2, 43A3, W46, 47A, W48D, W50, 51B, W51, W52, 52B, T53, 54V, W57P, 60P, T64G, T64P, W64R, T67, 67B, 68P, 71P1, 71P2, 74A, 78B: et ce ciel

185 MS4: Arrachez ce jour
71P2, 74A: Arrache-moi le jour et ce

187 MS5: honte, efface la mémoire;

187-190 43A2*<β>:
Que fais-tu Mahomet? Quoi ton âme étonnée
Des coups qu'elle porta paraîtrait consternée?
Reprenons nos projets, imposons aux mortels
Par de nouveaux forfaits méritons des autels.
De l'amour, de ses traits, repoussons la puissance
Des regrets, des remords bravons la violence.
Ma vaste ambition ne connaît point de loi
Et le premier degré n'est point assez pour moi.
D'une flamme importune étouffons la mémoire.
Cet instant de faiblesse obscurcissait ma gloire.

[19] In abortive endings for the play given in MS3 and D2408, we find the line 'Périsse mon empire, il est trop acheté', which owes at least something to earlier playwrights: 'L'honneur d'un si beau choix serait trop acheté' (Corneille, *Horace*, II.viii.701); 'Ce reste malheureux seroit trop acheté' (Racine, *Bajazet*, II.iii.595).

Cache au moins ma faiblesse, et sauve encor ma gloire;
Je dois régir en dieu l'univers prévenu:[20]
Mon empire est détruit, si l'homme est reconnu.[21] 190

*Fin du cinquième et dernier acte.*

---

Je veux régir en Dieu l'univers prévenu.
Mon empire est détruit si l'homme est reconnu.
[*above this, in fainter ink*:]
Mais dois-je des remords éprouver la puissance.
Mon cœur ne fut jamais né pour la dépendance.
Rendons-le à des projets illustres, immortels.
A force de forfaits méritons des autels.//

189 MS5 <β>, 42B1-42B3, 42B5, 42XX, 43A1, 43A2, 47A, 52B, 60B, 67B, 78B: Je veux régir
42B4: β

[20] In a suggested ending given in D2408, we find crossed out: 'Ah! donne-moi la mort et prends soin de ma gloire', which echoes Racine's *Phèdre*, I.iii.309: 'Je voulais en mourant prendre soin de ma gloire'.

[21] On 19 January 1741 Voltaire suggested to d'Argental the following ending to the play (lines 185-190) (D2408):

Périsse mon empire, il est trop acheté,
Périsse Mahomet, son culte et sa mémoire!
(*à Omar*)
Ah! donne moy la mort, mais sauve au moins ma gloire,
Délivre moy du jour, mais cache à tous les yeux
Que Mahomet coupable, est faible et malheureux.

On 21 January (D2411) he revised this to:

Vous êtes tous vanges, je me connois moy même,
Je me hais, je déteste et le trône et le jour.
(*à Omar*)
Frappe, ôte moy la vie, et sauve au moins ma gloire,
Frappe, et de tant de honte étouffe la mémoire
Prends pitié de ton maître et cache à tous les yeux
Que Mahomet coupable est faible et malheureux.

# APPENDIX I

Variant to III.ix.278-314.
This reading is found in MS4, MS5, 42X1, 42X2, 42B1-42B5, 42XX, 43A1, 43A2, 47A, 52B, 60B, 67B, 78B.

***

Remets-toi dans mes mains, trembles, si tu balances,
Suis-moi.

SCENE IX.
PHANOR, ZOPIRE, SEIDE

PHANOR

Seigneur lisez ce billet important,
Qu'un Arabe en secret m'a donné dans l'instant.

ZOPIRE *Il lit.*

Hercide! qu'ai lu? Dieux, votre providence,
Voudrait-elle adoucir soixante ans de souffrance? 5
(*après avoir regardé Seïde*)
Suis-moi.

SEÏDE

Quoi Mahomet...

ZOPIRE.

Viens ton sort en dépend.

SCENE X
OMAR *avec sa suite arrivant avec précipitation de l'autre côté du théâtre*, ZOPIRE, SEÏDE, PHANOR

3a MS4, MS5, 42X1, 42X2: *Il lit haut le seul mot.*

OMAR

Traître, que faites-vous? Mahomet vous attend.

SEÏDE

Où suis-je? ou suis-je? ô ciel? et que dois-je résoudre?
D'un et d'autre côté je suis frappé du foudre.
Où courir, où porter un trouble si cruel, 10
Où fuir?

OMAR

Aux pieds du Roi qu'à choisi l'Eternel.

SEÏDE

Oui j'y cours abjurer un serment que j'abhorre.

SCENE XI
ZOPIRE, PHANOR

ZOPIRE

Ah! Seïde où vas-tu?... Mais il me fuit encore,
Il sort désespéré, frappé d'un sombre effroi,
Et mon cœur qui le suit s'échappe loin de moi, 15
Seïde... cet écrit, ton aspect, ton absence
A mes sens déchirés font trop de violence.
Hercide devant moi cherche à se présenter,
Ah! les cœurs malheureux osent-ils se flatter?
Hercide est ce guerrier dont la main meurtrière, 20
Me ravit mes enfants, et fit périr leur mère.
Mes enfants sont vivants; et sans doute aujourd'hui,
Mon sort et leurs destins s'éclairciront par lui.

8 MS4, MS5, 42X1, 42X2: Où suis-je! ô ciel, où suis-je, et
9 MS4: frappé de foudre
14 MS4, 42X1, 42X2: Il sont de ses pères, frappé
19 MS5: ↑Ah! l'homme malheureux
23 MS4, MS5, 42X1, 42X2: leur destin

Mahomet les retient, dit-il, sous sa puissance,
Et Palmire et Seïde ignorent leur naissance? 25
Je m'abuse peut-être, et noyé dans mes pleurs,
J'embrasse aveuglement de flatteuses erreurs;
Je m'arrête; je doute, et ma douleur craintive,
Prête à la voix du sang une oreille attentive.

PHANOR

Espérez, mais craignez. Songez combien d'enfants, 30
Mahomet chaque jour arrache à leurs parents,
Il en a fait les siens, ils n'ont point d'autre père,
Et tous en l'écoutant, ont pris son caractère.

ZOPIRE

N'importe; amène Hercide au milieu de la nuit,
Qu'il soit sous cette voûte en secret introduit 35
Aux pieds de cet autel, où les pleurs de ton maître;
Ont fatigué des dieux qui s'apaisent peut-être.
Un moment peut finir un siècle de malheurs,
Hâte un moment si doux, vas, cours, vole, ou je meurs.

## SCENE XII

ZOPIRE *seul.*

O ciel! ayez pitié d'un destin que j'ignore, 40
Grands dieux apprenez-moi si je suis père encore!

36 MS4, MS5, 42X1, 42X2: Au pied

40-41 42X1, 42X2, MS7:
O Dieux, apprenez-moi si je suis père encore,
Ne m'abandonnes point, juste ciel, que j'implore.
MS5:
Ne m'abandonne point, juste ciel que j'implore!
O ciel! apprenez-moi si je suis père encore,

41 MS4: O ciel, apprenez-moi [*and lacks previous line*]

Rendez-moi mes enfants, mais rendez aux vertus,
Deux cœurs nés généreux qu'un traître a corrompus.

[*Fin de l'acte III.*]

42-43 MS4, 42X1, 42X2:
Rendez-mois mes enfants, rendez-moi les vertus
De deux cœurs généreux, qu'un traître a corrompus.
42X1*: →β
43A2*: →β [*while retaining some variants* (*see above line* 309), *line* 279 *is followed by lines* 286-291, *with a variant in line* 289 (*see above*)]

# APPENDIX II

Variant to V.i.5-57 from MS3.

MS3 consists only of act V, from which the opening lines are missing. It presents a version of events in which Seïde is poisoned in prison rather than before or in the course of his attack on Zopire. The variant from MS1 appears to follow this version rather than that of the base text.

***

OMAR

[...]
Tous ces premiers soupçons qui retombaient sur toi
De ce meurtre en ton nom j'ai demandé vengeance.
J'ai voulu faire encore adorer ta clémence.

MAHOMET

Mon ordre, sur Seïde, est-il exécuté?

OMAR

Tu peux t'en rapporter à ma fidélité. 5
Il est dans la prison et tandis qu'à la porte
Des peuples incertains la foule se transporte,

3 <admirer> V? adorer
6-11 MS1:

OMAR

et tandis qu'à sa porte
Des peuples incertains la foule se transporte.
Dans son sang odieux lui-même a fait couler
Le poison qu'en sa coupe on avait su mêler.
Il porte dans son sein la mort qui le déchire.
Cependant [...]

J'ai fait prendre en secret à cet infortuné
Le breuvage mortel qui lui fut destiné.
Seïde ne peut rien, et bientôt il expire. 10
Cependant en ces lieux j'ai su garder Palmire.
Vengé, maître de tous, sur le trône appelé,
Souverain dans les lieux dont tu fus exilé.
Législateur, prophète et Roi dans ta patrie,
L'amour achevera le bonheur de la vie; 15
Palmire à tes genoux d'un œil respectueux
Te voyant comme un dieu t'adressera des vœux.
En son âme en tous temps de ta grandeur frappée
N'aura pas seulement besoin d'être trompée.

MAHOMET

Je ne sais, mais peut-être il est un dieu vengeur 20
Qui de ce lâche amour empoisonne mon cœur.
J'adore malgré moi par un charme funeste
Ce reste infortuné d'un sang que je déteste.
Et dans les attentats de cet horrible jour
Le comble des fureurs est cet indigne amour. 25
Et comment me flatter que Palmire éblouie
Abandonne Seïde et le nœud qui les lie!

---

MOHAMET

Je ne le sais, mais peut-être il est un dieu vengeur
Qui de ce lâche amour empoisonne mon cœur.
Ma faiblesse me pèse, et par un nœud funeste
M'attache avec fureur au sang que je déteste,
Ce sang que j'ai versé, ce comble d'attentats
Rend ma tendresse affreuse, et ne m'en guérit pas.
Quoi! tu m'oses flatter que Palmire éblouie
Abandonne Seïde, et le nœud qui la lie,
Que ses respects forcés lui tiennent lieu d'amour,
Qu'elle cède à l'orgueil de régner dans ma cour.

21 [V]: de
26 <Et ils> [V]Et

Qu'elle n'écarte point ce voile redouté
Mis entre sa faiblesse et mon autorité,
Et qu'ignorant toujours le sang qui la fit naître 30
Elle ait l'ambition de captiver son maître?

OMAR

On l'amène à tes pieds. Tu seras éclairci

MAHOMET

Va rassembler mes chefs, et je t'attends ici.

SCENE 2

MAHOMET, PALMIRE, Gardes

Ciel, où suis-je!

MAHOMET

A mes yeux soyez moins consternée
J'ai pesé les décrets de votre destinée, 35
Ce que vous avez vu de moi vous effrayer.
Mais je n'ai pas besoin de me justifier.
Vous voyez en moi seul toute votre famille.
Je vous traitai quinze ans comme ma propre fille.
Un titre encor plus noble est destiné pour vous. 40
Seïde n'est point né pour être votre époux.
Le sort qui vous attend est l'objet de l'envie
De toutes les beautés que renferme l'Asie.
Vos premiers sentiments doivent tous s'effacer

33b <OMAR, Gardes>

# APPENDIX III

The following *avertissement* was printed in the Kehl edition of *Mahomet* (iii.121-22).

## *AVERTISSEMENT DES EDITEURS*

On trouvera des détails historiques sur Mahomet dans l'*Avis de l'Editeur*. On y reconnaît la main de M. de Voltaire. Nous ajouterons ici qu'en 1741 Crébillon refusa d'approuver la tragédie de *Mahomet*, non qu'il aimât les hommes qui avaient intérêt de faire supprimer la pièce, ni même qu'il les craignît; mais uniquement parce qu'on lui avait persuadé que *Mahomet* était le rival d'*Atrée*. M. d'Alembert fut chargé d'examiner la pièce, et il jugea qu'elle devait être jouée: c'est un de ses premiers droits à la reconnaissance des hommes, et à la haine des fanatiques qui n'ont cessé depuis de le faire déchirer dans des libelles périodiques. La pièce fut jouée alors telle qu'elle est ici. Quelque temps après, les comédiens supprimèrent le délire de Séide, parce qu'il leur paraissait difficile à bien rendre; et la Police trouva mauvais que Mahomet dît à Zopire:

> Non, mais il faut m'aider à tromper l'univers. [II.292]

En conséquence on a dit pendant longtemps:

> Non, mais il faut m'aider à dompter l'univers.

ce qui faisait un sens ridicule.

Le quatrième acte de *Mahomet* est imité du *Marchand de Londres* de Lillo; ou plutôt le moment où Zopire prie pour ses enfants, celui où Zopire mourant les embrasse et leur pardonne, sont imités de la pièce anglaise. Mais qu'un homme qui assassine sans défense un vieillard vertueux et son bienfaiteur, soit toujours intéressant et noble; c'est ce qu'on voit dans Mahomet, et qu'on ne voit que dans cette pièce. Le fanatisme est le seul sentiment qui puisse ôter l'horreur d'un tel crime, et la faire tomber entière sur les instigateurs.

## APPENDIX IV

The language of Voltaire's plays shows his deep knowledge of the classical theatrical tradition, if also the limitations of the alexandrine. The following list shows what may be conscious or unconscious echoes.

*Act I line 37*:

'Et te jurer aux siens une haine immortelle' (Racine, *Alexandre*, III.ii.770)

'Je conserve aux Romains une haine immortelle' (Racine, *Mithridate*, I.i.28)

'Quand je voue au Romains une haine immortelle' (Crébillon, *Rhadamiste*, V.ii)

*Act I line 54*:

'Mais songez qu'au port même il peut faire naufrage' (Corneille, *Pompée*, I.iii.258)

'Dans un pareil naufrage elle ouvre un heureux port' (Corneille, *La Toison d'or*, III.v.1347)

*Act I line 60*:

'Daignez d'un roi terrible apaiser le courroux' (Racine, *Esther*, III.v.1166)

*Act I line 77*:

'Je ne sais quel penchant parler en sa faveur' (Crébillon, *Sémiramis*, III.ii)

*Act I line 79*:

'Je ne puis sans horreur me regarder moi-même' (Racine, *Phèdre*, II.vi.718)

*Act I line 84*:

'Et haïr *Alexandre* autant que je le hais' (Racine, *Alexandre*, IV.iii.1172)

*Act I line 86*:
'Les autres dans le sein de leurs dieux domestiques' (Corneille, *Cinna*, I.iii.198)

*Act I line 99*:
'Chargées d'indignes fers vos généreuses mains' (Racine, *Athalie*, V.ii.1566)

*Act I line 102*:
'Sans elle trouve à dire au bonheur de ma vie' (Corneille, *Médée*, II.iv.570)
'Que j'attache à l'aimer le bonheur de ma vie' (Corneille, *Sophonisbe*, V.iv.1668)
'Vous m'avez envié le bonheur de ma vie' (Corneille, *Œdipe*, act III.iii.942)

*Act I line 153*:
'Faisons par vos travaux et ma reconnaissance' (Rotrou, *Venceslas*, III.vi.1087)
'Je fis parler mes yeux et ma reconnaissance' (Crébillon, *Electre*, I.ix)

*Act I line 163*:
'Oui, je crois voir en vous cet Ange impérieux' (Houdar de La Motte, *Les Macchabées*, III.vii)

*Act I line 212*:
'Rentre dans le néant dont je t'ai fait sortir' (Racine, *Bajazet*, II.i.524)

*Act I line 220*:
'C'est un exemple illustre aux siècles à venir' (Rotrou, *Cosroès*, I.iii.191)

*Act I line 302*:
'Elle a trop de vertu pour n'être pas chrétienne' (Corneille, *Polyeucte*, IV.iii.1268)

*Act I line 328*:
'Allons, allons, seigneur, les armes à la main' (Corneille, *Othon*, V.ii.1635)
'T'avait mis contre moi les armes à la main' (Corneille, *Cinna*, V.i.1440)
'Est-ce moi qui vous mets les armes à la main' (Racine, *Thébaïde*, IV.iii.1022)
'Il nous trouve partout les armes à la main' (Racine, *Alexandre*, II.ii.576)
'A forcé ce palais les armes à la main' (La Motte, *Inès de Castro*, IV.iii.886)
'En forçant ce palais les armes à la main' (La Motte, *Inès de Castro*, V.iv.1149)
'Ou mourir avec lui les armes à la main' (Crébillon, *Pyrrhus*, III.vi)
'Les armes à la main, volant sur notre bord' (Piron, *Gustave Wasa*, V.v)

*Act II line 34*:
'Il tombe sur son lit sans chaleur et sans vie' (Racine, *Britannicus*, V.v.1632)

*Act II line 43*:
'Et j'ose me flatter qu'entre les noms fameux' (Racine, *Mithridate*, V.v.1657)

*Act II line 49*:
'J'en vois une partie à mes pieds abattus' (Corneille, *Théodore*, IV.iv.1288)
'Par une main impie à leurs pieds abattue' (Corneille, *Polyeucte*, III.iii.858)

*Act II line 71*:
'Qu'être allié de Rome, et s'en faire un appui' (Corneille, *Nicomède*, III.ii.877)

*Act II line 90*:
'Et vous veut faire part de son pouvoir suprême' (Corneille, *Cinna*, III.ii.846)
'Et vous veut faire part de son pouvoir suprême' (Corneille, *Cinna*, III.ii.846)
'Il n'est que trop jaloux de son pouvoir suprême' (Crébillon, *Atrée et Thyeste*, I.v.301)
'Le bonheur peut conduire à la grandeur suprême' (Corneille, *Cinna*, II.i.477)
'Le plus illustre essai de son pouvoir suprême' (Corneille, *Agésilas*, V.vi.1990)

*Act II line 97*:
'Je viens contre un tyran, prêt à tout entreprendre' (Crébillon, *Electre*, IV.v)

*Act II line 102*:
'Nous nous aimions tous deux dès la plus tendre enfance' (Racine, *Thébaïde*, II.i.367)
'Nous étions ennemis dès la plus tendre enfance' (Racine, *Thébaïde*, IV.i.919)

*Act II line 159* (1742 version):
'Ah! Madame, il est vrai que les Dieux ennemis' (Racine, *Thébaïde*, V.iii.1284)

*Act II line 173*:
'Elle veut voir le jour et sa douleur profonde' (Racine, *Phèdre*, I.ii.149)
'Sans ce vœux, triste objet de ma douleur profonde' (Crébillon, *Idoménée*, V.v)

*Act II line 178*:
'Vois-je l'Etat penchant au bord du précipice?' (Racine, *Bérénice*, IV.iv.1003)
'Voyez tout mon espoir au bord au porécipice' (Corneille, *Agésilas*, I.ii.178)

'Le destin les aveugle au bord du précipice' (Corneille, *Pompée*, IV.i.1093)
'Donne-t-il à qui marche au bord du précipice' (T. Corneille, *Le Comte d'Essex*, I.i)
'Vous la verrez, brillante au bord des précipices' (Corneille, *Cinna*, I.iv.313)
'S'il entraîne l'Etat au bord du précipice' (La Noue, *Mahomet II*, III.vii)

*Act II line 184*:
'On lui fasse en mon sein enfoncer le couteau' (Racine, *Athalie*, V.vi.1782)
'Au sein de ton tuteur enfonças le couteau' (Corneille, *Cinna*, V.i.1140)

*Act II line 192*:
'Et commandez-vous même au reste des humains' (Racine, *Alexandre*, V.iii.1520)
'Ce héros, si terrible au reste des humains' (Racine, *Iphigénie*, IV.i.1096)

*Act II line 196*:
'Et je le sens trop peu, pour daigner t'abuser' (Piron, *Gustave Wasa*, IV.v)

*Act II line 247*:
'Tout ce qu'on leur souhaite au pied de leurs autels' (Corneille, *Rodogune*, V.ii.1550)
'Je vais moi-même encore au pied de ses autels' (Racine, *Phèdre*, IV.iv.1191)
'Montrez que je viens suivre au pied de nos autels' (Racine, *Iphigénie*, III.iv.871)
'Et chercher du repos au pied de ses autels' (Racine, *Athalie*, II.v.525)

*Act II line 255*:
'Sauver ce gentilhomme à tes pieds abattus' (Corneille, *Clitandre*, IV.iv.1136)

*Act II line 281*:
'Et c'est de vos leçons qu'il faut que je l'apprenne' (Rotrou, *Venceslas*, I.i.80)

*Act II line 300*:
'Etouffons nos discords dans nos embrassements' (Rotrou, *Venceslas*, I.i.254)
'Avecque le dernier de leurs embrassements' (Rotrou, *Venceslas*, V.iv.1589)

*Act II line 311*:
'La moitié du sénat s'intéresse pour nous' (Racine, *Britannicus*, III.v.905)

*Act II line 319* (1742 version):
'Vous me deviez servir malgré tout mon courroux' (Corneille, *Sophonisbe*, II.iii.577)

*Act III line 12*:
'Que de trouble, d'horreurs, de sang prêt à couler' (Racine, *Bérénice*, V.vii.1474)

*Act III line 26*:
'Et puisque vous voyez mon âme tout entière' (Corneille, *Nicomède*, III.ii.899)

*Act III line 30*:
'Et le hais d'autant plus, que je vois moins de jour' (Corneille, *Pertharite*, I.ii.173)
'Non, Seigneur, je vous hais d'autant plus qu'on vous aime' (Racine, *Alexandre*, IV.ii.1121)
'Je les hais d'autant plus que vous leur pardonnez' (La Motte, *Inès de Castro*, V.i.1098)

*Act III line 45*:
'Animé d'un regard, je puis tout entreprendre' (Racine, *Andromaque*, I.iv.329)
'En l'état où je suis, je puis tout entreprendre' (Racine, *Bérénice*, V.vi.1420)

*Act III line 46*:
'Prince, de ce devoir je ne puis me défendre' (Racine, *Bérénice*, IV.viii.1252)

*Act III line 48*:
'Enfin ce jour heureux, ce jour tant souhaité' (Crébillon, *Atrée et Thyeste*, I.ii.15)

*Act III line 63*:
'Parce qu'il va s'armer pour la première fois' (Corneille, *Le Cid*, V.iii.1620)
'Et crois toujours la voir pour la première fois' (Racine, *Bérénice*, II.ii.546)
'J'ose l'interpréter pour la première fois' (Crébillon, *Pyrrhus*, II.i)

*Act III line 64*:
'Du trouble où je vous vois ne puis-je être éclairci?' (Crébillon, *Atrée et Thyeste*, I.v.287)
'Qui peut-être rougis du trouble où tu me vois' (Racine, *Phèdre*, I.iii.219)
'Rassurez-vous. Chassez le trouble où je vous vois' (La Noue, *Mahomet II*, V.iii)

*Act III line 82* (1742 version):
'Je ne hais point Porus, Seigneur, je le confesse' (Racine, *Alexandre*, V.i.1290)

*Act III line 104* (first hemistich):
'Et de votre bonheur reposez-vous sur moi' (La Motte, *Inès de Castro*, II.i.338)

*Act III line 104* (second hemistich):
'Et fiez-vous à moi de vos vrais intérêts' (La Motte, *Inès de Castro*, IV.vi.1026 variant)

*Act III line 105*:
'J'ai vu favoriser de votre confiance' (Racine, *Britannicus*, IV.ii.1204)

*Act III line 106*:
'Ce n'est pas pour sortir de votre obéissance' (Corneille, *Rodogune*, V.iii.1568)
'Je ne veux point douter de votre obéissance' (Racine, *Bajazet*, IV.iii.1187)
'Seigneur, je vous réponds de son obéissance' (Corneille, *La Toison d'or*, I.ii.378)
'Mais je vous répondrais de son obéissance' (Corneille, *Agésilas*, II.iii.571)

*Act III line 111*:
'Mais à condition qu'il soit digne de vous' (Corneille, *Pertharite*, I.i.90)

*Act III line 112*:
'N'en doutez point, Seigneur, mon âme inquiétée' (Racine, *Alexandre*, II.i.421)
'N'en doutez point, Seigneur, soit raison, soit caprice' (Racine, *Bérénice*, II.ii.371)
'N'en doutez point, Seigneur, il fut votre soutien' (Racine, *Esther*, III.iv.1114)

*Act III line 121*:
'Et je plains seulement le malheur de ma vie' (Mairet, *La Sophonisbe*, III.iv.800)

*Act III line 124*:
'Victime infortunée et d'amour et de haine' (Mairet, *La Sophonisbe*, III.iv (903)
'Mon amour et ma haine, et la cause commune' (Corneille, *Attila*, III.vi.697)
'C'est à vous de choisir mon amour ou ma haine' (Corneille, *Rodogune*, III.iv.1023)
'Déclarer à la fois ma haine et mon amour' (Racine, *Alexandre*, III.ii.768)
'Sacrifie mon sang, ma haine et mon amour' (Racine, *Andromaque*, IV.i.1124)

'J'espérais étouffer mon amour et ma haine' (Crébillon, *Idoménée*, I.ii)
'Parlez, méritez-vous mon amour et ma haine' (Crébillon, *Xerxès*, II.v)

*Act III line 138* (variant):
'Le prêtre deviendra la première victime' (Racine, *Iphigénie*, V.ii.1606)

*Act III line 157*:
'Vous avez sur mon cœur une entière puissance' (T. Corneille, *Le Comte d'Essex*, III.iv)
'Je vous offre en ces lieux une entière puissance (P. Corneille, *La Toison d'or*, II.iv.933)
'Vous avez dans ces lieux une entière puissance' (Racine, *Mithridate*, I.ii.164)

*Act III line 174*:
'L'amour n'est point le maître alors qu'on délibère' (Corneille, *Pulchérie*, II.iv.650)

*Act III line 180*:
'Voici qui vous dira les volontés des cieux' (Racine, *Athalie*, IV.i.1263)

*Act III line 188*:
'Que traînée avec pompe aux marches de l'autel' (Corneille, *Tite et Bérénice*, III.v.937)
'Et, comme une victime aux marches de l'autel' (Corneille, *Horace*, IV.ii.1137)

*Act III line 206*:
'Le tyran m'a surpris sans défense et sans armes' (Racine, *Phèdre*, III.v.961)
'Elle nous croit ici sans armes, sans défense' (Racine, *Athalie*, IV.iii.1345)

*Act III line 211*:
'Amour, rage, transports, venez à mon secours' (Racine, *Thébaïde*, V.vi.1495)

*Act III line 214*:
'De leurs plus chers parents saintement homicides' (Racine, *Athalie*, IV.iii.1365)

*Act III line 215*:
'L'Ange exterminateur est debout avec nous' (Racine, *Athalie*, V.iv.1698)

*Act III line 216*:
'Comme je ne vois pas dans le fond de mon cœur' (Corneille, *Sertorius*, III.i.859)
'Que vous pénétrez mal dans le fond de mon cœur' (Racine, *Thébaïde*, I.iii.130)
'A caché les plus grands dans le fond de mon cœur' (Crébillon, *Idoménée*, II.ii)

*Act III line 220*:
'De ne vous point compter parmi mes ennemis?' (Racine, *Andromaque*, I.iv.296)
'Je ne vous compte plus parmi mes ennemis' (Racine, *Britannicus*, IV.iv.1413)
'Et ne le pas choisir parmi vos ennemis' (Corneille, *Attila*, IV.iv.1292)

*Act III line 234*:
'J'ai le cœur aussi bon, mais enfin je suis homme' (Corneille, *Horace*, II.iii.468)

*Act III line 263*:
'Ce temple est mon pays, je n'en connais point d'autre' (Racine, *Athalie*, II.vii.640)

*Act III line 266*:
'Quels effets voulez-vous de sa reconnaissance?' (Racine, *Britannicus*, I.i.87)
'Empêche les devoirs de ma reconnaissance' (Corneille, *Médée*, IV.v.1254)
'Que peut donc tout l'effort de ma reconnaissance' (Corneille, *Sophonisbe*, II.ii.535)
'Un juste et plein effet de sa reconnaissance' (Corneille, *Tite et Bérénice*, IV.i.1080)
'Où doit aller celui de ma reconnaissance' (Corneille, *Pertharite*, II.ii.492)
'Et le plus digne effort de ma reconnaissance' (Crébillon, *Pyrrhus*, IV.iv)
'Mais dois-je vous parler de ma reconnaissance' (Piron, *Gustave Wasa*, III.ix)

*Act III line 279*:
'Pour la dernière fois, venez, je vous l'ordonne' (Racine, *Mithridate*, IV.iv.1316)
'Pour la dernière fois vous voyez si je l'aime' (Racine, *Bérénice*, V.iii.1293)
'Pour la dernière fois, sauvez-le, sauvez-vous' (Racine, *Andromaque*, III.vii.960)
'Pour la dernière fois, qu'il s'éloigne, qu'il parte' (Racine, *Britannicus*, II.i.360)
'Pour la dernière fois souffrez que je le voie' (Crébillon, *Pyrrhus*, III.iv)
'Pour la dernière fois enfin je le déclare' (Piron, *Gustave Wasa*, IV.ii)

*Act III line 306*:
'Prêtez-moi l'un et l'autre une oreille attentive' (Racine, *Athalie*, II.v.464)

*Act III line 307*:
'Fait enlever Junie au milieu de la nuit' (Racine, *Britannicus*, I.i.54)

*Act IV line 40*:
'Dans le sein de sa ville, à l'aspect de ses dieux?' (Racine, *Mithridate*, III.i.890)

*Act IV line 52*:
'Mais un heureux destin le conduit en ces lieux' (Racine, *Andromaque*, II.iii.603)
'Qui t'amène en des lieux où l'on fuit ta présence (Racine, *Andromaque*, V.iii.1554)

*Act IV line 60*:
'Quel sera ce bienfait que je ne comprends pas?' (Racine, *Athalie*, I.i.161)

*Act IV line 64*:
'Il entend les soupirs de l'humble qu'on outrage' (Racine, *Esther*, III.iv.1053)

*Act IV line 97*:
'Je l'ai vu soupirer de douleur et de rage' (Racine, *Thébaïde*, II.i.376)
'Transportés la fois de douleur et de rage' (Racine, *Bajazet*, V.xi.1690)

*Act IV line 117* (1743 version):
'Malheureuse quel nom est sorti de ta bouche?' (Racine, *Phèdre*, I.iii.206)
'Même le nom d'*Esther* est sorti de sa bouche' (Racine, *Esther*, II.i.390)

*Act IV line 124* (1742 version):
'De ce spectacle affreux votre fille alarmée' (Racine, *Iphigénie*, V.vi.1737)

*Act IV line 129*:
'Et mon époux sanglant traîné sur la poussière' (Racine, *Andromaque*, III.vi.930)

*Act IV line 136*:
'Et vous offrir la paix pour la dernière fois' (Racine, *Alexandre*, II.ii (448)
'Céphise, allons le voir pour la dernière fois' (Racine, *Andromaque*, IV.i.1072)
'Et je vais lui parler pour la dernière fois' (Racine, *Bérénice*, II.ii.490)
'Et si je vous parlais pour la dernière fois' (Racine, *Britannicus*, V.i.1546)
'Prêt à me dire adieu pour la dernière fois' (Racine, *Bajazet*, II.v.692)
'Je vais donc voir mon fils pour la dernière fois' (La Motte, *Inès de Castro*, IV.i.802)
'Vains désirs, taisez-vous pour la dernière fois' (Crébillon, *Sémiramis*, I.vi)
'Et je cours l'embrasser pour la dernière fois' (Crébillon, *Pyrrhus*, II.ii)
'Elle vous parle ici pour la dernière fois' (La Noue, *Mahomet II*, V.iii)

*Act IV line 159*:
'Il n'en faut point douter, Auguste a tout appris' (Corneille, *Cinna*, I.iv.291)
'C'est lui-même, Achorée, il n'en faut point douter' (Corneille, *Pompée*, II.ii.568)
'Xipharès ne vit plus, il n'en faut point douter' (Racine, *Mithridate*, V.i.1474)

*Act IV line 161*:
'Du haut du ciel sa voix s'est fait entendre' (Racine, *Esther*, III.ix.1205)

*Act IV line 189*:
'Dans une heure au plus tard ce veillard vénérable' (Racine, *Esther*, III.iv.1133)

*Act IV line 195* (MS1 variant):
'Hélas, de vos malheurs innocente ou coupable' (Racine, *Phèdre*, III.i.773)

*Act IV line 199*:
'Et lui plonge trois fois un poignard dans le sein' (Corneille, *Pertharite*, V.iv.1757)
'Leur enfonce tous deux un poignard dans le sein' (Corneille, *Théodore*, V.viii.1782)
'Lui donne, au lieu d'encens, d'un poignard dans le sein' (Corneille, *Cinna*, I.iii.236)
'C'est lui mettre moi-même un poignard dans le sein' (Racine, *Andromaque*, II.v.699)
'Pour mettre votre fils un poignard dans le sein' (Racine, *Mithridate*, IV.iv.1366)
'A me plonger, barbare, un poignard dans le sein' (Crébillon, *Sémiramis*, V.iii)
'Sais-tu que pour plonger le poignard dans mon sein' (La Noue, *Mahomet II*, I.ii)

*Act IV line 212*:
'Il ordonne à mon cœur ce sacrifice affreux' (Racine, *Iphigénie*, V.i.1510)

*Act IV line 218* (1742 version):
'Voilà comme *Pyrrhus* vint s'offrir à ma vue' (Racine, *Andromaque*, III.viii.1006)

*Act IV line 244*:
'Et ma reconnaissance et l'excès de ma joie' (La Motte, *Inès de Castro*, V.vi.1232)

*Act IV line 254*:
'Pour qui? / Tu vas ouïr le comble des horreurs' (Racine, *Phèdre*, I.iii.260)
'Et pour vous élever au comble de la joie' (Racine, *Thébaïde*, I.iii.127)

'Par où je veux monter au comble de ma joie' (Mairet, *La Sophonisbe*, III.iv.928)
'Et pour mettre ton âme au comble de sa joie' (Corneille, *Théodore*, IV.v.1375)

*Act IV line 260*:
'Vengez-la, vengez-vous. Ah! dans ses ennemis' (Racine, *Thébaïde*, III.iv.753)
'Vengez-moi, vengez-vous, et vengez un époux' (Rotrou, *Venceslas*, IV.vi.1381)

*Act IV line 262*:
'Et donner à ma haine une libre étendue' (Racine, *Andromaque*, II.v.678)

*Act IV line 276*:
'Ils se jouaient tous deux de ma crédulité' (Racine, *Bajazet*, IV.v.1296)

*Act V line 14*:
'Où je vais vous jurer un silence éternel' (Racine, *Mithridate*, II.vi.698)

*Act V line 46*:
'Entre le ciel et moi, sois juge Sophronyme' (Crébillon, *Idoménée*, I.ii)

*Act V line 50*:
'Des secrets d'où dépend le destin des humains' (Racine, *Britannicus*, V.iii.1598)

*Act V line 96*:
'Ecoutez-vous, Madame, une foule insensée?' (Racine, *Bérénice*, V.v.1319)

*Act V line 97*:
'En poussa vers le ciel des hurlements affreux' (Racine, *Athalie*, III.iii.949)

*Act V line 102*:
'A ce combat fatal vous seul l'avez conduit' (Racine, *Thébaïde*, V.iii.1304)

*Act V line 109*:
'Depuis six mois entiers une fureur commune' (Crébillon, *Idoménée*, I.ii)

*Act V line 148*:
'De rompre des méchants les trames criminelles' (Racine, *Esther*, III.iv.1112)

*Act V line 163*:
'J'ai vu trancher les jours de ma famille entière' (Racine, *Andromaque*, III.vi.929)

*Act V line 164*:
'Me ménage avec soin ce reste de lumière' (Rotrou, *Venceslas*, IV.iv.1288)
'A peine lui laissait un reste de lumière' (Crébillon, *Idoménée*, I.v)

*Act V line 165*:
'Après que le transport d'un amour plein d'horreur' (Racine, *Phèdre*, IV.ii.1047)

*Act V line 192* (variant):
'Ne délibérons plus. Bravons sa violence' (Racine, *Iphigénie*, IV.vii.1429)

# *De l'Alcoran et de Mahomet*

critical edition

by

Ahmad Gunny

To the memory of Ira. O. Wade

# INTRODUCTION

*De l'Alcoran et de Mahomet* was first published in 1748, when it appeared in a collective edition of Voltaire's works, immediately following *Le Fanatisme, ou Mahomet*. Voltaire's interest in Islam had been fostered by this play and his reading of books on Islam and its Prophet, and the essay is intimately connected with the tragedy, being written in the same spirit and representing a continuation of the war waged on the charlatan Mahomet.

Both texts show Voltaire hostile to Islam and Mohammed, whereas in later writings such as the *Catéchisme de l'honnête homme* (1763), the *Examen important de milord Bolingbroke* (1766) and even section I of the article 'Alcoran ou plutôt Le Koran' in the *Questions sur l'Encyclopédie* (1770), this hostility has disappeared. Voltaire is by then better disposed and more balanced towards Islam. In *Mahomet* and *De l'Alcoran*, however, it suits his purpose to follow authors writing in the 'tradition dévote'. It is in support of his earlier suggestion that Mohammed is an impostor whose preaching rests on lies that Voltaire refers in *De l'Alcoran* to the fifty-fourth chapter about the splitting of the moon, attributing this event to Mohammed himself.

Although the apparent source of the information is George Sale's English translation of the Koran (1734), the real source is Jean Gagnier's *Vie de Mahomet* (1732), to which Sale refers. Voltaire, who possessed both works (BV1411, BV1786), relied more on Gagnier than on Sale.[1] Gagnier, Laudian professor of Arabic at Oxford from 1724, was hostile to Islam. In 1723 he had edited in Arabic, with a Latin translation, some chapters on the life of Mohammed extracted from the work of the historian Abul Fida

[1] Voltaire made numerous notes on his copy of Sale's Koran; see *Corpus des notes marginales de Voltaire*, iv.654-64; a note in the hand of Mme Du Châtelet shows that the volume was read during the Cirey period (*Corpus*, p.724, note 599).

(1273-1331), under the title *De vita et rebus gestis Mohammedis*. He then in 1732 produced his biography in a French version as a challenge to Boulainvilliers, who, in his *Vie de Mahomed* (1730), had been fairer to Islam.

It is therefore hardly surprising that in *De l'Alcoran et de Mahomet* Voltaire should attack Boulainvilliers for praising the Arabs, whom he chooses to describe as 'un peuple de brigands'. Publicly at least, Voltaire had to appear consistent: having denounced the impostor in his play and having only recently dedicated it to the pope as a son of the church, he could be expected to show hostility to Mohammed and the Arabs. Privately, however, he acknowledged that in *Le Fanatisme* he had made Mohammed appear worse than he was. In his letter to Frederick, for example, he said that he knew that 'Mahomet n'a pas tramé précisément l'espèce de trahison qui fait le sujet de cette tragédie' (D2386, 20 December 1740). To Mme Denis he wrote: 'Il n'appartenait assurément qu'aux musulmans de se plaindre, car j'ai fait Mahomet un peu plus méchant qu'il n'était' (D4597, 29 October 1751).

In *De l'Alcoran* one of Voltaire's aims is to discredit Mohammed by showing how he exploited the people's belief in the supernatural and how he himself had nothing supernatural about him. Hence he took great delight in relating the episode of the journey to the heavens and the scandalous tale linking the name of the Prophet's wife Aisha with Safwan. The latter episode, the incident of the injury Mohammed sustained in an early battle and all his alleged borrowings from other religions enabled Voltaire to destroy the idea that Mohammed's mission was divinely inspired. For these episodes, as for the marriage contract between Mohammed and his first wife, Voltaire could read all the details in Gagnier. Mohammed is shown to be vastly inferior to Voltaire's hero Confucius, who never experienced revelation, and *De l'Alcoran* ends with the statement that Mohammed lacked nothing to deceive people.

Yet this text does not show Mohammed in an entirely negative light. Voltaire seems to have grasped some of the principles of Islam relating to the unity of God, the necessity of praying and almsgiving, describing Islam as 'une religion si simple et si sage' (lines 43-44). He is also alive to the debate dividing Muslims in the ninth century on the question of the uncreatedness of the Koran, although he ridicules the idea. He is prepared to refute commentators on the question of the exclusion of women from paradise, which interested many people in the seventeenth and eighteenth centuries. He appears to justify Islamic polygamy, concluding that Mohammed's civil laws are good, although his methods are horrible. Again, Voltaire's stand is not surprising. The *Mercure de France* of April and June 1745 had published articles by him in which he described Mohammed more favourably. Voltaire's ideas on Islam in the 1740s, later developed in the *Essai sur les mœurs*, owe much to Sale and to the article 'Allah' in Barthélemy d'Herbelot's *Bibliothèque orientale*. What Voltaire says on Mohammed and Islam in *De l'Alcoran* must therefore be viewed in the context in which this text is written. Voltaire has laid the basis for a more balanced later reappraisal of Islam.[2] *De l'Alcoran et de Mahomet* later became section II of the article 'Alcoran ou plutôt Le Koran' in the *Questions sur l'Encyclopédie* (1770), and the same pairing is maintained when the texts are incorporated into the 'Dictionnaire philosophique' of the Kehl edition.

*De l'Alcoran et de Mahomet* first appeared in the *Œuvres de Mr. de V.* (W48D, iv.449-54), which is the base text. Subsequent editions make no particularly significant changes to this first edition; variants are recorded from the following editions: W39A, vii(49).132-39; W51P, vi.237-44; W52.ii.379-402; W56,

[2] On the whole question of Islam and Mohammed in French and English writings in the seventeenth and eighteenth centuries, see A. Gunny, *Images of Islam in eighteenth-century writings* (London 1996). See also Djavad Hadidi, *Voltaire et l'Islam* (Paris 1974), and M. G. Badir, *Voltaire et l'Islam*, *SVEC* 125 (1974). On Mohammed specifically, see Clinton Bennett, *In search of Muhammad* (London 1998), and Diego Venturino, 'Imposteur ou législateur? Le Mahomet des Lumières (vers 1750-1789)', *SVEC* 2000:02, p.243-62.

W57G.v(pt.1).228-34; W57P.iii.[298]-305; W57P.vii.423-32; W64G, W70G.v(pt.1).228-34; W68.xv(71).323-27; W71.xiv.323-27; W71P.vi.67-75; W72P.xvii.249-57; W70L.xxvii(72).281-88; W75G.xxxiii.395-400 and K.xxxvii.144-50. The work was also published in the pirated collective editions W50R, W64R and W72X.

The spelling of the base text has been modernised, but the original punctuation has been maintained. The following nouns are capitalised in the text: Charlatan, Lune, Verset, Philosophe, Peuple, Sage, Poète, Musulman, Docteur, Vulgaire, Moine, Négociant, Législateur, Souverain, Prosélyte, Religion, Vainqueur, Islamisme, Bonne, Ange, Mage, Jannat, Paradis, Prophète, Sectateur, Ange, Province, Morale, Loi, Comte, Brigand, Puits, Citerne, Généalogie, Ciel, Marchand, Pontiffe, Monarque, Empire, Univers, Veuve, Médecin. It is interesting to note that Voltaire spells 'Koran' with a 'k', perhaps influenced by the English model of George Sale's translation of the Koran.

## DE L'ALCORAN ET DE MAHOMET

C'était un sublime et hardi charlatan que ce Mahomet, fils d'Abdalla. Il dit dans son dixième chapitre: 'Quel autre que Dieu peut avoir composé l'Alcoran?' On crie, c'est Mahomet, qui a forgé ce livre. 'Eh bien! Tâchez d'écrire un chapitre qui lui ressemble et appelez à votre aide qui vous voudrez.' [1] Au dix-septième il s'écrie: 'Louange à celui qui a transporté pendant la nuit son serviteur du sacré temple de la Mecque à celui de Jérusalem.' [2] C'est un assez beau voyage; mais il n'approche pas de celui qu'il fit cette nuit même de planète en planète, et des belles choses qu'il y vit.

Il prétendait qu'il y avait cinq cents années de chemin d'une planète à une autre, et qu'il fendit la lune en deux. [3] Ses disciples,

[1] Voltaire, who had been reading George Sale's translation of the Koran as early as 1738 (see D1588), is referring to the following lines from ch.10: 'This Koran could not have been composed by *any* except God [...]. Will they say, Mohammed hath forged it? Answer, Bring therefore a chapter like unto it; and call whom ye may to your assistance, besides GOD, if ye speak truth.' Elsewhere quotations from the Koran;, unless otherwise stated, are from *The Holy Quran*, ed. A. Yusuf Ali, 2 vols (New York 1946).

[2] Ch.17 of the Koran (in Sale's version) begins: 'Praise be unto him, who transported his servant by night, from the sacred temple of Mecca to the farther temple of Jerusalem.' In the Koran the journey stops at Jerusalem, but in a footnote Sale remarks that from Jerusalem Mohammed was carried through the seven heavens to the presence of God, and brought back again to Mecca the same night. He insists that this journey of Mohammed to heaven is so well known that he may be pardoned if he does not describe it, adding that the English reader may find it in Dr Prideaux's *Life of Mahomet* and the learned in Abulfeda's *Life of Mohammed*.

[3] Voltaire is referring to the beginning of ch.54 of the *Koran* which does not attribute the splitting of the moon to Mohammed himself, but simply states: 'The hour of judgment approacheth; and the moon is split asunder' (Sale). In a footnote Sale says that this passage is expounded in two different ways. Some imagine that the words refer to a famous miracle supposed to have been performed by Mohammed, for it is said that on the infidels demanding a sign of him, the moon appeared cloven in two. Others think the preterite tense is here used in the prophetic style for the future, and that the passage should be rendered 'The moon shall be split asunder',

qui rassemblèrent solennellement les versets de son *Coran* après sa mort, retranchèrent ce voyage du ciel. Ils craignèrent les railleurs et les philosophes. C'était avoir trop de délicatesse. Ils pouvaient s'en fier aux commentateurs, qui auraient bien su expliquer 15 l'itinéraire.[4] Les amis de Mahomet devaient savoir par expérience, que le merveilleux est la raison du peuple. Les sages contredisent en secret, et le peuple les fait taire. Mais en retranchant l'itinéraire des planètes on laissa quelques petits mots sur l'aventure de la lune; on ne peut pas prendre garde à tout. 20

Le *Coran* est une rhapsodie sans liaison, sans ordre, sans art; on dit pourtant, que ce livre ennuyeux est un fort beau livre; je m'en rapporte aux Arabes, qui prétendent qu'il est écrit avec une élégance et une pureté, dont personne n'a approché depuis.

C'est un poème ou une espèce de prose rimée, qui contient six 25 mille vers. Il n'y a point de poète dont la personne et l'ouvrage aient fait une telle fortune. On agita chez les musulmans, si l'*Alcoran* était éternel, ou si Dieu l'avait créé pour le dicter à Mahomet.[5] Les docteurs décidèrent qu'il était éternel; ils avaient

13 W39A, W51P, W52, W56, W57G, W57P, W64G, W70G, W68, W71, W70L, W71P, W72P, W75G, K: craignirent
25 W39A: une poème

for this, they say, is to happen at the resurrection. This second interpretation is also Djavad Hadidi's, *Voltaire et l'Islam*, p.86-88.

[4] In the rest of the footnote to Jerusalem (see n.2 above) Sale refers to the dispute among Muslim divines as to whether Mohammed's night journey was really performed by him corporeally or whether it was only a dream or vision. Some think that the whole was no more than a vision. Others suppose that he was carried bodily to Jerusalem but no further, and that he ascended thence to heaven in spirit only.

[5] Voltaire is here touching on a fundamental point of belief which divided Muslims in the ninth century. Under the influence of the theological sect of the Mu'tazilites, the caliph al-Ma'mun (813-833) introduced the Mihna or 'Inquisition' which required all governors, judges and senior officials publicly to profess the doctrine that the Koran was the created word of God. The doctrine had political significance. For, if the Koran is God's uncreated word, as most of the *ulema*

raison, cette éternité est bien plus belle que l'autre opinion. Il faut toujours avec le vulgaire prendre le parti le plus incroyable. 30

Les moines, qui se sont déchaînés contre Mahomet et qui ont dit tant de sottises sur son compte, ont prétendu qu'il ne savait pas écrire. Mais comment imaginer qu'un homme, qui avait été négociant, poète, législateur et souverain, ne sût pas signer son nom?[6] Si son livre est mauvais pour notre temps et pour nous, il était fort bon pour ses contemporains et sa religion encore meilleure. Il faut avouer, qu'il retira presque toute l'Asie de l'idolâtrie. Il enseigna l'unité de Dieu,[7] il déclamait avec force contre ceux qui lui donnent des associés. Chez lui l'usure avec les étrangers est défendue, l'aumône ordonnée. La prière est d'une nécessité absolue; la résignation aux décrets éternels est le grand mobile de tout. Il était bien difficile, qu'une religion si simple et si sage enseignée par un homme toujours victorieux ne subjuguât pas une partie de la terre. En effet, les musulmans ont fait autant de 35 40 45

41-42 w57P (iii): La prière est une nécessité
45-46 w39A: autant des prosélytes

(scholars) believed, then it is in certain respects an expression of his essential being, but if it is merely a word he has created, it is not necessarily an expression of his character any more than are other created things. The practical conclusion is that if the Koran is created it does not have the ultimate validity ascribed to it by the *ulema*, who believed that the caliphate should be administered according to the Sharia (a God-given law) which included the Koran, and may therefore be discarded by the caliph. By 849 the Inquisition was abandoned as it did not effect a reconciliation of the opposing blocs. This political decision marked the consolidation of Sunnism. See W. Montgomery Watt, *What is Islam?* (London and Beirut 1968), p.126-28.

[6] In the seventh of the *Lettres philosophiques* Voltaire spoke of 'l'ignorant Mahomet'. But later, in the *Essai sur les mœurs* (ch.6), he declared that Mohammed was no illiterate. See also the *Lettre à l'auteur de la critique de l'histoire universelle* (M.xxiv.145, 479). The Koran itself speaks of the 'unlettered Prophet' (chapters 7, 62) in order to emphasise the divine inspiration of Mohammed.

[7] Compare the *Essai sur les mœurs*, ch.7: 'Le dogme surtout de l'unité d'un Dieu, présenté sans mystère, et proportionné à l'intelligence humaine, rangea sous sa loi une foule de nations et, jusqu'à des nègres dans l'Afrique, et à des insulaires dans l'Océan indien.'

prosélytes par la parole que par l'épée. Ils ont converti à leur religion les Indiens et jusqu'aux Nègres. Les Turcs même leurs vainqueurs se sont soumis à l'islamisme.

Mahomet laissa dans sa loi beaucoup de choses qu'il trouva établies chez les Arabes, la circoncision, le jeûne, le voyage de la Mecque qui était en usage quatre mille ans avant lui, les ablutions si nécessaires à la santé et à la propreté dans un pays brûlant où le linge était inconnu, enfin l'idée d'un jugement dernier que les mages avaient toujours établie, et qui était parvenue jusqu'aux Arabes. Il est dit, que comme il annonçait qu'on ressusciterait tout nu,[8] Aïshca sa femme trouva la chose immodeste et dangereuse: 'Allez, ma bonne', lui dit-il, 'on n'aura pas alors envie de rire'. Un ange selon le *Coran* doit peser les hommes et les femmes dans une grande balance.[9] Cette idée est encore prise des mages. Il leur a volé aussi leur pont aigu,[10] sur lequel il faut passer après la mort et leur *jannat*,[11] où les élus musulmans trouveront des bains, des

50 W52: la jeûne
59 W70L: encor

[8] In the Koran there is simply a reference to 'the day that the shin shall be laid bare and they shall be summoned to bow in adoration' (ch.68).

[9] In the Koran there is no question of an angel who will weigh men and women in a big scale, but 'the weighing of men's actions on that day shall be just; and they whose balances laden with their good works shall be heavy, are those who shall be happy' (Sale, ch.7).

[10] The Koran does not mention a narrow bridge to be crossed after death, but speaks of the straight way which is often the narrow way, or the steep way, which many people shun (chapters 1, 90). After Mohammed's time Muslims came to believe that both rewarded and condemned had to walk across a path or bridge stretched over Hell; the ridge of the bridge was fine as a hair and the wicked fell into Hell. See Watt, p.51.

[11] The Arabic 'al-Janna', literally 'garden', is the commonest term used in the Koran to describe Paradise. Voltaire's understanding of the term (which he uses again in the *Essai sur les mœurs*, ch.7) is rather particular, however, and is indebted to George Sale: 'But all these glories will be eclipsed by the resplendent and ravishing girls of paradise, called, from their large black eyes, *Hûr al oyûn*, the

appartements bien meublés, de bons lits et des houris avec des grands yeux noirs.[12] Il est vrai aussi qu'il dit, que tous ces plaisirs des sens si nécessaires à tous ceux qui ressusciteront avec des sens, n'approcheront pas du plaisir de la contemplation de l'Etre suprême.[13] Il a l'humilité d'avouer dans son *Coran* que lui-même n'ira point en paradis par son propre mérite, mais par la pure volonté de Dieu.[14] C'est aussi par cette pure volonté divine qu'il ordonne que la cinquième partie des dépouilles sera toujours pour le prophète.[15]

Il n'est pas vrai, qu'il exclue du paradis les femmes.[16] Il n'y a pas d'apparence, qu'un homme aussi habile ait voulu se brouiller avec cette moitié du genre humain, qui conduit l'autre. Abulfeda rapporte, qu'une vieille l'importunant un jour en lui demandant,

71 W39A: exclud

enjoyment of whose company will be a principal felicity of the faithful. These, they say, are created, not of clay, as mortal women are, but of pure musk; being, as their prophet often affirms in his *Korân*, free from all natural impurities, defects, and inconveniences incident to the sex, of the strictest modesty, and secluded from public view in pavilions of hollow pearls [...]. The name which the *Mohammedans* usually give to this happy mansion, is *al Jannat*, or *the garden*' (*The Koran* (1734), p.96-97).

[12] The Koran, ch.56.

[13] The Koran, ch.75.

[14] It does not seem that this is specifically mentioned in the *Koran*, but it may be inferred from the beginning of ch.48: 'Verily we have granted thee [Mohammed] a manifest victory: that God may forgive thee thy preceding and thy subsequent sin [...]. It is he who sendeth down secure tranquillity into the hearts of the true believers [...] that he may lead the true believers of both sexes into gardens beneath which rivers flow, to dwell therein for ever' (Sale).

[15] Voltaire's source is Sale, *The Koran*, ch.8: 'And know that whenever ye gain any spoils, a fifth part thereof belongeth unto God, and to the apostle, and his kindred, and the orphans, and the poor, and the traveller.'

[16] In the *Essai sur les mœurs* (ch.7) Voltaire again states that Muslim women are not excluded from paradise. In fact the Koran teaches not only that women enter paradise as a reward for their good actions, but that husbands and wives enter together (ch.43). See also A. Gunny, 'Montesquieu's view of Islam in the *Lettres persanes*', *SVEC* 174 (1978), p.152-55.

ce qu'il fallait faire pour aller en paradis: M'amie, lui dit-il, le paradis n'est pas pour les vieilles. La bonne femme se mit à pleurer, et le prophète pour la consoler, lui dit: Il n'y aura point de vieilles parce qu'elles rajeuniront. Cette doctrine consolante est confirmée dans le cinquante-quatrième chapitre du *Coran*.[17] 75

Il défendit le vin, parce qu'un jour quelques-uns de ses sectateurs arrivèrent à la prière étant ivres. Il permit la pluralité des femmes se conformant en ce point à l'usage immémorial des Orientaux. 80

En un mot, ses lois civiles sont bonnes. Son dogme est admirable en ce qu'il a de conforme avec le nôtre; mais les moyens sont affreux, c'est la fourberie et le meurtre. 85

On l'excuse sur la fourberie, parce que, dit-on, les Arabes comptaient avant lui cent vingt-quatre mille prophètes, et qu'il n'y avait pas grand mal, qu'il y en parut un de plus. Les hommes, ajoute-t-on, ont besoin d'être trompés. Mais comment justifier un homme qui vous dit: 'Crois que j'ai parlé à l'ange Gabriel, ou je te tue'? 90

Combien est préférable un Confucius[18] le premier des mortels qui n'ont point eu de révélation! Il n'emploie que la raison, et non le mensonge et l'épée. Vice-roi d'une grande province il y fait fleurir la morale et les lois. Disgracié et pauvre il les enseigne, il les 95

86 W57P (vii): c'est avec la fourberie
91 K: l'ange Gabriel, ou paye-moi un tribut?

[17] Voltaire really means ch. 56: 'Verily we have created the *damsels of paradise* by a *peculiar* creation' (Sale). In a footnote to this sentence Sale writes: 'Having created them purposely of finer materials than the females of this world, and subject to none of those inconveniences which are natural to the sex. Some understand this passage of the beatified women; who, though they died old and ugly, shall yet be restored to their youth and beauty in paradise.'

[18] See the *Notebooks*: after he has stated that the Muslim religion is inferior to the Chinese religion, Voltaire remarks that Confucius was all the greater because he was not a prophet (*OC*, vol.81, p.139); and he lists Confucius among the philosophers who alone had a religion, that is, recognised a God and were virtuous (*OC*, vol.82, p.635).

pratique dans la grandeur et dans l'abaissement, il rend la vertu aimable, il a pour disciple le plus ancien et le plus sage des peuples.

Le comte de Boulainvilliers,[19] qui avait du goût pour Mahomet, a beau me vanter les Arabes, il ne peut empêcher, que ce ne fut un peuple de brigands; ils volaient avant Mahomet en adorant les étoiles, ils volaient sous Mahomet au nom de Dieu. Ils avaient, dit-on, la simplicité des temps héroïques: mais qu'est-ce que les siècles héroïques? C'était le temps où on s'égorgeait pour un puits et pour une citerne, comme on fait aujourd'hui pour une province.

Les premiers musulmans furent animés par Mahomet de la rage de l'enthousiasme. Rien n'est plus terrible qu'un peuple, qui n'ayant rien à perdre combat à la fois par esprit de rapine et de religion.

Il est vrai, qu'il n'y avait pas beaucoup de finesse dans leurs procédés. Ce contrat du premier mariage de Mahomet porte qu'attendu que Cadishca est amoureuse de lui et lui pareillement amoureux d'elle, on a trouvé bon de les conjoindre.[20] Mais y a-t-il tant de simplicité à lui avoir composé une généalogie dans laquelle on le fait descendre d'Adam en droite ligne, comme on a fait

104 W52, W56, W57G, W57P (iii), W68: où on s'égorgeait

115 W56, W57G, W57P (vii), W64G, W70G, W68, W70L, W75G: on la fait descendre

115-116 K: comme on en a fait descendre

[19] In his *Vie de Mahomed* (1730) the comte de Boulainvilliers was no blind admirer of Mohammed and the Arabs, but tried to defend them against the unfair attacks to which they had been subjected. He not only attacked Christian doctrines such as those of the Trinity and the Incarnation but also stressed the fundamental teaching of Mohammed. D. Venturino has devoted three important studies to Boulainvilliers: a doctoral thesis on his religious and political thought, an Italian translation of his biography of Mohammed, and an article entitled 'Un prophète philosophe? Une *Vie de Mahomed* à l'aube des Lumières', *Dix-huitième siècle* 24, p.321-31. All date from 1992.

[20] See the *Notebooks*: 'Contract de mariage de Mahomet fait par Abul Motaleb son oncle. *Attendu que Mahomet est amoureux de Cadishea, et Cadishea pareillement amoureux de luy*' (*OC*, vol.81, p.382).

descendre depuis quelques maisons d'Espagne et d'Ecosse? L'Arabie avait son Moréri et son *Mercure galant*.[21]

Le grand prophète essuya la disgrâce commune à tant de maris; il n'y a personne après cela qui puisse se plaindre. On connaît le nom de celui qui eut les faveurs de sa seconde femme la belle Aïshca; il s'appelait Assuan.[22] Mahomet se comporta avec plus de hauteur que César qui répudia sa femme, disant, qu'il ne fallait pas que la femme de César fût soupçonnée. Le prophète ne voulut pas même soupçonner la sienne, il fit descendre du ciel un chapitre du *Coran* pour affirmer que sa femme était fidèle.[23] Ce chapitre était écrit de toute éternité aussi bien que tous les autres.

On l'admire pour s'être fait de marchand de chameaux pontife, législateur et monarque, pour avoir soumis l'Arabie qui ne l'avait jamais été avant lui, pour avoir donné les premières secousses à l'empire romain d'Orient et à celui des Perses. Je l'admire encore pour avoir entretenu la paix dans sa maison parmi des femmes. Il a changé la face d'une partie de l'Europe, de la moitié de l'Asie, de

121 K: Assan

131 W56, W57G, W57P (iii & vii), W64G, W70G, W68, W71, W70L, W71P, W75G, K: parmi ses femmes

[21] In his article 'Mahomet' in the *Grand Dictionnaire historique* (1683 edn), ii.504, Louis Moréri offers a caricature of the early years of Mohammed's life. The reference to the *Mercure* is not very clear. Voltaire may be referring to the *Dissertation sur l'auteur de l'Alcoran* read by the abbé Vertot at the Académie des inscriptions in November 1724. The *Mercure de France* of December that year gave a full account of the *Dissertation* which reproduced medieval clichés of Mohammed's preaching Islam by the sword and favouring loose morals.

[22] See the *Notebooks*: 'Il [Mahomet] fut cocu. La belle Hahissea couchoit avec Safwan. Mais le prophète fit descendre du Ciel un chapitre de l'Alcoran par lequel il fut déclaré incocufié' (*OC*, vol.81, p.382).

[23] 'Those who brought forward the lie are a body among yourselves' (ch.24). The incident referred to occurred on the return from the expedition to the Banu Mustaliq in 627. When the march was ordered Aisha was not in her tent, having gone to search for a necklace she had dropped. Next morning she was found by Safwan, who put her on his camel and brought her, leading the camel on foot. This gave occasion to enemies to raise a malicious scandal.

presque toute l'Afrique, et il s'en est bien peu fallu que sa religion n'ait subjugué l'univers.

A quoi tiennent les révolutions? Un coup de pierre un peu plus fort que celui qu'il reçut dans son premier combat donnait une autre destinée au monde.[24] 135

Son gendre Ali prétendit, que quand il fallut inhumer le prophète, on le trouva dans un état qui n'est pas trop ordinaire aux morts, et que sa veuve Aïshca s'écria: Si j'avais su, que Dieu eût fait cette grâce au défunt, j'y serais accourue à l'instant.[25] On pouvait dire de lui: *Decet imperatorem stantem mori.* 140

Jamais la vie d'un homme ne fut écrite dans un plus grand détail que la sienne. Les moindres particularités en étaient sacrées; on sait le compte et le nom de tout ce qui lui appartenait, neuf épées, trois lances, trois arcs, sept cuirasses, trois boucliers, douze femmes, un coq blanc, sept chevaux, deux mules, quatre chameaux, sans compter la jument Borac sur laquelle il monta au ciel. Mais il ne l'avait que par emprunt, elle appartenait en propre à l'ange Gabriel.[26] 145 150

138-139 W39A: prétendit qu'on trouva le Prophète, quand il fallut l'inhumer, dans un état

[24] The reference is to the battle of Uhud which took place in Medina in 625. The Muslims were nearly overwhelmed not so much by superior numbers as by lack of discipline. Mohammed was wounded in his head and face and one of his front teeth was knocked out by a stone thrown at him. But he rallied his troops and Abu Sufyan, leader of the Meccan pagans, decided to withdraw. Voltaire's source is Gagnier's *Vie de Mahomet*, i.353-72. Uhud was not the first battle fought by Mohammed. In 624, for example, he had won the battle of Badr, about fifty miles south-west of Medina.

[25] See also the *Notebooks*: 'Mahomet bandoit après sa mort, toutes ses femmes l'attestèrent' (*OC*, vol.81, p.383).

[26] 'Burak' is the name given by tradition to the fabulous animal, represented in pictorial art as a mare with a woman's head and peacock's tail, which the Prophet mounted on the night of his ascension to heaven. It is not mentioned in the Koran, which refers to the night journey from Mecca to Jerusalem and thence to heaven in chapters 17 and 53, but commentators say that Gabriel brought it to Mohammed in the precincts of the Ka'ba in Mecca. See the article 'Burak' in *The Shorter encyclopedia of Islam* (Leiden 1974).

Toutes ses paroles ont été recueillies. Il disait que 'la jouissance des femmes le rendait plus fervent à la prière'.

En effet, pourquoi ne pas dire bénédicité et grâces au lit comme à table? Une belle femme vaut bien un souper. On prétend encore, qu'il était un grand médecin; ainsi il ne lui manqua rien pour tromper les hommes. 155

# WORKS CITED


Alekseev, M. P., and T. N. Kopreeva, *Bibliothèque de Voltaire: catalogue des livres* (Moscow, Leningrad 1961)

Badir, Magdy Gabriel, 'L'anatomie d'un coup d'Etat ou la prise de pouvoir dans la tragédie *Mahomet* de Voltaire', *Eighteenth-century French theatre, aspects and contexts. Studies presented to E. J. H. Greene*, ed. Magdy Gabriel Badir and David J. Langdon (Alberta 1986), p.99-106.

– *Voltaire et l'Islam*, *SVEC* 125 (1974).

Barbier, Edmond-Jean-François, *Chronique de la régence et du règne de Louis XV* (Paris 1857).

Barnes, Bertram, *Goethe's knowledge of French literature* (Oxford 1937).

Bengesco, Georges, *Voltaire: bibliographie de ses œuvres* (Paris 1882-1890).

Bennett, Clinton, *In search of Muhammad* (London 1998).

Bernays, Michael, *Schriften zur kritik und literaturgeschichte* (Stuttgart 1895).

Bondois, Paul, 'Le procureur-général Joly de Fleury et le "Mahomet" de Voltaire', *Revue d'histoire littéraire de la France* 36 (1929), p.246-59.

Boulainvilliers, Henri, comte de, *La Vie de Mahomed* (London 1730).

Brenner, Clarence D., *A bibliographical list of plays in the French language* (Berkeley, Cal. 1947).

Brown, A., 'Calendar of Voltaire manuscripts other than correspondence', *SVEC* 77 (1970), p.11-101.

Cahagne, abbé de, *Lettre d'un comédien de Lille sur la tragédie de Mahomet. Contenant l'idée des caractères, de la conduite et des détails de cette pièce* (Paris, Prault, 1742).

Cameron, Keith, 'Aspects of Voltaire's style in Mahomet', *SVEC* 129 (1975), p.7-17.

Carr, Thomas M., 'Dramatic structure and philosophy in *Brutus*, *Alzire* and *Mahomet*', *SVEC* 143 (1975), p.7-48.

Clément, J.-M.-B., *Cinquième lettre à m. de Voltaire* (La Haye 1774).

– and Joseph de La Porte, *Anecdotes dramatiques* (Paris 1775).

Collé, Charles, *Journal et mémoires*, ed. H. Bonhomme (Paris 1868).

Conlon, P. M., *Voltaire's literary career from 1728 to 1750*, *SVEC* 14 (1961).

de Felice, Renzo, 'Trois prises de position italiennes à propos de *Mahomet*', *SVEC* 10 (1959), p.259-66.

Desnoiresterres, Gustave, *Voltaire et la société française au XVIIIe siècle* (Paris 1867-1876).

Doutrelant, Jean-Luc, 'L'Orient tragique au XVIII$^{e}$ siècle', *Revue des sciences humaines* 37 (1972), p.283-300

Gagnier, Jean, *La Vie de Mahomet* (Amsterdam 1732).

Glaesener, Henri, 'Goethe imitateur et traducteur de Voltaire au théâtre', *Revue de littérature comparée* 13 (1933), p.217-23.

Granet, François, and Pierre-Nicolas Desmolets, *Recueil de pièces d'histoire et de littérature* (Paris 1731-1732).

Gunny, Ahmad, *Images of Islam in eighteenth-century writings* (London 1996).

– 'Montesquieu's view of Islam in the *Lettres persanes*', *SVEC* 174 (1978), p.152-55.

– 'Tragedy in the service of propaganda: Voltaire's *Mahomet*, en marge du classicisme', in *Essays on the French theatre from the Renaissance to the Enlightenment*, ed. Alan Howe and Richard Waller (1987).

Hadidi, Djavad, *Voltaire et l'Islam* (Paris 1974).

Ibershoff, C. H., 'Bodmer's indebtedness to Voltaire', *Modern philology* 23 (1925), p.83-87.

Joannidès, A., *La Comédie-Française de 1680 à 1920. Tableau de représentations par auteurs et par pièces* (Paris 1921).

The Koran, translated into English by George Sale (London 1734).

– The Holy Quran, ed. A. Yusuf Ali, 2 vols (New York 1946).

La Harpe, Jean-François de, *Commentaire sur le théâtre de Voltaire* (Paris 1814).

– *Lycée ou cours de littérature ancienne et moderne* (Paris an VII [1805]).

– *Œuvres* (1820).

Lancaster, H. C., *French tragedy in the time of Louis XV and Voltaire* (Baltimore, Md, 1950).

– *The Comédie française, 1701-1774, plays, actors, spectators, finances, Transactions of the American Philosophical Society*, n.s. 41 (1951), p.593-849.

La Porte, J. de, and J. M. B. Clément, *Anecdotes dramatiques* (Paris 1775).

LeClerc, Paul O., *Voltaire and Crébillon père: history of an enmity*, *SVEC* 115 (1973).

Lefèvre, L., *Histoire du théâtre de Lille* (1905).

Lion, Henri, *Les Tragédies et les théories dramatiques de Voltaire* (Paris 1895).

Martainville, A. L. D., and C. G. Etienne, *Histoire du Théâtre français*, depuis *le commencement de la Révolution jusqu'à la réunion générale* (Paris 1802).

Martino, Pierre, 'Un réquisitoire contre Voltaire (1746)', *Revue d'histoire littéraire de la France* 35 (1928).

– 'L'interdiction du *Mahomet* de Voltaire et la dédicace au pape (1742-1745), in *Mémorial Henri Basset* (Paris 1928), ii.89-103.

Mason, Haydn, 'Fathers, good and bad in Voltaire's *Mahomet*', in *Myth and its making in the French theatre. Studies presented to W. D. Howarth*, ed. E. Freeman, H. Mason, M. O'Regan and S. W. Taylor (Cambridge 1988), p.121-35.

– *Pierre Bayle and Voltaire* (Oxford 1963).

Mézeray, François de, *Histoire de France avant Clovis* (1643-1651).

Nolte, Fred O., 'Voltaire's *Mahomet* as a source of Lessing's *Nathan der Weise* and *Emilia Galotti*', *Modern language notes* 48 (1933), p.152-56.

Pappas, John, *Berthier's 'Journal de Trévoux' and the philosophes*, *SVEC* 3 (1957).

Pomeau, René, *La Religion de Voltaire*, nouv. éd. (Paris 1969).

Pitou, Spire, 'Sauvé de La Noue: actor, author, producer', *SVEC* 117 (1974), p.89-112.

Prideaux, Humphrey, *The True nature of imposture fully display'd in the life of Mahomet* (London 1697).

Rezler, Marta, 'The Voltaire–d'Alembert correspondence: an historical and bibliographical reappraisal', *SVEC* 20 (1962), p.9-139.

Ridgway, Ronald S., *La Propagande philosophique dans les tragédies de Voltaire*, *SVEC* 15 (1961).

Roosbroeck, G. L. van, 'Une parodie inédite du *Mahomet* de Voltaire: *L'Empirique* [de Favart]', *Revue d'histoire littéraire de la France* 35 (1928), p.235-40.

*Shorter encyclopedia of Islam* (Leiden 1974).

Solbrig, Ingeborg H., 'The theater, theory and politics, Voltaire's *Le Fanatisme ou Mahomet le prophète* and Goethe's *Mahomet* adaptation', *Michigan Germanic studies* 16 (1990), p.21-43.

*Thomet ou le Brouillamini, parodie en un acte* [...] *Représenté pour la première fois sur le théâtre de* ***, le 7 mars 1755 (London 1755).

Tobin, Ronald W., 'The sources of Voltaire's *Mahomet*', *French review* 34 (1961), p.372-78.

Trénard, Louis, 'L'influence de Voltaire à Lille au XVIIIe siècle', *SVEC* 58 (1967), p.1607-34.

Venturino, Diego, 'Imposteur ou législateur? Le Mahomet des Lumières (vers 1750-1789)', *SVEC* 2000:02, p.243-62.

– 'Un prophète philosophe? Une *Vie de Mahomed* à l'aube des Lumières', *Dix-huitième siècle* 24 (1992), p.321-31.

Villaret, Claude, *Lettre à Monsieur de V***, sur sa tragédie de Mahomet* (n.p. 1742).

Voltaire, *Essai sur les mœurs*, ed. R. Pomeau (Paris 1963).

– *La Henriade*, *OC*, vol.2, ed. O. R. Taylor (1970).

– *Mahomet*, ed. Jean Humbert (Geneva 1925).

– *Notebooks*, *OC*, vol. 81-82, ed. Th. Besterman (1968).

– *La Philosophie de l'histoire*, *OC*, vol.59, ed. J. H. Brumfitt (1969).

– *Œuvres complètes*, ed. Georges Avenel (Paris 1867-1873).

– *Œuvres complètes*, éd. Louis Moland (Paris 1877-1885).

– *Œuvres complètes/Complete works* (Geneva, Banbury and Oxford 1968- ).

– *Zaïre*, *OC*, vol.8, ed. Eva Jacobs (1988)

Vrooman, Jack Rochford, *Voltaire's theatre: the cycle from Œdipe to Mérope*, *SVEC* 75 (1970).

Watt, W. Montgomery, *What is Islam?* (London and Beirut 1968).

Watts, George B., 'Notes on Voltaire', *Modern language notes* 41 (1926), p.118-22.

# INDEX

## INDEX